EARLY PRAISE FOR RAYMOND DUNCAN AND *PATRIOT TRAP*!

"*Patriot Trap*, based on real-life events in present-day Cuba, is a must read. For those looking for a better understanding of contemporary U.S.–Cuban tensions, this highly charged action-adventure is just the ticket. I strongly recommend it!"

—C. Fred Bergsten,
Former Deputy to Dr. Henry Kissinger
at the National Security Council

A LITTLE WARNING

McGrath got up to go to the men's room. He worked through the crowd around the edge of the dance floor, then down the narrow, dimly lit hallway to the men's room at the far end. He was half conscious of one, maybe two men close behind him. As he approached the door, his senses alert, he felt the presence of a body quickly closing the distance between them. Poised and balanced, he reached for the doorknob to see if it was locked. It wasn't, so he pushed the door open and stepped inside.

Suddenly he felt two arms wrapped around him from behind like a vise by someone powerfully built and bent on doing some serious damage. As the man thrust him forward, McGrath turned his head and saw in the mirror over the wash stand a tall black guy with a shining bald head, dark glasses and a goatee. The man was a head taller than McGrath, and looked vaguely familiar. Then McGrath remembered. One of the goon squad guys he had belted that first day in Havana when they were arrested. This was the same man he thought had been following him and Elena. McGrath could swear he saw a second guy, who stopped just inside the door and seemed to be holding it shut.

He struggled hard, but could not stop himself from being pressed into one of the stalls. The muscular black arms were pushing his head forward and down, as a low strong voice hissed in his ear, "We have a little score to settle, you and me. When I finish with you, you better get on the first plane and leave this place. Next time won't be so easy...."

ACKNOWLEDGMENTS

I owe tremendous thanks to the following individuals who have helped on this novel:

Mary Trone for her early encouragement and Cynthia Manson for seeing it through.

To those who helped so much along the way:

Mike and Sheilah Reynolds, Mel Goodman, Carolyn McGiffert Goodman, Rolando Cartaya, Miguel A. Rodriguez-Espi, Gina N. Grasso, Elisabeth Wilson, Ricardo Planas, Jose Alonso, James Hogan, Barry Recame, John Shiman, Paul Gimigliano, Alastair Worden, D.D. Davis, Sonny and Billy White, Claudia Vasquez, Jorge Perez Lopez, Judy Walker, Kathy Hogan, Sara Bogolin, Col. "Buck" Buckwalter, Col. Bill Marshall, Lt. Col. "Bear" Owen, Col. Alan Ricketts, Tom Stewart, Barry Waddell, Carlos Jensen, Romana Ahmed, Gloria Legvold, Roger Pajak, Ronald Endeman, Bucky Ackles, Jim Tillman, Kyle Duncan, John Kramer, John Izzo, Harry Shifton, Dena Levy, Andrea Rubery, Mark Chadsey.

And special thanks to my sons, Erik and Christopher, for their humor and support in this endeavor.

ONE

The Great Bahamas Bank

The steady whine of twin outboard engines screamed in Bernardo Alguero's ears, as he guided his thundering 60-foot speedboat through the shoals of the Great Bahamas Bank. Key West lay far behind by now, beyond the moonlit wake that trailed out from the stern of his boat, *La Mujer*. Leading a "V" formation of four other speedboats skimming over the dark water, he could see their high arcing rooster tails close by. Bernardo had made this run many times with these men. That is, with all but one—Sánchez—Miguel's new man who Bernardo neither liked nor trusted. Bernardo kept a worried eye on him off to the port side. His grip tightened on the wheel, matching the tension at the back of his neck. He could make no mistakes today. He was the man, el hombre, in charge of this operation.

With Sánchez on his mind, he focused on the job at hand—reaching Cuba's north shore about twenty miles ahead, undetected by the U.S. Coast Guard. Not that the coast guard could do anything if they found them now.

There was nothing to hide in their boats, but it would tip them off about the return trip and that spelled trouble. His eyes flitted between black water ahead and the green-lit radar screen in front of him.

Bernardo's heart jumped when dots suddenly popped up on the radar—indicating small, low-lying islands called cays. Stretched out like a string of pearls, it was here that U.S. Coast Guard cutters had been hiding when they seized two speedboats like Bernardo's last week. But the cutters were only half the problem, he thought anxiously. The other half was the coast guard helicopters now on the prowl. They were fast. Damn fast, he thought. Well-armed too. Everyone knew that Washington was hell-bent on bringing down Fidel Castro, especially since the 9/11 terrorist attacks on America. It was no secret that Washington believed Castro had terrorism on his mind. So in today's stormy U.S.–Cuba climate, Bernardo and his friends were flirting with danger, and they knew it.

Bernardo inhaled deeply and tried to relax. He wanted to tell Miguel about his worries, but knew it was out of the question. Miguel would think he had lost his nerve, had no cojones, and would drop him on the spot—at a time when Bernardo badly needed the money. Playing at weddings and banquets had not provided steady income at the level he had hoped for when he left Medellín, Colombia, for Miami, leaving his wife and four kids behind. An illegal alien, he was painfully aware of how much he had to rely on word-of-mouth referrals for his gigs. Lots of hustling. Lots of dead ends. Still, it sure as hell beat his former grinding life of working cocaine crops in Colombia with his parents. A million times better than shining shoes in Bogotá like his brothers.

He glanced at the other speedboats skipping along to his port side, confident that everyone out here knew what to do. This run was all about cocaine. Bernardo visualized the white packages of pure cocaine pressed into a "kilo-brick," each weighing a kilogram, or 2.2 pounds, worth around $20,000 wholesale in the U.S. Today's drop, 500 kilograms, would be worth around $10 million in the U.S. It would arrive at his pick-up point on a private twin-engine plane flying in from Colombia. The drugs began the trip from deep inside Colombia's southern rain forest as shiny green leaves from waist-high coca shrubs. Great crop for dirt-poor peasants, he thought, but a high risk game here at the receiving end of the line. His anxiety at times was nearly unbearable, a constant reminder that death hung like a curse over every one of these runs.

Easy for Miguel to demand more runs, he thought. Miguel was sitting tight in Miami. It's *my* ass on the line out here on the open sea. His heart jumped again when he thought he saw the telltale blip of a coast guard ship on the radar. The blip faded, his eyes were playing tricks on him. He leaned forward into the wind and tried to relax his fingers on the steering wheel, the hull vibrating rhythmically under his feet.

The trip from Key West passed swiftly. When he caught sight of the sweeping beam of the lighthouse on Cayo Paredon Grande, homing landmark inside Cuba's closely guarded territorial waters, he reached for his VHF radio microphone and selected the prearranged channel.

"*La Mujer* to Cuba Coast Guard," he said, a hint of nervousness in his voice.

The Spanish-speaker's firm response came instantly, and Bernardo breathed more easily. He throttled back and signaled the others to a holding pattern. Thirty minutes later he caught sight of the Cuban gunboat on the horizon motoring steadily toward them in the early light of dawn.

Cuba's coastal waters meant danger for those without proper papers and many foreign sailors wound up as

Cuba's long-term "guests" when they strayed this close to the coast. As the gunboat drew near, Bernardo could see the ship's chief officer braced against the railing on the port side of the rolling foredeck, a six-foot-five, lanky man with short black hair. In addition to the captain, Bernardo counted five security types on deck—members of Cuba's intelligence agency, the DGI, he assumed.

"*Hola! Capitán*," Bernardo shouted, reaching out to catch the thick, wet nylon line cast to him. They rafted *La Mujer* to the larger Cuban gunboat and Bernardo climbed up the rope ladder onto the lightly rolling deck above, where he shook hands with the captain and accompanied him to the bridge. Bernardo knew the captain well, liked him, and had been through this drill many times before. He looked forward to this part of the operation. The captain treated him as a special guest of the Cuban government. At least that segment of the Cuban government behind the drug business, Bernardo thought, as he stepped into the bridge. He often wondered how high up it went in Havana, but of course never asked. Instead, he enjoyed the rum and Coca-Cola Cuba libres and rich, fat cigar offered by the captain.

About an hour later the first officer came into the bridge and informed the captain that they'd picked up the incoming aircraft. Draining glasses and putting on their hats, the captain and Bernardo stepped outside into the cool early morning air, heads cocked to the sound of the distant plane ghosting toward them. It flew directly over restricted Cuban air space, where surface-to-air missile sites, SAMs, and airfields were located. The foreign twin-engine aircraft came in low, in full view of Cuba's military defense units, its distant droning engines growing louder as red wing lights blinked more visibly against the sun-streaked early morning horizon. As Bernardo turned to climb back down the rope ladder, the captain handed him a box of fine Cuban cigars, gave him a broad smile, and added, *"Buena suerte,* mi amigo . . . may you have a safe trip back."

Back on *La Mujer*, Bernardo gazed at the incoming plane as it passed over the flotilla, lifted the radio microphone from its holder, and checked in with each member of his group. They knew the drill. The Cuban gunboat meanwhile motored slowly from one speedboat to the next, dropping off a DGI official in each vessel. With the plane closing in for a second pass, Bernardo frowned as he checked Sánchez again to make sure his boat was in the right place.

On the aircraft's second pass, they watched the first white bundle, about the size of a bale of hay, tumble out the aircraft's open door into the lightening sky, rapidly followed by others. Like large dice rolled by a giant hand, the plastic-wrapped bales fell end-over-end and plunged into the sea like some huge seabird diving for fish. They did not use parachutes. They took too long for the drop.

The moment a bale hit the sea, men in boats went to work. They snagged the bobbing bales with grapples, pulled them to the side of the gentling rolling vessel, reached over the gunnel, and hauled them aboard. As Bernardo worked, he kept Sánchez ever present in his peripheral view. Wrestling dripping bales, DGI officials cut them open, verified numbers of the small, white packets inside, and entered information in spiral notebooks. It was all going smoothly, another well-rehearsed pick-up.

The drug pick-up was right on schedule. Just a few floating bales left to be retrieved from the sea. Bernardo hummed to himself, wiped sweat from his eyes with a red bandanna, and hefted another dripping bale over the gunnel. Miguel will be pleased, he thought—a good thing, given his brooding temper. Miguel had been in and out of prison and had beaten more than one man so badly they were disfigured for life. He quivered for a second, thinking of Miguel's dark, sunken eyes and unsmiling mouth as he hauled another bale aboard, letting it thump confidently on the deck floor. He stopped to rest for a moment and was about to say something to the DGI official standing beside him.

Then it happened. Out of the blue. A roar of twin outboard engines exploded to life off the starboard bow of Bernardo's boat. The noise so startled him that he stood there for a moment, staring in stunned disbelief at the giant rooster tail behind Sánchez's speedboat, bow raised as it shot forward at high speed. He could see the DGI official from Sánchez's boat treading water in the oily wake, waving his arms and shouting for help.

"Sánchez! *Puta, carajo!*" Bernardo muttered, pulling down the bill of his cap. "That bastard! Goddamn him!" he hissed, lunging for the wheel and reaching for the throttle to give chase. In urgent confusion he stumbled over a crate, knocked down the DGI official standing beside him and sprawled head first onto the slippery cockpit floor. Bernardo struggled to stand up, grabbed the wheel, advanced the throttle to keep Sánchez in view as his boat leapt forward. The DGI man scrambled to his feet and pulled out his own pistol, but it was of little use. Bernardo looked around for his rifle as *La Mujer* gathered speed. He hoped he could get close enough to take a shot. The other boat drivers apprehensively watched the chase, mesmerized by Sánchez's audacity, but stuck to their work as ordered.

It was not long before Bernardo realized that Sánchez was out of rifle range. Shit, he thought, what the hell do I do now? With no chance of closing the gap, painfully aware that he had to get back to keep an eye on the others, he sighed and methodically turned *La Mujer* around, wondering how he would explain all this to Miguel. His trembling hand removed the red bandanna from his back pocket and wiped his damp forehead. The DGI official looked at him sympathetically and said, "Jesus, man, this is bad . . . really bad. What are you going to do?" Bernardo stared at him bleakly, his eyebrows pinched. He had no answer to that cryptic question.

When all the bales had been fished from the sea and merchandise counted, Bernardo and the other boatmen said good-bye to the Cubans. The gunboat captain again explained to Bernardo that the reason he had not chased after Sánchez was because he had no authority in international waters. "But don't worry," he said, trying to put a note of confidence in his words, "I will report this incident to the right person when I return to port." Still, he appeared far from convinced that this would be of much help to Bernardo.

Bernardo and his crew watched the gunboat disappear over the horizon, nervously discussing the brazen actions of that bastard Sánchez and how Miguel would react. A careful counting of the drop indicated that he had gotten away with four bales. It was quite a haul, depending on how and where it would be sold, worth a small fortune. A huge loss for Miguel.

They spent the rest of the day anchored not far from Cayo Paredon Grande, waiting to return to Key West at night, in an effort to elude the U.S. Coast Guard cutters. The hours seemed endless as Bernardo, baseball cap pulled down low over his brow, eyes taking in the sea's light and dark shades of jade shimmering around him, played out one agonizing scenario after another on what he would say when he returned to Key West. Normally, he would have been elated about the drop and upcoming pay-off, celebrating with the others, joking and shooting the breeze as they waited out the day. Not this time. The only thing on Bernardo's mind was Miguel.

Bernardo slumped forward in the gently rocking boat, listening to the light waves slap against the hull, watching three large frigate birds with long wings and hooked beaks pester two sea gulls high above until they dropped their tasty catch, swooping in to grab the bait in mid-air. These winged creatures, known as "pirate birds" because they harvested the rewards of others' hard work, reminded him of Sánchez, and it kept going through his mind that his foreboding about Sánchez had come painfully true.

Jesus, he thought, why didn't I speak up when he mentioned that Sánchez would be the new guy? Why didn't I ask if we could trust him? He remembered that he *was* about to say something when the thought of Miguel losing his temper, going into one of his rages, silenced his words before they crossed his lips. Bernardo knew full well that Miguel could not *stand* having his decisions questioned. Still, what had taken place was not *his* fault. But how would Miguel see it? Yeah, that was the real problem.

As the day wore on and the sun rose higher, he struggled with dark thoughts about his inevitable meeting with Miguel, rubbing the knot in the back of his neck with his hand, wishing like hell he were home in Colombia with his wife and kids. The more he agonized over his situation, the more he felt like a trapped animal. Head drooped down, eyes half closed, staring between his legs, he wondered if he should just cut out and beat it fast back to Colombia and let them find somebody else to replace him.

Then again, money was the issue. God knows he needed it. Couldn't survive without it. If he wanted to cash in on this run, he had to go back and face Miguel. Could he talk his way out of this Sánchez problem? You never knew when Miguel would erupt, he sighed. Bernardo felt strangely entangled in a spider web with no escape. He sat there in gloomy despair until the sun began to set, his boat rolling gently on the swells. He listened to the sea lap against the hull and racked his brain for a story Miguel might buy.

Two

Havana

"Great day for the drop," General Manuel Ramiro said quietly, exhaling dark blue smoke. He brushed away the fly flitting along his left sleeve and stared intently over his desk at Victor, a cousin on Ramiro's side of the family, a colonel under Ramiro's command.

"*Sí* señor," Victor answered, removing his steel-rimmed glasses and laying them on the table he took an audible sip of his coffee.

"Weather's perfect." Ramiro turned his head, cocked it quizzically, and listened for a moment. He glanced warily at the closed opaque glass-plate door leading from his office to the main corridor outside. From the outside corridor came muffled conversation and footsteps of staff members, not all of whom could be trusted. The fan whirring overhead softened Ramiro and Victor's voices.

Ramiro's office was located in Cuba's Ministry of Interior's ultrasecret command center for internal security and intelligence operations. They talked just audibly enough to hear each other. Each wore the standard-issue olive green uniform of Cuba's Revolutionary Armed Forces. Ramiro cut a short and stocky profile, his face round and pocked-marked. He was known for his high, nervous energy and prone to emotional outbursts when not in the company of someone he wanted to impress with molasses-smooth courtesy. He rocked slowly back and forth in his squeaking desk chair, cigar stuck in the corner of his mouth.

Victor wiped small beads of perspiration from his

high, pale forehead with a clean, white handkerchief.
Tall and erect, he wore a gray, crisp-cut mustache and
full, but short, beard on his long face. His close-cropped
gray hair, intelligent clear blue eyes, and small, straight-
lined nose gave him more the appearance of a Jesuit
priest than security officer. He was in fact a closet
Catholic, but no one, not even Ramiro, knew. Victor
spoke in a terse, clipped accent, as if giving a lecture.
His manner of speaking, combined with austere face
and elitist air, tested the patience of the more outspoken
and volatile Ramiro. Something else about Victor: he
worried incessantly, not least about Ramiro and the high
stakes political games he played.

When the telephone rang, Ramiro picked up, listened
for a moment, and then asked quickly and tersely, "How
did it happen?" He leaned back in his chair, glanced at
Victor, and scratched at one of the reddish blotches on
his face, listening, deep in thought.

"So what did you do?" He paused. "That son of a
bitch." His voice was deep and mellow, like a 1940s
baseball announcer. It helped him offset his unattractive
features, or so he thought.

Ramiro hung up and said, "We have a problem."

"Oh?"

"One of the boatmen ripped off four bales from the
drop this morning . . . some guy named Sánchez.
Pushed our DGI guy overboard and took off. Headed
north for Key West or Miami."

Victor, wide-eyed, rubbed his hands and said anxiously, "My God . . . do you think . . . ?"

"CIA? Hard to say, more like someone out to make a
quick buck."

"Or a CIA agent now with proof of our operation. I
knew this would happen . . . just a matter of time. . . . I
tried to warn you. . . . Listen . . ."

"Goddammit, Victor," Ramiro hissed. "Relax for

Christ's sake. Stop pissing in your pants. Sure as hell it's some guy willing to take the risk. Cool it."

"But if CIA *is* connected, then we're in trouble . . . let's not fool ourselves," Victor said in a low, ominous tone.

A knock on the door that led to another inside corridor and its inner offices made Ramiro swing back around in his chair.

"What is it, Martínez? Don't just stand there, man. Come in!" He barked. "You finished that report yet?"

"Yes, sir," came the firm reply, perhaps less firm than intended.

"Good, put it on the desk," Ramiro snapped, jabbing his index finger at the desk. "Tell González to see me right away and alert the staff. I want everyone in here at eleven-hundred sharp."

When the door closed behind Martínez, Ramiro took a deep draw on his cigar, paused, and exhaled a long, thin trail of blue smoke. He pushed the newly arrived report across the desk to Victor and in a voice to convey the serious nature of the matter, said, "Take a look at this quarterly black market report. Doesn't look good. We got to crack down harder."

Victor took the thick report and began thumbing through it, not surprised by its contents. Havana's black market trade—a direct consequence of the country's scarce consumer goods and U.S. crackdown, unemployment, and huge demand for U.S. dollars—was no secret in Cuba.

Ramiro's office setting at the Ministry, where reports of this type were common currency, was what one would expect. His well-worn oak desk, polished by the cleaning crew and barren of papers, looked like something lifted from a U.S. Pentagon storage room. Across the room from his desk stood five shiny dark green metal filing cabinets, like ramrod sentinels guarding the office. Each had five drawers, a thick black iron bar running through the handles, secured by a bulky silver combination lock. The walls had multicolored maps of Central America and Colombia and a signed photograph of gray-bearded Fidel Castro. His watery dark brown eyes stared out from under neatly trimmed bushy eyebrows—a stern presence and reminder who was boss in this place.

Two thick-padded black chairs were arranged in front of the desk, one with the imprint of Victor's backside after he got up to start pacing the room. A large black couch took up one corner of the room, fronted by a short, spotless glass-top coffee table. On it rested a silver Cartier cigarette lighter and a crystal ashtray with the name *Lalique* etched in gold on its side. Ramiro kept his prized ruby-red Mont Blanc pen inside the top desk drawer in a dark back corner under several sheets of letterhead stationery. Their American origin made these items highly prized. Placed along another wall was a large black bookcase with books aligned in perfect formation, like soldiers in a close order drill. Most of the books were in Spanish, some in Russian. Arranged by subject matter, the Russian books were mainly on human behavior, psychic studies, and psychic research—as the Russians called it, psychotronics—or as anyone who had studied in Moscow like Ramiro knew, telepathy.

Ramiro's colleagues did not take seriously his claim of telepathic power and found his alleged use of it incomprehensible. But over the years Ramiro had become convinced of its power, which he projected with absolute self-confidence. Victor, for all his self-discipline and logical thought, seemed to believe in Ramiro's psychic abilities. It would be hard to say if Victor was totally under Ramiro's influence, but more than one person in that building had observed that Victor acted differently when he was around Ramiro than when he was not.

Still, Victor would be the first to say, as he had told his wife Isabella on numerous occasions that he was fortu-

nate to be Ramiro's cousin. Family connections were
everything in Cuba if you wanted to get ahead. Victor's
family tie paved the way to bask in Ramiro's aura, a *patrón,* used to his advantage. That's how you played the
game and climbed through the ranks here in Cuba—
identify a *patrón* and stick with him through thick and
thin. *Sí* señor, Victor knew that he could thank Ramiro
for his position in MININT, where personal contacts
ruled the day. Thank God Ramiro was *the* consummate
político, a master at political gamesmanship. In the old
days before Castro's revolution in 1959, Cubans called it
politiquería, the game of corrupt politics. Ramiro knew
every move on the chessboard.

Victor had witnessed Ramiro's extrasensory power
over people time and again—an uncanny ability to ease
them onto a path that appeared to serve their interests,
while never losing sight of his own goal. He had a mysterious style and grace, Victor thought, so different from
many others that he knew, more like a cobra than a
python. Victor could see it in Ramiro's manner—
authoritative, confident, and charismatic. He was very
macho. It was in his eyes—dark, piercing, calculating.
He had this way of staring you down, locking onto your
eyes with some ominous, fixed purpose.

It was eerie, Victor thought, even with that eye twitch
of his, which made it difficult to know if Ramiro was
winking on purpose or just couldn't control the corner
of his eye. But when they locked on, there was no mistaking it. They simply would not let go, exerting hyp-
notic control that made you feel vulnerable; at least
that's how Victor felt. He could swear that he had seen it
happen frequently with others too. Ramiro reminded
Victor of a Latino version of Russia's legendary psychic,
Rasputin, who during his own time exerted an improba-
ble influence that allowed him to control even the czar.
Even Machiavelli would have paid big bucks for that
kind of power, Victor mused.

"Enter!" Ramiro growled loudly at the knock on the door, jolting Victor out of his thoughts. A tall, thin, stiff-backed officer appeared somewhat timid in the doorway. The black security nametag clipped on the left pocket of his short-sleeved shirt read, COL. RICARDO GONZÁLEZ.

"Sir, we've completed that briefing paper on internal security," he said.

"So you made it on schedule," Ramiro replied.

"Right on schedule, sir," González said.

"*Bueno*," Ramiro shot back. "Give me your bottom line."

"Bottom line, sir? Just this," responded González in a clipped, no nonsense voice. "Our Counterintelligence Division thinks the CIA will try to slip one or more agents into Cuba over the next few weeks, most likely through Mexico or Canada as a tourist. They believe, from everything coming out of Washington lately, that the U.S. sees us weakened by food and fuel shortages, and of course escalating black market activities—so undermined in fact that we quite possibly are on the brink of collapse.

"But here's the key point, sir. Counterintelligence thinks the U.S. Republican president is hell-bent on bringing down our government. After all, he made 'liberating Cuba' a campaign promise in the last election. Since Florida delivered the votes in that election, our analysts think the President is obligated to Florida's Cuban exiles. So a U.S. military attack on Cuba would play out big in Washington. You know, for the president's party—and for the his brother, Florida's governor. He's a likely Republican candidate for the next presidential race, so military action against us would work well in a future election fight. Lots of votes in Florida."

The room turned oppressively quiet for a moment, only the whirring overhead fans breaking the silence. Ramiro sat in poker-faced repose. You never knew what he was thinking, Victor thought. He should be playing poker.

Spying on Cuba was nothing new in this Ministry's operations. Since the 1961 Bay of Pigs invasion, Cuba had been alert for espionage agents. Ramiro's Ministry had played a lead role in tracking down more than one scheme to assassinate Fidel—from exploding cigars to monkeying around with his scuba diving equipment. Ramiro himself had interrogated U.S. citizens visiting Cuba suspected to be U.S. agents, or Cubans who the Ministry believed worked for the U.S. No, it wasn't the spying that was new, Ramiro thought quickly. It was how the U.S. president would use the information.

The report was probably right on that score, he reasoned. Ramiro shifted the cigar in his mouth, removed it, and knocked off some ashes in the ashtray. What bothered him more than U.S. elections, he reflected, drumming his fingers on the desk, his mind racing like a computer, was the frenetic drug trafficking activities now running rampant in the Caribbean—transshipments through the Bahamas, Puerto Rico, Haiti, the Dominican Republic, Jamaica, U.S. Virgin Islands, St. Martin, St. Kitts, and Anguilla and Antigua—all of which he knew raised the DEA's attention to drug links with Cuba.

That kind of U.S. attention naturally threatened his own drug operation. Not good, he thought. Definitely not good. It was painfully obvious from all the monitored reporting out of Washington that the DEA suspected Cuba of drug trafficking. Hell, the CIA was even trying to pin terrorism on Havana after 9/11. Anything for votes, he thought. *Sonsabitches*. To try to diffuse that attention, Ramiro periodically ordered the seizure of a cocaine-loaded vessel transiting Cuba's territorial waters from Colombia to the Bahamas, and then transferred the cocaine to U.S. authorities who prosecuted the ship's crew members. Maybe he would have to step up those seizures.

"OK," he said, rubbing his chin, "good work, González. First of all, set up extra surveillance at José Martí Airport. Beef up personnel at customs. You know the drill. Same thing goes for foreign tourist operations. Let's give closer attention to incoming group tours and foreign education programs. Background checks. All that. We'll set up a meeting to discuss this report later this week. I want you to do the briefing at that meeting and this time, let's anticipate questions with more creativity. OK, dismissed."

Ramiro turned to Victor as the door closed and started to say something when Victor interrupted apprehensively with, "Jesus, more spies, just what we need. We got this place under more surveillance than a prison exercise yard, and the CIA still has people in here. How about those two arrests just last month? You think they suspect us?"

Rubbing the palms of his hands on his pants, shifting his weight in his chair, sitting straight, Victor added, "Maybe we should just get out of this drug business altogether. We got an awful lot of balls in the air, you know."

Ramiro locked eyes with Victor, a warning to calm down, and said, "You want to get out of it? How do you think your family will react? I don't see them complaining about the sweet life. Good food, plenty of clothes, nice jewelry. You think they'd be happy giving all that up? Remember how it was before we got into this business?" Ramiro flashed a thin smile at Victor and restlessly went to the window that opened onto the vast expanse of the Plaza de la Revolución below.

He took a long draw on his cigar and gazed pensively down at the great open space drenched in blazing sunlight, barren now, devoid of people save the tour buses pulling up at regular intervals and the weeds growing in cracks in the Plaza's uneven and bleak concrete slabs. He could see the cluster of Canadian tourists not far out

in front of his own Ministry of Interior, snap
tos, attracted by the monumental image of "Che
vara, one of Cuba's legendary revolutionary heroes
fought with Fidel, on the front of the Ministry building.
If he closed his eyes he could almost hear the young
heroic Fidel bellowing orations to the adoring masses
down there, sometimes numbering over a million, the
roar of their approval echoing his word. Ramiro remembered it as a time of ecstatic revolutionary fervor, everyone filled with hopes and dreams for the future. Such a
long time ago, he mused. What saps we were to believe
in him, he thought, momentarily clenching his teeth.

Off in the distance on the other side of the giant historic plaza stood the huge white monument towering
over the statue of José Martí, Cuba's famous nineteenth
century national hero. Martí, whom all adored still today, the moving force behind the 1895 War of Independence against Spain, was the man with whom Ramiro
knew Fidel fatuously loved to compare himself. Ah,
Martí, Ramiro thought, another misguided idealist, all
that democracy crap. He never understood the meaning
of power or how to use it.

Farther in the distance, behind the Martí statue and
monument he could see the squat, low-lying gray building of the Central Committee of the Communist Party
of Cuba where Fidel had his office. He sighed deeply,
nearly choking on inhaled cigar smoke, thinking how he
had come to loath the man. His toes clenched at the
thought, and, visualizing Castro sitting at the head of
the conference table in his office, Ramiro shook his head
in total disgust.

Ramiro reflected how he and Fidel once shared a common vision in the early days, but time had cooled his
trust in Fidel as a skilled leader. In truth, Ramiro seethed
in pent-up rage at playing a subordinate role in Cuba's
decision-making hierarchy. He had come to detest par-
ticipating in pro-Castro rallies. Ramiro blamed Fidel for

everything wrong in Cuba—not least his bullheaded pursuit of outdated communism after the Soviet Union fell apart. But it was not simply blaming Fidel for his stewardship of Cuba's destiny. In truth, Ramiro craved power. Absolute power—and he had a plan to get it.

The telephone ring snapped Ramiro back to the present. He picked up the receiver and said, "*Diga.*" A pause, followed by, ". . . OK, OK. Bring it in."

Seconds later a tall woman who looked to be in her late thirties opened the door separating Ramiro's office from the staff offices in the inner corridor. Dressed in a white skirt and light blue blouse, open at the neck in Cuban fashion, that flattered her trim, well-defined body, her pale green eyes bore the trace of carefully selected, quality makeup. She exuded a kind of regal self-confidence of someone who knew she was attractive, and her movement conveyed grace in motion. She was a looker all right, Victor mused.

Still, not even her long slender legs and satin complexion warmed the chill that greeted her entry into the room. Anyone could see that although she wore enough mascara to accentuate her eyes, her makeup did not disguise dark circles that had started to form in recent days. Taut, barely discernible worry lines etched the corners of her mouth, the effect of more anxiety than laughter in her life, Victor guessed. Well, she damn well had plenty of reason to be nervous, he thought.

Ramiro, wary of enemies around him, was certain that several days ago he had left open one of the secret file cabinets in this office. Not like him, but it had happened. Worse, Ramiro was convinced that while he was out of the office, this woman, Elena Rodríguez, had rifled through the files and likely come across compromising information. This meant one thing: she was a spy, some kind of goddamn agent.

Yet, as he had told Victor, he could not be one hundred

percent sure until he had more evidence. Besides, he needed to know *who* she was working for—Castro? CIA? Some other Cuban faction? God knows, the political infighting was rampant these days and factions were out there in scores, like a can of worms. So, he had put her under round-the-clock surveillance. But this woman was smart, real smart. She probably knew, or at least suspected, she was being followed, Victor thought. Yeah, in which case, she should be scared. Her life was in danger; make no mistake about it, he mused. Lucky she was still alive. But when the time came to take her out it would not be pretty, for Ramiro excelled in butchery.

Her poise, surprising under the dark shadow of suspicion that she must have felt, was checked by guarded deference to Ramiro. With an expressionless face, she responded calmly and cogently to Ramiro's questions about the letter she had just completed and then reminded him of a meeting within the hour. Despite her apparent, thinly-disguised anxiety, her cool demeanor impressed Victor. Ramiro, however, seemed impressed only by the fact that she represented some kind of treachery among his staff. If his convictions proved accurate, he knew exactly what to do with her and anyone connected to her.

"Will that be all, sir?" she asked in a flat-toned voice, standing erect, her jet-black hair combed to a sheen straight down between her shoulder blades.

"That's it," Ramiro snapped.

Dismissed, she turned gracefully and walked back toward her office, the echo of her high heels trailing her out of the room. The two men's gazes lingered closely behind. Observing this little scene unfolding reminded Victor of how her background was, to put it mildly, odd. Ramiro had been forced to hire her under pressure from Fidel Castro himself. As the niece of one of Castro's old friends, to whom he owed a favor, Castro had insisted that Ramiro make room for her on his staff. After all, Castro had argued, even though he hated Americans, he liked their system of higher education. Elena Rodríguez was well educated, had a master's degree in political science from Georgetown University in Washington, D.C. Her knowledge of international affairs and American foreign policy would be of unique assistance in Ramiro's Caribbean operations. She would be an asset on Ramiro's staff, Castro had insisted. So, under pressure, Ramiro reluctantly had brought her aboard, though he distrusted her from the beginning and this file thing sealed it for him.

Still, Ramiro had told Victor early on that her looks at least offered some compensation, as did her nice hip swing.

Ramiro glanced at Victor as the door closed. "She moves well, *Chico*. No?"

"First class," Victor responded, standing up to leave. He paused a second, a thoughtful look on his face, then asked in a low voice, "You really think she suspects something?"

Ramiro shrugged his shoulders and said, "Probably. Maybe I should speak to Moreno about her." His eyes narrowed over a thin smile that crossed his tight lips. "Which reminds me," he added coyly, toying with his diamond-studded gold ring, working it around his left ring finger. Ramiro gazed over the desk at Victor, his eyes narrowing, "Moreno's flying in tomorrow."

Victor, hand on the outside corridor doorknob, about to make his exit, stopped dead in his tracks. He turned slowly, deliberately, and stared at Ramiro like a deer in headlights. He went slightly pale and found himself trying to control his suddenly rapid breathing. "So . . . so soon?" he said, dry mouthed, hoping his voice sounded normal.

"*Correcto*. Mañana."

Victor struggled to remain calm and said, "I . . . I thought it was next month."

"Had to move things up," Ramiro replied, his eye winking away, a barely discernible grin playing along his lower lip.

Victor put his moist palms on his thighs and rubbed slowly. Uneasy, he wanted to say something clever that Ramiro would like. Instead, out came a simple, "I see. Mañana, you say?"

"*Sí* señor. You'll have a chance to meet him."

Victor swallowed hard. Moreno's image in his mind, a character whose scarred face and animal movements resembled a maximum-security escapee from death row, a mass murderer on the loose. Moreno gave him the creeps and events were moving fast. He felt Ramiro's eyes on him, knowing he dare not show fear. The thought jumped into his mind—was it wise to go along with this plan? He started to reach for his coffee, but his hand was trembling so much that he thought better of it.

Victor stared at Ramiro as he played with the large gold ring on his finger. He could not slip the feeling that they were now in uncharted and dangerous waters. Events had gathered a momentum of their own. The whole affair had an uncanny dreamlike quality. Jesus, it all had sounded so logical when they first discussed the plan, but now with Moreno actually coming to town, the future looked . . . well . . . to put it mildly . . . foreboding. Victor knew Moreno's file backward and forward. He had met him twice and knew enough to want to stay as far away from him as physically possible. In Moreno's presence, Victor felt like he was being stalked by some kind of predator that knew his every move and blocked all exits. He felt light-headed and found it hard to breath, like a vise had tightened around his chest.

THREE

Georgetown

Neal McGrath stood confidently at the podium in the Capitol Hill Club lecture hall and gazed out at his audience. A packed house—foreign policy wonks, legislative assistants from the Hill, think tank types, military brass, and a host of staffers from executive offices. It was Friday, eleven-thirty in the morning, and he had just finished his hour lecture on Cuba. He stuffed his white note cards into his inside coat pocket and prepared to take questions. McGrath wore his standard speaker get-up of gray trousers, white shirt, blue blazer, and flashy red-striped tie. He did not look like a stodgy political science professor at Georgetown, where he taught, but someone who more resembled Harrison Ford in *Raiders of the Lost Ark*. Even in tie and shirt, his tanned, rugged good looks made him appear as if he belonged more at the controls of a bush plane over the Amazon than in a university classroom.

McGrath knew what to expect. Castro's Cuba offered endless avenues for bitter disagreement over U.S.–Cuban relations. He had been in the thick of it many times. This morning would be no different, he thought, and sure enough, the man he recognized stood up and in a booming, strident voice launched a vitriolic anti-Castro monologue, arms waving, fists punching the air to make his points. McGrath shifted his weight, sighed, and smiled wryly at the man, mildly amused by the emotionalism, yet also somewhat sympathetic to him.

He assumed the man was a Cuban-American from his Latino accent and powerful, even poetic, manner in which he spoke. This Latino had an attitude, and Mc-Grath's sympathy quickly soured when he accused Mc-Grath of giving a lecture that supported "that two-bit dictator" who so dominated Cuban politics, imprisoned anyone who disagreed with him, probably harbored terrorists, and killed people at random. His attack went on in classic style that would have brought a standing ovation from conservative Cubans in Miami or LA. He should win an Oscar for this performance, McGrath thought, squeezing his toes to control his slow burn.

McGrath stared hard at the man, interrupted him, and said, "Listen my friend, now that you have made your position crystal clear, what exactly is your *question*?" Two minutes later and still no question, but still more colorful diatribe, McGrath ended the speech with, "This is more complicated than we have time for here. Let's move on. You and I can discuss it later. Next question?" Cuban politics, McGrath thought. Any issue on Cuba gets ten different points of view. He pointed to another raised hand.

McGrath answered a range of questions—rising tensions in U.S.–Cuban relations, Castro's aging, but still entrenched leadership, a tightened U.S. embargo, refugees fleeing for the U.S., domestic instability, and possible drug trafficking. The high number of refugees, he said, may indicate growing internal dissension and political instability. He reminded the audience that human rights activists had been treated harshly lately—beaten and jailed with little chance of release. He talked about the recent Cuban rally of over a million Cubans who had marched against the U.S.—the biggest protest rally since Castro took power back in 1959—a sure sign Castro was trying to shore up his regime in view of all the talk about a U.S. invasion. After all, he explained, we have a reelected Republican administration in office with its publicized view of Cuba as part of the "axis of evil." So Cubans have reasons to worry they might be next on the U.S. attack list—a possibility that Castro would play to the hilt to consolidate his power.

He ended the question and answer period by making it clear that Castro was the consummate politician. "He's as tough as they come. Tell you what, invite me back in a couple of months for another look at that question. I'm headed for Havana on a research trip myself shortly. I'll give you the straight scoop later . . . that is, provided I get back," he smiled, a ripple of laughter and round of applause to end the session.

McGrath's "Cuba trip" comment got the attention of a middle-aged couple in the back of the auditorium. The man, shorter than McGrath, wore a summer khaki suit. His thick black hair was combed straight back, and he had a distinct dark mole on the left side of his forehead. He had been watching McGrath's performance like a pointer flushing a pheasant. The woman seated beside him was slightly taller, slim, about five-ten. Attractive in her late forties, sitting erect in her fashionable short-sleeve, light blue business suit, she fit Washington's bureaucratic image perfectly.

While McGrath answered questions, Sam Goodwin turned to the woman, Kim McGinnis, leaned his shoulder into her and whispered, "So he's going to Cuba after all. The report was right." He looked at her closely, eyebrows raised.

McGinnis tilted her head toward Goodwin without taking her eyes off McGrath, and whispered back out of the corner of her mouth. "Didn't I tell you?" A pause. Then, "You sure this is a good idea?"

"I do." Goodwin said quietly, quickly, his usual pit bull confidence on fast-forward. "Look at the way McGrath's handling this crowd. He's back to normal."

"I'm talking about his emotional state," McGinnis said dryly. "I think he's still under tremendous stress. Another thing, the report says his research's slipping at the university. Teaching's OK, but he's making himself scarce to students and, more importantly, hasn't met his deadline with the publisher for his book. He's up for tenure and under the circumstances might not get it. I know McGrath's dean, Jack Robertson—friend of mine—doesn't like the look of things. Says there's no guarantee Georgetown's going to grant tenure to McGrath, despite his extenuating circumstances. He may look confident, Sam, but I'm not convinced that he's all that stable as you think. Hope you know what you're doing."

"Look," Goodwin replied, mildly annoyed, "What have we got to lose here? Even if he's hurting inside, he can separate his emotions from his professional life. That's all we need. He's in good physical shape. Plays tennis, jogs regularly. I say let's go for it."

McGinnis shot Goodwin a doubtful sidelong glance. They sat there for a minute, watching McGrath wind up and leave the podium, two hangers-on trailing him, locked in animated conversation. "Let's go," Goodwin said, standing up.

When McGrath stepped out of the air-conditioned Capitol Hill Club, the oppressive hot air of a steamy D.C. afternoon hit him like a steel mill blast furnace. He paused for a moment on the sidewalk, as a deep roll of ominous thunder echoed across the skies. He glanced at the huge, dark purple clouds piling up above him, then looked across the street and was reminded that his wife, Rebecca, had stood at this very spot two years ago—greeting him as he came out of the club from one of his lectures. A pang of remorse hit hard as he flashed on her presence. The first heavy drops of rain splattered on the sidewalk, and people dodged for cover. McGrath jogged across the street and headed for the Capitol South metro station, trying to outrace the predictable downpour. He reached the escalator as lightning cracked two blocks away and the skies unleashed a Niagara Falls deluge.

Goodwin and McGinnis pushed their way out of the club's revolving front door just in time to catch sight of McGrath disappearing down the escalator across the street. "So what do we do next, Sam?" McGinnis asked, standing close to him under the green- and white-striped canopy at the club's entrance as gray sheets of rain poured down in a torrent, more thunder booming across the leaden skies nearby.

Goodwin pulled a white handkerchief from his breast pocket, wiped his brow and said, "I'm going to make the pitch. I think he'll go for it."

Down at the metro's concrete first level, McGrath slipped his metro card into the turnstile, rode the second escalator down to the brightly lit platform and caught the train just before the doors hissed shut. He dropped into an empty seat, still feeling high from his lecture, a normal reaction he had come to enjoy since leaving the Army's Special Forces and entering university life. A "Join the Reserves" poster in the metro car reminded him about his combat in Panama not so long ago, thoughts that he quickly swept back into the dark corner of his mind. Soon the ride would be over, he mused, and then he would walk to his empty town house. Rebecca would not be there.

The thought of Rebecca brought a wave of melancholy, and he stared blankly straight ahead, watching the Metro tunnel lights flash by on his right as if he were in a daze. He saw her clearly in his mind's eye: tall, trim body, long, dark hair, and hazel eyes; the soft tone of her laughter, always sunny and upbeat. Life after the army had been sweet, he the consummate new professor relishing the university world of ideas, Rebecca fresh out of Georgetown School of Law, driven by a passion for congressional human rights legislation, especially in the Caribbean—a promising career ahead of her. *What a great time we had*, that is . . . he thought, until Rebecca . . .

As the metroliner sped through two more crowded stations, the adrenaline power surge from his lecture dropped swiftly, and he felt more and more drained. He focused on Rebecca as if gazing through a crystal ball of diffused light and sound. He listened robotically to the metallic voice of the metro driver droning out announced stops, "Federal Triangle . . . Metro Center . . . Farragut West," that fused in McGrath's mind with the doctor's whispered words, "I'm so sorry to have to tell you this, Professor McGrath . . ." He blinked twice and forced himself not to think about it.

At Foggy Bottom, twenty minutes later, he came out from the metro tunnel and squinted in the light, glancing up at the still-cloudy skies. The street gutter rushed with water from the passing downpour, but by now the cloudburst was over, and he began walking listlessly toward his town house in Georgetown several blocks away. This was the part of the day he dreaded most. When he reached the red brick steps of his two-story town house, he hesitated, swallowed hard and ran his hand through his hair in a vain effort to ease the sick, empty feeling that now engulfed him. He turned the doorknob hesitantly, pushed open the door, tossed his sport coat over the stairway banister and walked slowly into the kitchen, looking for something to eat. He made a sandwich from the leftover roasted chicken, poured himself a large glass of milk, sat down at the kitchen table, finished his meal, and then shuffled upstairs to the bedroom to try to take a nap.

McGrath slumped down on the edge of the bed, kicked off his shoes, sighed, and fumbled gloomily through the CDs on the end table, where he kept his black portable two speaker CD cassette player. Most of the CDs were big band music from the 1940s, the rest pop hits from the 1950s. He found the Benny Goodman selection he was looking for, slipped in the CD, and lay back on the pillow as strains of one of the songs, "What's New?" wafted through the bedroom. *What's new?* he asked himself morosely, just about everything, not least of which his disturbingly vulnerable position at the university. He visualized that dark, unexpected meeting with his department chair two months ago when the spring semester ended. What a disaster.

He had just collected his mail from his slot in the department mailroom, most of it new textbook advertisements from a dozen or more publishers and a batch of uncorrected final blue book exams he had tucked under his arm. After he had stopped a minute to say hello to Sue Longman, the department's secretary, he had started back to his book-lined office down the hall with its large window looking out onto the plaza two stories below. His intent was to pull out the red ink ballpoint pen and dig into the blue book exams. At that moment Dr. Bill Hudson had stepped out of the chairperson's office, motioned for him to come in, and closed the door behind them, a dead serious look plastered on his face, not the typical jovial smile and goodwill bantering. He looked flushed, like a bad case of roseola—not a good omen—McGrath remembered. He would never make a good poker player, he mused.

In a nutshell, Hudson's message was stark and clear. The department's Appointment, Promotion, and Tenure Committee, and Hudson himself, had agreed that if McGrath had any shot at tenure, he simply would have to get off the dime and tie up the loose ends on his book on Cuba. It must be published—or least it had to be in the works for publication. Otherwise, that was it for his teaching career at Georgetown.

"Sorry Neal, publish or perish still rules," Hudson said soberly.

McGrath lay on his back, hands resting on his chest, and gazed wistfully up at the off-white ceiling where he and Rebecca had hung the mobile of little wooden sailboats. They stirred softly in the faint breeze coming through the open window, and he unhappily recalled last summer when they had spent those two incredible weeks of idyllic sailing on the Chesapeake Bay down around Solomon's Island. He pictured her sitting across from him in the cockpit, silhouetted against the pink and blue fading sunset, their boat at anchor in Mills River. His gaze wandered to her picture on the dresser.

Then came the automobile accident that took her life this past January. Bad timing, McGrath thought. Lousy freak weather. Black ice. Drunk driver. McGrath had found himself in a hospital emergency room waiting area, awaiting word on Rebecca.

Nothing had prepared him for anything like Rebecca's death, not even his years of combat training in the U.S. Army. He turned on his side and stared at his army medals neatly arranged on the bedroom wall across from the bed—the Purple Heart (for wounds received in Panama), the Bronze Star with "V" device (valor), Meritorious Service Medal (for successful company command), and Army Commendation Medal—wondering if he had made the right decision to switch careers after Panama.

He hated feeling sorry for himself, for he came from a long line who took pride in self-reliance and a stiff upper lip when times where tough and when you needed to hang in there. But the way things were going lately, he wasn't sure he had it in him to push on with his academic life, with Rebecca now gone. Recent events had piled up, and at times he felt like throwing in the towel. It crossed his mind that maybe he should dump the university with its grinding demands on research and publishing and look for something else. Maybe teach sailing out in Annapolis. He could do that, he reasoned. It made sense. He would not make as much money, he thought sardonically. Jesus, he suddenly said to himself, you damn well have *got* to get your act together, man.

When the telephone rang, he reached out, half asleep, fumbled for the receiver and mumbled, "Hello?"

"Neal! That you? Great news," Don Samuels, his old college buddy, gushed heartily. Samuels lived in San Diego, fertile land for lawyers. He had agreed to go to Cuba with McGrath, who could use his company. The two of them had taken some crazy trips together in their college years, like hitchhiking across the country, hooking up with that old Greek ship to Europe for more hitchhiking on the continent. They had bought an old 1938 British motorcycle in Belgium, ridden it through Germany and France, slept in hay fields, and crashed it outside Versailles, which produced a close scrape with the law. All that when they were just nineteen.

"Neal, listen," Don said. "My visa and clearance papers just arrived. I'm all set on this end." Don was excited, looking forward to poking around in Cuba and learning about how the law operates in an authoritarian system.

"My visa and papers arrived two days ago," McGrath said, trying to muster a semblance of enthusiasm. "Looks like we're ready to go. Plane reservations out of Miami, right?"

"Right on, *compañero*. Havana, here we come!"

"Fantastic. It's gonna be great. I can hardly wait." McGrath said with more excitement, but thinking it was unconvincing. Still, going to Cuba with Don was a bright spot in McGrath's life. They were tight. He flashed back to the incident on the Colorado River when their rubber raft had flipped upside down, flying through the awesome and frigid Lava Falls rapids deep inside the Grand Canyon. Don had nearly drowned before McGrath, a strong swimmer, dragged him to shore. Maybe this trip would jump-start his book on Cuba, he thought, spike his motivation, "unjam" his writer's block.

He swung his legs over the edge of the bed, trudged into the bathroom and splashed water on his face; then returned to the bedroom and changed into tennis shorts and shirt. He was sitting on the edge of the bed, bent over tying the laces of his tennis shoes, when the telephone rang again.

It was Sam Goodwin. Goodwin? he thought. Why would his old CIA friend call? McGrath had worked for Goodwin as a scholar-in-residence in the Intelligence Directorate during a sabbatical leave two years ago. The CIA liked to bring in a few university scholars now and then to develop new analytic angles in their own research activities. Now Goodwin was calling, because he wanted a word with McGrath. Would he meet him at Dean & DeLuca's tomorrow morning, Saturday, for a cup of coffee?

"What's up?" McGrath asked, his curiosity on full alert.

"Just a little something I'd like to fly by you," Goodwin answered casually.

Ten minutes later as he locked his town house door behind him, he was still pondering Goodwin's call. CIA people don't just telephone out of the blue to pass the day, he thought, especially a serious, all-business type like Goodwin. He took a deep breath and sighed heavily. The call seemed ominous. One more thing he did not want to have to worry about. Not these days. Now what the *hell* did *he* want?

FOUR

Over the deep green Caribbean Sea, a sleek MiG-29 exploded out of a double roll across the cloudless blue sky. Its twin Sarkisov RD-33 turbo engines generated 18,300 pounds of thrust, driving the jet fighter over 1,520 miles per hour. The pilot had not tested the outer 1,300-mile range of this fifty-six foot Russian-built multi-role combat plane, but had put it through its paces under its ceiling of 55,000 feet. Time to return to base. Sun glinted off its trim twin tails, each emblazoned with the blue and white stripes of the Cuban flag. The pilot breathed deeply, slammed into a one hundred and eighty degree turn and lined up with Cuba's southwest shoreline.

"Baños approach, this is MiG two-oh, sixty miles south at angels ten. Requesting radar vectors for approach to Antonio de los Baños. Over."

"Roger two-oh. Radar contact. Proceed inbound on heading three-sixty, descend to five thousand, over."

"Roger. Descending to angels five."

Brigadier General Julio Herrera turned his head and looked through the cockpit at Cuba below. The island stretched out like a giant salamander headed east, angling out the Gulf of Mexico, it made its way against the Gulf Stream flowing northwest toward Florida.

"MiG two-oh approach. Report ten miles with a visual."

Fields of deep emerald green shimmered below into the distance, evidence of sugar cane fields ready to harvest. He sucked in a long breath.

"Approach, MiG two-oh. I have the airport in sight. Over."

"Roger, MiG two-oh. Continue inbound. Descend to three thousand feet. Contact tower on channel three."

"Roger. Leaving five for three, switching tower."

To the northeast, he could see a Russian Aeroflot flight banking to land at Havana's José Martí International Airport, sunlight glinting off its wings. You didn't see Russian planes so much these days, he thought.

Switching his VHF radio frequency to channel three as instructed, he transferred his control from approach to the tower at Antonio de los Baños. "Tower, this is MiG two-oh at three thousand feet, six miles. Over."

"Roger, MiG two-oh. Visual contact. Proceed to the initial."

"Roger." He pressed the stick slightly forward, descending.

At this lower altitude he could see Havana etched out in a mosaic of rectangular blocks and streets stretching away from the sea that separated it from Key West, ninety miles north. Old Havana, the easternmost section of the city, bounded on the east by the harbor and west by the old city walls, was clearly visible. Two castle fortifications near the mouth of the bay led into the harbor. From up here the scene reminded Herrera of Havana's older and more glamorous times, alluring in its Spanish colonial beauty of elegant public buildings, majestic Catholic churches and patio residences. Not so elegant these days, he thought. He glanced down at the huge, busy harbor jammed with freighters from Europe, South and Central America, China, and Japan. His thoughts shifted back to the days when he would have seen it filled with Soviet destroyers and submarines. He could see the Panamanian-registered freighter that had gone aground recently, stuck in the shallow sea not far off from El Morro Castle, the old Spanish fort at the harbor's entrance.

"MiG two-oh. You are cleared to break."

He descended to 1,000 feet and decreased his speed, leaving a roar in its wake. Then, in a stunning maneuver over the airfield, in one of his traditional moves, he braced himself and threw the plane into a gut-wrenching 6-G turn, a 180-degree level left turn, pulling back hard on the stick. Vapor trailed off the wings and tail. His face mask tightened and he grit his teeth, fighting to stay conscious. The inflatable bladder in his G suit automatically expanded to counter blood rushing from his torso to his feet. His aircraft headed downwind, 180 degrees from its ultimate heading of the runway, and raced parallel with the landing strip clearly defined below.

Herrera lowered the landing gear and flaps, set the speed brakes, and throttled back to near idle on downwind. A tight 180-degree descending turn to final, and the plane reached landing speed.

As he set the landing gear gently onto the tarmac, wheels squealed, blue smoke kicked up and the plane's weight settled in, its nose tilted up off the ground. Traveling at 135 miles per hour, with 8,000 feet of runway remaining, the whine of engines thrown into reverse announced this ride was about over. Rudders had controlled the descent, throttle set at idle, he nudged the stick forward until the nose touched ground at which point Herrera cleared the duty runway, shifting his radio to ground control.

The uniformed ground crew awaited Herrera at the military hangar, his designated place to park. Engine cut, Cuba's senior test pilot opened the cockpit canopy, unhitched his ejection seat safety harness and yanked his helmet off as soon as possible. He hoisted himself smartly out of the cockpit to the waiting ladder, climbed down and grinned as his foot touched the steamy tarmac runway. Anyone around would recognize this pilot as General Julio Herrera. Much taller than most of his countrymen, with dark eyes edged by deep laugh wrinkles, thick black hair, he had a jovial disposition and infectious smile. Like other jet pilots he had developed a partial hearing loss from engine noise.

"Works great," he said to the squadron's commanding officer and his own personal aide who stood waiting for him. "One hell of a plane."

"It looked shit-hot from down here," said the C.O. "Bet it gave your hemorrhoids an extra little squeeze on that hot dog break you pulled," he chuckled, grinning at Herrera.

Herrera replied with a huge smile and walked with knees bent and bowlegged for a couple of strides, face contorted, teeth showing, mimicking pain.

"Nice job, General," a crewman yelled at him. Herrera smiled back. With five confirmed South Africa kills years before in Angola, he was one of a handful of military officers who had earned the title of "Hero of the Republic of Cuba," a flying legend.

"You haven't lost it, sir!" he heard from an enthusiastic smiling crewmember as he walked by. Herrera grinned back, but he knew he was getting older. No point in kidding yourself, he thought. He *had* nearly lost it on that last stunt.

They went straight to the flight office where he filed his report. Herrera noted that this test flight had taken him south of Cuba out over the Isle of Youth into international air space. He had put the plane through rolls, split S's and high "G" barrel rolls. He had experimented with various maneuvers at high angles of attack, utilized full rudder control approaching zero air speed and recovery from near spin situations. He had exercised the radar weapons system's search and track automatic acquisition features. He paused, pen in hand, and signed his name.

Herrera hit the showers, dressed, and walked out to the parking lot, looking for his boxy, Russian-built white Lada, for the drive home. He had a ways to travel northeast back to Havana on the main highway into Vedado. Vedado was a district in the city—more upscale than Central or Old Havana, but hardly as posh as Miramar, home of embassies and foreign diplomats. Many tourist hotels were in Vedado, in addition to residences and mansions left after Castro's revolution. These had been converted to public use, some into homes for Cuba's communist power elite. Herrera had been offered a mansion out in Miramar, but had declined. He selected instead a modest traditional two-story white stucco residence in Vedado, with small black metal balconies on the second floor.

He had refused most of the privileges the state wanted to bestow on him. Rather than a member of the power elite, Herrera saw himself as one of the people. The austerity of his dwelling made this point quite clear. His lightly furnished home had no rugs, expensive paintings or other costly works of art. He and his wife were content with inexpensive furniture, an old Sony television set and some small African figurines, souvenirs to remind him of Angola. "Why should we live better than anyone else?" he would tell his wife when expensive gifts were offered. "After all, aren't we the Cubans who fought for equality?"

Herrera's reputation as a selfless military leader dedicated to his men's well-being was locked in concrete. A decorated hero of 1980's Angolan War, he was known as an officer of unique character—highly principled and devoted to solving problems for his men stuck in the steaming heat and battle of Angola. Today, he was the top officer in charge of military morale at the Ministry of Defense, located at the Plaza de la Revolución, not far from the Ministry of Interior. He was in daily contact with Cuba's officer ranks and deep in the bureaucratic thicket of problem solving for his men and their families trying to survive under Cuba's stagnating living conditions.

With Latino warmth, charm and good looks difficult

to resist, his acid criticism of Cuba's deteriorating economy and willingness to go to any length to help his men had spawned a throng of loyal followers, especially within army and air force ranks. Cuban newspapers described him as a larger than life macho individual—charismatic, self-confident, articulate and daring, a leader of heroic proportions, the most influential military officer in the country, apart from, of course, Fidel Castro and his brother Raúl. The press had lapped up his high profile personality with so many reams of newsprint that by now his reputation extended beyond the barracks to every city and hamlet in the country. In Cuba, personalities counted more than political parties, and Herrera's backers were recognized as "Herreristas," die-hard individuals who would follow him as if he were Alexander the Great himself.

But would they follow him under any condition? He wondered, pushing his sunglasses up on the bridge of his nose, impatiently beeping his horn and accelerating around the huge, overloaded public bus creaking along up front, one of those giant pink "People Movers" Cubans call a "camel."

How deep did his men's loyalty really go? Would they stake their lives on him? That thought had haunted him in the past two weeks. He was not sleeping well, two nightmares in just the last three days. The more he thought about his men's loyalty, the more he felt another headache coming on with the tension in his back muscles. For the hundredth time in a month, he asked himself if he was doing the right thing. Could he pull it off? Was he walking on a volcano ready to explode? If he could get out of this thing gracefully, he thought, he might be half tempted to do it. Then again, *something* had to be done. Things simply could not go on like this. Got to concentrate, he thought, rubbing his moustache with his right hand, pondering his situation. Keep you head on straight, man. His foot punched the gas pedal in frustration.

* * *

It was not a good day for Bernardo. He was standing—well at least he was doing his best to stand up—in the back office room of a weather-beaten warehouse in Key West, facing the withering ridicule of an infuriated Miguel.

"So he simply pulled in the cargo, lit himself a big fat cigar, revved up his engines, said 'adios mothafucks,' and beat it for South Florida. Is *that* how it happened?" Miguel glowered menacingly at him.

Miguel's looks reminded most people of an ex-con, sent up the river for God knows what. His small, sunken, snake-like, eyes peered out from within two dark caverns created by black bushy eyebrows that hung over his drooping eyelids. Three knife-wound scars stood out distinctly on the left side of his face and his straight-line mouth, with a vertical line running down from each corner, created the illusion of a creepy nut-cracker you might find in the dark corner of a pawn shop. His ears lay back against his square head like a junkyard dog, and he stared as if he were about to cut your throat. Everyone who knew him understood that Miguel in fact *was* capable of killing anyone anytime if they got in his way. He had done precisely this in the past and could do it again. The cobra tattoo on his right shoulder mirrored his personality.

Tension filled the room. One man shuffled his feet uneasily. Three other *lancheros* who had been on the last run with Bernardo stood nearby, nervously eyeing Miguel as he inspected the results of this latest transaction. He cut into one of the packets with his switchblade.

"Do you know how much your stupidity will cost us, my friend?" he asked, his eyes narrowing into two slits, index finger jabbing at Bernardo. "Our Colombia contacts won't be happy about this little fiasco." His face was hard and angry, mouth tight, as he examined the white powder.

Bernardo felt sweat trickling down his back. He had a knot in his stomach, and his heart pounded uncontrollably. He had seen Miguel in a dark rage like this on other occasions, when he was displeased with the performance of some hapless member of the organization. But never had he been the recipient of one of "Miguel's moods." If this were a bad dream, he wished that he would wake up. But it was not a dream, and his spirits were sinking fast. His head was light, confused, and nausea swept over him.

Would his knees hold up much longer? He knew he was about to vomit, as Miguel barked one question after another. Bernardo would have kissed Miguel's ass, if only he would stop this inquisition. He tried to say that it was Miguel who had insisted that Sánchez go along as the new driver, not him. The words came out as an incoherent mumble. It made him look even more pathetic and weak.

Terrified, Bernardo caught Miguel's raised eyebrow directed at his three thugs standing in the shadows. He saw them coming toward him, moving on cue. The larger one pulled from his baggy pants a black leather bag just large enough to hold a bowling ball . . . or a man's head. The two men seized Bernardo in one easy motion, while the third snapped the bag down sharply over Bernardo's face, muffling his words as he thrashed out in panic. Choking and gasping for air, Bernardo's arms flailed wildly, tearing at the thing over his head as the larger man cinched the leather bag tighter while the second wrestled Bernardo to the floor.

"Get rid of him," Miguel snarled. The two giants nodded and started to drag Bernardo, thrashing madly, toward the door that led to a garbage truck parked outside, engine running, driver ready.

When they reached the doorway, Miguel snapped, "OK. That's enough. Let him go."

One of the men uncinched the bag over Bernardo's head, jerked it off and stepped back. Bernardo gasped loudly for air, as if he were half-drowned and pulled from the sea, his eyes wide and wild. He slumped, back against the wall, wheezing, trying to get his breath as the others looked at him curiously. He had wet his pants.

Bernardo's mind tried to grasp what had happened and why, as he wiped the saliva from his lips with the back of his trembling hand. His heart pounded wildly.

Then Miguel spoke to him in a low, deliberate tone. "You know I could kill you right now. Maybe I should. But, my friend, I am a generous man. I grant you this one time mercy. Let this be a warning. Don't screw up again."

Bernardo slumped against the wall, trying to collect himself as the other men left the room. The fear that had consumed him only moments ago slowly ebbed, replaced by a building anger fanned by the visions of what Sánchez and Miguel had just done to him. He looked down at the large wet spot in the crotch of his linen pants. If he ever caught Sánchez, he vowed he would cut him into little pieces. But even more intense was his seething hatred of Miguel. He swore he would never forget this horrifying humiliation.

FIVE

Georgetown

McGrath arrived at Georgetown's Dean & DeLuca's coffee shop at ten A.M. Saturday. Splashy, expensive, and populated by D.C.'s yuppy crowd—not his kind of haunt. But Sam and Kim loved it, so what the hell. He pushed the crystal clear glass door with its posh brass handle and entered the noisy dining area, grateful for the cool condition air that washed over him. He wore Levis, a dark blue polo shirt, and running shoes. He looked like a yuppy, but sure as hell did not feel like one.

"Neal . . . over here." Goodwin waved from an inconspicuous table at the far back of the busy main dining room. McGinnis was with him.

Five minutes later, after a round of good-natured banter, Goodwin's face turned somber. "Look Neal," he said softly, slowly stirring his black coffee. "Something has come up. Little problem down in the Caribbean. We think you might be of help."

McGrath caught the faint smile playing at the corner of McGinnis's mouth, a look of encouragment that masked something serious about to come. Instinctively he felt defensive and braced himself against being dragged into something he knew deep down he should avoid like the plague.

"And what might that be?" McGrath asked. He slumped nonchalantly in his chair, staring impassively across the table at Goodwin. He tried to look totally bland and disinterested. He suspected this meeting had something to do with his Cuba trip. The last thing he needed now was to be wrápped up in some kind of CIA business in Havana. He did not need that kind of pressure hanging over him on what was supposed to be a legitimate, university-backed research trip.

"Actually, you might find it interesting, Neal."

"Might even help your book project," McGinnis added smoothly.

McGrath raised an eyebrow and sipped his coffee. Under other circumstances, he might have been intrigued. On this trip he wanted to keep his nose clean, conduct interviews, and talk with locals.

"Look," Goodwin said, "We were in the audience yesterday at the Capitol Hill Club. Great job. Your talk was right on target. But, um, here's the point. When we heard you were going to Cuba, we thought you could do something for us."

McGrath looked dubious.

"Let me put it this way. I don't have to remind you that Cuba's internal politics is a tough nut to crack. We of course interview a defector now and then. But you know all that." He had McGrath's attention, although he could read his body language. Distinctly noncommitted.

"Listen," Goodwin said, chuckling, "It's no big deal, Neal. Really. I'm not talking a *spy* mission, for God's sake. No fake moustache. No trenchcoat. Call it *information gathering*. Nothing more, nothing less. Why are you grinnng at me like that," he said.

"I was just thinking about the difference between information gathering and spying," McGrath quipped dryly. "A fine line, don't you think? You want me to go down there and check out the quality of beaches for you? Count the number of American tourists in Havana? Jesus, Sam, you, of all people, know Cuba's at the boiling point."

McGrath remembered his days out at highly guarded, secluded Langley off the highway, back in the thick woods. He had worked for Goodwin for a period of time, and when Goodwin first raised the prospect of his staying on permanently, he had toyed with the idea. Given Special Forces training and his fluency in Spanish, McGrath could have had a regular slot in Goodwin's Latin America Division. But in the end he had opted for academia, with its classroom give-and-take and the freedom to speak openly.

At CIA, you had to keep your mouth shut inside and outside the building. They could drop a polygraph on you at any minute. Writing and research was strictly inhouse, for a restricted audience. Never break the oath of secrecy was the golden rule. So McGrath opted for Georgetown where he felt liberated and free to speak his mind. But he knew Goodwin and McGinnis well, knew how they thought and acted.

"Of course," Goodwin said. "But look. Here's the story. Our concern, Neal, is *drugs*. More and more pouring through the Caribbean. Cocaine, marijuana, and heroin. Stuff's coming in by the boatload. Tons of it. Puerto Rico and the U.S. Virgin Islands are two big transshipment areas. So's Haiti. We want to know if and how deep Cuba is implicated in all this trade. State and the DEA have asked us to dig deeper. Not that we haven't been trying." He took another sip of coffee.

"I thought Cuba had been given a clean bill of health on drugs earlier this year," McGrath replied. "No conclusive evidence. Anyway, what's drug trafficking in Cuba got to do with my trip? Besides, that's DEA's problem child, right?"

McGrath looked at Goodwin quizzically. Why would Goodwin think he would be able to find out anything useful about the drug trade just by staying alert? But he knew Goodwin was a pro in this business. He would not drag him in here unless it was serious. Kim's presence made the point even stronger.

"Look," Goodwin said, "DEA, FBI, CIA—*everybody's* trying to get a handle on this thing behind the scene. All we're asking is that you keep your eyes and ears open while you're down there. You know . . . with this drug trafficking issue in mind. We're just trying find out whether or not Cuba's implicated."

"Let's get real, Sam," McGrath said. "Why would a professor on a research trip run into anything related to drugs? How the hell am I supposed to find anything helpful while I'm chasing down legitimate information for my book? You want me to watch for Americans buying drugs on the streets? Maybe try to buy some myself? How far would that get you?" His curiosity was rising, but not any inclination to get involved.

"OK, OK," Goodwin said, locking eyes with Mc-

Grath. "There is more to it. But first, let me make a coupla points crystal clear. We suspect Cuba's engaged in transshipping the stuff, partly because at least seventy percent of cocaine smuggled into the U.S. passes through the Caribbean. That's twice as much as five years ago, a gigantic jump in volume. Point is, smugglers use the Caribbean islands more and more for transshipment."

"Lots of people think Cuba's involved," McGinnis said softly.

"You both obviously agree," McGrath said.

"We aren't sure," McGinnis replied. "Nobody can find the smoking gun. Cuban authorities flatly deny any connection."

"Maybe they're telling the truth," McGrath said.

"Maybe they are," Goodwin added. "Maybe not. Sure, could be they're not involved. Castro wants to stay in power. He knows that if he gets too hung up with organized drug crime, he could find himself facing an alternative power base in Cuba. He knows what happened to their old buddies in Russia. Russia's infested with criminal groups. Drugs became big business there, and look what happened. Besides, after this Iraq business, Castro knows this is not the time for the U.S. to catch him engaged in heavy-duty drug trafficking."

"That's the point," McGrath said. "Castro would be nuts to get tangled up with drug traffickers. He would be better off cooperating with the U.S., at least on this key issue, just like he claims."

"From that perspective, you're right, Neal," McGinnis chimed in, "But you know as well as we do that strange things happen. Maybe someone—or some group not connected with the government is involved. Who the hell knows for sure?"

"Hard to imagine," McGrath said, "Castro's got that placed wired up tighter than the FBI. He knows everything."

"You might be right," McGinnis replied, "but like I said, anything's possible. We just need to get a better handle on it."

"Exactly," Goodwin said. "All of which means we need more evidence. The facts, man, just the facts," he grinned broadly. "That's all we want."

"So we're back to square one," McGrath said softly. "Why bother with a university professor? I just don't see how I could find anything useful for you, short of burglarizing the Ministry of Interior. You want me to put on a black suit and dark face paint, maybe try to slip in there to crack some safes?" He grinned at Goodwin.

"Don't be funny. *Mission Impossible*, this ain't. Still, you can help. First, you worked at CIA. You had a top security clearance. You know how we operate. Second, your book project gives you a legitimate excuse to interview people that might shed a little light on this thing. Never know what you might see or pick up in talking with people down there. Third, you're a bona fide college professor who likes to ask questions—a nonthreatening kind of guy. And . . ." he paused, ". . . actually, there is something else."

About time, McGrath thought. This should be interesting.

"Our background check tells us that there's one person who *will* be mighty pleased to see to you in Havana."

"Oh?"

"Remember a former graduate student of yours, a woman named Elena Rodríguez?" Goodwin reached inside his blue blazer's coat pocket and handed McGrath a photograph. A small white index card, typed address and telephone numbers in Havana, home and work, was paper clipped to the picture. "Ring any bells?"

"Elena Rodríguez?" He paused. "Sure," McGrath said, looking at her picture, a replica of her Georgetown yearbook photo. Ring any bells? he thought. Was Goodwin kidding? Of course it did. "Yeah, I remember her.

Good student. One of my best M.A. candidates. Wrote a great thesis on the Batista period. We were friends. Real dedicated to Cuba. Intelligent. Cuban parents. Lost touch with her some time ago."

Jesus Christ, he thought. They kept tabs on *Elena*? Now why would they do that? Goodwin obviously hadn't told him everything.

"*We* did not lose touch," Sam said. "As it turns out, Elena Rodríguez works in Havana. Nothing less than in the Ministry of Interior. One hell of a contact, huh? Perfectly placed. Even better, you know her personally."

"Sure, but . . ."

"Wait, just think, Neal. Maybe she's got an angle on this thing. Maybe she knows something she might share with you. All we ask is that you look her up. In fact, you could say we're giving you your best lead for your book project," he smiled. "A golden opportunity to hook up with someone who can arrange interviews with Cuban officials. Chances are, she would love to help." Relaxed and more comfortable now, Goodwin grinned at McGrath as if he had just handed him a brand-new, free laptop computer with all the bells and whistles.

McGrath was thinking fast now. "Let me get this straight. You're asking me to waltz down to Cuba, look up an old graduate student, who just happens to be working in the Ministry of Interior. How convenient. And you think all I need to do is pick up the hotel phone, give her a call, and she's going to spill her guts to me about everything she knows about Cuban drug trafficking? Come on, Sam. Get real. What's going on here? Something's missing. What makes you think that she's going to talk to me at all . . . about anything? Folks over at Langley don't make a habit of telling their next-door neighbors how their work's going. You think Elena's position in Cuba's security agency's any different?" He gave Goodwin one of his whimsical smiles, like he was talking to a five-year-old . . .

"OK, you're right. There *is* something else." Goodwin paused, his voice calm, matter-of-fact. "Turns out, Elena may be in some kind of trouble." He shifted his weight in his chair. "Maybe it's nothing . . . but she could be in some difficulty. We aren't sure what, but anyway she may be glad to see an old friend about now, might be vulnerable, willing to talk, wanting to talk . . . who knows?"

His words hung in the air like a casual afterthought. He gave McGrath a quick smile, sipped his coffee, and turned to ask if McGinnis wanted a refill.

McGrath stared at Goodwin's poker face for a minute, caught his tense jaw muscles, and wondered again what was going on here. Goodwin was about to say something else to McGinnis, when McGrath flashed the palm of his hand like a cop stopping traffic.

"Wait a minute," he whispered sharply, leaning forward over the table. "What do you mean, she's in trouble? What kind of trouble?" He looked hard first at Goodwin, then McGinnis, "And how do you know that much about her personal life?"

Goodwin answered in a tone that McGrath thought sounded a lot like a pencil-moustached used car dealer explaining the small print in the contract to a redneck. "Look, I said she *could* be in trouble. Let's just say that we have our sources, OK? I'll be honest with you." Yeah, sure, McGrath thought. "We debriefed a Cuban defector last week," Goodwin continued, "that claimed to know one of Elena's uncles, who lives in Havana. The defector says her uncle told him that he had a niece who worked at the Ministry of Interior and that she might have some kind of problem over there. Our defector mentioned it when we asked him about his contacts in Cuba. Naturally it got our attention because she works so high up.

Not some local librarian. We're always interested in anyone at that level. That's all we've got. Slim, I know, but that's it."

"That's it?"

"That's it. Nothing more."

"Where's her uncle if she's in trouble?"

"Apparently off in the Middle East somewhere."

"Not a hell of a lot to go on," McGrath said, rubbing his chin. He was now more suspicious than ever. It occurred to him that he should get up, tell Goodwin to take a hike and get out of there, get his life back together, and finish his book project. But his old graduate student and friend, Elena, was in trouble, and he might be in a position to help her. He could not ignore that basic fact, but he needed more information.

"Tell me, Sam. Does Elena work for you? Is she CIA?" McGrath settled back in his chair, stared hard at Goodwin, and waited for an answer.

"Work for *us*? What *have* you been smoking, man? I see you haven't lost your knack for creative thinking."

"That doesn't answer the question," McGrath said tersely, not letting Goodwin off the hook. McGrath never liked being set up and kept in the dark. He could walk away right now if he wanted to, but then, he thought again, he'd probably never forgive himself for it if something happened to Elena. What kind of trouble was she in? he wondered.

"Does she work for us?" Goodwin's voice sounded astonished that McGrath would ask such a question. "Of course not. Why would we ask you to contact someone who works for us? If she were CIA, we'd already have any information she had to offer. Jesus, Neal, use your head."

Goodwin sounded convincing, but McGrath was well aware of the range of human emotions Goodwin could pull out of the hat to serve his purpose. Elena might in fact be a CIA spy. Goodwin might be using him, a civilian, to make contact with her because an agent would be too dangerous. Absolutely logical, he told himself. In a low voice, as if he were serving a subpoena, he asked, "What do you know about Cuba's Ministry of Interior?"

"Well, for openers, its mission is internal security. Elena works in the General Directorate of Intelligence, aka DGI. Collects foreign intelligence. Worldwide operations. Orchestrates foreign front companies, in Panama, for example, that buy products to improve Cuba's economy. Computer equipment and so on, you know."

"Secrecy to the max," McGrath said.

"Right. Real hush-hush, tough characters run the show."

"Smooth running?" McGrath asked. "Efficient?"

"Smooth running? Maybe not," Goodwin replied. "Defectors tell us DGI interdepartmental battles have flared up lately. Plus they don't get along with Cuba's military. Heavy-duty infighting, we hear."

"Not so strange," McGrath said, ". . . from what I've seen around this town."

Goodwin lowered his voice. "A DGI agent shot and killed another agent last week because the guy supposedly was stealing livestock in a city about twenty miles outside Havana. Local residents say the guy who was killed wasn't stealing anything. But one thing's certain, he was in a different division within DGI than the fellow who killed him. All we know is that the Ministry seems stressed to the max, probably because so many Cubans are disgusted with the way things are going. Morale's real low, y'know. Economic conditions and all that."

"Place sounds like a snake pit."

"Yeah," McGinnis smiled.

With stoic obstinacy, McGrath pressed on. "Who's her boss? What do you know about him?"

A dark shadow flit across Goodman's face. "Smart

questions," he responded solemnly. He looked at
McGinnis. "The top guy she works for is a General
Manuel Ramiro. Bio on him says he's highly intelligent
and manipulative, a leader who knows how to get others
to follow him. Has a reputation for some kind of psychic
power, but that sounds far-fetched to me. Anyway, he's
suspicious of everyone and everything, cunning, real
snake in the grass. Actually, a classic paranoid personality. Defectors tell us the word on Ramiro is don't get too
close to him. He's got a deep capacity to hate and goes
after anyone he thinks has crossed him. He's eliminated
at least three people and . . . uh . . . he has a reputation
for torture. Seems to murder at times for pure pleasure."

"Sicko," McGinnis chimed in.

"Great," McGrath said. "Just what we need. Elena
works for a psychotic creep, and we think she's in some
kind of trouble."

"Right."

"Anything else?"

"Nope. That's it, pal. What do you say?"

"So let's summarize the situation. You're basically
telling me that you've learned about Elena Rodríguez
from a defector?"

"Right."

"And because she works in this highly secretive spook
center, you just want me to establish contact with her,
since she's my old graduate student? A natural entrée?"

"Right."

"You think that she'll be pleased to see me, apart from
being my friend, because she's in some kind of trouble?"

"Right." Goodwin could read McGrath's face like a
book. He was skeptical as hell, with those half closed
eyes and slight, upturned chin, like he was examining a
plagiarized student paper. Oh, he's suspicious all right,
he would tell McGinnis later, but curious enough to go
for it, especially with the Elena factor.

"And when we meet, I gently inquire if she might

know anything about Cuba as a transshipment point for Caribbean drug trafficking?"

"Exactly. Well, I mean, maybe you can frame the issue more discreetly."

"And . . . I am a natural way to obtain that information, because as a civilian I might be able to get it without compromising Elena . . . assuming that she would tell me anything of importance in the first place?"

"Absolutely. Right on the mark."

"No danger for Elena. No danger to me."

"You got it. None whatsoever. Piece of cake. As harmless as a stroll through Georgetown on a hot summer day."

McGrath sat back in his chair, looked quizzically at each of them for a minute, knowing he didn't have all the facts. Lots of bullshit here, he thought, but he knew one thing for certain. If Elena was in trouble, given this cutthroat Ramiro character, her life, and probably his, could be in danger. Yet how could he not agree to Goodwin's request? He had to do it.

"OK Count me in."

"Great," Goodwin replied. "Here, this is a contact telephone number in Miami. Call it, and the party will get the message to me in D.C., OK?"

McGrath took the small white index card Goodwin handed him, smiled at them, got up, and headed for the door.

He left Goodwin and McGinnis in the coffee shop and began his walk back to his Georgetown town house. It was baking hot as he waited for the red light to cross M Street and seemed all the more humid because he now worried about Elena and kept wrestling with his conversation with Goodwin. Goodwin was holding back.

The signals for his trip to Cuba had just changed, like shifting a freight train from one track to another. The stark truth was that he had just agreed to play spy for the CIA. What he really wanted to know now was, why?

SIX

Havana

General Herrera saw Colonel Ernesto Garcia waiting for him as he turned the corner and drove up to his small home. Garcia, Herrera's devoted senior staffer, was standing inside the rusting iron housegate like an impatient terrier. Shorter than Herrera, his thinning dark hair topped a pudgy, round baby face. Everyone close to General Herrera knew that he depended on Garcia to cut through Cuba's red tape over at the Ministry of Defense.

"Hey, Ernesto!" Herrera boomed out as he approached the house, "Who do we have on board this fine afternoon?" He grinned, opened the squeaking gate and glanced toward the porch. Several officers were there, locked in muffled conversation, gathered in clusters of twos and threes.

"Looks like a full house today, eh?" Herrera smiled. He shook Garcia's outstretched hand, handed him his briefcase, and closed the gate behind them.

"Lots of action in the bull pen, sir," Garcia replied. He spoke in rapid, clipped sentences and nodded in the direction of the porch, keeping step with Herrera's long strides. Garcia was a textbook type A personality: stressed to the max, sweat-drenched, unable to throttle back.

"Beg pardon?"

"Lot's of action today, sir!" Garcia repeated loudly to Herrera's cocked head. "Captain Rivera has hit a logjam trying to nail down an apartment. His wife, Maria, you know. Pregnant, third child. Yes, *pregnant*, sir. They're stuck in temporary housing. He needs help bad."

"OK, *chico*, let's see what we can do." He pulled a
white handkerchief from his pocket and wiped his brow.
"Jesus, we got more people here than the unemployment office."

Herrera was a hero to these men. Many believed he
should be *up to bat*—that he should be running the government. Why not? Herrera had proved time and again
that he could get things done when others failed. This
was the kind of intense loyalty Herrera counted on in
the days ahead. He knew he was going to need it.

They returned to Ramiro's villa from a private dinner at
a place outside Havana through driving rain and wind.
The villa was much like those of other high-ranking officials and political elites in Cuba's chain of command.
A prerevolutionary luxury dwelling located in fashionable Miramar, the stately two-story white painted residence surrounded by palm trees was well-groomed
with gardens and lush green bushes. Fidel's revolutionaries had confiscated it after they came to power back in
'59. Elite members of Ramiro's personal security staff
were posted at the front and back entrances. This security measure made Ramiro feel more self-confident and
safe.

Seated in the living room, Ramiro leaned forward to
extend the humidor filled with Cuba's finest. "Cigar?"
He offered his guest a long fat Cohiba. A pot of coffee
and earthenware cups had been set on the table by
Ramiro's housekeeper. "More coffee?"

While Ramiro poured, Moreno twirled the cigar between his thumb and fingers and gazed around with the
eyes of a cobra mesmerizing its prey. He took in
Ramiro's eclectic art collection—crude paintings of
naked women and grotesque Native American masks
from Mexico. Heavy wood furniture from Spain was
prominent. An enormous TV screen and a top-of-the-
line sound system with quality speakers stood in the far

corner. Ramiro wore designer jeans, a bright red polo shirt and flashy Rolex watch on his left wrist. He loved to entertain in this room. It demanded respect and deference. At least that's how he saw it.

Ramiro had toyed with the idea of meeting with Moreno in his personal office down the hall from the living room. There he could show off his other symbols of power and wealth. He imagined himself seated behind his huge dark Spanish-style desk with ornate lion heads carved on the legs, facing Moreno in the chair opposite the desk. Ramiro's own desk chair was built up higher than normal, where he looked down on anyone seated across from him. On the desk, near the gold-plated pen set was the clear bowl with dried human ears of men Ramiro had tortured in the past, something that might impress Moreno. But in the end, Ramiro ditched the whole idea of bringing him in there, knowing Moreno was too intelligent. He would see through the whole power thing and think less of him for trying that sort of stunt.

Moreno wore a white Cuban-cut shirt, a *guayabera*, open at his muscular neck, hanging loosely over dark linen trousers on his physically powerful frame. Moreno's unblinking black eyes and four-inch scar on the left side of his face gave him a sinister look, magnified by long black hair combed back in a ponytail. Ramiro watched Moreno cautiously. His body movements—walking, sitting, reaching for something— were executed with balance and poise as if ready to attack at any moment. It reminded Ramiro of a skilled assassin slipping up on the sentry in the dark to slit his throat.

"How's the leg?" Ramiro asked casually. He had met Moreno three years ago when Moreno had come to Havana for medical help. He exhaled a thin trail of blue smoke and tried to sound confident. "No doubt you found our medical services satisfactory?" A note of pride echoed in his deep voice, as he ran his left hand through his greasy kinky hair.

"Leg's fine. Your hospital staff was exceptional," Moreno replied.

"Good thing we got you here." Ramiro liked this remark. It drew attention to how much Moreno owed him.

"*Sí* señor. I nearly didn't make it."

Ramiro recalled the event in vivid detail. Moreno was a member of a leftist group struggling against local Mexican land-owning political bosses in southern Mexico backed by Mexico's government. Moreno had led a small group of Mexican guerrillas on a mission to destroy a power station near a small town in the mountain near San Cristóbal de las Casas. After the explosion, Mexico's local army commander tracked Moreno's guerrillas trying to get back to their Mayan jungle base. One of Moreno's injured men limped along, holding them up. Moreno slit the man's throat. An hour later a Mexican Army helicopter caught them on open ground stumbling through a shallow rocky stream. Moreno took a bullet in his left leg that caused him to bleed heavily. Moreno's luck held, however, and he managed to reach the jungle rendezvous point. A clandestine flight arranged by Ramiro landed him in Havana two days later.

Ramiro blew a smoke ring and gazed at Moreno. The airtight background check and daily contact left no doubt in Ramiro's mind that Moreno was the man for the job he had in mind. Moreno, a Marxist revolutionary, would stop at nothing to accomplish his goal: overthrow Mexico's government and replace it with communist rule. Moreno was the key piece that had been missing on his chessboard of deception. The trick would be to convince Moreno to follow a path of action that would seem in his best interest, but in fact lead to Ramiro's ultimate goal: power. Ramiro would use his telepathy on Moreno. Still, he had to admit in the darkness of night, lying in bed in the early hours of the morning, that maybe, just maybe, he did not have as much control over this man as he wanted to believe.

Ramiro knew Moreno's background chapter and verse. A product of Mexico's university system, formerly a young university professor, Moreno was now a "true believer" in violent revolution. Moreno had joined in acts of civil disobedience and street riots in a number of small villages and towns to demand Indian rights. When an agreement with Mexico's government failed to deliver promised reforms, Moreno dropped out of society, broke with his family and joined the Indian guerrilla movement. At first an idealistic revolutionary, over time his personality had changed. No one knew exactly what had happened. Ramiro's best guess was that Moreno had been deeply affected by his special training in the art of killing. He had met his assignments with such gruesome finality that even Moreno's fellow guerrilla leaders feared him.

Ramiro leaned forward over the coffee table to flick cigar ashes into the ashtray. He stole another glance at Moreno. Strikingly handsome except for the scar tissue, poker-faced, he was of light brown complexion, a mestizo, half Indian, half Spanish. His eyes were something else—two tiny opaque spheres that barred the inquiring minds of others—windows through which Moreno saw out, but allowed no entry. Even for Ramiro, a tough intelligence operative with a record of interrogation by intimidation and torture, a man who had seen and done it all in the domain of brutality, Moreno's eyes warned him to be wary.

"Well, mi amigo," Ramiro said, shifting in his chair, "I managed to set up the training session at the Sports Center you requested. It's scheduled for tomorrow at ten-hundred hours. My driver will pick you up at your hotel. Ricardo Diaz, our top karate expert, is looking forward to working out with you."

"Excellent. I'll need the weight room," Moreno said nonchalantly, sipping his coffee.

"By all means. I'll tell Diaz. He'll fix it up. How about the swimming pool?"

"*No.*" Moreno's quick, curt answer reminded Ramiro that Moreno had a distinct distaste for water. An uncle had thrown Moreno into a river and ordered him to swim at an early age.

"My sources," Ramiro said casually, "report that your people are experiencing problems since your president launched his peace offensive. Your president," he added, "seems to have created some kind of popular impression that all problems between his government and guerrillas are negotiable. I hear he's negotiating directly with your organization—even on power sharing and land reform. So it seems that popular backing for a revolution is declining."

"Your sources are correct," Moreno sighed, leaned back in his chair. "It doesn't matter if the president makes *promesas* that he can't fulfill. If the masses believe it, that's what counts," Moreno replied in disgust.

"So what do you intend to do?"

Moreno leaned forward. His jutting chin tilted slightly upward, his body tensed. He gave Ramiro a long, icy stare and set his coffee cup and saucer down on the table separating them. Ramiro's heart skipped a beat, but he had that small pistol strapped around his right ankle.

Moreno spoke in low, deliberate, calculated tones, a razor edge to his voice. "You, more than anyone, understand what we face in my country. We've tried everything to pressure the president and win mass support—strikes, bombings, general insurrection—all carefully planned and executed. But you're right. Momentum's slowing. The president's stalling tactics are working for the government."

Ramiro looked at Moreno sympathetically.

"The president has duped our people," Moreno said, "of that I am certain. But the masses aren't the only problem. Our guerrilla leaders disagree on what to do."

"It's the same story throughout Central America. Revolutionary morale has declined everywhere," Ramiro replied. His voice oozed compassion.

Moreno nodded in agreement, inhaled deeply on his cigar, and stared at Ramiro, as if to ask where this cat and mouse game was going.

"Hmmm," Ramiro said reflectively, "you know, your cause is supported by many of us here in Cuba. We've discussed alternate scenarios which might ignite your revolution. We agree that something *really dramatic* must happen. How about you? Can *you* envision *anything* so dramatic that it would produce a huge following for your movement?" Ramiro wrinkled his forehead, like he was deep in concentrated thought on Moreno's behalf. He gazed intently at those impenetrable eyes.

"What exactly do you mean?" Moreno said, looking out from half-closed eyelids.

"I mean," Ramiro said slowly, his words deliberate, "some event to fire up Mexico's masses, make them furious, willing to come to the jungle to join you, prepared to die for the cause."

"Do you have anything specific in mind?"

"Look, the old policies won't work," Ramiro said, leaning forward, intent to make his point clear. "You know, strikes, sabotage, demonstrations, those things. No, you need a new path. Action that would turn the whole country toward the road of violent revolution." He shifted his weight on the sofa, his eyes narrowed to slits of brooding focus."

"What is your point?" Moreno said darkly. Ramiro almost did not hear him, as just then thunder boomed off in the distance.

"As it turns out," Ramiro said, pausing to play with

the giant ring on his finger, "I do know of one way to jump start your revolution."

"Oh?"

"Think back through Mexico's history to when the *military* ran the show—long before civilian politics. Remember how it was? How did the average Mexican feel about the military?"

"Scared and disgusted," replied Moreno.

"*Correcto.* So how would Mexico's masses react to a military dictatorship today?" Ramiro smiled knowingly, aware that Moreno was not buying his act entirely.

"They would be furious." Moreno responded.

"Quite so," Ramiro said. "And what would that discontent mean for your guerrilla revolutionaries?" Ramiro forced another smile on Moreno.

"Our revolutionaries would be positioned to lead a revolution against the military. A revolt of the masses." He paused, as the idea sunk in.

"Well then," Ramiro said confidently, "from that perspective, would it not be advantageous to have the Mexican military back in power?"

"Of course, but that's as likely to happen as my becoming president of Cuba." Moreno did not smile.

"So the next question is obvious. How can we put the Mexican military back in power?"

"You mean some act to return to military rule?"

"Exactly. That's the point." They almost jumped as a lightning bolt stuck close by, lighting up the yard outside. Thunder rattled the window frames, and night seemed to close in.

"Something orchestrated, say, by a movement like ours?"

"Not necessarily *everybody* in the movement. Not the *whole* movement, my friend. More like *one person*," Ramiro said cryptically.

"If the military *were* in power again, that would set up conditions for a popular counterrevolution?"

"*Sí* señor."

"Our movement naturally would lead the popular counterrevolution."

"*Correcto.*"

Seconds passed in silence. The antique grandfather clock chimed down the hallway, and Ramiro said, "Isn't it obvious, *chico*? The key to bringing in the military is to make Mexico's *el presidente* disappear." There, he thought, it's out.

Ramiro thought a minute. "Don't you mean *eliminate* the president?"

"*Sí* señor."

"Even more to the point, *assassinate* him?" Moreno sat back deep in his chair and took a long draw on his cigar, staring at Ramiro, his eyes deep in thought.

Ramiro knew exactly why this plan would work. Under normal conditions the army would *not* intervene in politics. But would it stage a coup if Mexico's president were assassinated? Yes, Ramiro thought. It would. Well, at least if not definitely, the odds were high for a military coup. In this age of terrorist threats, hell, the U.S. probably would encourage military rule to stabilize Mexico after the assassination. Got to keep those borders safe.

Ramiro and Moreno both knew that army insubordination had been growing in the past two years. The army even spied on government peace negotiations with the guerrillas. So if the Mexican president were *assassinated*—the ultimate threat to national security—Mexico's armed forces likely would stage a coup in order maintain stability. Then, with the military in power, Mexico's public, who wanted no part of military control, would be incensed. Exactly what Moreno needed to lead a popular counterrevolution.

Moreno broke the silence. "How about the U.S. response? Wouldn't they suspect that the guerrillas were behind the assassination?"

"No," Ramiro replied confidently, with a negative head wag. "First, the U.S. knows the Mexican government has been negotiating with the guerrillas. The U.S. will reason that the guerrillas would not kill the person who publically cooperates with them. Second, given the string of assassinations in Mexico over the last two years, the U.S. will think that it could have been done by anybody, perhaps a drug lord or political opponent. A guerrilla link is far down the list."

"Still, Washington will push for new elections as soon as the military takes over."

"Of course. Like all mighty hell. But with the level of instability that will follow the assassination, Mexico's military won't let go the reins of power easily. No sir. You and your friends can think of plenty of ways to keep the country destabilized and, consequently, the armed forces in power. All of which means more support for your revolution."

"But why would Cuba want to see Mexico in revolution, with the Zapatistas coming to power? What's in it for you?" Moreno's face was a mask of suspicion.

"What's in it for Cuba?" Ramiro was prepared. He expected nothing less from Moreno. "Simple, my friend. Cuba is extremely sympathetic to your movement and its drive for social justice and a better life for Mexico's poor. Cuba is totally opposed to the capitalist system now operating in Mexico and so many other developing countries around the world. We don't have to remind you how capitalism has brought suffering worldwide, with more and more people dying of hunger and preventable diseases. You heard about Castro's speech last week?"

"No. What about it?"

"Jesus, man, he blasted global capitalism. You know, how it's the cause of worldwide poverty and terrible conditions for the world's masses. Mexico's a classic case in point as you know. Just look at how government-backed wealthy *hacendados* in Chiapas have confiscated land from the poor. It's the very causes for which you fight. I tell you that with capitalism tamed by your movement, we in Cuba will be pleased indeed. Just read Castro's recent speeches. You'll see. He likens American capitalism to the Holocaust. For Christ's sake, Moreno, your movement could produce a *showplace . . . a . . . a focal point* of how to beat U.S. capitalism. Right here in the Caribbean. Right next to Cuba. Incredible!" he blurted. "What's in it for us? Nothing less than all we believe." Would Moreno take the bait? Ramiro's plans depended on it.

"So you mean I just walk up to the Mexican president and shoot him," Moreno said skeptically, as if he were talking to a snake oil salesman. He smiled at Ramiro in a way that was more frightening than friendly. Yet Ramiro saw the shift in his body language that signalled he was interested.

"Oh no, nothing like that, hombre. We can be far more creative."

That was the turning point. From then on their conversation focused on how Mexico's president could be eliminated. Once removed, Mexico would slide into chaos, they agreed. It was clear the Mexican military would *have* to step in to maintain order—at least in the short run—to hold the place together. With the line of logic clear, they turned to the details of how Moreno could carry out the mission.

Standing on the porch as Moreno turned to go, Ramiro noticed under the porch light that the pupils of Moreno's black eyes seemed to glow like tiny flecks of eerie seaborne phosphorescence. The look and tone of voice in Moreno's good-bye signalled a lingering suspicion of what Ramiro was up to. Ramiro knew he had more work to do on Moreno, but the bait was out. He watched as

Moreno walked down the path into the dark, stormy night that swallowed him. He had an uneasy feeling that he was not in total command of this creature.

Victor telephoned an hour later to ask how the meeting went. Ramiro said that their "guest" would be departing soon, after a few more days in Havana to tie up loose ends.

"Operation Rebirth," as Ramiro intended to play it out, was now complete. Moreno unwittingly had stepped onto his stage of deception in a leading role. The trick now would be to keep him moving in the right direction. Could he pull it off? He knew he must.

SEVEN

Miami = Havana

Air Florida's Flight 28 roared down the runway and lifted off. McGrath stretched back in his seat and gazed out the window. After meeting with Goodwin and McGinnis, he had gone back to his paper-strewn office at Georgetown, jumped on the Web and downloaded every report he could find on drug trafficking in the Caribbean. Several news releases pinpointed high-level Cuban officials as possibly implicated, but most of the reports originated with right-wing Republicans or Cuban Americans in Miami, no friends of Castro. Besides, top Cuban leaders *were* cooperating with the U.S. Inconclusive evidence, he reflected, just like Goodwin and McGinnis had said. Anyway, he at least had a handle on what the press had reported.

He and Goodwin had agreed not to bring any

telecommunications equipment into Cuba. A mini computer, cell phone, satellite phone, that kind of stuff, would be confiscated at the airport and raise suspicions. "We'll simply use the Miami telephone contact," Goodwin had said. Besides, it's not as if you're going in there for the rest of your life; you'll be back in Washington inside a month."

His thoughts turned from drugs to Elena. Since his conversation with Sam, she had been in the back of his mind. Let's see, he mused. She must be in her mid-thirties by now. Attractive, he reflected, smiling as he remembered how amusing it was to watch how the male students acted toward her. It occurred to him that now she was no longer his student and he no longer happily married.

He visualized Elena when he first met her as an alert, vivacious, graduate student. She had taken his advanced seminar on Latin American nationalism, and her contribution had been enormous. Cuban-born, she possessed a razor sharp analytic mind and unique ability to express herself clearly. To McGrath she represented the personification of the Cuban woman—intelligent, proud, self-reliant. He was delighted that she had taken his class and pleased to have been her advisor on her master's thesis.

When had he last seen her? Let's see, he thought. Ahh, yes. She had come to his office to say good-bye when she had finished her degree. He had to admit that when she leaned over to hug him, despite Rebecca, there was a fleeting moment of warm sexual impulse, which he instantly repressed and put into neutral. Truth was, he was sad to see her leave, because he enjoyed her company. But after a few months went by, for the most part he had put Elena out of his mind. That is, until this recent conversation with Goodwin and McGinnis.

She had arrived in Miami with her parents, disillusioned with Castro's turn toward communism. The par-

ents had done well, her father joining an uncle in the
restaurant business, her mother working at the University of Miami. But they, like many other Cubans, always
remained a family that dreamed of returning to Cuba
when Castro no longer was in power.

McGrath knew all about her political convictions,
which he reviewed as he listened to the drone of the
plane's engines. She believed that as the world became a
global community, Cuba one day would play its part.
She had told McGrath that she was planning to return to
Cuba to be part of the country as it moved into the
twenty-first century, convinced that she could contribute
to Cuba's future in a positive way. As far as she was concerned, Cuba would shed its communist ideology in
time and move toward a less hard-line version of socialism. Castro would change, she argued, and become less
ideological, and she wanted to be a part of it when it
happened. Elena had explained to McGrath that she had
an uncle connected to Fidel who could help her find
suitable employment once she returned.

McGrath took out the 3 × 5 index card with the name
and address and telephone number of the family in
Cuba that Rebecca had told him about. Rebecca. God, he
thought, thinking of her, how in the hell can I look forward to seeing Elena at a time like this? Instantly he felt
a wave of heartache over Rebecca and was glad Don was
reading a newspaper. He swallowed hard and concentrated on the index card. Looking at the card, Juan and
Martina Espinosa. He remembered his meeting with
Martina Espinosa's sister in Rebecca's office last year.
Her name was Alicia. They had discussed the case.
Their brother was in prison outside Havana for a human
rights street demonstration calling for free elections.

Rebecca had gotten the facts of the case from Alicia
Espinosa and had worked to have the evidence of the
case placed on Amnesty International's list and into a
Congressional Research Service information packet on

human rights violations in Cuba. Alicia Espinosa had
told Rebecca how grateful she and her sister, Martina,
were for all Rebecca's help, and if she ever came to Cuba
she must look them up. McGrath thought he might as
well call the Espinosas and pay his respects. Why not?
Maybe they could shed some light on his questions
about Cuban nationalism. Hell, maybe they knew something about drug trafficking on the island. Might as well
go for broke, he thought.

When they reached the island, the plane banked and
McGrath could see the old Spanish port of Havana below. Anxious faces pressed against the aircraft's plexi-
glass windows. Most of the passengers, returning
Cubans, strained to scour the terrain below for familiar
landmarks. From his side of the cabin, McGrath could
see dark purple thunderclouds piled up in the distance.
A downpour later in the day, he thought.

"Here we are, old buddy. Let the fun begin!" Samuels
punched McGrath lightheartedly on the shoulder as the
plane rapidly descended.

When the wheels squealed in a puff of smoke on the
landing strip and bounced once, the cabin erupted in relieved applause. Even before the plane stopped rolling,
half the passengers were out of their seats, ignoring the
announcement to remain seated until the plane had
come to a full stop. Mild pandemonium ensued as passengers yanked open overhead compartments, grabbed
bags, barked instructions and ducked the luggage tumbling from overheads, everyone eager to get out and get
going.

The first crack of brilliant sunshine pierced the opening doorway, and McGrath and Samuels joined the others who surged forward. Within minutes, they
stepped—more or less were carried—from the aircraft
onto the rickety roll-up gray metal stair ramp. They
made their way down the shuddering steps in the
steamy heat onto the hot cracked tarmac, eagerly look-

ing around, taking it all in. They were here. The Caribbean isle of sugar and tobacco.

Loud shouts greeted the plane's passengers from the crowd of wildly-waving and screaming Cubans up on the airport's sagging second story balcony. A colorful mix of whites, blacks, and mullatos in high emotion—it looked like the whole bunch might topple over the weathered railing at any minute. Nothing McGrath could have done would have prepared him for this lunatic human drama that unfolded before his eyes as they made their way toward the low-slung, desperately-in-need-of-paint terminal.

Inside the crowded baggage claim area, they waited impatiently for their luggage, as arriving Cubans waved, jumped up and down, and shouted to relatives beyond the custom booths. Once the Cubans had collected their luggage, they were waved through quickly. McGrath and Samuels had to wait for a more thorough customs check of travel documents. These stipulated that they were on a research trip rather than strictly tourists.

When they finally found themselves in the run-down waiting lounge, they entered a melee of Cubans embracing, crying, kissing, greeting one another in an explosion of welcome. The sheer size of the mob left them literally dumbfounded. *What to do next?*

"Guard yourself," Samuels said, grinning. "They might sweep you away here as somebody's uncle. *Jesus,* it does make you feel good to be surrounded by so much happiness, don't you think?"

They picked their way through the crowd to the sun-drenched parking lot laced with tall royal palms. "There's the cabs. Let's go." McGrath led the way as they crunched across the gravel toward a 1955 fire-engine red and white Chevy Bel Air, a flashy four-door sedan with a yellow license plate and black letters that beckoned under two tall, gently swaying palm trees.

The cab driver, a mulatto with a grizzled white beard, leaned out his window and asked, "Where to, amigos?"

"The Havana Libre Hotel," McGrath said.

"*No problema*, señors!" came a lively reply. "Hop in. Here, I put bags in trunk, *no problema*."

The cab had a distinct odor—an animal stench that suggested to McGrath that a wet goat might have slept in there recently. Samuels gagged as he slid into the front seat, but before he could get the door open again to get out and try another cab, the taxi coughed, sputtered, backfired and gave a slow lurch forward in the direction of downtown Havana like an old burro who knew exactly where he was going.

The driver, confident his passengers were *Americanos*, not *Cubanos* who might report him, launched into an energetic litany of complaints about the ancient relic he drove, his own car, as indicated by its yellow license tag. State-owned cars had blue tags. Yet despite his bitching and moaning, he spoke of his Chevy as an old friend.

"This taxi older than my grandmother," he intoned in broken English, relaxing, his elbow on the window ledge, right hand lightly on the steering wheel. "I put her on orange crates and rewire her every Sunday. Otherwise, she fall apart. I have for thirty-seven years. Some days I work two, three hours to make her run." He coughed, turned his head and spat out the window, as if to underscore his statement. McGrath ducked in the back seat. His window was open.

When the driver wanted to make a turn, he started cranking the steering wheel well in advance of the upcoming corner. This guaranteed that the car wheels actually aimed in the desired direction by the time they reached the critical point. He was flawless in this intricate maneuver.

McGrath was struck by the number of old 1950s cars on the highway. Not all cars were old, because newer European makes were scattered here and there. So were

Cubatur vans and other swish air-conditioned tour buses filled with foreigners on packaged tours. But the number of 1950s cars was pronounced. "An antique car lover's heaven," McGrath said, leaning forward to talk to Samuels.

"Right," Samuels replied, speaking out of the corner of his mouth.

"Cuba probably imported more U.S. automobiles—Cadillacs, Buicks, Chevys and Dodges—than any other country in the world during Batista's dictatorship in the 1950s."

"Yeah, I read about that somewhere. Jesus, just look at them. Like a museum."

"The U.S. blockade after Cuba's revolution in '59 prevented new U.S. car imports," McGrath said, watching the countryside fly by, billboard after billboard proclaiming the glories of Cuba. "So this place is frozen in time."

"Get a load of the bicycles," Samuels said. "Looks like China."

"You're right. China sells lots of bikes here. Gas prices skyrocketed after Soviet oil subsidies ended," McGrath added. "So the average family uses bikes."

"Yes sir," said the taxi driver, "we take care of our automobiles like newborn babies."

"Not what I expected," Samuels said, staring out the window at the well-worn buildings sagging in disrepair. In some cases, they could see that whole pieces of Spanish-style homes and apartments had simply vanished. "Kinda looks like a war zone in places," he added. "Still, you got to say it's enchanting . . . I mean, there's still plenty of buildings intact. Broken down, but intact. Look at that one on the corner there. Sure, they need paint, but they're still standing."

"Oh, we love our cars," said the driver.

"What's the story on all these billboards?" Samuels asked, pointing out his window as they flashed by on the highway into town.

You couldn't miss them, some twenty or thirty feet high, forty to sixty feet long. Giant political posters plastered along the palm tree route by the side of the road, on central squares and vacant lots. Slogans in Spanish barked out: WE FOLLOW THE RIGHT TRACK, FURTHER ALONG THE RIGHT TRACK, and ones with pictures of scowling Cubans carrying guns.

"The NRA would love this place," Samuels said. "Get a load of this one coming up." Painted in dark red on a white background, it read SOCIALISM OR DEATH. The next sign close by read, SOCIALISM'S BANNERS WILL NOT BE SURRENDERED WITHOUT A STRUGGLE.

"If you believe signs," said the taxi driver, "you think everyone was together in Cuba with no *problemas*. That big joke. Look! See the next banner?" His arm pointed out the window.

McGrath peered out the open backseat window and read out loud, "IF HISTORY SHOULD ASSIGN US THE ROLE OF THE LAST DEFENDERS OF SOCIALISM IN THE WORLD, WE SHALL DEFEND THIS BULWARK TILL OUR LAST DROP OF BLOOD."

"What *I want*," said the driver, "is not to give my last drop of blood for socialism, but some of my sweat for new parts for this car. For new parts I give *mucho* sweat!" He hawked again, and McGrath moved to the center of the back seat.

"So how's socialism working these days?" McGrath asked casually.

"Is not worth much," the driver replied. "Maybe Castro want defend to his last drop blood. But rest of us? No way," he said, chuckling.

"Do you worry much about the U.S.?" Samuels asked.

"Mostly about baseball," the driver said. "We march around mucho and protest Americano government like Castro wants. But really, we like Americans like you." Then he added, "if you meet Señor Fidel, do not say I tell you this!"

Traffic picked up as they drove into downtown Havana. Crowded streets and palm-lined plazas and parks—whites, blacks, and mulattos strolling, talking, visiting—all the sights and smells you would expect in the sunny Caribbean. More bright-colored cars and bicycles now.

McGrath's thoughts were interrupted by the driver who pointed his arm out the window again and remarked, "Look! See long *cola* by store?"

"You mean over there?" McGrath said. He could see groups of two to four, talking amongst themselves, not smiling much. The line extended twice around the building, the size of a large city block.

"*Sí* señor. New shoes on sale today," the driver said smiling. "Not good shoes. But you got to wear something on feet, no? Can no wear palm leaves on feet. Ha! People stand all day. Maybe later today lucky ones get shoes. But," he added with a big grin, "They get wrong size, wrong color, and style. It rains and shoes fall off." He smiled knowingly.

"Not much fun," Samuels said.

"But what can we do?" the driver said. "No help to complain. Things not get better. Castro say we got to tighten belts more. Says things gonna get better. God, my belt so tight now, I think I going to choke," he said, laughing out loud.

When the taxi approached the half circle driveway in front of the 25-story Havana Libre Hotel at Calle L and 23, the driver began spinning the wheel to the right, timing it perfectly to angle into the driveway. The brakes cried out in agony, and they came to a stop in front of the glass front doors, with its security guards, leading into the spacious, polished lobby.

"Here we are amigos. Beautiful Havana Libre Hotel." He hopped out, ran around the side and opened McGrath's door and moved smartly to the trunk to retrieve their luggage. He was delighted with Samuels' five dollar tip.

McGrath paused beside the taxi and looked up, reminding himself that this was the old Havana Hilton before the revolution and still Havana's largest hotel. A tall, well-kept building, it was painted pale blue and white, 1950s style. It had opened only a couple of years before Castro's revolution in 1959. Fidel had actually taken over one of the top floors early in 1959 to run his operations. The circular driveway was busy with taxis and tour buses that weaved in and out, uniformed doormen and bellhops busily attending to patrons and luggage. While the Havana Libre did not have the 1940s charm and grace of the Hotel Nacional down the street by the ocean front, a reminder of early Humphrey Bogart movies, it remained a stark, if not austere, contrast to the more neglected Spanish colonial architecture in old Havana not far away.

Two hours later McGrath unpacked. He decided to go ahead and try to make contact with Elena Rodríguez. He pulled out the slip of paper with Elena's telephone numbers, sat down on the edge of his bed by the nightstand, took a deep breath and dialed the hotel operator. It took several minutes to put the call through. He glanced at his watch. Close to noon. Would she be home?

The telephone rang five times.

Not there, he thought.

He sighed and started to replace the receiver, when he heard a faint voice at the other end of the line. A familiar voice. Low. Sultry. Definitely feminine. *"Bueno?"*

General Herrera and Colonel Garcia emerged from Antonio de los Baños Flight Command Center and crunched across the gravel parking lot toward the general's car.

Garcia broke the silence. "Sir," he said quietly, glancing around to make sure nobody was near, "I'm almost finished with the report. Should be ready later this week. I've made two lists, one with names of loyal officers, one of who might be suspect."

"Good. How many on the first list?" Herrera asked.

"Eighty, sir. Top ranks are ten colonels, twenty majors, twenty-five captains."

"*Bueno.* Security still tight?"

"Concrete solid, sir. Business as usual up and down the line."

"How about your friend on Ramiro's staff. Still working that angle?"

"Yes sir. But Ramiro's office is tight as a clam. No whispers. No rumors. You'd think it was a cemetery over there." Garcia said.

"We know he has no affection for me. We need reliable information. We got to know what he sees in this for himself, and who's in it with him," Herrera said darkly.

"He's not in it for love of country, that's certain."

"Hell no," Herrera snapped. "He says he is, but that's bullshit."

"I never trusted that guy. Look at how he weaseled his way to the top. One big-time ass kisser. Rolex watch giveaway king. Passes 'em out like candy." Garcia said. The watch bonded giver and receiver together as *socios*, best buddies. It was why many observers called Cuba's political system *sociolismo*, not *socialism*—a system of buddies who watched each other's backsides. A well placed *socio* could save the watch-giver's hide. "He's a snake in the grass."

"But he's our snake, Ernesto. Stay on it, man. Try to find anyone else over there who might know something. Time's getting short." Herrera was massaging the back of his neck as they approached the car. "I just don't trust that son of a bitch."

EIGHT

Havana

McGrath and Samuels walked toward the huge plaza with its imposing marble-covered Capitolio Nacional—a wide-stairway, Washington, D.C.-lookalike capitol building built in 1932. They crossed with the green light to the broad sidewalk leading to the front of the building. McGrath saw nothing unusual aside from the sheer width of the boulevard in front of the Capitolio, divided by the long line of old parked cars that separated the boulevard itself. Most of the brightly painted autos were 1950s variety—green and white 1959 Ford station wagon, 1956 Rocket 88 Oldsmobile, and the '54 black-and-white Chevy just in front of him. Parked nearby were the pedicabs, bicycle taxis imported from China.

Across the boulevard stood a row of two and three-story, washed out, scruffy looking buildings with lower level columns that formed a lengthy pedestrian arcade. In front, a crowd boarded one of Cuba's so-called "camels," pale orange, truck-driven people movers that carried up to 250 passengers and resembled a two-hump camel. Clusters of people hung out around the pedicabs and taxies. A light breeze off the sea rustled their shirts, and from the looks of the gray clouds building up overhead, it would be raining soon. A white, blue-trimmed, modern Cubatur tourist bus whizzed by, faces plastered against the windows.

McGrath was surprised when Samuels nudged him, picked up his pace and said, "Neal, look up the sidewalk there. What the hell's going on?" He pointed to some kind of demonstration up in front of the wide Capitolio steps that led up to the building's main entrance. McGrath could make out about a dozen middle-aged men and women marching up and down the sidewalk carrying posters on what looked like sawed-off broom handles. As they drew closer, they could read the signs that protested Cuba's human rights violations, demanding freedom of expression and release of individuals—indicated by name—jailed for speaking out.

McGrath was dumbfounded. For Christ's sake, how in hell could these people even dream of pulling off a stunt like this? Today? So soon after that anti-American rally right here on this spot? With Castro on the warpath for human rights activists? They must be out of their frigging minds. Tension was in the air, and his practical instinct said get out of here.

Several bystanders stood by gawking, along with taxi drivers by their cabs in the parking area in front of the Capitolio. They kept looking up and down the street as if they expected something and wanted no part of it. A policeman on a radiophone and two others started to block pedestrians from walking toward the demonstrators.

"Take a good look," McGrath said in hushed voice. "Here's exactly what we've been discussing . . . you know . . . police state. You don't see something like this every day in Cuba. Frankly," he whispered, "these people are nuts. Courageous, but nuts."

McGrath translated the Spanish language signs for Samuels. One demanded release of three prisoners jailed for a human rights demonstration last month. "And that one," McGrath said in his hushed voice, "advocates more rights for freedom of expression." Jesus, he thought, there's a poster with the name Enrique Maceo on it. Wasn't he Martina Espinosa's brother, the guy from the family Rebecca had helped? Incredible, he thought. It felt odd to be associated with that family through Rebecca, then to stand here on the street curb in downtown Havana and watch the name played out in a street demonstration. Ironic, he thought, bending down to tie his shoelace.

"So what next?" Samuels whispered.

Before McGrath could answer, two pickup trucks screeched around the corner, loaded with tough-looking thugs wielding guns and nightsticks. They roared up in front of the small band of protesters and slammed on brakes. Three heavyset men from each truck leaped onto the sidewalk, and in seconds a full-fledged melee erupted. The thugs lunged methodically and violently into the demonstrators, men and women alike, flailing away with nightsticks and fists. They knocked two of the demonstrators to the ground immediately, one an attractive young woman now bloodied. She was dazed from a blow to her head.

"Those mother *fuckers*," Samuels muttered. His old college football instincts seized control, and he shot down the sidewalk at full tilt. He pushed by the restraining policeman, picked out the first thug in his line of sight, put his shoulder down and rammed him like an NFL linebacker. He took the thug to the pavement and started pounding him in the face with his right fist, using his left hand to hold him by his shirt collar. The Spanish film crew who had crossed the street to watch the brawl shouted encouragement, but stayed cautiously on the sidelines.

McGrath, aware that he was about to do something utterly insane, adrenaline pumping, followed Samuels at full tilt. He charged the two guys hanging on Don's back who looked as if they belonged in the ring of worldwide wrestling and let fly a solid punch to the kidneys of one of them. He pulled the guy off Don and punched the other one. He turned just in time to see a right fist coming at him from someone else, sidestepped and used the assailant's momentum to send him flying several feet into the air and onto the pavement. In a blur of action, he deflected another swinging arm coming at him and smashed the nose on the face, heard the satisfying crunch and found himself spattered with blood. He caught sight of Don out of the corner of his eye, pounding the hell out of a black thug he had pinned on the sidewalk, just as he slipped out of a bear hold someone had put on him from behind. McGrath reached back, got his arm around the man's neck and flung him over his shoulder.

He was still on his feet, not breathing particularly hard, looking left and right for the next attacker when a green pickup truck came skidding up to the curb to unload a swarm of security types with nightsticks and revolvers. With the revolvers aimed at them, he let go of the man whose arm he had bent up behind him in a totally unnatural position and raised his own arms to the sky. McGrath knew they were in deep shit.

Ten minutes later he and Samuels and three protesters bounced along in the back of a pickup truck. Four goons looked impassively at them, weapons drawn. One was a big black shaved-headed man, the others shorter and stockier, hairy arms, one with a missing front tooth. McGrath stared at the large revolvers and wondered where they were going. He had a good idea.

They pulled up in front of at a nondescript weatherbeaten two-story gray building on the outskirts of Havana fifteen minutes later. They were unloaded, herded through a steel side door, and marched down a poorly lit hallway to a room, then roughhoused through the doorway. The door slammed and locked behind them. McGrath assumed the other protesters had been taken to other rooms, but he couldn't be certain where everyone wound up. The room was barren save for two fivefoot old wooden benches and a stinking latrine in the corner. The smell of urine was distinct in the dim cell. Two dirty windows with rusting black bars blocked the light high on the walls.

Within an hour McGrath and Samuels were hauled out from the foul-smelling room and marched back down the hall to a smaller room. The guards pushed them in and gruffly told them to sit down on the two brown wooden chairs under a bright light hanging by a long black electric cord from the ceiling. The chairs faced the more dimly lit large desk behind which sat a tough looking military type wearing dark glasses. His hat lay on the edge of the desk. The insignia on his shoulders indicated he was a colonel.

McGrath's mind raced, thinking what to say or do to get them out of here. The room with its single light smacked of an old gangster B movie McGrath might have seen as a kid, something starring Edward G. Robinson or James Cagney. He would have laughed had he not been in Castro's Cuba, cast in the starring role as victim. He stared blankly back at the interrogator, who leaned forward across the desk, pen poised in hand, ready to ask questions and make notes. The colonel thumbed through McGrath's passport, then picked up Samuels' and slowly and deliberately, poker-faced, pondered the stamps on each page. For five minutes the only sound in the room was the ticking of an old clock up on the cracked gray paint wall.

"Why are you here?" The voice was somber in correct English, with no trace of friendliness. McGrath wondered if this guy was DGI. Did Elena know him? Maybe he was one of her friends, he thought in a second of bitterness.

"We're here as tourists," McGrath answered, trying to sound calm. "I'm a professor at Georgetown University, Washington, D.C. My trip's been cleared with your government."

"And you, Mr. Samuels, a lawyer," he said, looking at his passport.

"That is correct." McGrath had heard that voice before in the courtroom. He called it Don's lawyer voice, loaded with objectivity and reason. It sounded like, "Yes, your honor," to McGrath.

"Interesting. A lawyer who, it seems, begins his stay in Cuba by breaking Cuba's laws." He turned back to McGrath. "What kind of people did you intend to interview?"

"I have written to the Ministry of Foreign Affairs and to labor officials and two or three party leaders," McGrath answered.

"I see. And what did you plan to do with the information you collect?"

"My research is on how Cubans interpret their past, present, and future as a people."

"You will find our people very busy here. They may not want to waste time with you."

"Yes, that *could* be a problem," McGrath answered. He tried to sound neutral.

"Do you understand the serious nature of the crime you committed this morning?" His words were ominously laced with threat, like offering them arsenic at gunpoint. "It is a major national security violation to engage in public protests, but even more serious to assault Cuba's security forces. I am afraid you are in deep trouble. Deep trouble indeed," he repeated. He thumbed the passports, stared at them in steely-eyed gravity. He drummed the table with the fingers of his right hand.

McGrath thought fast, cleared his voice, and then said in a tone that he hoped sounded sufficiently contrite but not pleading, "We understand the seriousness of the situation, Colonel. It's clear we acted hastily without thinking, Would it be possible to telephone the American Interest Section?" But he feared his request was more hopeless than reasonable, as if he knew the answer before the question. Like thinking you're going to whiff a golf shot or blow a return lob in tennis. Then doing it.

So it hardly came as a surprise, when he heard, "Out

of the question." Then the colonel put their passports in his desk drawer and suddenly barked to the security guards standing just inside the door, "Take them away."

Back in the lockup room, the door slammed behind them, and McGrath and Samuels slumped down against the dank wall. "So what do you think, man? What are the odds on our getting out of here?" Samuels whispered glumly, arms folded and resting on bent-up knees, the left one poking through the rip in his pants.

"I don't know. Let's hope these guys contact the U.S. Interest Section. Maybe someone there can help."

"How long you think it will take?"

"Hard to tell. This isn't exactly a five-star hotel."

"Too bad they wouldn't let you call the Interest Section. Great idea."

McGrath was silent. He raced through the possibilities. *Goodwin*? Maybe Sam alerted the U.S. Interest Section about him before they arrived. Maybe they'll do something. Elena? He did speak to her. She knew he was in town. They arranged to have lunch tomorrow. Had she heard about their arrest over at the DGI? Could she do anything if she knew? Maybe she knew the guy who interrogated them. Long odds, he thought. Sam's the best bet. They'd just have to wait and see. He stood up and checked the door just to be sure it was locked.

"God, it stinks in here," Samuels said, gazing gloomily around the room. "Hotter'n hell . . . I'm sweating like a pig . . . could sure use a shower . . . tell you one thing . . . if they had habeas corpus, we'd be out of here by now. What a moth-eaten legal system."

They looked up when one of the protestors, a tall, lean guy, wearing a blue and white T-shirt approached them. His T-shirt had the words "Cuba Libre" in fire-engine red on the front, and he wore black pants. The guy shuffled over and slouched down beside them against the dank wall. "*Hola*, amigos," he said, extending his hand. "You *Americanos*, no? I guess this is not what you expected to see in beautiful downtown Havana. Hemingway's *Floridita* this is not. My name's Ricardo. Yours?"

He has a sense of humor, McGrath thought, shaking the man's hand. He looked to be in his late forties, maybe early fifties. Hair thick with salt-and-pepper, skin light brown, and dark hazel eyes that gleamed with intelligence and high energy.

After McGrath and Samuels introduced themselves, Ricardo said, "Thanks for diving into that brawl to help us. *Muchas gracias*. You were brave. Not many foreigners would have taken the risk. I hope you get out of this OK Maybe you will, because you are foreign."

"I'd like to think so," Samuels said. "How about you and your friends?"

"We no doubt are in for a longer stay. I hope not. But who knows these days?"

"I don't suppose we can be of much help to you, given our track record now," McGrath said with a straight face.

"So what happened when they took you away a few minutes ago?" Ricardo asked.

"About what you'd expect," McGrath answered. He told him about the colonel. As he was talking about their brief interrogation, he remembered the sign he had seen one of protestors carrying, this man maybe, before he had rushed into the melee after Samuels. "One of your signs read Enrique Maceo," McGrath said. "Do you actually know Enrique Maceo?"

"I should," the protester replied seriously, looking McGrath square in the eyes. "He's my brother." McGrath instantly recognized the distinct resemblance to Alicia. "Why do you ask?"

Well, I'll be damned, McGrath thought. This guy's

Martina Espinosa's brother. "Then . . . Señora Martina Espinosa is your sister?"

"That is correct, my friend. Do you know her?"

Did he know her? McGrath thought. "Well . . . yes and no," he said.

He explained how he knew about Ricardo's brother and family in Havana through Rebecca, and Ricardo's jaw dropped. He knew all about Rebecca's efforts on behalf of his family—and of her death through her Washington office. With tears, he said, "She was an incredible woman." Pausing, he added with passion, "This . . . this . . . is absolutely incredible . . . that we should meet in this room, in this lousy prison, under these circumstances. Who would believe it?" He stared back at McGrath for a minute, trying to take in the situation.

They talked animatedly, and Ricardo said, "Listen, if they let you out, and I sincerely hope they do, you *must* go to my sister's home to meet Martina. You have the address and telephone number, yes? She will be delighted to meet you. She'll want to learn everything she can about Alicia. My God, this is fantastic that you have come to Cuba, Professor McGrath. We know all about what your wife has done for our family. Alicia has written everything. I can't tell you how indebted we are to her, and now to you. We can never repay you."

McGrath was no less effusive in his praise of Ricardo and his family. He praised Ricardo and his family for their battle for human rights under Cuba's notorious state security system. The more he expressed these feelings, the more McGrath felt connected with everything Rebecca had fought for back in Washington. He long had identified with her work, but now for the first time he felt personally, intimately, involved—right in the thick of it. Nothing like rotting in a dirt-hole jail to focus your thoughts, he thought ruefully.

They stopped talking abruptly when two guards brusquely pushed through the door and barked at Ri-

cardo to get to his feet. Without ceremony they hauled
him off for questioning. Before they pushed him
through the door, Ricardo grabbed McGrath's hand,
squeezed it between the palms of his own and winked.

They waited. Two hours. Time for McGrath to reflect
on Ricardo and his family's courage. Patriots, he
thought, fighting for the right cause against heavy-
handed authoritarian rule. Cuban versions of Patrick
Henry, battling for principles like those of American patriots in our own early revolutionary history. He suddenly wanted to help Ricardo and people like him,
involved in Cuba in ways that he would not have
dreamed just two days ago.

Another hour waiting when agitated voices exploded
in the hallway just outside the gloomy room. Two men
arguing. Just then, the door suddenly opened and a pair
of hands shoved a wide-eyed Ricardo back inside.

"How did it go?" McGrath asked, as the door
slammed shut. Ricardo said that he had experienced the
same line of questioning as McGrath, only more in-
depth. He was worried, he said, and the purple swollen
eye underscored this point. Ricardo confessed it did not
look good.

"Can't your protest group here in Havana help you?"
Samuels asked.

"Afraid not," Ricardo said quietly, "You saw what
happens to public protestors. They are helpless in situations like this, that is, outside of working with somebody like Professor McGrath's wife, you know,
somebody in Washington."

"Jesus, what a dumb ass situation. What kind of country is this anyway?"

"It's a great country," Ricardo said defensively, "Run
by the wrong people. Look, when you think about . . .
wait a minute . . . listen . . . what's going on out there?"

"Sounds like somebody's really steamed up," Mc-
Grath said.

"I think it's someone from the U.S. Interest Section here in Havana," Ricardo said, then added, "and someone else from the Cuban Ministry of Interior. They're both pissed. I heard your names mentioned when the guard hustled me by them. I forgot to tell you."

The row outside escalated into loud vigorous arguing, but they could not hear the words distinctly from inside the cell room. "What's the deal? Can you understand what they're saying?" Samuels asked.

"Wait a minute." McGrath put his ear to the door. He couldn't hear completely, but caught snippets in Spanish.

"You try that, my friend," he heard one deep voice say, "and we'll burn your ass on the front page of the *New York Times*."

"That must be the guy from the Interest Section," McGrath whispered.

Then the Cuban retorted with something about "If this happens again, we won't give a good goddamn what you print in your stinking *Yanqui* imperialist newspaper."

It went on like that for another five minutes, at the end of which they heard the Cuban storm off down the hall. They backed away as keys jangled in the outside lock, quickly sliding down the damp wall into a sitting position, as the doorknob turned, and the room door violently flew open, through which stomped an American and two Cuban guards. The balding, short, thickset American barked out in a heavy New York City accent, "McGrath, Samuels . . . let's go."

He motioned to follow him, and as they departed, McGrath gave Ricardo a wave and a wan smile. "Good luck," he whispered, as the guard slammed the door. The last words McGrath heard as Ricardo clasped his hand were, "May God go with you."

They followed the American down the hall, out the door, and into the fresh air.

"I'm Bob Kincaid," the American said testily, as they walked along the broken sidewalk. "You, know, the guy you were supposed to contact quietly, your back up, the one you called this morning?"

Oh shit, McGrath thought.

Kincaid stared at them in disgust for a minute. "What I want to know is this. What in the fuck do you think you were doing?" He scowled at each of them in turn. "Do you have even the remotest goddamn idea of the problem you've created for us? Where the shit do you think you are, anyway? Miami-fucking-Beach?"

They said nothing at first. McGrath was the first to reply. "Listen, we're sorry if . . ."

"Shut up," Kincaid snapped back, cutting him off. "I'll do the talking here. Welcome to Cuba. Here are your passports." They were damp with perspiration. "You may not know just how lucky you are. The fellow you heard in the hallway is from Cuba's Ministry of Interior. He was all set to throw your sorry asses into prison and put the both of you on trial for espionage."

"Espionage?" McGrath said.

"Right. Espionage. They would have trumped up charges against you as CIA agents sent here to destabilize the government. The jury would have found you guilty. You're a lawyer, Samuels. You would have learned some hard lessons in Cuban jurisprudence. The first lesson is forget your rights."

"It was a dumb move," Samuels began, but Kincaid waved him off.

"You should know the drill, McGrath." His tone of voice and face hinted that he knew who they were and why they were here. "Dissidents get beaten up by mobs or plainclothes security thugs down here every week. Prisons are bursting. Need a shoehorn to squeeze more in. Public discontent's growing fast too, and the government's uptight as all hell. Its been getting worse, but the government intends to stay in control. It's no secret. But instead of avoiding trouble, you numbskulls waltz in from Miami and throw yourselves square into the middle of it. I swear to God I've never seen anything so goddamn stupid."

"Will they deport us?" McGrath asked.

"You lucked out this time, McGrath. That's what we were arguing about in the hallway. If the Interior Ministry had it their way, you'd stay in jail. But his higher-ups don't want to blow it out of proportion. They sure as hell don't want you looking like heroes here or back in the States. So they agreed to bury this incident. It'll be suppressed in both presses."

McGrath looked at Samuels and let out a sigh of relief. He turned back to Kincaid. "So where do we go from here?" he asked.

"OK, look. First, for Christ's sake be careful down here. This place is as tense as a chicken coop with the fox inside. There's not much we can do if you get arrested again. Keep your noses clean, whatever you do. Now then, you've been fully briefed on Elena Rodríguez, Goodwin tells me. That right?"

Fully briefed? McGrath thought. He doubted it, but he replied, "Far as I know."

"Good. Maybe she's got information we can use. See what you can learn."

"Sam said she's in some kind of trouble. What's the story?"

"I don't know anything more than Goodwin probably told you. One of our defectors knew her uncle, mentioned something's going on in her office. Whatever it is, she'll be pleased to see an old friend."

The tone of Kincaid's voice sounded as if it were a vote of no confidence in their ability to do anything right, like whatever they might do for Goodwin would be half-assed.

"You mean, find out everything she knows, and is willing to discuss, about drug trafficking?" McGrath asked.

"That's the idea," Kincaid replied laconically. "We believe someone high up is deeply involved in moving drugs through Cuban territory in some way, facilitating the Colombians who produce the stuff. We've got all kinds of circumstantial evidence, some of which you may have seen yourself, or run into, just walking the streets as tourists. You know, drug pushers in the tourist areas. In some areas they're like fleas, not only here in Havana but up and down the island. Lots of smoke. We want to find the fire."

They reached Kincaid's beat-up green Ford and got in. "I'll give you a ride back to the Capitolio. You can catch a cab back to your hotel. Safer that way. After this little incident, we don't want to be seen together. They'd think you're CIA for sure."

"Sorry we had to meet this way," McGrath said, feeling stupid.

"We'll use better judgment in the future," Samuels said from behind.

"So how do we contact you if we need to?" McGrath asked.

"Open the glove compartment."

McGrath opened it, reached in and pulled out what looked like a cell phone. "It's a satellite handheld telephone, made by Global Star. Programmed security frequency, all calls secure. Use it to call me, won't be monitored. Write this number down. There's a pencil and pad in the glove compartment. Grab that little knapsack in the backseat. You can put the phone in it and carry it around, safe and sound."

"I can call Goodwin?" McGrath asked.

"Yes. Got his number?"

"Yes." McGrath thought a minute. "Tell me one thing.

Does Elena work for you?" He got the same surprised look Goodwin had given him and pretty much the identical verbal response. There were still a lot of question marks hanging over her head.

It was then that he remembered. Tomorrow. He would meet Elena.

Victor poured himself a cup of steaming black coffee, glanced at his watch and sat down in front of Ramiro's desk. It was four in the afternoon, the corridor outside Ramiro's office filled with people briskly going about their business.

Ramiro wheeled around in his swivel chair, put down the thick manila folder he was reading, and took a deep, audible breath. He leaned forward over his desk, resting his chin on the palms of his hands, elbows braced on the table. His eyes probed at Victor. "I suppose," he said in a low sinister voice, "that you heard the latest on Quintero?"

"You mean his finally getting Elena into his apartment last week?"

"Precisely. That goddamn fuckhead. What kind of bullshit is that? Haven't we got enough problems with her?"

Victor detected the fury in Ramiro's tone of voice. "Certainly I heard. Hell, by now everybody knows. Quintero couldn't keep his mouth shut about something like that, even if he wanted to. You know Quintero."

"What in the *hell's* the matter with him?" Ramiro said, his words dripping with venom. "He should know better, the little prick. And at night? With those Defense of the Revolution Committee watchdogs hanging around his block, sniffing at anything that moves, just *waiting* for something to happen. You been over to his place lately? *Jesus,* its loaded with stuff. She's got to be asking herself where the *fuck* does he get all those things? TV, new stereo, CDs. There's a goddamn embargo on, for Christ's sake," Ramiro hissed, throwing up his hands in utter frustration. "Sometimes I think that man's brain's hanging between his legs."

"Yes, I know," Victor said, "I was at his place just last week. Kitchen looks like a warehouse. I saw two new cases of Jamaican rum, a couple more of Heineken beer and a case of top quality Mexican tequila—stacked in the corner like some kind of monumental trophy case. Look, that's the way the guy operates. He *lives* for that stuff. That's why he works so damn hard in this office. That's why he's made himself so indispensable. He works for the payoff, *chico*. He loves all that merchandise. You know, symbols of power. Thinks that's the way to get women. But I agree. He's a high profile skirt chaser for sure. Yeah, it was a dumb move all right. *Really* dumb. Especially at a time like this."

"You mean especially if she's spying?"

"*Sí chico.* I don't think Quintero had to work so hard to get her to come to his apartment. I think it's the other way around. She cozied up to Quintero, wormed her way into his apartment to see what he had there. After that, she got into my file cabinet, which I know someone was in because, you will remember, the Mexico file was left on top."

"You're still certain she's spying for God knows who?"

"*Absolutamente.*"

"So . . . a spy for who?"

"I don't know . . . could be anybody. Castro? Wouldn't put it past him, but I doubt it. CIA? Maybe. After all, her parents are Cuban refugees? She studied in the U.S. Sure, she could be a CIA plant. Now wouldn't that be something? Right here in this office."

"It's possible. But what about Herrera? Maybe Herrera's got her in his pocket."

"Yeah . . . yeah . . ." Ramiro mused, ". . . could be. *Es posible* . . . maybe she's working for Herrera. But *quién sabe*? Maybe somebody else we haven't considered? We'll find out. She'll make a mistake soon."

Victor could tell from the look on Ramiro's face that he would enjoy interrogating Elena, a time when he, Victor, would just as soon not be present.

"Hang on a minute," Ramiro said. "Don't leave yet. Let's get Maria in here and see what she knows. Ramiro reached down and buzzed Maria without missing a beat. A minute later, they heard the soft knock at the door, and Ramiro shifted in his chair, barking out, "Come in."

A well-dressed, alert, rather attractive woman in her mid-forties entered the room. She made eye contact with each man and waited attentively.

"Ah, Maria," Ramiro intoned confidentially. "I want to ask you a couple of questions. Elena's still away from the office, right?"

"Yes sir," Maria replied.

Maria Gonzalez looked like a typical middle-aged Cuban woman. She was short and stocky, dressed in a pastel blue suit with crisp white blouse. She was tidily put together, although her clothes and shoes had that well-worn look. Widowed and alone, her co-workers had taken on the role of family in Maria's life. She was well liked and trusted by everyone. Maria was now Elena's confidant. That relationship had evolved as a result of the stressful organizational culture of MININT and the tension that was so evident every time Ramiro was around Elena.

What Elena did not know was that Maria's sole objective in life was to serve Ramiro as a *persona de confianza*, someone who could gather information for Ramiro through office gossip and on weekends spent with office personnel.

Maria smiled at the two men, as Ramiro motioned her to sit down.

"Maria," Ramiro said in a gentle voice, smiling pleasantly, "so what have you heard about Quintero and Elena lately?"

NINE

Havana

A 1956 blue and white Chevy taxi pulled up in front of the Havana Libre Hotel the next day at one in the afternoon. The driver jumped out and rushed around to open the door for his passenger—a woman with dark, shoulder-length hair, dressed in a pale blue skirt, short-sleeve white blouse, and black platform shoes. So stunning was her appearance that she caught the eye of two businessmen standing by the hotel's glass doorway. They tripped over themselves to open the hotel door for her and get a closer look. She walked confidently through and rewarded them with a smile.

McGrath, waiting inside the lobby entrance, spotted her instantly. His face broke into a giant grin. His heart picked up pace as he walked toward her.

"Elena, so good to see you!"

They shook hands awkwardly, as if they wanted to embrace, but didn't know how the other felt. "You . . . you look wonderful!" She had changed since he last saw her, now more beautiful than he remembered. But she still had that intelligence in her face, that warm smile and remarkable posture. He did not recall the dark shadows under her eyes.

Elena took his hand and said, "Professor McGrath, this is incredible! Who would have dreamed we might meet here in Havana? I thought I'd never see you again!" She smiled broadly and stepped back.

"Let's drop the professor stuff. That's the past. Call me Neal. Let's go to lunch," McGrath said. "We've got lots to talk about."

"Absolutely," Elena replied. "But let me take you to a place I know. A *paladar*. Not far from here, OK?"

"*Paladar*?" Neal asked as they jumped in a taxi.

"Privately run restaurants. Typically seat no more than ten or twelve people. Fixed menu. Quaint. Away from the crowd. We can talk there."

Fifteen minutes later, they walked up the concrete steps of a two-story white stucco home in Vedado and rang the bell. A young woman greeted them, ushered them into the marble floor living room, through the home's dining room and out backyard to a cozy eating area. Three tables for four, thatched roof, small bar, and one mangy gray cat who took little interest in the goings-on. Tacky, but it would deliver the goods.

"Our menu today is *pargo*, red snapper, vegetables, rice, and black beans for ten dollars. Beer is two dollars per can. Crystal." The young woman took their orders and disappeared.

"So, Elena," McGrath started, "been a long time, too long. How's life treating you?" From the looks of those eyes, not well, he thought.

"So-so," she replied. "Can't complain." She waved her hand in the so-so way that everybody understood. Her voice sounded matter-of-fact, but McGrath caught a slight edge to it, the tone slightly unnatural, tentative. "How's it going for you?" she added.

"Same here," he said. "I'm getting along. The university's still standing. Lots of blue books. You know the drill."

"You always loved university life," she said.

"So what exactly do you do to make ends meet down here? Did you land a great job? Did that Georgetown master's degree pay off?"

She shifted slightly in her chair, uneasy. "Well . . . I . . . uh . . . lucked out." McGrath thought he saw a faint shadow cross her face, like a passing cloud on a sunny sidewalk. "Found a position with the government. Took awhile, but it eventually worked out." A hesitant smile played at the corner of her mouth as if she were trying to appear calm and as natural as a summer breeze, but the smile, or whatever it was, quickly vanished. It reminded McGrath of the *Mona Lisa*. He could not tell if her lips were a grin or a frown. She sat straight-backed in her chair, looking professional and in total control.

"What kind of position?" McGrath asked, pressing.

"It's . . . ah . . . in the security field."

"What kind of security?"

"Intelligence," she said, "Something like CIA. I work for the Ministry of Interior."

She hesitated, took a sip of water and for a second looked distracted, as if she were trying to collect herself before replying. "Well, as you can imagine, much of the work they do there is classified, so I'm not at liberty to discuss it in detail. You can use your imagination." She definitely was not jovial now.

"Sounds exciting," McGrath said.

"At times," she replied, but the tone of her voice and body language telegraphed that this subject was off limits, and she smoothly shifted gears. "So what do you think of Havana so far?" She unfolded and placed the red- and white-checkered napkin on her lap.

"Before we get into that, Elena," McGrath said, not letting go, "and I can appreciate your not wanting to discuss your work if it's classified, but can you just say whether you find your work interesting and challenging? I mean are you enjoying it?"

"You sound like 'Professor McGrath' in your office up in D.C." she replied. "I remember you used to ask your graduates that question when they came back to visit, after they were out there in the big world."

"Well, yeah, that's right, and you are my former student, no?"

Again she hesitated, then said, "OK, fair question. Yeah, I guess, sure, it's interesting, certainly challenging at times. Do I enjoy it? You bet. At times I like it, but who enjoys their work every minute of the day? Are you happy all the time in what you do?" The defensive edge in her voice was unmistakable, and she sounded less than confident as she brushed back her hair and fidgeted with her hands. McGrath now was convinced that she was in trouble.

"Good enough," McGrath said. "You asked how we like Havana. Well, I'll say this. The place is full of surprises." He picked his words carefully, not wanting to offend Elena. "As a matter of fact," he added, "My friend Don and I managed to get ourselves arrested yesterday."

Elena's mouth dropped open. Recovering herself after a second, she said, "What? Arrested? Good God, what on earth happened?"

Elena listened with a look of total amazement. "You mean you literally ran down the sidewalk and started pounding on the Rapid Action guys? On the side of the protesters?"

"That's about it," McGrath said. "You might say we didn't give it much thought. But it seemed the right thing to do."

"Were you hurt?" she asked in a voice of concern.

"No, nothing more than bumps and bruises."

"How long did they hold you?"

"About four or five hours," he replied.

"My God, do you realize how lucky you were to walk out so quickly?"

"Oh yes," McGrath said. "The guy from the U.S. Interest Section made that point crystal clear."

"What was his name?"

"Robert Kincaid."

Elena looked at McGrath, paused a second. "The protesters they arrested probably won't be so lucky. Sorry your visit got off to such a rotten start." Then she added, "apart from your skirmish with the law, have you had time to form any other initial impressions of beautiful downtown Havana?" Their waitress arrived with food.

"No offense, Elena," McGrath said, "but I didn't expect to find the city so dilapidated. I knew it would be run-down and all that, but I have to tell you that I was really surprised when we drove in from the airport. Not just the old cars, but the general disrepair of everything, except of course the new modern hotels. It seems so neglected."

Elena's cheeks turn pale red . . . defensively red, McGrath thought. "To quote the guide books you can read," she said, "Havana is an ancient and majestic, once-proud Spanish city now in sad disrepair." She paused, brushed away a fly, then added, "But remember that life is strained here—really strained, thanks to the U.S. embargo." She said, ironically.

McGrath found himself emotionally charged by her presence. He loved the sound of her voice and literally was bowled over on seeing and interacting with her again. He hadn't had this kind of a reaction to a woman since his wife's death. He still didn't know what was going on with her, but it was clear to him she was in a bad situation, and he was determined to find answers. He took a long draw on his cold beer.

As she talked, his mind jumped around from seeing one minute his old intelligent student, next as somebody he needed to talk to because of his CIA assignment. She sounded so fired up on the embargo and the country's crummy conditions that she talked like a Fidelista. If she was, then what kind of trouble could she be in and why the hell would CIA want him to talk to her as a contact? He ordered another round of beers.

"Sorry to get on this soapbox," Elena said. She looked embarrassed, pouring the last of her beer into her glass. "The bottom line is, and I repeat, that people are better off now than before the revolution." She pulled a pack of cigarettes and small silver cigarette lighter from her purse, lit up, and flipped the lighter shut with a distinct clink. She exhaled a stream of smoke, and drew the glass ashtray across the table toward her.

The cigarettes got McGrath's attention. He remembered that she had smoked when he first met her back in D.C., but she had broken the habit while a graduate student. She had been proud of her steel will on that issue and had mentioned more than once that she would never again smoke.

Forty minutes later they paid the bill, got up, and walked back through the two rooms in the private home to the front door. There, they hailed a taxi from the curb. When they reached their hotel a few minutes later, they stood in front of the hotel entrance awkwardly. McGrath decided to get to the point and find out what was wrong with her. "I see you're smoking again."

She looked embarrassed, then defensive, and replied, "A woman's got a right to change her mind, doesn't she?"

"Sure, but when a person returns to that old habit, y'know, it usually means something's not exactly right in their life."

She gave him a sidelong glance, paused, took another draw on her cigarette, then said hesitantly, "Neal, I . . ." She paused, looked away.

"Yes, what is it?"

"Look," she said, "I just want you to know that I'm *really* so happy that you have come to Havana." She glanced suspiciously around the half-moon hotel driveway as if looking for someone. "Your timing is really remarkable."

"What do you mean?"

"I hesitate to bring this up, especially after what happened to you yesterday," she said, still casting glances in different directions, obviously trying to look unruffled.

"Jesus, Elena, if you've got something on your mind, let's talk about it."

"You're right. Do you have time to walk with me for a couple of blocks before I get back to work?"

"Absolutely, let's go."

She walked McGrath down to the busy corner of "L" Avenue and 23rd Street, turned left on 23rd and when the light changed, crossed the street to the Coppelia Ice Cream Park. He glanced up at the thick gray cloud cover that had taken over the skies, with rain likely, not unusual for this time of year. After all, it was hurricane season. When they reached the park, long lines of people waited their turn to order ice cream, but McGrath and Elena walked by them into the lush tropical setting and found a free bench where they could talk in private.

They seated themselves on one of the black steel-grated benches in the park, shushing the seagulls away. Elena sat close to McGrath, legs crossed, clearly restless. The other visitors in the park were older Cubans who sat in twos and threes, chatting, smoking cigars.

"Listen," she said softly, but swiftly "the last thing I want to do is complicate your life, but I've got to tell you something. I'm not certain who else I can trust at this point, except for my uncle, and he's out of the country." She paused for a moment, her lips drawn tightly closed, leaning forward, arms crossed, hugging her body, as if apprehensively trying to protect herself against something menacing. She looked grim.

"Must be serious," McGrath said.

"Dead serious," she said darkly, her somber eyes locked on his.

He tilted his head close to hear her whispered words as she leaned into him, her eyes filled with premonition. The fragrance of her perfume overpowered the smell of cigarettes.

"Look, this may sound foolish," Elena said, lower lip

slightly sucked in. "Maybe I'm imagining things. I don't know. I'm not even sure how to tell you . . . but." She glanced around again. "I think I'm being followed." She looked at McGrath anxiously.

TEN

Havana

"Followed?" McGrath whispered. "Why would anybody want to tail you?" He was all ears. Goodwin, he thought. Questions bounced around his head like a pinball machine. She'd done something. And Goodwin had heard about it from one of his expat informers and hoped Elena would confide in her old college professor. Or she worked for Goodwin as a mole. He couldn't rule that out. Where did Kincaid come into the picture? Suspicions stacked up in the back of his mind like a long line of grounded jetliners waiting out a Chicago thunderstorm.

"Exactly. I noticed a few days ago. The same guy." McGrath saw a thin, pale blue blood vein running along her temple. This is no act, he thought. She's damn scared.

"Why would anyone want to follow you?"

"Sounds odd, I know."

"But you work for the government. Interior Ministry, right? Aren't you the people that do the surveillance? You're not supposed to be followed, right?"

"Exactly. That's the point. But . . ." she drew closer to him, and he could hear her controlled breathing. "Something's going on in my office, Neal. I haven't quite figured it out yet. Maybe it's connected."

"What do you mean something's going on? What's going on?"

"I think. I mean . . . Oh, God, this is all so stupid and confusing." She took another long draw on her cigarette.

"If you're in trouble, Elena, for God's sake, tell me."

She sighed and pursed her lips as a hint of foreboding crossed her face. "OK here goes. First," she paused, "I think the man, actually more than one, a different person different times, following me may actually work for my boss. And you're right. My office is full of high-level secret service types, highest in Cuba. Whoever's following me probably works out of my own building, maybe even out of my own office."

McGrath looked at her with grave concern, and in a quiet tone of voice, he said, "Go on."

A few seconds passed. Then she said, "OK," smiling wanly, her hand slightly trembling on his arm, she stared directly into his eyes, "let me try to explain. You know me pretty well, right? All those times in graduate school we worked together. You know I'm fairly well organized, don't go around getting into trouble, balanced, straightforward and all that, right?"

"Of course. Definitely not the wacky type," McGrath smiled, trying to make her feel comfortable, but thinking all the time, what's she getting at?

"Well, as background to all this, I should tell you that the Ministry of Interior, they call it MININT, where I work, as you might well imagine, deals with a lot of classified information. Hush-hush stuff. Intelligence business. Well, the thing is, I have always sensed that some people at the Ministry have never completely trusted me from the very first day I arrived. Certainly that seems true of General Ramiro."

"Your boss?"

"Right. During the time I've been there, Ramiro has given me mostly routine work—typing reports, running down background information, digging up material at other offices and sometimes at the library. At first I thought he was simply breaking me in, giving me a chance to pay my dues. When I was hired, I was hired to do research. But after all this time, that certainly hasn't happened—despite my academic degree." She tossed her cigarette down and squashed it under her foot.

"Waste of talent," McGrath said. "Why the lack of trust?"

"It's hard to put in plain words, but I know for a fact that General Ramiro and his cousin, Victor, who is also a big gun at the Ministry, were not pleased when *El Comandante* arranged to place me in Ramiro's office."

"*El Comandante*. You mean Fidel Castro?"

"Right. Ramiro doesn't take kindly to having an outsider—especially someone from the U.S., whose parents were classified as *gusanos*—rammed down his throat. I can tell you, it's been no picnic working for General Ramiro. He's no life of the party."

"OK So you think that's why you're being tailed? Routine security check?"

She looked at him, puzzled. "No. It's something else." She paused again and gazed reflectively off in the distance, collecting her thoughts, hesitant to bare her soul.

Then she whispered, "I've done something truly stupid. We're talking monumentally idiotic here."

McGrath stared at her. "Oh? Like what?"

Elena cleared her throat, pushed back her shoulders, and spoke softly. She told McGrath that for several weeks odd events had been occurring in Ramiro's office. Long telephone calls, meetings in hushed tones with Ramiro's cousin, Victor, and high-ranking officers behind Ramiro's closed doors. "It has been so out of the ordinary routine of the office," she said. "Lots of unexplained activity. Highly unusual," she said.

"Maybe some kind of special operation requiring secrecy."

"Uh-uh . . . something else's going on in there. Anyway, on top of all that, a few days ago Ramiro had to leave his office in a hurry—I think it was a phone call from Castro or something. Anyway, he left in a big rush. I had to go into his office a little while later to return a completed report to him. That's when ... when I ..." she removed her dark glasses, ". . . when I saw it."

"Saw what?"

"His file cabinet." Elena took a breath. "One of his classified file cabinets was open. What I mean is, the safety bar that locks it was in place through the handles, but I noticed the lock was still open. He must have thought he locked it, but the lock didn't catch, and he was in a hurry to leave. It was the first time ever I remember seeing his file cabinet open when he wasn't in the office. Like I said before, there's something going on, and he's under some kind of pressure that made him overlook the lock."

"So you ... just casually strolled across the room and took a peek in the open file cabinet?" It was difficult for McGrath to picture his former student taking such a reckless risk ... unless she had an ulterior motive. It crossed his mind that she was being disingenuous, but he didn't call her on it.

"*Yes.* I know it was a rash move, but the truth is I was worried something illegal was going on, and I was curious to know what it was. With all the strange comings and goings in that office, I simply couldn't resist the temptation to take a look. The opportunity was just too great."

"Good God, weren't you *frightened?*"

"*Frightened?* Are you kidding? Of *course* I was. I was *shaking.*"

"So? What happened?"

"Two things. First, I saw a thick file on Mexico's president—one of the bulkiest files in the cabinet. Lots of clippings about the guerrilla war in southern Mexico. Other clippings on a previous president, you know, Carlos Salinas de Gortari, and his brother Raúl, the one arrested for all that drug trafficking and corruption. Then there were a bunch of reports on those high-level assassinations in Mexico. Mexico's very unstable politically. But I don't have to tell you that."

"What else?"

Elena tossed another cigarette and ground it out with the toe of her shoe. "The file had a *lot* of information on all those political assassinations. Oh, and lots more on the Mexican military and how they've criticized the government. Internal reports of military discontent, clippings of that type."

"Ramiro's paying attention to Mexico's political problems. That's for certain."

"Right. And get this. There was a big report on drug trafficking in Mexico and Colombia. Loaded with information on how drugs travel from Mexico to the U.S. and how drugs get shipped from Colombia."

"So Ramiro follows Mexican political assassinations *and* drug trafficking."

"That's what it looks like to me."

"But why? Maybe something deeper than Cuban security? Could be Ramiro's involved in illegal drug operations in or around Cuba. It's not that far-fetched, you know. Wouldn't be the first time something like that has happened."

If Ramiro was connected to illegal drug activities, the obvious question, he thought, was how far-reaching they were in Elena's office and how high up they went.

"Yes, but on the other hand maybe those reports make perfect sense. Drugs, after all, are a national security problem, right? Ramiro would want to know in general about drug trafficking activities near Cuba."

"How detailed were the files?"

"Very. Delivery routes. Shipment dates, drop-off places, the works. Jesus, I know what you're thinking. It certainly crossed my mind. I didn't want to admit it before, but I think you might be right. Truth is, as far as I know, our office's mission is not to follow drug trafficking," she said gravely. "Never has. That's the job of another office. Ramiro covers CIA infiltration, black market activities, operations in Panama, those kinds of things."

"So the files are definitely out of place, then, from what you know to be your office's mission, right?"

"Right."

"Looks like you stumbled onto something Ramiro doesn't want anybody to know, Elena. Damn good reason to have you followed."

"Yeah, I know. But there's something else," Elena said.

"More?"

"Afraid so. When I opened the bottom drawer of the file cabinet, there was a large paper bag."

"A large paper bag?"

"Sound strange?"

"Depends on what was in it. Dirty laundry?" A little humor might ease her tension, he thought.

"No. Money. Piles of it. So much I couldn't believe my eyes."

"My God," McGrath whistled. "*How much* is how much?"

"Bundles and bundles of one hundred dollar bills. Probably thousands and thousands of dollars."

McGrath let out a low whistle. "Not exactly a petty cash fund. Could it be for his special operations?"

"Well, I don't know, but definitely something illegal. "I've got a horrible feeling it's *drug money*."

"Could be. Tell me more about the Mexican file," he said.

"Besides the drug business, it had a bunch of clippings on the Mexican president's upcoming visit to the U.S. I don't know what that was all about, since it has not been public knowledge in the rest of the office. Also, get this, several reports on a guy named Moreno, a guerrilla leader from Chiapas, Mexico. I didn't read everything. No time. Just glanced at the headings. Anyway, Moreno's a well-known guerrilla, a specialist in martial arts. Killed lots of people. And," she added, her voice quavering, "I *saw* this man Moreno in Ramiro's office last week. I had to take a report into Ramiro's room, and he was there. Neal, he has the eyes of a cobra, I swear to God, scared the daylights out of me when he looked at me."

"What possible connection would information about Mexico and Moreno have to do with drug trafficking in Cuba?" McGrath asked.

"Haven't a clue," she replied.

McGrath thought a few seconds, decided not to push it even if she wasn't telling the truth, then said, "Must be some kind of connection, but meanwhile you're convinced that your boss, Ramiro, suspects that you were digging around in his classified file."

"Right."

"So he has you followed to see who you talk to and where you go."

"Right."

"But why you? Why you in particular?"

"Lots of reasons," she murmured. "I'm one of only a few of the staff besides Maria who goes into his office. But here's the real problem. I was glancing through the file when I heard Ramiro coming back down the hall—I could see him right outside his door, back early from his meeting—I *panicked*. I was *sure* I'd be caught. I tried to stuff the file back in the drawer, but it wouldn't fit. So I just put it on top of the cabinet. I guess I hoped Ramiro would think he had left it out. I did get the bottom drawer shut."

"*Jesus*," McGrath replied. Now he was genuinely concerned for Elena. "Then what happened?"

"I closed the file cabinet drawers as quietly as I could and ran back to my office!"

"Ramiro didn't see you? Sounds like you ran right by him."

"No. My office connects with Ramiro's through an inner corridor. Our staff offices are there, and nobody was in their office at the time. That's why I thought I could get away with it."

"Oh, I see. So what happ—"

"God, I was absolutely *petrified*. Thank heaven, somebody asked Ramiro a question out in the hall before he opened the door to his office, and that saved me. But I had left *my* report on his desk and that big file on top of the cabinet. Ramiro can add two and two together and draw the conclusion that it must have been me in his office at the time."

"But he doesn't know for certain that you got into his cabinet, right? Could be that he doesn't suspect anybody, that he thinks he may have left the file on top himself, kicks himself for doing it."

"That's possible."

"In which case, you're being tailed could be routine. Or just the highly suspicious Ramiro who doesn't like you and would like to get some dirt on you to fire your— and do it in a way that he can justify to Castro who put you there in the first place, no?"

"Interesting possibility."

"Yeah . . . interesting possibility. But I don't buy it. Elena, you're in one helluva serious situation." He asked himself if she were reaching out to him to help her escape from Cuba. Did she know that he was connected with CIA and sent to see her? Was his former graduate student just a dedicated fly caught in a web . . . or one of the spiders? He could use a good stiff shot of bourbon right now, he thought.

"I know."

"There's something I've got to ask you," McGrath said.

"What's that?"

"Are you telling me *everything*?"

"What do you mean, everything?"

"I mean . . . is there anything else you need to tell

me?" McGrath refrained from directly bringing up any connection she or he might have with the CIA, but wanted to give her an open door on the subject if she chose to enter.

"Nothing else," she said, in a voice with just the hint of ice, McGrath thought.

"OK, OK. Sorry. Had to ask, that's all. Look . . ." McGrath paused and then said, ". . . maybe you ought to leave Cuba for a while. Have you thought about that possibility? Why not pull out and blow this Popsicle stand?"

"Yes. Yes, I have. I agree that this is potentially dangerous, but remember I work for Cuban intelligence. If Ramiro *is* running a drug operation, if he's doing something illegal that threatens Cuba's security, it's my job to try to find hard evidence and get it to the right people."

"Sure, sure, but . . ."

"Look, when my uncle returns, I'll have the security I need and a conduit to the right authorities. I know what I've got to do, Neal."

"Wait a minute," McGrath said, "If Ramiro *is* drug trafficking, then for sure his boss, the president, Castro, must know all about it too, right?"

"Oh, no. Impossible," she said passionately. The top political leaders would *never* approve of drug trafficking. For God's sake, the Cuban government officially is *cooperating* with the U.S. on drug trafficking down here. No, no, quite impossible. If Ramiro's involved, Fidel most certainly does not know about it."

"Well then, why not go straight to him right now and report it?"

"I *can't* do that," she said plaintively, throwing her hands up in the air. "I have no *proof* of anything. They might not believe me, then I would really look brainless."

"Your uncle's out of the country you say?"

"Unfortunately, yes. But I have some friends who might be able to help me if this thing escalates." Elena said in a voice of resignation. "I just basically wanted you to know what's going on. If I act a little strange while you're here, at least now you know why."

"Do you see the guy who has been following you around now?" McGrath said, looking around casually. "One of those men on the bench over there?"

"No," she replied, glancing nervously at the bench. "Too old. Anyway, I've been keeping an eye out since we left the hotel. Nobody's around now. It's curious. I don't think I'm followed every minute, but I know at times I am being watched."

As they stood on the sidewalk by the park, waiting to hail a taxi, she switched the subject to McGrath's research. "What kind of people do you want to interview?" she asked. "What's the nature of your project?" Her voice sounded to McGrath as if she were trying now to put on the face of self-assurance, maybe uncomfortable for showing so much fear earlier. But he could see apprehension in her eyes.

McGrath explained not so ardently that his subject was Cuban nationality, how individual Cubans, leaders in particular, perceived Cuba. How do they interpret Cuba's past and what kind of Cuba do they see in the future? But he was not thinking much at all about his research, far more engrossed in getting answers to the drug trafficking mystery and Elena's situation.

"So it's a study of how individuals identify with the *patria*?" Elena asked with an obligatory smile. "How Cubans relate to the *patria*, our fatherland?"

"Exactly."

As the 1957 red and white Chevy taxi rattled up with its smiling driver, Elena took hold of McGrath's hand and said, "Thanks for listening, Neal. I'll be OK, really. Meanwhile," she added, "let me see what I can do for you. I have some contacts that might be willing to be interviewed."

"Thanks," he said. "I'd really appreciate it." But

they both knew what they were talking about. Interviews would be a good excuse for him to stay close to her, and obviously she wanted that. Why else would she have told him her story?

She drew him to her, embraced him affectionately, and said, "I'm so pleased you're here," as her lips brushed his cheek. "Can you give me a call tomorrow?"

"Certainly," McGrath said, "That would be fantastic."

She handed him her little white professional card, her *tarjeta*, with its red and blue work address after writing her home number on the back. "Let me be your sightseeing guide too," she added. "I'd love to show you and your friend Don around Havana."

McGrath could not help asking himself how safe they all would be under the gathering storm Elena had created.

"How about dinner tomorrow night with Don and me?"

"That would be grand," she said.

McGrath took her cold hand, leaned to her ear and whispered, "Look, I will help in any way I can, OK? Just let me know how and when."

As he watched his former graduate student drive away, he had to admit that he still didn't know what was going on exactly, or why the CIA had sent him, but it was clear Elena was in deep trouble. He walked along the sidewalk, jaw firmly set, determined more than ever to help her.

Still, he felt a tinge of anxiety about the situation. When had he felt this way before? It wasn't like going into combat. In combat jumpy nerves were expected. In combat you were well trained, surrounded by plenty of support and lots of friends. It would be chaotic, that you knew, but you accepted what was to come. No, this trepidation was different, more sinister. Like something unpredictable and bad was about to happen, something evil that he could not control. He looked around to see if anyone was following him. He picked up his step. Somebody *was* back there—someone he thought he recognized.

ELEVEN

Havana = Mexico City

"Señor McGrath . . . Señor McGrath . . ." penetrated his tormented sleep. He awoke from a nightmare where he saw Rebecca slammed by the drunk driver, heard the metal crunch and ambulance sirens. He struggled to open his heavy-lidded eyes to the sound of a strident voice of a panicked male hotel employee banging furiously on their door, yelling at them to get out of the room immediately. At first he thought the voice was part of his bad dream, Rebecca crying out to him, but the yelling intensified, accompanied by agitated commotion in the outside hallway.

He dragged himself out of bed, glancing at Samuels who had just sat up. He thought he heard the word "fire," which got him moving fast. They pulled on a pair of pants and T-shirts and opened the door to a confused scene of half-dressed hotel patrons herded down the hall to the stairwell by three hotel staff members. Nobody seemed to know what the problem was. Some said fire, others thought it was a bomb.

In the melee, as they stumbled down the staircase with the others, they bumped into a nervously energetic man in his mid-forties, short, thin, grey at the temples, horn-rim glasses. "Name's Larry Diamond," he said. "What's yours?" They struck up a lively conversation on the way down to the lobby, during which Diamond made clear that he was an old Cuba hand and this whole business was a false alarm. "Happens all the time," he said.

"I've been through this drill twice before . . . just this year. Believe me, if it's a bomb, we'll know soon enough, but I doubt it is, and I guarantee you it's no fire, just hotel staff incompetence. I sometimes wonder how this place holds together."

Diamond explained that he owned a used bookstore in Toronto, Canada. He came to Cuba to trade western technology books for old Spanish tomes that he sold in Toronto as antiques. "Just got back from a week's trip out to the eastern end of the island, a big book-swapping tour up and down the Central Highway," he said. "Stopped at Cuba's major universities along the way. I rented a van and driver from Cubatur—the state tourist company. Subsecretary of Cuban libraries, Lourdes Morales, went with me. She's black, you know," Diamond explained. "Smart as hell. Great trip. Saw parts of Cuba tourists rarely get to visit."

They killed an hour down in the hotel lobby while things settled down. No fire. No bomb. False alarm. Diamond suggested that if they were interested, if they had the time, he would be pleased to show them some of the sights they might not normally catch, like the nightclub scene.

The more they talked, the more McGrath saw Diamond as a potential source of information, somebody that might know know something about drugs here on the island. He seemed familiar with the nooks and crannies of Cuban life, black market included, had Cuban contacts, and spoke fluent Spanish as far as McGrath could tell. Why not use him? Maybe he could hook them up with a drug dealer.

Next morning they checked out of the Havana Libre

at seven o'clock in the morning and moved to the Hotel Florida to throw off any surveillance.

They had their breakfast at the café on the Florida's first floor, just off the hotel's main courtyard. Outside, a light slow drizzle fell from low, pewter gray, overcast skies, while inside, as if to match the weather, the café had a laid-back, languid atmosphere, like time was moving at a half-time beat. Despite its calming environment, McGrath had spent a restless night, wrestling with everything Elena had told him yesterday, thrown into more turmoil by the false alarm fire. One thing stood out, however. Goodwin was right on the mark about Elena's situation.

At this point in the game, as he confided to Samuels over breakfast, he had more questions than answers about Elena and Goodwin. Why did she look into that classified file cabinet? He didn't buy her story that she thought something illegal was going on in her office and wanted to take the opportunity to find out more. Why was she being followed? It did not take long for them to conclude that if Elena *was* under suspicion by General Ramiro, then he would see McGrath as a threat too. Ramiro might conclude that McGrath was a CIA agent working with Elena. Hell, it wasn't a far stretch to reason that Samuels could be suspect too.

"Did she come right out and say she suspects Ramiro of drug trafficking?" Samuels asked.

"She thinks odds are it's a distinct possibility."

"Ah-ha," Samuels replied. "The old drug allure. Wouldn't be the first time a high level government official got tangled up in drug activities. Happens next door in Mexico all the time, y'know. Tell me again about the evidence."

"Purely circumstantial. Just the files in the safe and the money."

"She certainly works in the right building for suspicions."

They talked for awhile over coffee, then McGrath said, "Know what I'm thinking?"

"Tell me."

"I'm thinking that maybe you should catch the next plane and beat it out of here."

"Are you nuts? No way, man."

"Look, given the circumstances, especially since she's been seen with me, and since we've already been arrested, you would be a lot safer if you went back to the States now and call it a day. Besides, Elena's not your problem. I'm the one that dragged you into this thing."

"What about you?"

"Me? I'm going to stick around and see if I can help Elena. One person in her company won't draw as much attention as two."

Samuels munched on his toast, took another sip of coffee, paused, reflected, then said, "Look, Neal, I don't mind telling you again that our little visit to the Cuban lockup scared the piss out of me. I still got the jitters about this place. I don't feel real comfortable even walking the streets now . . . all this closed society business and police on every corner gives me the willies . . . know what I mean? But no, absolutely not. I'm not ditching you now, just because the heat's on. Besides, it's kinda challenging."

McGrath could see that he was still shaken, but he was gutsy, he thought. True grit. "I know what you mean, Don," McGrath said. "Nothing to be ashamed of. Can't say I'm totally comfortable either. You get your ass thrown in jail in a foreign country, and you don't walk out with a big comfort zone grin on your face. I hear you. There's a side of me that would just as soon pack it in and go home right now. But then there's Elena. I don't feel as if I can just fly away and abandon her."

"I don't know what kind of difficulty she's got herself

into or what kind of problem it might cause for us, but I'll tell you this," he gave McGrath a broad smile, "I respect your commitment to integrity, Neal. I can't possibly ditch you. Especially after you jumped in with me when I went after those government goons. Leave you stranded in Havana now? No way, Jose. I'm going to stay. Besides, you need somebody to watch your back."

"But you have a wife and kids back home. I don't. That's a Grand Canyon difference, my friend. I think you should scoot back. I mean it. I'm serious."

They argued for another five minutes, but it was clear Samuels would not budge. He would stay. Case closed.

"Thanks, Don. I appreciate it," McGrath said, reaching across the table to shake Samuels' hand warmly.

"Glad to do it. Anyway, I could use the good karma."

"What do you mean?"

"You know, what goes around, comes around. I've got some bad karma going now," Samuels replied, jokingly. "I defended a couple of scumball brothers recently, who should not have been defended. Got them off a prison term. My instincts tell me they should be rotting in prison. Like the one we visited here in Havana. They didn't murder anybody, but stole tons of public funds. Anyway, maybe I can balance things out by doing a good deed down here. We'll see, won't we?"

McGrath smiled. "We can start by helping Elena watch her back. Next, see if we can dig up more information on drugs. At least we can contact Kincaid with the satellite phone, even Goodwin if we have to."

"Right. Now about that tail on Elena. You think maybe it could be just a routine thing? Maybe they don't have lie detectors down here, so an intelligence office like hers, that Ministry of Interior, has to go labor intensive. Instead of a polygraph, they put a tail on their employees for a couple of days, write a report, and there you go, no need for all that high tech stuff. Too bad, though. I've found polygraphs useful despite their limitations."

"Uh-uh, Don. Elena thinks it's more serious. I believe that part of her story. She's into something bizarre, that's for sure."

"Worth a call to Kincaid?" Samuels asked.

"Not just yet, but in time, yes. We'll call when we've got more information. Let's see what we can learn from Larry Diamond."

"Diamond?" Samuels asked. "Seems interesting enough. Talks a big game. Didn't he say he spent a lot of time out at Veradero? Maybe some action out there, who knows? Yeah, he might be able to produce something."

"We obviously wouldn't say anything to him about Elena or the Ministry of Interior. We don't have to hit him over the head with it, y'know, just light, inquisitive remarks here and there."

"Sounds like a plan," Samuels said, reaching for his wallet to pay his bill, just as Larry Diamond strolled into the room. He was dressed in a faded yellow *guayabera*, Cuba's choice of shirts, open at the neck and hanging loosely over his well-worn khaki trousers, and old Sacony Jazz running shoes.

"Morning, gentlemen. Ready to do a little sightseeing?" Sightseeing, McGrath thought, as they walked across the hotel's patio through the lobby and out onto the wet street. The idea had taken on a totally new meaning since his encounter with Elena yesterday. He glanced up and down the street to see if the guy he thought might have followed him back to the Havana Libre yesterday was anywhere to be seen.

The morning sightseeing went well enough with no surprises. The surprise came when they returned to their room at the Hotel Florida shortly after noon. There was a message at the reception desk for one of them to call a señor Morales at the Havana Libre. Samuels said he'd make the call, while McGrath took the room key and went upstairs. When he unlocked the door and walked in, he knew immediately something was wrong. The closet door was ajar and his suitcase was not on the suitcase stand as he had left it. It was on the floor next to the dresser. He went to the top door of the dresser, opened it carefully and found the carefully folded shirts less carefully folded and slightly wrinkled. McGrath was a meticulous folder of shirts, and this work was distinctly not his. Someone had searched the room. Who and for what? he wondered.

At that moment Samuels walked in, a worried look pasted across his face. "You'll never guess what," he said.

"Neither will you. You go first."

"The call was from the bellhop we met at the Havana Libre. Remember, the one we gave a hefty tip?"

"I do."

"Well, he called to say they caught somebody over there trying to break into our old room."

"Jesus."

"Yeah, but they let him go. Paid somebody off and disappeared."

"Great. That's just great," McGrath said. "Wonder if it was the same person who got in here." He explained the folded shirts scenario.

Time to put a call through to Goodwin and a second to Kincaid. McGrath waited until nightfall, when he walked down to the Malecon beachfront walkway and found a spot out of sight behind a statue of José Martí. Waves rolled in from the dark northeast and pounded the long concrete wall angling along the northern edge of Havana. McGrath was certain no one had followed them and he had taken a roundabout route to make it less likely. McGrath dialed Goodwin's number.

Goodwin sounded delighted with what McGrath had learned from Elena. "She sounds gutsy," he said, "and obviously onto something we can use. Now look, Neal, you've got to give her all the support you can, but for

God's sake be careful. Tell Kincaid about your room being searched. He'll know what to do."

Kincaid did not seem greatly surprised that their room had been searched. "The security guys are probably just following up your little incident and jail stint. They gotta be pissed they couldn't hold you, so it's likely they're harassing you, maybe hoping to come up with something they can nail you with and haul you back for questioning."

"So about Elena," McGrath said. "Do you want to talk to her if I can arrange it?"

"No way, man," Kincaid replied. "First off, she won't want to get anywhere near me or my staff. She gets caught doing that now and it's the kiss of death. Our best bet is for you to stick close to her, give her all the help you can. You're her friend. She's gonna trust you. Meanwhile, now that we know she suspects Ramiro, given what you say she found in his file cabinet, we can at least focus on him. Who knows, maybe some defector will turn up with credible information. Keep your nose clean, McGrath. Like I said, we won't be able to bail you out next time."

McGrath packed the telephone back in the bag, looked around, and started back to the hotel. He had not walked more than a block, when a car he thought he recognized passed slowly by him under the street light.

The Zocalo. Historic giant main square and center of bustling Mexico City. Indeed, its very center. You could feel the heat and humidity engulfing its ancient worn stone plaza and buildings. Today, as yesterday and the day before, weary Indian women, some with babies they nursed openly, and small children, had staked out their place on the dirty cobblestones. They squatted behind their handmade trinkets carefully displayed on dark blankets for maximum effect. Here they sat in silence for hours, hoping to make enough money to buy frijoles and tortillas. Oblivious to the noisy confusion of buses and cars roaring around the multi-laned boulevard that enveloped the plaza, they focused instead on pedestrian—*turistas* and locals alike—who might stop to buy their merchandise.

Light, brown-skinned mestizo men, Mexico's mixed white-Indian class—busily arranged lottery ticket displays and hawked the day's newspapers meticulously laid out on the spit-spattered sidewalk. Rather than wait for people to stop like the patient Indian women, they hawked their wares by pacing around their displays, shouting out what they had to offer. Customers were middle- and upper-class Mexicans rushing by to begin desk jobs in the Zocalo's government offices. Sweating shoe-shine men plied up and down the plaza, lugging metal star-studded wooden shoe-shine boxes loaded with polish, rags, and old brushes, barking out prices and services.

The Zocalo. Official name: Plaza de la Constitución. It occupied center stage during the Aztec Empire before Spain's conquest of Mexico. In fact, not far from here, a few short blocks away, the Spanish conquistador, Hernán Cortés, met Aztec ruler, Montezuma, many years ago in the sixteenth century. In those days, Mexico City was called Tenochtitlán, a clean, healthy, bustling city, one of the world's largest with roughly 200,000 people. Only four European cities—Paris, Venice, Milan, and Naples—had populations of 100,000 or more. Today, its neglected seventeenth century buildings symbolized a fading tribute to a more glorious past. Even the imposing National Palace, where Mexico's president resided, seemed wasted by pollution. The gigantic Catedral Metropolitanio was sinking. Not strange, for a huge lake once occupied this area.

Moreno crossed the street in front of the Zocalo. He dodged noisy bumper-to-bumper traffic, entered the giant plaza, and stepped carefully around the Indian women. Years ago as a university student, he would have stopped to give the Indian woman nearest him a peso or two and wished her *buena suerte*, maybe patted the baby's head and smiled. Not today.

Today Moreno was a man who had killed too many and too often for his own good, a man with much blood on his hands who passed the Indian women without a word. He had gone into the revolutionary movement as an idealist, but the movement and its violence had washed away all traces of idealism. What was left? That depended on who you asked. Some would say he was a man who loved revolution for its violence, not its goals. Others would say he was a calculating tactician in the art of local war. Others? They would tell you he was a cold-blooded killer—a psychopath.

Moreno walked across the sticky hot Zocalo, passed in front of the busy, sinking cathedral with all the vendors and beggars lining its entrance. He turned left on Pino Suarez, the avenue running between the cathedral and Temple Mayor. He elbowed his way efficiently for two blocks through thick pedestrian traffic, made a right on noisy Justo Sierra, then another block to Correo Mayor. There he took the green light across the street and made a left. Two blocks later he caught sight of the hanging sign in bright red letters down the block, buried in all the other signs. It boldly announced, SHOE REPAIRS. He smiled inwardly, pulled a fresh white handkerchief from his pocket and wiped his brow, pleased to see that the shop was still there, warming to the vital role it would play in his future. He ignored the frail Indian woman with a baby in her arms, no shoes, who approached him holding out her thin hand.

He paused for a minute to make certain this was the place he had visited two years ago. It was. Two ruby-red neon signs in the glass window beckoned customers with the words, REPAIRS and CIGARETTES. Fifteen different types of soles you could get here, all lined up neatly in the window beside the neon signs. Another sign in the window announcing KEYS MADE HERE. Keys? Moreno thought. He can make keys all right. Keys and even more complicated objects. He smiled to himself and turned to step down and enter the dingy shop interior.

When he opened the door and entered the room, the aroma of leather, grease, and shoe polish hit him. He waited calmly for his eyes to adjust to the dim light. The only other customer in the shop was a grandmother type, who stood in front of a shelf of shoe polish cans stacked in the corner. She held the hand of a little girl, who played with the rows of shoestring packets hanging on hooks. The older woman was trying to decide on the right color of polish to go with her new pair of shoes. Moreno walked over to the counter and stared at the shelf behind the counter that displayed stacks of brown paper bags with shoes inside. He waited until the proprietor looked up from his work at what appeared to be a large, old-fashioned sewing maching. He looked over his spectacles at Moreno.

"May I help you sir?" No hint of recognition.

"Yes," Moreno said, "I need a pair of riding boots. You come highly recommended."

The shopkeeper stood up and carefully wiped his hands on his apron. "Ahhh. Yes. Of course. This is the right place. Riding boots, you say. We'll have to take measurements in the back and select the right leather. Just a minute. Let me get my daughter. "Rosa! Come to the front."

A teenager entered through a black curtain that separated the shop from the living quarters. Malmierca, the shopkeeper, lifted a hinged part of the counter to allow Moreno to step through. He pulled the curtain covering the door aside and escorted Moreno into a separate room in the back and quietly closed the door behind them. He reached up and turned on the single hanging lightbulb and turned to face Moreno. "So, my friend, what can I do for you today?"

Malmierca had not changed much since Moreno last saw him two years ago. He was short and burly, badly in need of a shave, eyes popping out of his head, and still wearing that dark, greasy apron. His arms, covered with black curly hair, seemed too long for his body. He looked like a character out of a 1920s film with that old green shade on his shiny balding head. His body movements communicated a man of nervous energy. Like an overweight ferret.

Moreno spoke quickly. "A special order."

Malmierca raised his eyebrows.

"A forty-four caliber automatic. With silencer. Built into this kind of apparatus." Moreno pulled a photograph out of his coat pocket. "I need it within the week."

Malmierca took the photograph in his rough, calloused hands, adjusted the glasses on his nose, flattened it out on the table under the light and studied it intently. He viewed the photograph no more than a minute, traced the image with a stubby index finger, and then spoke in a soft voice that would not travel through the door. "This is a television camera, no? Like TV cameramen use. Looks like an ENG model, a Betacam SP set up, inside of which, I take it, you want the weapon concealed?"

"Precisely."

"Umm. Let's see. A forty-four caliber automatic. With a four-inch barrel. Effective killing range of sixty yards easy. Firing mechanism would go here." He pointed at a rough diagram and sketched as he talked. "Trigger on the outside. That way it can be squeezed easily with the camera on your shoulder. Ah yes, the silencer will fit nicely inside here. Yes . . . Yes . . . interesting. Your sight setting could be placed at this point, allowing access through the camera and onto the target. From the outside it appears as a standard model television camera. Correct?"

"Correct. Is it possible?"

"Oh yes, yes," he murmured, deep in thought. "Quite possible. An interesting challenge. But doable. Oh yes, doable indeed. By the way, will you be taking this camera through airport metal detectors?"

"Yes."

"Then I suggest that we make your pistol entirely of a composite plastic material. Like the German Glock Seven, renders it undetectable. A remarkable innovation. I can use a similar approach in your weapon."

Moreno nodded agreement. Then he added, "I'm prepared to pay you two thousand dollars. That's dollars, not pesos." They always dealt in dollars. More stable.

"Two thousand? Oh, no, no, my friend . . . hardly enough. It'll cost me five hundred dollars alone for the materials, and then there's the labor. I must construct a calibrated barrel, make up the firing mechanism assembly, build a device for the trigger, and the sighting arrangement will cause some problems, but I can do it. Also, you know my reputation, señor. My work is absolutely guaranteed. The finest. Never a complaint about my jobs. No, this job will cost much more. And look, I've got to use my contacts to get the camera. You can't do that for nothing, you know. No, this job will cost five thousand dollars. Naturally, as always, no questions asked."

In the end they agreed on the sum of four thousand dollars.

"Done." Malmierca's grin revealed gold on a front tooth glittering under the light. "Leave your photograph with me. Come back Thursday. I will have a better idea of where we stand."

After Moreno departed, the elderly woman paid for her shoe polish, took the little girl's hand and left the shop to resume their shopping. Moreno scarcely noticed the woman. She, however, watched his movements discreetly from the corner of her eye.

TWELVE

Havana

"She's gone. Just got into a taxi," Victor said, as he watched Elena from high up through Ramiro's office window at the Ministry of Interior in the Plaza de la Revolución . . .

"So let's have the update," Ramiro said authoritatively.

"She's meeting him after work today. Maria says she overheard her on the telephone again, talking with the American, McGrath."

"Getting to be a regular thing," Ramiro said, his mouth a lurid grin.

"But not unusual," Victor answered. "After all, from what Elena told Maria, he's her old professor from Georgetown University. Maria says he's here on a research trip. Elena's showing him around Havana. Helping him set up interviews. The other guy, McGrath's friend, has been out sightseeing with them at least twice."

"Does the sight seeing include their little visit to prison?" Ramiro gave Victor a rueful smile. "They should have left them there."

"No. We're talking straight sightseeing. The real thing."

"So he's a professor, huh? Makes you wonder, no?" Ramiro said, his words dripping with suspicion. "But, yes, maybe he is just that. Think, if he *were* CIA or spying for someone else, he obviously wouldn't make such a scene in downtown Havana, draw all that attention to him." He paused. "But I still don't trust him."

"Exactly, and Elena's made no secret about seeing the man, according to Maria." Victor walked slowly across the room, back erect, eyes half hooded behind the dark circles underneath. Worried furrows lined his high, freckled brow, as he cracked his knuckles. "Look, I've been giving this matter a lot of thought," he said. "Maybe she's clean. Maybe she didn't see a damn thing in here. Why not just transfer her out of the office? Get her out of our hair."

"Uh-uh . . . no go . . . I want her right here where I can watch her. Let's keep her under twenty-four hour surveillance. I want to know every move she makes. My instincts tell me she damn well did get into the files. Everything points to it. Think," he said, tilting his head and pointing his index finger to his temple, staring at Victor. "The report she put on my desk while I was gone. Those out of place files in the cabinet. The Mexican file left on top of the cabinet. Nothing to give away Operation Rebirth of course. But she's capable of putting two and two together about our drug operations, and she's smart enough to suspect Moreno. Hell, I still say she may work for CIA. We can't rule it out. You saw that report on renewed CIA activities. Maybe this McGrath guy's CIA too. Maybe they're in this *together*. A professor title is perfect cover. Use your head, man."

"But why would someone who had spent all this time worming her way into this office risk everything by pulling a dumb file cabinet stunt like that?" Victor asked. "She'd blow her cover in a second. She hasn't made any visits to the U.S. Interest Section as far as we know. No telephone calls from her apartment. Just hangs around with this McGrath character, who gets himself jailed as soon as he hits Havana."

"You *never* can be certain, Victor. Never. The fundamental rule. The fact remains," Ramiro said, "that if it *was* Elena, then she's got to suspect what's going on here. She could tell anybody."

"Sí, señor," Victor replied, "You are correct, of course. With that information, she *could* blow the whistle," he added thoughtfully, slumping into a chair. "No telling who she might contact. It does complicate matters."

"That, my friend, is precisely the point," Ramiro said. "Don't forget, she saw me talking to Moreno right here in this office last week before he left for Mexico," Ramiro said, leaning back in his chair, looking up at the ceiling in thought.

"So she might have seen his photo in the file, maybe read some background bio information and saw the file on Mexico. On top of all that she could have seen the money in the bottom drawer," Victor said dejectedly.

"Correct. Moreno's whole dossier was in the file cabinet. His photograph. Background info. The works. She probably has heard about him through the grapevine. It's that photograph I worry about. Now she knows what he looks like and that he was the man I was talking to. And don't forget his file was in the same drawer as the file on Mexico's president."

"You're thinking that she could draw a connection between Moreno and the Mexican president, on the one hand, and on the other, our drug operation here in Havana," Victor replied, always seeking space on Ramiro's good side.

"Right on the money, *chico*. Now this guy McGrath shows up. Here's the big problem. It's obvious, no? She could tell *him*. Doesn't matter if he's *not* with CIA as far as we're concerned. He can take the information back to the U.S., tell somebody in Washington, no? So now we've got a problem with both of them."

"So we keep her under surveillance and see what develops?"

"Exactly."

A knock at the door brought Quintero into the room. Sensing the tension, the little man with his balding head stood by the door, somewhat subdued, not his characteristic bravado. Ramiro stared intently at Quintero, five feet, two inches with thin moustache, skinny build, weighing in at a good 123 pounds. The office joke was that he looked like a rat, walked like a rat, acted like a rat. He had a slight lisp when he talked, his shoulders slumped forward, and to look at him one would wonder how he came to gain any power whatsoever in this office. Truth was, he had an encyclopedic memory and knack for getting things done that Ramiro ordered. He had earned his place in the pecking order by becoming the world's greatest "gofor" for Ramiro. His only problem, a big one, was his tendency to puff himself up around anyone he thought he could impress. Plus, he had a tough time keeping his penis in his pants. Ramiro knew all about Quintero's bad habits, but tended to overlook them, because Quintero delivered the goods when Ramiro needed him.

"OK, smart guy," Ramiro said tersely, forgoing pleasantries, "tell me about you and Elena Rodríguez. What the shit were you thinking? Your *apartment?* With all that stuff you have in there? Did you really think you could get her between the sheets?" He glowered at Quintero, eyebrows pinched together, jaw muscles tense.

Quintero flushed and wiped his brow with his left hand, shuffling his feet. Ramiro let him stand by the door.

"As a matter of fact," Quintero replied defensively, his voice louder than necessary, an edge of shrillness to it, "I did get a little action. I slept with her. No harm in that, is there?" He gave them a wan, greasy smile.

"No harm unless you opened your big mouth. I don't give a rat's ass what you *did*," Ramiro said in low, rapid-fire, sinister tones. He knew Quintero was lying. "What matters is what you *said*. Your mouth and your *pinga* will land you in big trouble one of these days, Quintero." Ramiro sat back, pulled out a cigar, and lit up.

"I told her nothing, General. Absolutely *nothing*. Just bed talk, fooling around, little lies. Nothing more. Hell, I can't even *remember* what I said." Confidence had returned to his voice.

He did not impress Ramiro. Quintero's shuffling feet and squirming around like his bladder was about to explode told a different story. The little sonofabitch surely had said something to to show off, raising Elena's curiosity, Ramiro thought. It confirmed what Ramiro already feared. She was getting too close for comfort. The Mexico file. Money in the file cabinet. Moreno's photograph. Now this night in Quintero's apartment. It all added up to one thing. *She might have to go.* You could not afford to have her walking around Havana with that kind of information. Stakes were too high. Risks too great.

"Look," Ramiro kept his voice steely. "We can't afford loose ends. No slip ups. No mistakes." He drew two or three times on his cigar, thinking. Then he walked over close to Quintero—so close that the red hot end of his cigar almost burnt Quintero's nose. "You try my patience, little man," he said, giving him a push. "Don't ever date Elena again or talk to her about all your perks. Understand?" He wheeled around. Quintero stumbled backward, swallowed hard, and said, *"Sí mi General. Absolutamente. Nunca. Lo siento,"* as he tried to melt into the wall. His feeble apology went unanswered.

Ramiro paced slowly back and forth in front of his desk, speaking in a low voice, his face a study in concentration.

"Victor, stay on her, but not too close. Don't spook her."

"Certainly. We think she spotted us when we first began to shadow her, but I've changed tactics and men. She doesn't know the new guys. They're much more careful. As far as she's concerned, her shadows have disappeared. Besides that, she's all wrapped up in the American."

"Bueno. In the meantime, we treat her with absolute respect. Go out of your way to make her feel comfortable and useful. Throw her off guard. Give her nothing to worry about."

Victor and Quintero nodded soberly, Quintero relieved that the focus was off him.

"Now to another subject," said Ramiro, looking at Quintero, whose shoulders suddenly straightened, body erect, "I'm sending you to Cali to meet with Pedro Esteban. Here's his file. Memorize it. One of Colombia's top cocaine dealers. Deal with him exclusively."

The plan was to increase drug operations, Ramiro explained. Use the same routine as always, but larger deliveries and stepped-up schedule. Esteban should be prepared to ship as much as he could deliver through Cuba.

Quintero listened carefully, then said, "How about *El Señor*, our president."

"What about him?" Ramiro snapped. "Let me worry about him," Ramiro said, jabbing his chest with his right thumb.

Victor nodded in agreement.

"One more thing, make sure Esteban uses at least one ship to bring in the stuff. We don't want it to arrive exclusively by plane. You're in charge of logistics on this one, Quintero. Any questions?"

"When do you want me to leave?"

"Tomorrow. And don't fuck it up," Ramiro added sharply, glaring menacingly at Quintero, and slapped the back of his right hand noisily into the palm of his left.

Elena took them out that evening to another *paladar*, and in no time the *señora* of the home produced three steaming lobsters, side orders of black beans and rice, fried plantains and a touch of pork. They chose a Crystal beer to wash it down. The dining room was small, off in the corner stood a two-foot dark green palm, soft guitar music played in the background, and the little wooden dining table was covered with a white imitation lace tablecloth. Elena knew its owner, a friend of her uncle's. Quiet and secluded. A place to talk unobserved.

Since yesterday, McGrath had come to the conclusion that Elena was braver than those shadows under her eyes suggested. As he gazed at her now in the dim light of the dining room, he could appreciate that despite the pressure she was under, she did not appear as if she was about to crack.

"Think we were followed over here?" Samuels asked.

"No. Of course I can't be sure," Elena answered in a less than confident voice. "Let's just say that I didn't see anyone suspicious."

"How was it at the office today?" McGrath asked.

"Funny you should ask," Elena replied, taking a sip of her beer. "Ramiro was quite friendly. In fact, downright civil. He asked me how my work was going and for me to make any suggestions I wanted in order to make the load bearable. Strange. It's a big change. Even his cousin, Victor, who frequently stops by Ramiro's office, said hello to me today. He rarely says a word. It's almost as if the place is thawing out a little bit. Oh, get this, Ramiro says he trying to get tickets for the Tropicana nightclub. They're hard to come by, even for a guy like him with all that rank. Well, we'll see what happens. The fat lady hasn't sung on that one yet."

"So why the change?" Samuels asked, forkful of lobster poised in midair.

"Beats me," Elena said. "But all Ramiro's nicey-nicey doesn't change a thing about the facts. I know what I saw, and I believe he's certain it was me."

"You seem convinced," Samuels said.

"Why else have me followed? Listen, there's something else I should tell you," Elena said, lowering her voice. McGrath and Samuels looked at her expectantly. "I'm not proud of this, but shortly after the file cabinet incident, I accepted an invitation to go to this Quintero guy's apartment for dinner. A real scuz ball who works for Ramiro, a skirt chaser who most of us in the office can't stand to be around."

"If he's such a jerk, then why did you . . ." Samuels asked.

"Wait," Elena said, holding up her hands. "Let me explain. This guy knows everything. I mean he's on Ramiro's *first* team. I went because I thought I might learn something. That file cabinet stuff was driving me crazy."

"And . . . ?" McGrath asked, more questions flying around in his mind than wood chips in a sawmill. Why is she so damned determined to get the bottom of things? So committed that she goes off to this dork Quintero's apartment? At the same time he felt . . . what was it? Jealousy? He felt himself actually experiencing resentment that Elena had dated Quintero.

"Just this," she said. "His apartment's loaded with stuff the average Cuban never could touch here in Havana. Expensive stereo equipment, liquor, fancy television, beer, two or three crates of the stuff. So I ask you, how does he have the money to buy those kinds of things? Jesus, he even wore a Rolex watch, pair of Levis, and fancy polo shirt."

"Drug money," Samuels said.

"Could be. I wouldn't be surprised. There's something else. Quintero managed to get himself absolutely loaded. He started boasting about his boss and his big plans for . . . guess who?"

"You?" Samuels asked.

"Cute," Elena replied. "No, this man Moreno."

"Moreno?" Samuels asked, eyebrows raised.

Elena took a minute to explain to Samuels what she had previously told McGrath about Moreno.

"This fellow Quintero . . . he didn't get more specific?' McGrath asked.

"Nope. Just that Moreno was going to play a huge role in Ramiro's future."

"Connected with drug trafficking?" McGrath asked.

"Hard to say. Could be. Moreno's from Mexico, that's true. So sure, there could be a connection. But his MO's not so much in drug deals. He's more into terrorism and guerrilla activities."

"Wow," Samuels whistled. "Now that's *really* interesting. Wouldn't you love to know what that's all about," he said. McGrath was thinking exactly the same thing.

"Did you see Moreno today?" McGrath asked.

"Uh uh," Elena replied. "Haven't seen him for some time. Maybe he's left the country."

"Left Cuba?" McGrath asked. "To go off and do what?"

"Maybe we should liquor up Quintero and ask him," Samuels quipped.

McGrath saw the shadow cross Elena's face when the discussion turned to Moreno. So many missing links here, he thought. What *was* going on in Ramiro's office? This whole goddamn thing was becoming more complicated by the hour, and it didn't hang together.

Elena's voice brought him back to the dinner. "Neal . . . Neal, I do have some good news. I've set up two interviews for you. One tomorrow at six-thirty PM at the Foreign Ministry, the other is for the day after tomorrow. Top guy at the National Assembly."

"Oh . . . great, just great," he said, trying to sound upbeat. But he had other priorities on his mind now.

THIRTEEN

Veradero, Cuba = Havana

The twin engine aircraft landed at Veradero's Airport, approaching from the northeast against a stiff offshore breeze. It was still dark, early morning, as three men quickly began to transfer bales of cocaine to a blue and gray Ecoline van parked at the last hangar on the far side airstrip, away from where charter tour jets landed. The van would drive to docked speedboats not far away. The boats, sent by Miguel and led by Bernardo, head *lanchero*, or boatman, delivered the merchandise to Key West.

Two Cuban guards stood by languidly, smoking, talking quietly with each other at a distance from the pilot and Enrique Ventura of the MININT. Ventura's men did the unloading.

"Step it up!" Ventura barked, checking his watch. "Time's money." He turned to the Colombian pilot and said, "Boats got here an hour ago. They're good to go. I take it you have our payment for the last transaction?"

"Yes, sir. Safe in my flight bag—the whole four hundred thousand. I'll turn it over to you later in private. Your cut of the cocaine is over there, twenty percent of the shipment." He nodded in the direction of bales stacked up to the side of the plane "You'll want to count it."

"*Absolutamente*, señor. General Ramiro will be pleased. Remember, we need precise information again for your next delivery to file your landing permit authorization. The cargo request will show computer equipment."

"All set, *Capitán!*" shouted a voice.

"*Bueno!* We'll follow you in my car." He turned to the pilot. "Let's go. I got to supervise this boat business and take care of our stuff. Afterwards we'll get you some dinner and a beer. You'll spend the night at our border patrol house. Weather looks good tomorrow."

Ventura's raspy voice exuded confidence, but in truth he felt little pleasure in this lucrative task. He had grown more and more uneasy about this drug business. It started out small time, a few extra bucks here and there, but now it was an all-consuming monster. He could see its effects right here in Havana. Ramiro's twenty percent cut was supposed to be sold directly to his own contacts in Miami, for a sum of money ten times as much as he received to facilitate transshipments through Cuba. None of it was supposed to wind up in Cuba, but it did.

He wasn't certain whether or not Ramiro was using a middle man to sell some of it on the island, or if somebody was ripping off Ramiro's warehouse before he transshipped it to Miami.

Either way it was bad. Drug pushers prowled the streets at night, prostitutes got hooked, young folks tried a snort and wound up addicts. He thought of his own children and the risk it posed to them and their friends, and it bothered him terribly. But what the hell could he do about it, he wondered. It seemed so high up in the political system, and the money was fantastic. Still, he wasn't certain how long he could keep up his pretense of loving this work. He felt as if he were stuck in the bottom of a deep well with no escape. How do I get out of this? he had asked himself more than once lately, feeling a headache coming on.

Castillo del Morro, Havana's most famous colonial landmark, on the elevated headland at the mouth of Havana Harbor across the bay from the city. The sun's early morning rays cast long shadows on the giant ramparts of this imposing, weather-beaten, gray stone fortification built between 1589 and 1630. Its lighthouse flash could be seen thirty kilometers out to sea. On El Morro's harbor side, down by the water, stood its giant ancient cannons known as Battery of the Twelve Apostles. Although a popular tourist attraction, there were no visitors at this early hour. A breeze whipped up little cloudlets of gritty sand that played around the massive stone walls and ancient castle walkways.

Standing in an El Morro alcove out of sight of any passerby, Kincaid cupped his hands as a shield against the wind and lit a cigarette. He took a deep drag and exhaled a stream of smoke that instantly disappeared in the breeze. He stared hard at the person standing near him.

"That's as much as I know at this point," the shadowy figure told Kincaid. "All I know is that a coup is in the making. General Julio Herrera likely will play a lead role. He's an obvious choice to become the new Cuban president. But I can't say for certain. Who else is involved? How deep does this thing go? I don't know."

Kincaid studied *El Caimán* closely. "*El Caimán*," or "crocodile" in Spanish, a code name well-suited to this individual. Crocodiles float quietly in the mouth of rivers, only two big bubble eyes and upper snout showing as they watch for their prey to drift into reach. The job of this *caimán* was to gather morsels of information—an assignment tailor-made for this informant. Their conversation ended, and they parted casually without further conversation. They went their separate ways like two rattlesnakes slipping into the underbrush.

Martina Espinosa lived on O'Reilly in Old Havana, a narrow cobblestone street that ran parallel to Obispo, not far from the Hotel Florida. Most of the old two- and three-story Spanish buildings were cracked and chipped with age, tiny black iron balconies hanging perilously from second and upper story apartments, with just room enough for two or three people to stand and chat with neighbors down on the street. Looking up, McGrath could see the ever-present tangle of black electric wires hanging on the sides of buildings. Some balconies supported old-fashioned television antennae that stuck out over the street below. The worn concrete sidewalk was narrow, so people walked in the street.

"That's right," McGrath replied to Don's question, as he stepped aside for a speeding moped, "her name's Martina." He explained that Martina's sister, Alicia, had contacted Rebecca in Washington and all the work Rebbeca had done on Martina's brother's case, how she manged to get his record placed on Amnesty International's list and into a Congressional Information Pact on human rights violations in Cuba. "I promised Rebecca a long time ago that if I went to Cuba I'd look up the Espinosas and pay her respects. But the main thing now is if they know anything about the drug situation here. You never know."

"What's the name of the brother again, the one locked up in prison?" Samuels asked, hopping over a pothole of dirty water.

"Enrique. But if Elena's right, Martina's other brother, Ricardo, the guy we met when we were arrested, will be locked up for a long time too."

"Poor family."

"Not a lot to cheer about, that's for damn sure."

They took a roundabout way getting to Espinosa's apartment. They split up twice, met at the prearranged department store, ducked out a side door, walked swiftly down an ally, looked back, and—fairly certain the coast was clear—quickly reached the address on the card and rang the bell. Juan and Martina Espinosa were waiting for them with enthusiastic anticipation.

Their wooden street-level apartment door opened, and McGrath and Samuels received hearty hugs, *abrazos*, and profuse thanks from the emotional Espinosa couple. They ushered them into the tiny, clean living room facing the street. The family resemblance of Martina to Alicia and Ricardo was striking, McGrath thought. Same tall and lean frame, thick salt-and-pepper hair, light brown skin, dark hazel eyes that reflected intelligence and high energy.

A fruit tray of mangos and bananas lay on the small wooden table covered with a frayed white linen tablecloth. Offered café or fruit juice for drinks, they soon were locked in hurried conversation—deepest sympathy to McGrath for the loss of his beloved wife, Rebecca. Undying gratitude to this woman, who was, ". . . a saint," Martina said. She crossed herself.

"She did so much for our family," Juan said.

"We owe her so much . . ." Martina added somberly.

The subject turned to Ricardo, Martina's other

brother. Neal explained again, as he had earlier by phone, how they had met when arrested together, how impressed he was with Ricardo's bravery and coolness under stress.

Martina started to cry again, and Juan put his arms around her. "First Enrique, now Ricardo. I told him not to go to the streets."

"It's like he just disappeared," Juan added. "We're numb from this thing."

Martina pulled out two small photographs from her purse and showed them to McGrath and Samuels. "This is Ricardo, as you know," she said, pointing to the first photograph. "This is Enrique, who Rebecca helped so much. We are not allowed to see him."

"Political prisoners are treated badly," Juan said. "That's why we worry so much."

"We know," McGrath said.

"Oh yes, you can wind up in prison without batting an eye here," Juan said. It was clear he had a great deal to say about Cuban prisons, and McGrath had no inclination to stop his venting, given his family history. "The authorities can accuse you of almost anything," Juan said. "You know . . . slander, enemy propaganda, or acts against state security. You can be arrested even for disrespect, like writing anti-government graffiti on a public wall. In prison, you receive psychological pressure too," Juan continued. "You know, solitary confinement, long ugly interrogations, threats and insults, and of course the beatings."

"From what we saw, prison conditions aren't pretty," McGrath said, "but we were in for only a few hours."

"They're terrible," Martina said. "Poor sanitation and nutrition, bad water sometimes. The guards hold back medical attention and food as punishment." She put her face in her hand and turned away for a second, sniffing.

McGrath and Samuels learned that the human rights protest movement was strong, but underground, and, frankly, Martina said, not with much impact on government policy. "Did they have any contact with the CIA," McGrath asked. "Help from the U.S. on the protests?"

"No, no, too risky," Juan said. In fact, foolhardy. McGrath felt a little foolish himself for even raising the question. Of course, it would be nutsy to be linked with the CIA, Juan pointed out. A death sentence for certain. But, McGrath asked, could they get word to the U.S. Interest Section in Havana for him if he needed to? Oh yes. Absolutely. They knew two people who worked there. *No problema*. McGrath tucked away that information. Although he had Kincaid's telephone, alternate possibilities were a definite plus.

McGrath set his glass of orange juice on the table. He asked if they would mind if he raised another issue, rather sensitive, he said.

"Fire away," Juan replied enthusiastically.

McGrath explained that rumors were flying up in Washington, D.C. that Cuba might be involved in drug trafficking in the Caribbean, along with Puerto Rico and Haiti. He wondered if the Espinosas had any ideas on that matter. Had they heard of any high level Cuban officials being involved in drug running? Any rumors in the grapevine on the streets?

Juan said drug use in Cuba definitely had increased. "He's right, Professor McGrath. You can see drugs on the streets late at night."

"I've heard it's a big problem with high school and university students," Juan said.

They discussed the rise in drug use for another five minutes, then Juan said, "You know, it's interesting you should ask about possible official involvement. About two weeks ago a couple of taxi driver friends of mine mentioned that they'd heard rumors that someone or a group high up in the government might be mixed up in it."

"How high?" McGrath asked. Juan didn't know. Just

a lot of suspicion that maybe somebody with government connections was pulling strings. "Something's going on," Juan said. "I personally heard from another friend of mine, a fisherman, who says he actually has seen a plane flying in off the coast of Cuba dropping cargo into the water. It doesn't take a space scientist to know what that cargo is. 'Course nobody talks about it in public. Nobody wants to get arrested on trumped up charges. We got enough trouble in this family without putting that kind of noose around our necks."

Juan offered to show them around, maybe drive them out to Matanzas or Veradero or anywhere else they'd like to go. His taxi, an old yellow 1956 Buick, was still going strong. "She's got plenty of miles left in her," he said.

"If there's anything we can do for you, Professor McGrath, and you too, Mr. Samuels, please call us," Martina said. "Think of us as your family here in Havana."

Before they left, McGrath explained to them that it was quite possible he and Don were being followed. Likely connected with their involvement in that human rights demonstration and stint in prison, he said. He mentioned that their room had been searched and not very well covered up, like someone wanted them to know it had been searched.

"Scare tactics," Juan said. "Sounds like what they would do. It's a message to let you know that they know where you are and that they're watching you. Nothing new. Jesus, half the country is watching the other half. Heard about our neighborhood block committees?"

"Oh yeah," McGrath said. "Committees for the Defense of the Revolution. We know all about them."

"Well, now that you can consider yourself part of the family, you'll be watched like all the rest of us. Except maybe more exclusively since you are foreigners." Juan thought for a moment, then said, "Look, any time you want me to pick you up somewhere and give you a ride back here to our house, just telephone us, OK? It might be more safe to come here that way rather than risk being followed if you're on foot."

The Espinosas showed them a way to leave their apartment without being observed from the street outside. Martina gently opened the side door to their apartment that led to a dark alley littered with trash cans and litter. As they picked their way along the damp and slick asphalt, McGrath looked back over his shoulder. Instinctively he knew that he would take the Espinosas up on their offer of help sometime soon.

It was toward evening that day, wind gusting outside, light rain falling from a steel gray sky, when McGrath and Elena exited the Ministry of Foreign Affairs after an interview with the assistant secretary for foreign affairs, Rafael Caldera. He took Elena's arm to jump her over a pothole and headed for a small café down the street.

"I agree," she replied to his comment, tiny worry lines crossing her forehead. "I didn't realize drug dealing was as bad as Caldera suggested. Some reports come into our office, but nothing to suggest it's as widespread on the streets as he implied."

"So we now know drugs *are* getting into Cuba," McGrath said, "which means somebody's behind it."

"It's Ramiro," Elena said. "He's most likely not the only one, but a big fish, nevertheless. It all adds up. If so, he's a real sonofabitch. Probably dumping some of the stuff right here in Cuba. He'll ruin us all before he's through, the bastard. God, I wish we had more direct evidence."

With the rain stopped, locals poured out from streetside apartments, a young mother in T-shirt and pink slacks, hair tied back in a white bandana, carrying a little boy; two young men in jeans, four old guys bringing out the little table to set up a game of dominoes.

A 1951 brown Chevy pickup truck bounced noisily along the potholed street beside them, spewing black exhaust fumes, loaded with gunny sacks of potatoes and a bunch of bright green bananas. It lurched around two youngsters on beat-up bicycles, wearing short-sleeved shirts and baseball caps turned backwards on their heads; and in turn was passed by an old red and white Buick taxi with the word "Habana" neatly painted in white on its red hood. Its large rearview mirrors on the fenders and what McGrath thought looked like a bulky silver eagle mounted on the front of the hood made him suddenly wish he had the money to buy it and ship it home. Fat chance.

Elena glanced at the taxi that drove close to curb where they were walking before speeding up to pass the truck. It startled her, and she squeezed his arm sharply. "What?" McGrath said.

"Uh . . . nothing. Sorry," she said. "My mistake. Thought I recognized the taxi driver. Just panicked a little. Can't shake the feeling that we're being watched again . . . but so help me God, I can't prove it. Don't mind me. Just a little jumpy after our talk with Caldera."

"If, as you say," McGrath pressed on, "Ramiro's involved, then this drug conspiracy must go very high up, maybe to the top of the mountain, no?"

"If you're suggesting that our highest officials are involved, Neal," Elena retorted archly, "then you're dead wrong. They wouldn't dare compromise themselves that way, not when they want to cooperate with the U.S. and Western Europe."

"So we're back to square one. We need more information."

"You're right. We do need more information, that's for sure, and I've been giving it a lot of thought. As it turns out, I know one thing we could investigate."

"And that would be?"

"Just this. Look, our office keeps track of domestic and foreign shipping. Our records indicate that a Colombian freighter's due in port soon, and someone from our office will visit it, probably Victor. He's high up in the MININT too. We could try to take a closer look at that ship. Pretty obvious, don't you think? Colombia? Drugs? You never know what we might find."

"Colombian freighter?" He immediately wondered why Elena would propose something this risky, and how much extra digging around in her office did she have to do to come up with that kind of information? The first thing out of his mouth was, "And how the hell do you suppose we could pull off a stunt like that with you and Don and I being watched? Don't forget somebody's broken into our rooms. So it's not like Don and I are innocent tourists down here. We're in somebody's limelight too. Still, it's an idea, Elena. Let me think about it, OK?"

"I think we should check it out," Elena said. "We might find evidence that could nail Ramiro. I'd like that. Anyway, here we are. I think you're going to like this place." McGrath opened the restaurant door to let Elena go in first, glanced up and down the sidewalk, thought he spotted a man following them. But he disappeared around the corner behind him too soon for McGrath to get a good look. Maybe it was his imagination, he thought. Then again, maybe not.

FOURTEEN

Havana

They left the restaurant after a light dinner. Elena took Neal's arm and said, "Would you mind seeing me home? It's only ten minutes by taxi. I'd really appreciate it." The net upshot of the taxi ride to Elena's place, a third floor flat on Linea Street, named for the path where the old railroad used to run, was that McGrath found himself in her small, tastefully decorated apartment, seated on the sofa with her, having a cup of coffee.

"I just can't understand the change in attitude at the office," she said somberly, sipping her coffee, sitting close to Neal, shoulder to shoulder. "It's hard to explain. Ramiro and Victor are polite enough on the surface, but their whole demeanor seems phony. Like playacting and they're not good at their parts. In some ways the atmosphere is more unsettling than before. At least then I knew what I was dealing with. God only knows what they're reading into *our* relationship. Everyone in the office knows I've been seeing you." A brief smile played at her lips, then faded.

McGrath had his own stray thoughts about that interpretation of their relationship. But of more pressing concern to him at the moment was to flush out her possible CIA connection, which had been hounding him, and one way to do that was to shed light on his own CIA connections. He was on the edge of letting that cat out of the bag, when she interrupted his thought.

"Neal," she said ominously, "do you realize how grave this whole thing might be? I mean, if Ramiro's deeply implicated in drug trafficking and has dragged this Moreno character into some aspect of a game he's playing that's connected with Mexico, and he suspects I'm onto him, then my life isn't worth a damn. I know the way he thinks. He could have me eliminated with a single phone call. I'm beginning to wonder if I shouldn't try to get off the island," which was precisely what McGrath had been thinking about over the past hours himself. The quiver in her voice was a dead giveaway that she was scared.

McGrath decided that the time had come to tell her about his connecion with the CIA. Since he did not know precisely the story behind Goodwin's interest in

Elena, he was tired of speculating and wanted answers. Besides, Elena was a friend and former student— sufficient leeway for him to raise the subject. He would trust his instincts.

"Look," he said, "there's something you should know." Elena cocked her head quizzically, sipping her coffee.

"After you left the U.S., I worked for awhile with CIA, short-term position as scholar-in-residence." She tensed, her facial expression one of subdued surprise. She edged away from him. "So as it turns out," he continued as if he had not noticed her reaction, "before I came down here, a couple of friends of mine who work with CIA asked me to . . ." the sentence hung in midair, as Elena's eyes opened wide, her mouth suddenly ajar. She leaned back in hushed disbelief and gave him the look of an iceberg.

"My God, Neal, you worked for the CIA? You must be joking," she snapped. "How could you *not* tell me . . . I . . . I don't know what to say. By now Ramiro will know all about you. After all, you *were* arrested the first day you arrived! Surely they've done a security check on you. Now you're in contact with me? That makes me guilty as all hell as far as he's concerned." She pulled farther away from him on the sofa and retreated to the far end. "What possibly could you have been thinking?" she said accusingly. "Dumb, Neal. Really dumb," she added, punctuating her remark with a finger jab at him. He could see her biting her lower lip, breathing rapidly, crossing her arms across her chest in that defensive posture he had seen before.

"They asked me to talk to you about drug trafficking, Elena." McGrath spoke in a measured tone. "So before you fly completely off the handle," he said forcefully, trying to keep his own anger in check, "tell me this: Why would CIA know you had that kind of information? How would they know? The question is not why I contacted you, but are *you* working for CIA? Is there something you don't want me to know?"

"Me? CIA? Don't be ridiculous. What do you take me for? Some kind of total fool?" She looked hard at him, then stared off into space. "Jesus, you've got some nerve, Professor McGrath. First, you totally endanger my life by coming down here for your CIA buddies, land yourself in jail, draw attention to assure that the authorities will find out all about you, then look me up. Second, you tell me only now that you're connected with the CIA. I can't believe it." She got up from the sofa, walked to the window, and looked down on the streeet. "Why didn't you tell me before? Now I've got a death sentence hanging over my head for sure, that is, if Ramiro suspects me, and I don't see how he cannot."

"So if you are not working for the CIA," McGrath retorted, "then why did you go into that file cabinet? And why go to Quintero's apartment? And, again, how would CIA know you might have information on drug trafficking and that I should contact you? You aren't telling me everything, Elena, and you damn well know it."

Silence. She stood at the other side of the room looking tense, perplexed, rubbing her forehead with her hand. She turned her head and gazed across the room, shoulder turned toward him. Then she said in an cold, hard voice, "Look, I work for a high-level security agency. Any half-brain idiot would suspect that someone working for MININT might have information on a security issue like drug trafficking. Nothing super bright about that kind of deduction. So if somebody I know were to have told anyone else with links back to CIA, of course they would think I might have information of that type. If you're so damned worried, you can leave right now and go back to your CIA buddies."

Dead silence. After a painful pause, McGrath answered in a softer voice. "I'm not worried, Elena. Concerned, yes. Concerned for you, for myself, for Don. I just need some answers here. I'm fumbling in the dark."

She walked back to the sofa and sat down at the end away from McGrath. "Well, for one thing, as I told you, let's get it clear in your head that I do *not* work for CIA. For another, Ramiro's up to his armpits in something, and if he's doing what I think he's doing, then he must be stopped. At this point I don't have much evidence or many resources to work with, but I'm still going to try to stop him. I'm fumbling in the dark too."

"OK, I apologize. I believe you."

"Good. That's better." Her tone of voice suggested the ice had begun to thaw. She sat down beside him. "Look, Neal, I never meant to drag you into danger. I'm sorry about all this. But I needed help, and of all the people I know, you were the one person I felt I could trust. So when you showed up, I just jumped at the opportunity. You seemed like the brass ring on the merry-go-round."

"I haven't been much of a help so far," he grinned. "Just asking a bunch of questions."

"Good ones too," she half grinned, chuckling to herself.

"Sherlock Holmes in Cuba," he replied, smiling. "Seriously, I'll help all I can. We're in this together now, and we damn well will get out of it . . . somehow . . . I'm not clear on that last part."

"OK," she said, reaching for her coffee cup, "we can be friends again. All I can say is that Ramiro scares the hell out of me. He . . . Oh my God, Neal, how clumsy of me, I'm so sorry. Let me get a cloth to clean that up."

Having spilled coffee on McGrath's pants, she put her cup back on its saucer, got up and went to the kitchen for a wet cloth. She returned, sat down beside him and began to dab at the coffee stain on McGrath's trousers, both of them laughing. "What an oaf I am," she said, and he replied, placing his hand on hers, "You're no oaf,

Elena, far from it." Impulsively, he leaned closer and kissed her on the cheek. With his hand still resting on hers, she turned to him, her face close to his, breathing more rapidly than normal, and gazed silently into his eyes. A new emotion unexpectedly replaced the anger of just moments ago. McGrath could see the blush in Elena's face, and his heart began to race.

Hesitantly he pulled her closer to him and gazed into the depths of those mesmerizing eyes. Elena slipped into his arms like a soft kitten, and McGrath whispered "My God, Elena . . . I . . . never dreamed . . ." They kissed tentatively, then McGrath traced his finger gently across her lips, kissed her again, behind her ear, down her neck, back to her lips. "Neal, Neal . . ." she whispered between kisses. "I'm so sorry for what I said. I didn't mean it. Please forgive me. Just hold me," she murmured. His hand came to a rest on her thigh, caressing gently. It was all happening fast, and as Elena's hand moved along inside his thigh, McGrath felt his pulse racing. He kissed her deeply and ran his hand along the inside of her long, tan leg, as Elena felt for his fly. Neal's heart raced faster as Elena's finger gently found its way inside.

McGrath sighed, his breath short and rapid. One of his hands discovered her panty lining underneath her skirt. She parted her legs for him, and he slipped his hand inside to the soft hair of her mound, letting it curl between his fingers. His other hand, now around her back, raised her blouse and snaked up inside to unclip her bra. The bra slipped languidly off her shoulder and he began caressing her bare breast while his other finger explored deep inside her now thick, moist hair. Elena moaned and thrust her own hand fully inside his shorts, groping until she found what she was searching for and wrapped her hand around, gently but firmly. She was breathing hard now. She pulled off his shirt, as McGrath, his heart beating wildly, kissed her mouth, her eyes, her neck, and unbuttoned her blouse and stripped it off with her bra. He tugged her panties over her writhing back-side and down her legs, until one leg kicked free, panties slipping down the other, entangled around her ankle. She moved to help him slip out of his pants, their shoes already kicked off.

"Elena," McGrath whispered, breathing hard, "what about . . ."

"Don't worry," she shot back, "I take birth control pills."

They were on the floor now, Elena's skirt knotted up around her waist. McGrath tried to hold back as long as possible, wanting to please her, kissing her nipples. His fingers worked rhymically inside her, between her legs, where her black hair was wet, moving his lips down her stomach, below her navel, removing his fingers and re-placing them with his lips and tongue. Elena's moans were coming rapidly and then, softly begging him to come inside. There was no need for McGrath to part Elena with his fingers, her opening so wet and receptive that he glided in smoothly as they began to work to-gether, slowly at first, then faster and faster. At last Elena's back arched, her eyes opened wide, locked onto his, and panting heavily, she smiled at McGrath and let out a soft cry of joy. McGrath followed instantly and ex-ploded inside her.

They lay there for some time, exhausted, locked in each other's arms, soaked in perspiration, swept away in a stardust dream with no dark shadows of Ramiro or CIA, only the sound of two hearts beating like one and the soft notes of a guitar floating toward them from somewhere down the hall.

An hour later McGrath telephoned the Hotel Florida registration desk from Elena's apartment and asked to speak to Dizzy, one of the clerks who had befriended them. The phone rang and McGrath heard, "*Sí*, Profes-sor McGrath, it's me, Dizzy."

"Listen, Dizzy, would you please tell *Señor* Samuels

when he comes in that I will not be sleeping in the room tonight. I'll catch him tomorrow morning. Tell him I'm fine and will explain everything tomorrow, OK? He will understand. Thanks."

McGrath hung up the bedroom receiver. He smiled at Elena who was lying naked on her side next to him, one arm draped over his leg. He hadn't felt like this for months. He did not want to ask himself how long it might last. But he did confront himself with one overriding question. How the hell could he get Elena, himself, and Don off this island in one piece?

It was eleven-thirty P.M., and the strategy session at Herrera's home was under way. "You are right, Julio," General Gómez said, "conditions for the coup are absolutely ripe. Timing could not be better. We've got three key conditions going for us."

"Name them," Herrera said authoritatively.

"First, we got the sympathies of the armed forces. They're restless, not least because they haven't had much to do lately."

"Precisely," Herrera said in a quiet voice.

"Second, public opinion favors it. All you have to do is walk the streets of Havana or any other city in Cuba and look at the faces. Listen to the whispers. *Hell*, count the refugees trying to make it across the water to Florida. Public opinion will support it, of that we are confident. Look at all the turmoil and uncertainly we've been going through in recent months. The economy's in a state of collapse. Sure, the president has some support, but not much, and it's fading fast. Correct me if I am wrong."

"Right on the mark."

"Third, the international situation favors a military coup. What more could we ask for? No more aid from Russia, the U.S. embargo, and the rest of Latin America riding the tides of democracy and a globalized economy. All the while we remain stuck in the mud, stinking in the sun like rotting fish on the beach. We know damn well the U.S. would be delighted with a coup. Probably the rest of Latin America too."

"I agree," Herrera said. "Once we seize the state-run media, confine the president and vice-president to their homes, take over the homes of other top ministers, gain control of major government buildings, cut the international telephone lines and block the airports, we're in business. The rest should fall in place. Remember, once we launch the coup, we must act swiftly. Oust the current government and institute the new as fast as possible. Neutralize any forces that might oppose us before and *after* we go into action. Speed is critical, I mean *zip*, like zapping a mosquito."

This team had been hard at work many days now. They had painstakingly recruited the right men. Men with training and equipment to act swiftly and firmly in all the separate operations that had to be carried out *simultaneously*. They *personally* knew each man involved, had worked and trained with them for years. Each recruit detested Castro and his brother for personal reasons. Close coordination with Ramiro played a major part in Herrera's strategy. The subject at this planning session, however, was the post-coup phase, and they discussed it into the early morning hours.

When they were winding down, one of the officers said, "Listen, my friends, let me change the subject," he looked at Herrera. "Julio, tell us honesly, how far do you *trust* Ramiro? I tell you straight off that the more I see and listen to him, the more I distrust him. Too ambitious. Reminds me of Batista himself. At times he even acts like a fucking Batista."

"Couldn't agree more, Julio," another member of the coup said.

"They're right, you know," two others chimed in.

"Look," Herrera said, relaxing his shoulders and rubbing the back of his neck. "Let's not fool ourselves. Of course we have to be on guard—especially once the coup succeeds. The risks are high—both in terms of possible failure *and* success. My guess is that we'll have to clamp down on Ramiro immediately following the coup. Remove him. We aren't risking our necks to lead this thing only to turn it over to Ramiro and *his* men. We use Ramiro until his utility runs out. We all know his lust for power. He would never agree to our kind of *patria*."

"Fuck Ramiro. We deal with him when the time comes," an officer said.

Herrera looked around the room. The faces indicated he had total agreement on how to handle Ramiro. But he was savvy enough to know that thinking and doing were two different things. Ramiro was evil personified, a man who would stop at nothing to have his way.

Ramiro had informants everywhere, and given his resources, Herrera wondered if he *could* handle him A side of him was not so sure. A cold shiver shot up the back of his neck.

FIFTEEN

Miramar = Mexico City = Havana

Jorge Fuentes pulled up to the curb and parked his flashy 1957 red Chevy by the curb off Fifth Avenue. It was windy and mid-morning under a pale blue sky out in upscale Miramar, in western Havana. He got out, locked the doors, and walked down the sidewalk lined by palm trees swaying high above toward the three story gray mansion—one of MININT's official buildings. Fuentes, a civilian, wore his best white *guayabera* and faded brown trousers, fake gold necklace and two-tone brown and white shoes. He worked on the Havana Harbor docks, a dock workers' foreman who loaded and offloaded cargo. Today's meeting with "The General" made him uneasy. After all, he had been setting aside small amounts of cocaine from Colombian deliveries for his own business with Veradero tourists. Just enough, he thought, not to be noticed. He assumed his little operation was safe and secure.

Fuentes suspected that the General might question him today. Discrepancies in his reports did occur now and then. He would have to be on his toes. He wanted today's meeting to go as smoothly as they had in the past—a cordial professional meeting to discuss business at hand. If it went well, the best part would come after the meeting, when Ramiro would provide one or two attractive women for his pleasure. So as Fuentes walked toward the "The Mansion" for his appointment, the cocaine matter was distinctly on his mind.

"The Mansion" offered nothing unusual from the outside—standard three stories, black wrought iron guard fence, and high palm trees and colorful gardens. Inside was different. Ramiro, under the Interior Ministry's "Office Improvement Program," had ordered the construction of a large aquarium—to satisfy his fascination with predatory fish and sea snakes. The aquarium featured a glass observation hall below, in pale blue, for easy viewing of the species—piranhas, moray eels, and sea snakes. Ramiro enjoyed watching the action at feeding time, relaxing with a cigar. He especially prized his sea snakes, brought in from the mangrove swamps of Australia, one of the most venomous snakes in the world, ten times more venomous than the cobra. Up to seven foot in length and usually calm, they turned aggressively defensive when threatened. When hungry and threatened they became doubly aggressive. One bite means death if not quickly treated with antivenom.

Ramiro greeted Fuentes cordially and asked him

about his godchild—Fuentes' youngest son. Fuentes shared a humorous incident about the boy that had just happened, which brought a smile from Ramiro. Fuentes took the opportunity to thank Ramiro for the Rolex watch, which he proudly showed him. Ramiro informed Fuentes of the upcoming increase in shipments and need for more dock workers. Fuentes inquired if the president was comfortable with the scheduled increase. Without saying a word, Ramiro simply looked Fuentes squarely in the eyes and tilted his head ever so slightly in the affirmative. The meeting eased Fuentes' concerns. Fuentes' little side action apparently had not been discovered.

Ramiro pushed back his chair from the desk, stood up and said, "But enough of this business talk. Let's go meet the women. I think you're going to be pleased." He walked casually to the door of his office and stepped aside to let Fuentes pass. "Look, my friend, why don't you go on down to their room. I've got a little matter to attend to. I'll catch up with you." He patted Fuentes on the back and gave him a wink and a smile.

Fifteen minutes later, down in the aquarium observatory, Ramiro casually strolled up to the viewing window and cooly looked upwards into the shimmering aqua green water. He tapped his cigar ashes in the tall, silver-plated ash stand and moved a few inches closer to the glass, then reached out to press a button on the control panel. "Bring him," he said authoritatively.

Above at the deck level, a door opened and four men emerged. One was completely naked, blindfolded, one arm bound behind him, the other attached at the wrist to a long, ten-foot chain at the other end of which was bolted a large metal bucket filled with concrete. The bucket of hardened concrete and chain was carried by one of the large men. The naked man's ankles were bound, which forced him to hop along on the wet-tiled deck, helped by the two men who half-carried, half-dragged him toward the pool's surface. One of the men held a coil of rope around his shoulder. It was clear now that the naked man's wrists had been cut, because both were bleeding profusely, and his whole body had been smeared with fish guts.

Ramiro checked his watch and gazed up through the water to the shimmering silhouettes of the four figures, three large men struggling with a fourth. Ramiro could barely make out his face, but could not hear his screams. They now were standing on the four-foot wide gray-metal walkway that ran straight across the pool, used for observation and feeding. The view for Ramiro was clear enough, despite the bucket of slimy fish entrails that had just been dumped into the pool. Then he saw what he was looking for—a large, heavy bucket of hardened cement being lowered down into the pool by the ten-foot chain attached to the naked man's wrist. At the upper end of the chain near the surface, he could see the man's flailing arm and a Rolex watch glistening as it entered the water. Dark red blood oozed from the slash on the wrist and turned the water pink around it. On the walkway the three men had forced the fourth to his knees on the metal grating, making certain that the arm attached to the chain went into the water up above his elbow. The screams were deafening, but the captors seemed to be enjoying the show.

Ramiro pressed the second red button on the control panel and watched as a glass panel on the far side of the aquarium slid open. Within a minute twelve seven-foot long sea snakes entered. Tails flattened, extremely hungry from not having been fed in the last day, they glided from their container tank out into the main viewing chamber. With their forked tongues flicking for scent, like their land-based relatives, they instantly picked up the fish entrails and sped gracefully for them faster than one would imagine. As they fed, the man's arm attached to the cement bucket came deeper into the tank, followed by his wide-eyed face, torso, thrashing free arm and wildly kicking legs now cut free. Attached tightly to one ankle was a rope with plenty of slack to let the body sink down into the pool.

The tank's tranquil waters suddenly erupted in a maelstrom as if hit by a typhoon. The submerged free arm thrashed out at one of the snakes that had come close to the man's eyes and took a painful deep bite, followed by two quick strikes on his legs. Sea snakes bite repeatedly when provoked, and it was this show that Ramiro so relished—that twisting, turning, flailing body intertwined with a mass of angry coiling sea snakes on the attack. As they bit again and again at the fish pieces drifting down, along with the man's arms and legs, Ramiro once again marveled at the aggressiveness of these normally passive sea creatures. But now it was time to signal the men above to pull the victim out of the water before he drowned. It was important to get him out before he drowned so he would die more painfully from snake venom.

The men knew what to do. They hauled Fuentes up and threw him on a stretcher. They carried him to a locked back room with its single bed and wall toilet. In thirty minutes he would suffer stiffness, muscle aches, and spasm of the jaw. Next would come moderate to severe pain in his arms, legs, and face where he took the strikes. Soon he would experience progressive central nervous system symptoms of blurred vision, drowsiness, and finally respiratory paralysis. No antivenom would be administered in the back room. Fuentes, Ramiro purred to himself, would juggle reports of incoming cocaine no longer. Ramiro put out his cigar, turned and walked casually down the hall to the room where the two women awaited him. Aroused by what he had just witnessed, he knew it would be a pleasurable encounter. As for Fuentes, Ramiro mused, when word got out, others would think carefully before trying to cut into his drug operation. When Fuentes body was found down by the docks, Ramiro knew that he would have sent the message he wanted.

As he strolled down the hall, his footsteps echoing along the passageway, it occurred to him that it would be fascinating to see a naked Elena forced into the tank, along with her equally naked professor friend. What a show that would make. He made a point to mention it to Victor that he had decided to eliminate Elena. She had to go and, maybe, the professor with her. He could not risk Elena learning anything more a this critical stage of Operation Rebirth. As for the professor, he *had* to be connected with CIA. But was he? Information on this guy was lacking. What if he was just another of the thousands of tourists pouring in these days, something the government wanted to promote. Maybe he should try to scare the American off the island. Give him a good reason to leave. Soon. Sounds like a good plan, he thought.

Before he left his room on the sixth floor of the Willow Hotel in Mexico City, a block off the crowded Zocalo, Moreno used the public phone in the hotel lobby corner to place a long distance call to Key West. On the fifth ring, a voice answered. "Hello?"

Two minutes later, satisfied with his U.S. plan, everything in order, he walked across the lobby floor. He passed in front of the large black metal statues of Don Quixote and Sancho Panza, nodded to the bellhop dressed in his red and brown uniform, standing by the main door entrance, and stepped briskly out to the busy street. The sky as ususal was polluted, muggy air that hung like a giant gray brown shroud. The traffic was snarled with green Volkswagen Beetle taxis, and the sidewalks jammed with businessmen, tourists, and vendors.

When he arrived at Malmierca's shop, he found it empty except for Malmierca, who was hunched over, busy at work. The shoemaker broke into a broad smile when he saw Moreno. "I've been expecting you. We're in luck." He carefully set aside his work, got up, and beckoned Moreno to follow him into the back of the store. "Let me show you."

"The parts are here on the table." Malmierca removed the cloth to uncover what he had collected—a gutted television camera, its components carefully lined up.

Moreno picked up the camera frame, shouldered it, and looked through the sighting mechanism.

"I have a friend who works for one of our news stations," said Malmierca. "He owed me a favor. I persuaded him to find this little gem for us. What do you think?"

Moreno replaced the camera on the table. "*Perfecto*. And the gun parts?"

"Over here on this table." Malmierca's voice was laced with excitement. On a second work bench, he pointed to the four-inch calibrated barrel, firing mechanism assembly, trigger device, sighting lens, and silencer.

"You foresee no difficulties in constructing the gun inside the camera?"

"A project of this kind is never completely problem-free. But problems are challenges. Rest assured. When I've finished, this weapon will work flawlessly. Guaranteed. One hundred percent guaranteed."

General Ramiro walked swiftly toward the back of hangar Number Two shortly after 2:00 P.M. where a mechanic was working on a jet engine. It belonged to one of the two Soviet-built Mi-24 *Hind-D* helicopters parked nearby. The general called out to the mechanic, "*Hola*, Ricardo, how you doing?" As he spoke, the general checked out the hangar to see who else was around. Empty. Ricardo Agramonte turned around, saw who it was, and wiped off his hands with a greasy rag.

"Sir. Good to see you. Well, here I am, sir, working as usual. Always working, General. Working for the glory of our country, no?" His voice was low, in fact conspiratorial.

"And how's the family?"

"Good. My wife is constantly looking for clothing for the children. And we can't find those special shoes that Juan needs. But what do you expect?"

"Well, we hope to change all that in the future, don't we?"

"Most certainly, *mi General*."

The general's voice lowered to a whisper. "How is it coming with the device, Ricardo?"

"I have all the parts. I've started to put it together. It's going a little slower than I thought. But it should be finished and tested by this weekend."

"It will detonate at the level we require?"

"Sir, the explosion will totally obliterate the helicopter, no question about it."

"*Bueno*. The timer is accurate?"

"*Absolutamente*."

"You're still hiding the device at your uncle's house?"

"Yes sir. It's very safe. My uncle does not know about it. But if he did, he'd be for it one hundred percent."

"Why's that?"

"Well, sir, two of his brothers are in prison. Too outspoken about the lack of freedom in this country. If my uncle knew what I'm doing, he'd roll up his sleeves and say, 'Move aside and let me build this thing!' "

"Better not get him involved, *chico*. We can't be too careful."

"Don't worry, General. I am honored to be in this plan to help our country."

"Any second thoughts?"

"No sir. But I do wake up sometimes in the middle of the night, wondering if I've said or done anything that might give us away."

"That's natural. Try not to worry too much about it. You're doing a great job, Roberto. When we complete the task, we're going to turn Cuba around. Don't worry!"

"I believe that with all my heart, sir."

"Need anything? Parts? Electronics?"

"No sir. I'm in great shape."

"Good. If you need help . . . or equipment, let me know. I'll take care of it."

"Yes sir!"

The general snapped a salute and strolled casually out the hangar into the sunlight. Ricardo stepped outside and watched him drive away. Adjusting his sunglasses, he could see giant dark clouds piling up in the distance for the daily afternoon thunderstorm. When he walked back inside to his workbench, where the radio was playing, he heard the first national weather report about the possibility of a hurricane out east of Cuba. Could be severe if it continued to develop. They would have to watch this one closely, he thought.

At 7:30 P.M, Ramiro was in his office at MININT headquarters, sipping hot black coffee. He checked his Rolex watch, impatiently awaiting his appointment. Finally the knock came as a shadow crossed the opaque glass in the door connecting his office to the main corridor on his floor. "Come in," Ramiro barked.

"Evening, General," the man said in a firm voice as he entered the room.

"Good evening, Enrique. How did it go?"

"Not a hitch."

"*Bueno*. You have the money?"

"*Sí General*. Four hundred thousand as agreed," he replied, patting his briefcase.

"No problems? The landing?"

"No sir. Everything in order."

"Our stuff transferred to the warehouse?"

"*Correcto*. No problems."

"You're meeting Bernardo for the sale in Florida?"

"All set, sir."

"*Excelente.*" Well done, *chico.*" Ramiro opened the briefcase, pulled out a stack of bills and handed them to Enrique with a smile. "Here's ten thousand for you. See to it that Eduardo and Luis get their share."

"Yes sir."

"As you know, we're going to expand. Quintero's in Colombia setting it up. Miguel in Key West will have to line up more *lancheros.* How's control at the airport? Anybody getting nosy?"

"No sir. Not as far as I can tell. We're still using the border patrol house in Veradero. No one's asking questions. The pilots like that arrangement. Gives them a chance to rest before the return flight."

"Good. OK, keep me posted on the next flight. Remember, don't flaunt any stuff you buy with that money. Use your head. Don't draw attention. For God's sake, don't do anything to make our military friends suspicious."

"Yes sir. I know. I'll watch it."

When Enrique left the room, Ramiro carried the money over to the secure file cabinet, ran through the lock combination, removed the bar and pulled open the bottom drawer. He double-checked the amount again and stuffed it into the brown paper bag, shut the door and resecured the file cabinet. He made a mental note to remind Victor to move the money.

Five minutes later he was back at his desk, deep into the recent surveillance report on Elena and McGrath. He turned the pages slowly, studying every detail. The report convinced him that McGrath was something other than an innocent college professor doing legitimate research. Elena by now probably had spilled her guts to him about what she had discovered in his office. McGrath must be eliminated. He relished that possibility as he licked his index finger and turned the next page.

* * *

Cabaret Las Vegas was hopping at 9:00 P.M. Jam-packed and jumping with salsa music. Larry Diamond led the way as they elbowed across the small dance floor, a mix of locals and tourists, laughing, shouting, gyrating, dancing, weaving in and around each other in the intoxicated swirl of body sweat and cigar smoke. They could hear several languages—English, Italian, a little German, and Spanish—a celebration of international escapism.

Diamond pushed through the crowd as though he knew every nook and cranny of the place. He held up his hand for them to follow like a Japanese tour guide lacking only the little flag held high on a stick in this mass of tangled humanity. Diamond knew Cuba inside and out, and tonight was no exception. He had invited them here with a promise to introduce them to a drug dealer he knew who might be able to give them information. They'd have to pay the guy, but that was negotiable. Not much of a lead, McGrath thought, but something. Samuels and Elena were with him. A sizeable tip to the waiter magically produced a table at the rear of the smoke-filled room, not far from the stage where the band was belting out yet another popular salsa number. When they reached their table, Diamond excused himself to go look for the guy he had contacted.

"Elena," McGrath said, "Let's talk about that freighter. *El Tesoro*, you said? She's in berth from Colombia?"

"Right. Colombian ships are rare here. Most freighters are from South and Central America, Mexico and China. Once in awhile we get one in from Russia."

"Think it's worth the risk?"

"It's not as crazy as it sounds," Elena said confidently. "Listen, Maria mentioned that Victor would be going down to the harbor himself to go aboard later tonight. Around midnight. So if we positioned ourselves down there, we could watch what he does. No telling what we might learn."

"Sounds like it *is* worth the risk," Samuels said.

"We'd have to get down to the docks without being seen or followed," McGrath replied. "That's the first hurdle. But, yeah, it's possible. Number two is getting a good look at whoever goes aboard. Number three, how to go aboard and get off the freighter without being spotted."

"Neal, I've been down there many times," Elena said. "There's an abandoned warehouse right across from the pier from where *El Tesoro* docks. If we can get there without being followed, we could watch the boat from a safe place inside. I have a friend who works on the docks. He can help us get in and probably aboard the ship."

"Reliable?"

"Absolutely. He's a friend of my uncle's. Name's Frank, or Pancho. A true patriot. If he thought for a second there were cocaine shipments coming in here, he'd go through the roof. Knows freighters inside and out."

"Might work," McGrath said. "Can you get hold of a pair of binoculars?"

They kicked it around another five minutes, then McGrath said, "OK. Let's do it." He paused. "Now listen, Elena. I want you to agree to one thing. Once we check out this freighter, you've got to leave the island with us. We can't wait any longer for your uncle. Once we're out of here, you can call your uncle in safety. We might be able to broker a deal with the CIA, too. The main thing now is to get off the island alive, in one piece."

"I'm not sure I like the idea of brokering a deal with the CIA, Neal. But yeah, if we come up with solid information, you're probably right. We should get off the island, at least until somebody nails Ramiro. I could always come back after that. I'm not giving up on Cuba."

"OK, let's get hopping. There's a public telephone in the lobby. Call your friend, and tell him to meet us tonight, say around eleven-thirty?"

"Great." Elena paused as she stood up. "I assume you have a plan to get off the island? We can't exactly use airline tickets, y'know. Well, I mean, you and Don can. Not me."

"I'm working on it," McGrath said.

Elena smiled, picked up her purse, and headed through the crowd to the telephone, just as Diamond returned. Don ordered another round of Cuba libres, as Diamond sat down and said, looking around the room, "Well, I don't know where the hell he is. But he'll show up. He seemed awfully cooperative when I talked to him."

McGrath got up to go to the men's room. He worked through the crowd around the edge of the dance floor, then down the narrow, dimly lit, hallway to the men's room at the far end. He was half conscious of one, maybe two men close behind him. As he approached the door, his senses alert, he felt the presence of a body quickly closing the distance between them. Poised and balanced, he reached for the doorknob to see if it was locked. It wasn't, so he pushed the door open and stepped inside.

Suddenly he felt two arms wrapped around him from behind like a vise. He was powerfully built and bent on doing serious damage. As the man thrust him forward, McGrath turned his head and saw in the mirror over the washstand a tall black guy with a shining bald head, dark glasses and a goatee. The man was a head taller than McGrath and looked vaguely familiar. Then McGrath remembered. One of the goon squad guys he had belted that first day in Havana when they were arrested. He instantly thought of Ramiro, because this was the same man he thought had been following him and Elena. McGrath could swear he saw a second guy, a body who stopped just inside the door and seemed to be holding it shut.

He struggled hard, but could not stop himself from being pressed into one of the stalls. The muscular black arms were pushing his head forward and down, as a low, strong voice hissed in his ear, "Remember me, Yankee boy? I been looking all over for you. We have a little score to settle, you and me. When I finish with you, you better get on the first plane and leave this place. Next time won't be so easy."

McGrath's heart raced, adrenaline pumping furiously. The black man had kicked up the toilet lid and was forcing McGrath's head toward the toilet bowl. The toilet had not been flushed since its last occupant. McGrath used his legs to brace against the man's pressure to give the impression that he was trying hard to resist, but clearly losing the struggle. Then he made his move—a bone crunching stomp with the heel of his shoe on the black man's right toe, simultaneously heaving his arms straight up in the air to slide under the black arms while dropping down.

All this came in one smoothly executed move, followed by slamming his right elbow sharply into the black man's groin. That brought a distinct groan, allowing McGrath time to come up from the floor with a solid knuckle-leading punch to his testicles. McGrath let fly in rapid succession another powerful fist straight up to his Adam's apple that produced the desired results. The body lay on the floor choking, gasping for air, eyes wide and portruding. Neal found himself actually enjoying all this. Self-defense was self-defense, he thought, as he stepped over the writhing body and grabbed a handful of toilet paper for his bleeding nose and gash over his right eye.

When McGrath stepped from the stall, the pugnacious guy holding the door shut faced him. His scars and missing front tooth looked like he was anticipating the thought of kicking McGrath's ass around like a soccer ball. He charged suddenly, but McGrath sidestepped him, grabbed his left arm and in one quick move bent it up behind his back. He used the force of the man's forward momentum to bend over and ram his head into the porcelain washbasin. The blow knocked him out cold.

McGrath took a good look and thought he recognized him as another thug who had beaten up the human rights protesters. Ramiro crossed McGrath's mind again. The black guy on the floor in the stall was still gasping and choking, but he sounded like he was coming around.

Time to go. McGrath held the wad of paper on his nose, stepped outside, and made his way swiftly back through the crowd to the table. Now he was determined to get whatever the hell evidence they could find at the freighter and beat it out of Cuba fast. He was worried about Elena, but could see from the distance that she was safe at the table. So was Diamond.

When he reached the table, they took one look at him and Elena jumped up, "Neal, my God, what happened?"

"Just a little accident," he said, running his hand through his messed up hair, sweat trailing down his temples. He looked quickly and methodically around the club. As he sat down, he spotted two more of Ramiro's goon squad, two men who had been with them in the truck ride to the prison. They were seated across the room and pretended not to see McGrath and his friends. "Larry," McGrath said, turning to Diamond, his voice firm. "We have to ditch this place. Now. There's a couple of guys across the room we need to avoid. Think you could create a distraction over there?" he said, indicating with a nod of his head the direction where the two men were sitting.

"A distraction? Like what?" Diamond said. "Do a dance like John Travolta in *Saturday Night Fever*?"

"Uh-huh," McGrath said. "But we need to distract them."

McGrath shook his head. "Just walk over by their table and . . . let's see . . . start an innocent conversation like you're half-loaded. Get them talking for a minute. That should do it. We'll take the opportunity to beat it. Then you get the hell out of here fast."

It worked. They slipped out the club's main door out onto the crowded sidewalk, where the *jineteras*—young women in tight slacks or miniskirts and platform shoes—were working the tourist crowd. Elena said, "But Neal, we've got to get you to a doctor."

"No time," McGrath said. "Did you call your friend?"

"Yes. He said he'd meet us around eleven-thirty to-night."

SIXTEEN

Havana = Matanzas

It was 11:30 P.M., windy, light drizzle falling on the whitecaps dancing across a choppy Havana Bay. They used an elaborate switch taxi and car plan to dump any tail, thanks to Juan Espinosa's help, to reach the harbor. McGrath had called Juan from the café where the taxi they had caught at the club had dropped them. In ten minutes Juan was there with his beat-up taxi. He had no trouble getting Elena to her apartment to pick up the binoculars and back down to the docks, where she met up with McGrath, Samuels and her friend, Frank. Mc-Grath and Samuels had jumped in three different taxis in Old Havana, going in and out of stores to shake any-one who might have trailed them.

Frank was a short, burly, potbellied black guy, in his early fifties. His frayed Levis and dull red T-shirt blended with the rusty railroad tracks that ran in front of the faded pink two-story warehouses and crumbling double-decker Spanish-style archways. He led them to the pale yellow, long, customs house with its sign, "*Adu-ana*," over the chipped paint entrance, where he stealthily pulled out a ring of keys, carefully selected one, and gently unlocked the door.

They stepped inside and made their way in the dark through a giant hallway out to the dimly lit wet docks on the other side. An eerie, surrealistic scene greeted them, backlit by dock lights up on weather-beaten wooden poles that looked like giant ghoulish eyes peering at them from the dark, the drizzle and night blocking any real illumination of the dock area. The docks were jammed with rusting foreign freighters of every size, color, and description, many rafted together side by side in Technicolor oil slick water. In the murky gloom, they reminded McGrath of giant wraithlike insects; their booms and cranes frightening arms and legs ready to reach out to grab unsuspecting prey. The place was deathly quiet, save for the sound of rain and light wind whipping around the freighters hugging the wharf, secured by thick hemp mooring lines.

So far it had gone without a hitch. The place was deserted, most of the workers long gone home, silence broken only by a rundown forklift truck that rattled by. The driver said hello to Frank, who told him he was taking his friends on a little tour, and the guy moved on down the wharf into the gloom. They stepped around cargo crates, a huge old off-loading crane, metal containers already off-loaded, thick hemp dock lines with metal rat-stopping shields, and a couple of large Dempsey dumpsters. Elena jumped with a muffled yelp when a large, well-fed rat dashed by from behind a container and brushed her leg to join an even larger furry mate and vanish into the night.

"There she is," Frank whispered, gesturing to the red rusting hull of a freighter with the name, *El Tesero* painted in faded white up on the bow. It looked as if someone had intentionally tried to paint the rust on this phantom ship that had wandered in from the sea, but botched it royally, as the rust ran in great wide streaks down the side.

"How big is it?" McGrath asked.

"Manifesto says a hundred and sixty-one meters. Almost five hundred feet . . . oops," Elena replied, as she tripped on a dock line.

"What did you say she's carrying, Elena?" Samuels asked in a hushed voice, stepping around a crate, as Frank indicated the warehouse building they should enter.

"The manifesto says general cargo," Elena replied. "Probably canned food and textiles."

"We don't get many freighters from Colombia," Frank said. "One every two or three months."

"That's the point, Frank," Elena said, as he led them into the old warehouse across the dock from *El Tesero*. "This makes two from Colombia in one month."

Nobody was in the large dusty building, at least nobody they could see. Frank led them up the grimy, creaking stairway to the second floor that put them higher up so they had a better view of *El Tesero*'s deck. From their vantage point in the clerk's office, not more than fifty feet from the vessel's deck, they could see the white metal containers up on the ship's topside, faded blue wheelhouse way back at the stern and the three high yellow deck cranes used to load and unload cargo and containers. All this was lit by the ship's lights, not well, but sufficient illumination to make them out. The containers were still in place awaiting off-loading as the ship had just berthed earlier this afternoon. Because she lay lower in the water than she would without cargo they had a fair view of things. The deck area seemed vacant of activity, except for the deckhand sitting in a folding chair where the gangway met the ship's deck. "The guard," Frank whispered.

They settled in for the wait, murmuring in quiet conversation. Frank told them that hardly any Russian vessels berthed these days, not unusual, he added, given Russia's circumstances. He mentioned to Elena that he was thinking of quitting the dock and joining the tourist staff at one of the new Spanish hotels where he figured he could make a fair living. Did McGrath or Samuels have any contacts with the Spanish tourist industry? Most of his friends had become bar tenders or van drivers, he added. How he would love to get a position out at that new Melía Habana in Miramar, he smiled. Just then Elena rested her hand on his arm. "Shhh, Frank . . . here he comes."

None other than Victor himself came strolling down the dock. Elena pulled out her binoculars. "This should be very interesting," she whispered. "It's Victor. No doubt about it." They could all see him in the halo of the deck light, as he walked up the clanking, swaying gangway, using the ropes that served as handrails to steady himself. McGrath knew that the problem would be seeing the action up close if he started poking around on the deck. "Here, Neal, take a look."

McGrath focused in on the face, with its high cheekbones, gray beard cut short. "He looks more like an intellectual than a tough guy. Maybe he wound up in the wrong profession," he whispered. "Frank, you're certain the surveillance cameras are on?"

"*Absolutamente*," Frank whispered back. We got several here on the docks. Well-hidden. Most people don't know about them. Got to keep a sharp eye on incoming cargo. Theft's a big problem."

"You run them twenty-four hours a day?" McGrath asked in a hushed voice.

"*Sí* señor. Tape's connected to a VCR. We change the tape every twenty-four hours. That's my job."

"So whatever he does on deck will be taped?" Samuels asked.

"That's the idea," Frank whispered.

"But wouldn't Victor know about the camera?" Samuels asked.

"For sure," Frank murmured. "But he won't worry about it. He can get the tapes any time he wants. He's probably been around them so long now, he just doesn't see them as a problem."

"We're going to need that tape," McGrath said. "If we go aboard *El Tesoro* after Victor, the camera will catch us. That's a huge risk. But if you can handle the tape, Frank, then we're OK."

"*No problema*," Frank answered. "If what happens tonight is what you think is going to happen, I will be pleased to get it for you."

"He's stopped to talk to the guard," Elena whispered.

"Right," McGrath nodded.

"What now?" Samuels asked.

"We wait and see what he does," McGrath says. "Then we go aboard ourselves and check it out. OK. Look. Victor and the guard are walking back to the stern. Looks like they're heading to the wheelhouse."

"Makes sense," Frank said in a tense voice. "Probably going to meet the captain."

Frank was right. Forty minutes after Victor entered the wheelhouse, he emerged with the captain, and the two of them strolled down the deck toward the bow.

"Here they come," McGrath whispered, taking the binoculars back from Elena who had been observing the guard seated by the gangplank.

Halfway between the nav station and the bow of the freighter, they stopped. Then they stepped between two containers. "What are they doing now?" Frank asked.

"I can just make out . . . looks like the captain's left arm . . ." McGrath said. "He seems to be . . . yes . . . he's unlocking a door to the container. He's got it open. OK . . . OK . . . they're standing by the open door now. Victor's pulled something out . . . can't tell what it is . . .

could be a cocaine packet. Now he's putting it back. OK, now the captain's locking the door ... yes, see ... see ... they're back out on the deck now. If it's cocaine, it sure as hell isn't well disguised. But they don't have to worry much about disguising it here in Cuba. It does make sense."

They watched as Victor shook hands with the captain under the ship's standing lights, signed documents on a clipboard covered with plastic, turned, and walked back toward the gangway. Five minutes later he was back on the docks, then gone. The captain went back in the wheelhouse, probably turning in for the night, McGrath whispered, and the guard, seated at the top of the gangway, was nodding off. "Not a committed kind of guy, is he?" McGrath said.

"Now what," Samuels asked.

"Only one thing to do," McGrath said. "I'll go aboard and check out that container."

"Not by yourself, you're not," Elena said. "I'm going with you."

"The hell you say. Not on your life, my friend. This is a one man job. Safer that way."

"I insist," Elena retorted sharply. "Look, you need someone to watch your back. Besides, if we get caught, maybe I could talk us out of it."

"What? Jesus, Elena . . ."

"No, I mean it Neal. I could claim to be working for Ramiro and Victor. It might work, y'know. I insist. I'm going whether you like it or not."

"Well, dammit, we can't stand here and argue about it all night."

"OK then," McGrath said. "Here's the drill. Elena, you and I will go aboard. Don, you and Frank stay here. Frank, in exactly one half hour, do you think you could approach the guard as a dock manager and drum up something you need, maybe some kind of form, so the guard would have to go back to the wheelhouse for a minute? That would keep him occupied long enough for Elena and I to get off the ship, OK?"

"Leave it me, Señor McGrath."

They waited another five minutes, discussing how they would handle it, watching the guard. It wasn't long before he stood up, stretched, and slowly made his way toward the bow of the ship, opened a metal door and stepped inside.

"Great. He's probably going to the bathroom. OK Elena, let's go."

McGrath led the way up the gangway, two figures hunched over, moving swiftly, hearts racing, holding onto the rope lines. They reached the top just as they heard a metal door opening about fifty feet from them up toward the bow. "The guard," McGrath whispered. "Quick, duck in here between these containers before he sees us."

By the time the guard returned, McGrath had led them through a narrow space between the containers to the other side of the wet and slippery deck, where they crept forward, bent over double, to about where McGrath estimated they had seen Victor and the captain examining one of the containers. "Through here," McGrath gestured, turning left, leading the way between two rows of containers back to the dock side of the ship.

When they reached the end of the row, McGrath signalled for Elena to stay put between the containers in the shadows, while he poked around to try to find the right container.

Three minutes later they were crammed between two rows of gray metal containers, face to face with the one Victor had examined not long before. McGrath nodded to Elena, then took one of the three master keys Frank had given him to try to open the giant box. "Lock looks standard," McGrath whispered. "But see how this container is different from the others? Less metal. Thinner.

Not as wide. Sealed with this kind of lock. The others are built for much heavier wear and tear. This one's designed for fast loading and transshipment in a smaller boat."

"Like one headed for Miami," Elena whispered, nudging McGrath.

The third key worked. McGrath cautiously reached in and pulled out . . . a large packet wrapped in white oilcloth. "Open it," Elena indicated. McGrath took out his pen knife, slit the packet, and out tumbled . . . white powder.

"My God," Elena whistled quietly. "There's a ton of it. Worth millions."

McGrath placed the slit packet back inside the container and removed another unopened one that he put in his knapsack. He closed the door and locked it. "We'll keep it for evidence." He bent down and brushed the white powder off his hands and pants. Standing up, he whispered, "OK."

Elena said. "Now let's get out of here."

"Shhh . . ." McGrath mouthed, putting his index finger to his lips. "Someone's coming." Over their shallow breathing, the sound of footsteps on the metal deck grew louder, and Elena tensed, squeezing closer to him.

Out in the port city of Matanzas, it was exactly midnight. Bernardo felt uneasy, as he stood there in his yellow slicker under the gray-haze lights on the dock where *La Mujer* was tied. His boat rocked gently in the oily water, debris floating alongside the hull—a waterlogged wooden crate, some plastic bags, small dead fish belly up—protruding watery eyes glistening dully in the faded light. He watched the men in green military uniforms load the packages of cocaine into his boat, which he counted and marked on the file attached to the clipboard he held in his hand. A senior Cuban officer, his old friend, Enrique Ventura, stood off to the side supervising the transfer of cocaine from the two-story warehouse, one of several operated by MININT.

An hour later Ventura walked over to Bernardo and said, "That's it, my friend. All loaded and accounted for. Here's my count. May I see yours?" Bernardo showed him his clipboard. "Good," Ventura said authoritatively, "exactly the same. You're good to go. You have the payment?"

"*Si* señor," Bernardo said, as he jumped in *La Mujer*'s wet cockpit, stepped over to the dashboard, reached underneath to his secret compartment, and returned to Ventura with the plastic pouch sealed with waterproof tape. "Please count it," he said to Ventura. It occurred to Bernardo that Ventura seemed troubled and weary.

Bernardo did not know for certain who the top officer was in this operation, but he suspected General Ramiro. It was logical. He knew Ventura worked for the general, whose name was mentioned more than once among the *lancheros* who worked in and out of Veradero and made the sea pick-ups off Cuba's north coast. He also knew that this particular shipment, which he would deliver to Miguel, who was waiting for him on the cay northeast of Key West, was different from the larger hauls out of Veradero and the north coast area. This shipment, and others he had worked from this warehouse, were connected to MININT, because this, after all, was a MININT storage area, another lead linking General Ramiro. So the general gets partial payment for his Colombian transshipments in cocaine, Bernardo mused. And for that he makes many times more dollars than straight hard cash for helping the Colombians. Sweet, he thought. Real sweet. Good deal for Miguel too, because he works for both the Colombians and Ramiro.

Forty minutes later, Bernardo stood at the steering wheel checking his new GPS as he motored cautiously by the lighthouse at the entrance to the Bay of Matanzas.

He pulled the slicker hood down more closely over his eyes and listened to the marine weather report. He made a mental note to tell Miguel that this would have to be the last run for a few days. The sea swells were larger than they were two days ago, and Miami's weather center had issued storm possibilities for the upcoming week. A hurricane was brewing out in the northeast, still far away, but worrisome nonetheless. A sailor would have to be a goddamn fool to ignore it, he thought.

Clearing the harbor, Bernardo pointed his bow for Key West and gunned the engines. This run would pay handsomely, he thought, as *La Mujer* leapt forward into the dark of night, its high rooster tail flying off the stern. He felt of thrill of power surge through his body as his boat picked up speed, hull skimming over the ocean surface, vibrating under his tennis shoes, his body leaning forward over the steering wheel, eyes squinting into the blackness. He still worried about getting caught by the U.S. coast Guard, but still, he thought, his income recently had shot up with the rise in prices of cocaine. And it was quite clear that whoever was in charge of the Cuban shipments had decided recently to increase the flow.

McGrath motioned to Elena to flatten herself against the containers as heavy footsteps approached. If anybody looked their way, they would be spotted instantly. Two men passed by their hiding place, short skinny guys, chatting quietly, followed by a third, who stopped not ten feet away. The man, a giant, looked like he weighed at least 300 pounds, well over six feet tall. He paused right in front of the space they were wedged into, in plain view, turned to grip the ship's railing in his huge hands, and looked out over the docks. McGrath felt Elena nudge up close to him.

The deckhand stepped back, pulled out a packet of

cigarettes, flipped one out, cupped his hands, and lit up with a lighter. McGrath could see the cigarette lighter reveal his face—a long scar on the left cheek, huge nose, unshaved jutting jaw. Not somebody to tackle with, he reflected, his hands pressed against the container behind him. The man exhaled a puff of smoke, then stepped away and walked casually toward the stern and gangway where the guard was posted. McGrath could feel Elena's warmth and heard her audible sigh as the guy shifted his weight and walked on.

"What now?" she whispered.

"We wait," McGrath said quietly.

Elena elbowed McGrath and pointed to her watch, a question mark in her eyes.

Twenty minutes, McGrath signalled with his hands.

Exactly twenty minutes later, McGrath peered from behind the container to catch sight of the guard standing up as Frank made his way up the gangplank, saying something to the guard as he approached him. After a brief conversation, he heard the footsteps of the guard coming, then saw him in silhouette as he passed before the opening in the row of containers, then continue on back toward the wheelhouse.

McGrath put his head out just far enough to check both directions on the deck. Nobody near the guard place; he was still walking in the other direction. "Let's go," he whispered. "Hustle. Stay low. Not much time." They stepped out from behind the containers and saw Frank give them the hurry up sign. McGrath took Elena's hand as they made their way swiftly toward the end of the gangplank. "Lead me to the promised land," Elena whispered, grinning at McGrath.

"Hurry . . . hurry!" Frank urged in a hushed voice, when they reached the spot where he was waiting at the top of the gangway.

McGrath made the turn off the deck onto the gangway, Elena right behind him. That's when things went terribly wrong. Frank reached out to help Elena onto the gangway and knocked over the guard's chair that crashed onto the metal deck with a loud, sickening noise. Their running footsteps on the gangplank echoed off onto the night and docks below.

To their horror the guard stopped dead in his tracks. He stood silently under a ship's deck light not forty feet away from them, his eyes locked on McGrath and Elena running down the clanking gangway.

McGrath glanced back to catch sight of the lone figure standing there in a green rain jacket silhouetted under a ship's hazy light. The guard pulled a whistle from his pocket and blew it loudly, then shouted at them to stop. He made enough noise to wake the dead, and in the confusion Frank opted to trot down the gangplank after them, just as a distinct "pop" sound split the air. A bullet whizzed by McGrath's shoulder and ricocheted off a dockside Dempsey dumpster, which they jumped behind for cover. McGrath was certain that Frank had shouted something to the guard, but gave it no more thought when, suddenly, Samuels appeared out of the gloomy rain and jumped behind the Dumpster with them. "Thought I'd join the party," he said. A few seconds later, Frank came trotting up, his breath coming in loud wheezes.

"You OK?" he asked, panting. "Listen," he said, gasping for air, "I know a place we can hide. C'mon, let's go." He answered McGrath's questioning look by saying, "the guard thought I was chasing you." He motioned to follow him as he darted in the dark toward the warehouse, sticking in the shadows where the lights did not penetrate. "We got to move fast," he urged.

As they jogged apprehensively alongside the warehouse wall, Elena grabbed at McGrath's shirtsleeve and asked, "Listen . . . what's that back there?"

McGrath turned his head, narrowly missed tripping over a huge iron, orange-colored, dockside cleat, leaped over it, and said, "Mopeds. Sounds like two of 'em. Probably security types. Just came around the corner. Hurry, Frank."

Frank led them through an open wooden door into a huge warehouse, the other side of the pink building that they had passed on their way into the dock area earlier. They followed Frank into the shadowy, dank, foul-smelling building with its wall-to-wall containers piled up one on top of the other. Small lights along the upper walls near the ceiling gave off just enough illumination so they could make their way between the rows of stacked up containers.

"Down this way," Frank said. "Hurry now. They'll be here any minute. Did they see us come in?"

"I don't know," McGrath said, looking around the half-lit building.

From inside the warehouse, they heard the mopeds roar up outside.

"See that ladder?" Frank whispered. "Quick . . . hurry now. Give me a hand. Stand it up here. Elena, you first. Up you go. That's it. Climb up and lay down flat on top, OK?"

"You next, Don," McGrath said. "Right. There you go."

"You next, Señor McGrath," Frank said.

"What about you, Frank?" McGrath whispered, one leg poised on the first rung of the ladder. He had a two foot piece of lead pipe in his hand picked up from the floor.

"I'm going after the tapes. I know a back way out of here. *No problema*," he said. "Stay down flat now. They're almost here." When McGrath stepped off the last rung, Frank swung the ladder to the floor and started trotting with it down the corridor between the containers back toward the back side of the building. He turned the corner between the last row of containers just as four security guards stuck their heads through the dockside door, flashlights in hands, revolvers drawn.

"Spread out. Search every row," a deep voice barked out.

From where they lay on top of the container, they could see the reflection of the king-size flashlights darting around, probing down one corridor, then another, light beams bouncing off the ceiling in ghostly shadows. One man passed right under their hiding place, and they could see three other lights darting around forty or fifty feet away from them in different locations. The rain had started falling hard outside, pounding on the tin roof above them, insistent, unsettling. Elena got McGrath's attention and pointed to the huge rats skittering by on the container next to them. Her eyes were wide, her lower lip tucked in sharply.

A commotion at the far end of the warehouse broke out. They heard the sound of struggling, someone running, a gunshot followed by a cry of pain and body thudding to the floor.

"Oh my God, Neal," Elena whispered, "Frank. *Lo mataron.*"

"What?" Samuels whispered.

"She said they killed him," McGrath whispered back. He could feel Elena groping for his hand down by his right side, finding it, squeezing it hard. Her palms were moist, and her hand trembled as she turned her head sideways and buried her face in the nape of his neck. She was lying on McGrath's right side, and in the process of taking her left hand in his right, McGrath's hand slipped over her thin wrist. Something odd, he thought, lying there, trying not to breath hard as his heart raced. What was it? He thought for a moment. Then it hit him.

"Elena, where's your watch?"

"What?" she whispered, as light reflections bounced around, coming their way down the corridor where they had climbed the ladder. At least two men talking, maybe three, McGrath thought, and he started to catch snippets of conversation.

"My watch?" A pause. "Oh Neal, I've lost it," she whispered. Must have come off when we ran in here. Jesus, think it's on the floor down there . . . ?"

"Shhh," McGrath intoned. "Too late now."

He made out two, maybe three men, walking under their spot. They were obviously carrying something heavy from the sound of their labored breathing. "You sure he's dead?" One voice said.

"Absolutely," came another voice.

"How about the others," another voice said.

"Probably got away. That back door where we shot this guy was wide open. Led right out to the street. They're blocks away by now. General Ramiro's going to be pissed. Truly pissed. Glad I'm not the one to bring him the news."

McGrath focused on the voices below. He saw the reflection of light trailing along behind the first two men who had just passed underneath. The others were now outside the building, taking Frank's body away. Another light came closer, probing every nook and cranny. When it reached directly under their hiding place, it stopped. A long pause, as if the guard were picking up something, studying it, thinking. They could feel his presence, as the light shined upward on their containers, paused, then started back from where it had come, where Frank had gone.

Shortly it returned, this time more slowly. They could hear the guard wheezing, as if he were carrying something. Something that banged on the floor every five or six seconds. Something, McGrath thought, heart racing, that sounded distinctly like the end of a ladder.

The light stopped right under them. They heard the ladder scraping against the side of their container, and in seconds the end of a ladder popped up in front of them, banged against the top edge of their container, not a foot away from their faces. Outside the building, by the door, came the sudden urgent shout of what probably was the head guard yelling, "Hurry up, Fernando. They want us back at the ship. Victor's there." The sound of a moped motor jumped to life outside the building.

McGrath swallowed hard and took a long, slow breath, trying to center himself. Perspiration poured from his forehead, and he felt his heart beating against his rib cage. Must be 120 degrees in here, he thought. He tried to control his breathing, feeling for certain it could be heard echoing off the warehouse walls. His eyes flitted left and right across the top of the container they were lying on, calculating distance. He released Elena's hand to take a firm grip on the lead pipe, indicating to Elena to roll away from him, so he could manuever. He shifted his weight to his left side, freeing his right arm with the pipe, his muscles tensing. He visualized how it would happen and filled himself with confidence and a trusting instinct that it would work. Heavy footsteps on the rungs grew closer, as the ladder creaked and moaned with the weight of a man climbing up toward them.

The hand with thick, curly black hair on the back of it that appeared on the rung of the ladder was clasping a woman's watch. Then the top of a shiny bald head appeared, eyes staring at them. McGrath saw the man quickly shift hands on the ladder, holding onto the rung with his left, dropping the watch, grabbing a revolver in his right.

It was over in seconds. At precisely the instant man peered over the top of the container, McGrath squeezed the pipe firmly so it would not slip from his sweaty hand and swung it as hard as he could directly at the side of the man's head. After the pipe thudded into the skull with a sickening crunch, Samuels grabbed the gun from the man's hand and reached for his shirt collar, helped by McGrath. Between the two of them, with Elena's help, they wrestled the unconscious body off the ladder up over the lip of the container.

"Is he dead?" Elena whispered.

McGrath felt for his pulse. "Slight pulse," he said. "Quick now. We have to move fast." He signalled to scramble down the ladder, McGrath bringing up the rear. Back on the warehouse floor, McGrath picked up Elena's watch that the guard had dropped and handed it to her. The three of them hustled the ladder to the back of the warehouse and shoved it between a row of containers.

"The door," McGrath said, "the one the guards were talking about . . . there it is, over there. Let's go." They darted out the open door to the street out in front of the warehouses and ran down the railroad tracks between the two rows of beat-up railroad cars toward the side street up ahead. There Juan Espinosa was waiting.

"You think they know it was us?" Samuels asked.

"Depends on how the camera was angled and how clear the image. Elena wore a baseball cap. She could pass for a man. Jesus, I just don't know. Maybe they'll think Frank was trying to rip off some cocaine. But we got to assume the worst case scenario." One thing was clear. They must leave the island. Fast. But how?

SEVENTEEN

Havana = Mexico City

Juan Espinosa parked his taxi on a side street, a block away from the Hotel Florida at two in the morning. "I'll wait here," he said, "hurry."

Not that they had to be told to get a move on. "It shouldn't take long," McGrath said. "Elena, wait with Juan, OK? We'll be right back." She nodded in agreement.

Exhausted, McGrath and Samuels walked swiftly along under the dim amber streetlights that cast furtive shadows on the wet cobblestones. When they reached the hotel, they went straight to the registration desk to speak with their friend, Dizzy, a young mulatto, who was on duty. McGrath kept the revolver, now wrapped in an old copy of *Granma* he had found in a trash can, out of sight in his hand below the desk. The clerk did not comment on their scruffy appearance and unusual time of arrival, but greeted them with upbeat cordiality.

"Good morning, Professor McGrath . . . and Mr. Samuels." He reached behind him to the dark brown panel of room mailboxes. "Just a moment," he said, "I believe I have something here for you . . ." From McGrath's box, he pulled out an envelope with "Neal McGrath" printed in black ink on the front, and handed it over the counter to him. "There's something else . . . just a moment." He stepped away from the desk to go behind a partititon to the hotel safe, while McGrath opened the envelope.

"Jesus Christ," he whispered, "read this." He handed Don the note, his brow creased in worry lines.

The note was from Larry Diamond and read simply, "Neal, I have left the airline tickets and passports you gave me in the Hotel Florida safe. I dare not keep them as you asked. Can't guarantee their safety. Am in deep shit. Sorry. Good luck . . . Larry." Samuels, puzzled, handed the note back to McGrath.

"Here you go," Dizzy said, returning from the safe. He wore a big smile of accomplishment. McGrath took the manila envelope, double folded with a rubber band, thanked him very much and gave him a five dollar tip, which produced an ear-to-ear grin.

"Listen, Dizzy," McGrath said, "we're going to check out, but we may be back in a couple of days. So we'll square away our bill right now, OK?"

"No sweat, amigos," Dizzy said.

They paid the bill and went straight up to their room to collect their belongings.

As they walked up the stairs, Samuels said softly, "So what's up with Larry?"

"Don't know," McGrath said. "Sounds ominous. Notice the note? Hastily written. He was under pressure for certain. I got a sick feeling it has something to do with us. After all, we did ask him to introduce us to a drug dealer, right?"

"Yeah, and then that whole business at the club. You're right, sounds bad."

They walked down the hall to Room 222, slipped in the key, and opened the door. When they turned on the light, it looked like it had been hit by a tornado. Mattresses lay half off the bed as if two, maybe three, gorrillas had made love on it in the middle of the storm, sheets and pillows on the floor, two chairs turned over, clothes strewn everywhere. "Looks like they wanted to make a point," McGrath said.

"Look at the room safe," Samuels said, as he walked over to the open closet and the safe's half open door, hanging lopsided, blown off its hinges by a small explosive. They could see the powder and caps lying on the floor near the safe. "Bet they were pissed they didn't find anything," he added, smiling at McGrath.

"Small victory for the good guys," McGrath said, as he ripped off the rubber band and tore open the paper of the envelope. Their airline tickets and passports they had given to Diamond for safekeeping were intact. Most of their cash was with the Espinosas.

"At least we can still get out of here," Samuels said.

"You got that right, my friend. The quicker the better."

Moreno dialed the familiar number in Havana early in the morning. Ramiro picked up the phone on the first ring and immediately recognized the voice. "Ahh, my friend. And how is your vacation?"

"Well, the hotel is comfortable, and I have done a lot of sightseeing. Even met our mutual acquaintance, José."

"Excellent. And how is José?"

"Business is thriving. He is developing a new line of merchandise for overseas markets. I've seen the prototype, and it looks promising."

"Good, good. Great news. Glad to hear it. José is a talented man. Highly creative."

"Indeed. Also, I have made the reservations for the second leg of my trip."

"*Excelente*. You will be able to keep your schedule?"

"Oh yes. I will stay in touch along the way."

"One thing before you go," Ramiro said. "Do you remember the little matter about the young lady, my . . . ahh . . . niece?"

"The one you said was so lively and . . . inquisitive?"

"Precisely. Well, I thought you'd be interested to know that she soon will be making a long trip of her own. She won't be here when you return."

"A pity," replied Moreno, smiling at Ramiro's reference to Elena. "Stay in touch."

Moreno hung up the phone, laid back and stretched out on his bed, hands behind his head. Elena, one less thing for him to worry about.

By 7:30 A.M. they managed to rouse themselves after a few hours sleep at the Espinosas. Elena slept on the living room couch, McGrath and Samuels on blankets on the floor. They washed up for breakfast and sat around the small wooden table in the Espinosa kitchen.

"So what did he say?" Samuels asked. "Can he do anything for us?" Elena looked on expectantly, along with Juan and Martina. McGrath had just stepped back into the kitchen from the living room where he had phoned Kincaid on his satellite phone.

"One thing's for sure," McGrath said. "We have his attention. Can't say he was exactly pleased with our little stunt last night, but mighty interested in what we found. He wants that packet of cocaine. He'll tell us how to turn it over to him."

"What else?" Samuels asked, eyebrow raised.

"Just this. He can get a fake passport and papers for Elena. Maybe airline tickets too. Can't say he was one hundred percent enthusiastic, but he's going to give it a go. Elena, you'll have to disguise yourself, but it is not out of the realm of possibility. It's gonna take time, and he admits that could be a problem."

"You tell him where we're staying?"

"Hell no. I didn't use Elena's name either."

"So what do I do between now and then?" Elena asked. "Just go back to work and act like nothing's happened? After he's had a good look at the videotapes?"

"Which leaves another question unanswered," Samuels said.

"I know. I know. How do you and I get out?" McGrath said. "I mean, with our handsome faces splashed all over the tapes, along with Elena's."

"Precisely. How do we get out?" Samuels let out a long breath of air.

"I can think of one possibility," McGrath said, a hint of a smile playing at the corners of his mouth.

"And that would be? Why are you smiling? I don't see any humor in this," Samuels snapped.

"We use our regularly scheduled airline flight. Go right on out of here by air, assuming that is what Ramiro and his boys want us to do."

"Oh sure," Samuels retorted. "Right smack into the hands of Ramiro's security thugs. Holding a one-way ticket back to prison."

"Maybe not," McGrath said. "I have a little surprise for all of you." They looked at him expectantly.

"Listen, Kincaid told me something incredible. Incredible, but pleasing." He paused to let the mystery sink in.

"Well don't just stand there, damnit," Samuels said, "out with it."

"OK, get this. Kincaid said that he had heard about our little incident down at the docks last night."

"What?" Elena exclaimed.

"Right. Says he didn't know it was us, until I told him so, but he had heard about the *Tesoro* scene."

"Now how would he know that?" Samuels asked.

"We can only guess. He's obviously got an informant on the docks. He knew that Frank had been shot."

"What else did he say?" Elena asked quickly.

"Well, here's the really remarkable part," McGrath answered. "He knows for a fact that the video cameras were not working last night. They filmed absolutely nothing. He says they've been busted for several days now."

"What?" Samuels and Elena exclaimed simultaneously.

"My sentiments exactly," McGrath said.

"Jesus," Samuels exclaimed. "I just can't believe it," Samuels said, letting out an audible sigh as he sat back in his chair. "What total dumb luck."

"Yep," McGrath said, "Ramiro knows nothing . . . about who was on the ship, that is."

"So where do we go from here?" Samuels asked.

"Good question," McGrath said, sipping the hot black coffee Martina had poured for him. "First, we know damn certain that our buddy Ramiro is up to his armpits in drug trafficking. But does he know that Elena knows? Jury's still out on that one. 'Course, Ramiro would stop at nothing to get rid of Elena—or us if he thought we knew about him."

"He's right," Juan said, looking at Martina, who nod-ded in agreement.

"So Elena may still be safe at present."

"I agree," Elena said, leaning forward in concentrated attention.

"Second, Don and I are not exactly at a birthday party. That little scene in our hotel room is a healthy reminder that we've overstayed our welcome in Havana. For all we know, Ramiro may suspect right now that I'm a CIA agent in cahoots with Elena."

"There *is* another possibility, Neal," Elena said, stand-ing up.

"Oh?"

"Ramiro still might assume that I was involved in the ship incident last night, even if he has no proof. I can see him reaching that conclusion. Maybe he thinks you guys were with me. In his paranoid world, it would make sense to him. He sees threats in every corner, Neal."

"I know. I know," McGrath said. "It's entirely possi-ble. On the other hand, wouldn't another scenario come to him?"

"What's that?" Elena asked.

"*Locals* trying to steal some of the cargo."

"Obviously tempting,"Samuels said.

"Right," McGrath said. "Don't forget, it was *Frank* they actually caught and shot. Frank, a *Cuban* dock worker."

"Yeah, you have a point," Elena said. "Let's hope that's the prevailing theory he buys. You know what? I'm going into work. That calling in sick idea we had last night won't fly. I've got to act normal. Yeah, I'm going. It's the smart thing to do. If I don't show up, then Ramiro's going to be all the more suspicious."

"You're right, Elena," McGrath said. "Maybe you could leave the office early. Have a headache, or go to see a sick friend, run an errand, anything. Martina, is it

OK if Elena spends the night here?" Martina nodded. "Great. I'll give Kincaid another call in a couple of hours. I'm going to phone my contact in the States too. Tell him what's happening. He might have an idea on how to get out of here fast . . . in one piece. And don't forget our meeting with General Herrera you promised. This afternoon after work, right?"

"Right," she said. "Think we should cancel it, in view of our circumstances?"

"Hell no," McGrath said. "I want to meet this guy. Besides, we must act normal. That's our best course of action at this point."

"Yeah, I suppose you're right." Elena said. And yes, you certainly will find General Herrera an interesting figure. If ever there was a José Martí look-alike in character and outlook, a true patriot who loves his country, it's Herrera."

"What I'd really like to ask him," McGrath said, "is for a plane ride to Miami for the three of us and how to nail that sonofabitch Ramiro."

"Juan, can you give me a ride to my apartment? I've got to change clothes."

McGrath hugged Elena just before she walked away with Juan down the alley. "Be careful, OK?" he said, gazing into her dark-shadowed eyes. "Try to keep a low profile. We'll get out of this somehow." He tried to sound more confident than he felt at the moment. They both knew the next hours would be crucial. He resolved to pressure Kincaid like all mighty hell. He stood there and watched Elena walk away. Just before she disappeared around the corner, she turned and gave him a brief wave. Then she was gone, and McGrath was left with a moment of anguish and a pit in his stomach. Could he get her out safely? The question haunted him.

It was close to two o'clock in the afternoon at the MININT safe house just outside Havana when Ramiro began the meeting in the conference room with his own group of coup conspirators.

They were all alone in the safe house, a pale pink Spanish colonial mansion out in Miramar, surrounded by lush tropical plants and tall elegant palm trees now swaying in the brisk breeze. It was a meeting of Ramiro's Groupo Z. That meant Victor and four other high-ranking intelligence officers violently opposed to Castro and his brother. Ramiro had selected them to execute the countercoup against Herrera. Herrera was vital to the overthrow of the old leadership, for that would require his kind of contacts. But once the old leaders were gone, Ramiro planned to replace Herrera with his own men. Some, of course, would be bribed. But with all the money coming in from the drug trade, Ramiro reasoned that bribes posed no problem. The bottom line was that Herrera was dog meat once his job was done. At that point Ramiro intended to rule by absolute military power.

An hour later, Ramiro declared the countercoup plans to be "*excelente*." He looked around the room, pleased with these men and their organization. Soon he would be in power, in total power, he mused, in position to dominate Caribbean drug trafficking. If Moreno acted the way he predicted, Ramiro soon would have a strong ally next door in Mexico, not under Moreno's control, but under compatible military forces. The Mexican military was primed to seize power when Moreno assassinated the Mexican president.

That assassination would be blamed on the Zapatistas and, in any case, Moreno would soon be eliminated. The consequence would be a Mexican carbon copy of Cuba. With Ramiro's extensive ties with key figures in Mexico's corrupt military and their intimate ties to massive Colombian drug operations, Mexico under military rule would support Cuba under Ramiro's military power. Ramiro would be sitting on a pile of gold, in total political control, allied with Mexico next door. He sighed deeply and pondered smugly the eurphoria of absolute power. He would sleep well this night.

That is, until he remembered Elena. She's got to go, he thought. Oh yes, she must go. Soon. The image of Elena and McGrath in the aquarium with the sea snakes came to his mind again, and he smiled, relishing the thought of her and the American thrashing around underwater. Maybe he should put Herrera in there, too, when the time came. Then he glanced over at Victor, who seemed more nervous than usual lately. He wished Victor would stop rocking back and forth in his chair so much. He created an air of uncertainty, and that was not good for this operation. As he watched Victor crack his knuckles one by one for the second time in the last half hour, the thought crossed his mind that maybe he was a liability for Operation Rebirth.

Elena waited at the prearranged busy street corner in the afternoon after work, when Juan arrived with McGrath and Samuels to pick her up. She had taken two cabs and ducked through at least five department stores to get here, checking and double-checking to see if she was being tailed. She jumped in the back seat with McGrath, face flushed, excited, folding up her umbrella as she slammed the door.

"How'd it go?" McGrath asked. "You still seem to be in one piece," he added, smiling.

"*No problemas*," Elena said, slipping the umbrella under her legs on the floor. "But I can tell you tensions are running high in that office. I overheard Ramiro and Victor arguing over something this afternoon. The staff's real edgy."

"Maybe its all these weather reports about that stalled hurricane out in the Atlantic. Could shift and come this way they say," Samuels said from up front.

"Who knows?" Elena said. "But have I got something to tell you. It's just unbelievable." McGrath looked at her quizzically. "Ramiro has invited us to go with him to the Tropicana. Says he wants to do something nice for me, for all the hard work I've been doing in the office. Can you beat that? Caught me totally by surprise."

"Cuba's famous nightclub?" Samuels asked.

"Exactly. We have to accept it," Elena said.

"Absolutely. We got to act as if everything's normal," McGrath said.

"Who does he mean by us?" Samuels asked.

"Neal and I," Elena said. "Sorry Don. I didn't feel like I could push it."

"When does he want to go?" McGrath said.

"Soon as he can get the tickets. Could be anytime. He said to have my best dress out and ready to go."

They kicked the invitation around another five minutes as Juan peered through the windshield with its slapping wipers fighting a losing battle against the rain. "We're going to have to be on our toes with this one," McGrath said. "I don't like the sound of it, but we must go despite the risk."

"I agree," Elena said. "Hey, did you call that guy Kincaid again?"

"I did. He told me he's pulled out all stops to get your papers, a fake passport, and airline tickets. He doesn't know exactly when, but he's working like hell on it."

"That's comforting," Elena said ruefully. If we have them before this Tropicana scene, I say we leave."

"Absolutely. I telephoned my friend at CIA, told him where we stand. He says he's in touch with Kincaid. So we get extra help from that quarter. Let's keep our fingers crossed this thing gets done fast."

Two hours later they greeted Juan and jumped back into his taxi after a visit with General Herrera at his home, where Herrera's officers gathered on a regular basis. They climbed into the taxi, with Samuels in the middle of a sentence. "Yeah, I agree, Herrera sure seems popular, Elena, just like you said. Quite a bunch of high-powered brass gathered there. So, he holds these gatherings regularly." They slammed the doors, and drove off.

"Oh yes," she said, looking over her shoulder through the backseat window, wiping the rainwater off her forehead with a kerchief. "Everybody's talking about him. He's outspoken about conditions in Cuba and government inefficiency."

"Outspoken is an understatement," McGrath said. "Man, he really lays it on the line. You hear those remarks he made about economic conditions? Wow."

"He uses strong language, that's for sure," Samuels said.

"What impressed me was his take on nationalism," McGrath said. "This guy's truly committed to Cuba, loves its history, heroes, and struggles for independence. I'm convinced that he would die for his country. He's completely out of step with Fidel's policies."

"Yeah, but not in a position to do much about it," Samuels said.

"He's hard to believe in some respects," McGrath said. "Imagine in this police state how he's still alive with all his public loathing of present policies. His vision of Cuba is so at odds with Castro's. He's one disgusted individual." McGrath looked at Elena. "You got to wonder how he gets away with his negative remarks."

"You have a point," Elena answered. "If you listen to the grapevine, Herrera would win an open election for president hands down. Some people say he should be up at bat, meaning in charge of things. He's that popular."

"Sounds like a thorn in the side of the leaders running Cuba with all that public appeal," Samuels observed.

"Not necessarily," Elena explained. "Castro's solidly in control. He need not fear somebody like General Herrera. No one person or group is about to challenge this government. Fidel is number one. Everyone knows that. He still has respect and support from millions of people, except maybe some of our younger folks. But they have no idea what it was like before the revolution. I guess you can't please everyone."

"So Herrera's popularity isn't something Fidel would worry about?" McGrath asked, rocking with the jolt of the pothole they hit.

"I think not," Elena said. "There's room on the island for lots of popular leaders—in all professions, from film and dance to singers and the military. I should think Fidel and the top guys in politics would be pleased that a military leader would be as popular as Herrera. He makes everyone proud of Cuba."

"What about that home of his?" McGrath said. "Not the kind of place I would expect a decorated general to live in."

"He sees himself as a man of the people," Elena said.

"He's not pretentious," McGrath said. "But didn't you think he looked kind of tired? Did you see those dark circles under his eyes?"

"He's known as a hard worker," Elena explained. "Juan, you think that red Chevy back there is following us?"

Back at the Ministry of Interior late that night, Ramiro and Victor firmed up plans for Elena.

"Everything set up? Ready to go?" Ramiro asked.

"Totally under control. Everyone has their assignment. Good men. You can depend on them. How about your end? How did she react to the invitation? She took the bait?"

"The Tropicana? She was surprised and delighted. Especially when I told her she could bring a friend. She asked if she could bring her U.S. visitor along," he said, his eyes narrowing.

"You still think that was them on *El Tesero* last night?"

"Who the hell else? Too bad they killed the one guy. We could have made him talk. Anyway, the guard saw four people. He's certain one was a woman. Had to be her."

"How about the fourth guy?"

"Who knows? Your guess is as good as mine. Maybe McGrath's friend. But we can't be certain. The damn wharf surveillance cameras aren't working."

"Who do you think she's working for?"

"I don't know. Maybe CIA. At this point, I don't give a shit. She's history."

"So we take out Elena and McGrath together?'

"Right. Two for the price of one. He now knows as much as she does. He's got to go."

"So you want me to make the telephone call to get you out of there?"

"Right. The performance starts at nine-thirty. Ends at eleven. Give me a call at ten forty-five sharp. Call the front desk at the Tropicana. They'll send a waiter to tell me I've got a call. Make sure your driver and the tail have cell phones."

"You don't think it's dangerous to be seen in public with her right before her death?"

"No. Not at all. Everybody goes to the Tropicana. Just a night out on the town with a member of our staff. Giving the Americano the royal treatment. Person-to-person diplomacy. No, it's all perfectly understandable. We'll feign absolute sorrow about her and the American's death. We'll throw a huge funeral service for them. Make it look like real genuine regrets. It'll work. It would be more interesting to put her in with the sea snakes, but this way is more efficient," he said, smiling at Victor. "We'll blame the incident on a jealous lover. The public will buy it in a minute." Ramiro could hardly wait for the show to begin.

EIGHTEEN

Havana

Tropicana tickets had come through sooner than expected. Tonight was the night, twenty-four hours after their meeting with General Herrera. At 8:30 P.M. Juan dropped McGrath and Elena off at her apartment on Calle Linea. They had just returned from a *paladar* dinner in Central Havana with Samuels, trying to look and act as natural as possible. Samuels headed back to Espinosa's apartment with Juan. Samuels, worried sick over the way things were going, tried to talk McGrath and Elena out of it, but McGrath insisted that they had to keep up the front. None of them liked the idea of going to the Tropicana, but what else could they do? Kincaid was still working on Elena's tickets and identification papers.

Elena's apartment was located in a fourteen-story building on a wide boulevard with three traffic lanes running one way in each direction. The lanes in turn were separated by a narrow, three feet wide concrete median with tall streetlights shaped like a "T" running down the median with its tufts of grass clawing up through cracks in the concrete. Traffic was heavy this evening, the sky overcast, and that ominous rising wind. Was he imagining that it was getting stronger? As a sailor with his own sailboat moored in Annapolis, weather was second nature to McGrath, and he automatically paid attention. It occurred to him that the hurricane they had been talking about might be closer than they thought.

Her apartment building was in typical Cuban disrepair. Cracked walls, peeling paint, poor maintenance. They walked into the poorly lit foyer, stepped inside the beat-up elevator and punched the button for the third floor. Listening to the groaning elevator cables, McGrath wondered how much longer they would hold. As it creaked upward, he realized that his heart was racing, and when Elena stepped toward him and embraced him, he was about to say they should cancel the club, grab a cab, and go back to the Espinosas and hole up for the storm. But suddenly, in the middle of a long passionate kiss, the elevator lurched to a stop. They stepped out, walked down the hallway, half listening to muffled conversations and music behind closed doors.

When they entered her apartment, they went to the kitchen together to mix a rum and coke, and then returned to the living room.

"We've got a few minutes before General Ramiro arrives, Neal. Let's talk," her voice a low serious whisper. She signalled that the room might be bugged. With drink in hand, she led him into the tiny bathroom, turned on the shower, and sat down on the floor, indicating to McGrath to sit close next to her.

Elena leaned forward and whispered. "Neal, listen, I'm really nervous . . ."

"That makes two of us," McGrath said in a low voice, squeezing her hand, smiling, trying to ease her fears.

"Ramiro is absolutely ruthless, you know. I've heard rumors about how he gets information from people. Apparently he's got this place where he keeps sea snakes in a giant aquarium. He gives me the creeps. So I'm just saying, we have to be on our toes tonight. He's capable of anything."

"Look, I know the type. Of course we'll be careful. Just try to relax if you can. The last thing we want is to act nervous around him."

"Listen, I've been thinking about that shipyard business. Knowing the way Ramiro thinks, there's a good chance that he suspects it was me, maybe with you, down there on *El Tesero*. This guy sees conspiracies everywhere. He's paranoid. We're in real danger, Neal."

"I know." He paused. "Let me ask you again," Mc-Grath whispered. "You're absolutely certain you can't use your contact with Castro himself? After all, you said he helped you land your job with Ramiro?"

"Right. He owed my uncle a favor. Don't forget, my uncle's high up in the government."

"Then what's the problem? Why not go straight to Fidel and tell him all about this business? Go to the top."

McGrath saw her shoulders slump. She sighed, "Sounds logical, I know. But it won't work," she took a deep breath. "I can't go to Castro. First, I don't know him personally. I only met him once when my uncle introduced us. No way could I see him privately. Problem is, even if I could speak with him, he'd never believe me. After all, Ramiro's one of the old boys. Don't forget, Cuba's still a man's world, despite what you read about women in the revolution. Castro would dismiss my story as female hysterics." She stared at him wistfully. "Mind if I smoke," she added and pulled a cigarette package from her purse.

"I see what you mean," McGrath replied.

"And furthermore," she said in a whisper, tapping ashes into a tiny blue ashtray on the edge of the tub, "imagine if Castro got mad and to prove his case confronted Ramiro. Ramiro would deny everything—and then his original suspicions about me would be locked in concrete. Uh-uh, it won't work."

"And your uncle is of course . . ."

"Out of the country . . . for weeks. I'm not even sure where he is. He goes away often, doesn't always tell me where he's going."

"OK, then, we stick with Kincaid and hope the papers come through soon."

"Look, Neal, there is one other outside possibility. I've been thinking about it."

"I'm all ears," he said and gave her hand a squeeze.

She inhaled deeply on her cigarette and let the smoke come out slowly. "You told me that you know how to sail, right?"

"Right."

"Well, I mean, how strong a sailor are you? Lots of experience?"

"I'd say so. I have my own sailboat. Keep it in the Chesapeake Bay."

"Think you could sail from Cuba to Florida?"

"I suppose so. It would depend on weather and the boat. What are you getting at?"

"Well then . . . that's good. Look, my uncle has a sailboat."

"What?"

"Yes, and I think it's large enough to make the Florida Straits crossing. Well equipped too. Electronics. All that. What do you think?"

"You mean as a back-up plan?"

"Yeah. You know, if Kincaid doesn't come through with those papers pretty soon, we could use a another way out of here, no?"

"Absolutely right," McGrath said, visibly interested.

"Well, it's moored out at Cojimar, east of here, a forty-five minute drive."

"How big is it?"

"Thirty-two feet, older model wooden vessel, inboard engine. My uncle keeps the fuel tank full, ready to go . . . and . . . ," she said, glancing at her watch, stumping out her cigarette. "Look at the time. We have to run. I promised Ramiro that we'd wait out front!"

The sailboat, McGrath, thought, as he got up, Elena's hand in his, pulling her up, a nervous look on her face. Yeah, they might just make it by boat if it came to that option. One thing he knew he could do well—sail a boat. He'd been in dirty weather. Wind and high seas were no strangers. But they would have to wait until this storm passed. Too threatening.

Ramiro weaved in and out of traffic on Linea Street in his shiny blue 1958 Cadillac Eldorado convertible, its white top up, because of the weather. The most elegant Caddy ever built, Ramiro's Eldorado set the standard for ostentatious consumption among Ministry of Interior elites. No one drove a car like it. In fact, only a few of his colleagues had ways to import the whitewall tires that carried this class act through Havana's streets. The shiny tail fins alone turned more than one pair of eyes in his direction. But driving along in a car that snubbed its nose at Cuba's economic woes, Ramiro was basking less in the glory of his convertible than turning over in his mind his decision on how to eliminate Elena. He smiled and honked impatiently at the red and white Chevy in front of him.

He gestured angrily at the next car, a taxi, and accelerated around it, thinking about her relationship with the American. So he's her ex-professor from the U.S.? Or so she says. Must be CIA, another agent slipped into Cuba. Well, after tonight, he'll be a *deceased* professor and one less CIA spook too.

Ramiro pulled his convertible up to the curb and came to an abrupt stop. It was the first time Elena had seen him out of uniform—dressed in light blue sport coat, open white shirt and dark trousers, hair greased back, his neck displaying a gold chain. He jumped out and walked swiftly around from the street side to the sidewalk, greeted them with a quick flash of teeth and a short but civilized smile.

"Good evening, Elena. All set?"

"Good evening, General Ramiro. May I introduce Professor Neal McGrath."

"Elena speaks highly of you," Ramiro answered in his deep voice and extended hand, eyes piercing McGrath's. His handshake tested McGrath's response.

"Good to meet you too, General Ramiro. Thanks for this great invitation. I know how hard it is to get tickets. I'm so looking forward to the evening." He met Ramiro's smile and sinister, pockmarked face with a direct look into his eyes.

The trip to the Tropicana went easily enough, Ramiro showing oily courtesy. He pointed out various landmarks, and drove the Caddy like a racecar. People along the route gave him plenty of space, because the car was so impressive, a remarkable contrast to the other museum pieces on the streets. Ramiro dropped them off at the entrance. Mambo music played in the background. A uniformed doorman opened the door for Elena. Ramiro parked the car, not trusting the valet service.

They waited outside for Ramiro to return. "Quite a crowd," McGrath said, gazing around at the people gathered in clusters, chatting, women in evening wear, lots of high heel shoes, ruby red lips, all decked out. "A different side of Cuba."

"It's the old Cuba," Elena replied, squeezing his hand, trying to look confident. Mostly foreigners, McGrath observed. Probably too expensive for most Cubans, he thought. Three loudmouthed, young Americans with drinks embarrassed him. The ticket area was noisy confusion, cars pulling up, dropping off, and driving on. The doorman, who looked like a decorated navy admiral, collected his tips with a toothy smile. Lots of old-fashioned, and in some ways cheesy, glitz, McGrath thought, kind of like Maryland's Ocean City boardwalk where your shoe might stick on bubble gum.

"Shall we go in?" Ramiro offered upon his return. They strolled into the flashy Hollywood-style entrance, down a wide marble floor lined with mirrors with blue-fringed neon lighting. They passed by a stand selling cigars, resting in colorful boxes, and entered an amphitheater with a giant, circular dark wooden stage in the midst of huge royal palms that swayed up above in the open air. More bright blue neon lighting in the trees off in the distance blared out "Tropicana: 1939–2005." Off to the back of the stage he could see the full orchestra tuning up for the evening, as the officious nose-in-the-air waiter led them to their table.

Multilevel staircases and bridges led off the stage up into the trees. Best seats in the house went for ninety dollars and an additional ten dollars if you wanted to take photographs of the performers. The waiter tried to seat them at a table far back, mistaking the young woman and two men for tourists, arrogantly insisting this was their table like it or not. That is, until General Ramiro told him who he was and nearly took his head off with a no-nonsense, one-two insult of his own. Seats closer to the stage immediately became available. In that short burst of razor-edge language and emotion, McGrath got a glimpse at Ramiro's dark side. It was clear that he did not suffer fools lightly.

The waiter produced the obligatory bottle of Havana Club rum and three cans of Coca-Cola. Included in the price, he explained with a big smile.

Ramiro turned to McGrath, "I do believe you will enjoy this evening, Professor McGrath. The show is distinctly Cuban in music, song, and spirit. Lots of mambo and cha-cha-cha. It'll put you inside the Cuban *soul*. You're going to hear music and see dancers with an attitude tonight."

"I'm already enjoying it, General," McGrath responded upbeat, despite the tension he could feel.

"One of the big attractions here are the *mulatas*," Ramiro said.

"*Mulatas?*"

"Right. *Mulatas*—the dancers. Beautiful brown-skinned ladies. A mixture of white and black parents.

Tall. Statuesque. Wait, you'll see." He poured rum and Cokes. "So what's your impression of Havana so far?"

McGrath thought a second before responding, then said he was impressed with Cuba's education system, how everybody seemed to have a chance to succeed through higher education. He liked Cuba's health services, too.

"So you think our education is better than in the U.S.?" Ramiro asked.

"Well, we do have free elementary and high schools, but a college education can be costly."

"It's *all* free here," interjected Ramiro defiantly. He leaned back in his chair and snapped his fingers for their waiter and ordered two cigars. "We're turning out doctors, engineers, and teachers right and left. Many go abroad to help in poor, Third World countries—like Angola, Mozambique and Nicaragua. Something like your Peace Corps, but we send professionals."

"Most impressive," McGrath said.

"I've heard how U.S. education is deteriorating," Ramiro remarked. "Fewer and fewer qualified teachers producing poorly educated students. Lots of functional illiteracy. Too bad. You'd expect more from the great *colossus of the North*."

"We're making improvements, though," McGrath said

They had to talk loudly over the 20-piece orchestra, which had just launched into its first number. Suddenly, with thunderous applause, the stage filled with strutting long-legged, scantily clad women dressed in alluring Caribbean attire displaying more flesh than fabric. Not exactly Las Vegas, McGrath thought, but a good try. A Vegas wannabe, he thought, with a mambo beat. The headgear alone looked like something from outer space—giant blazing candelabras two feet high, lit up like the Rockefeller Center Christmas tree. But all the while, McGrath kept Ramiro in the corner of his eye.

Toward the end of the first half of the performance,

General Ramiro said offhandedly between numbers, "Elena, look who's over there. One of Cuba's heroes."

Elena looked over and exclaimed, "Oh my goodness. It's General Herrera. There was another article about him in yesterday's *Granma*."

"Right. He's in the press often," replied Ramiro nonchalantly, like it was the last thing on his mind. At that moment their waiter came up to the table and said, "General Ramiro, sir, you have a telephone call at the front desk."

"Certainly. You will have to excuse me for a minute," he said, pushing back his chair and standing up. He took a deep breath. "I'll be right back."

When Ramiro left the table, McGrath turned to Elena. "So what do you think? How's it going?"

"Don't trust him for a second, Neal. He's putting on his Mr. Nice Guy face. Peel it away and you see something much scarier. Seems antsy to me. I can't put my finger on it. Like he's preoccupied with something."

Ramiro returned. "I am *so* sorry. One of those things that seem to come up when I'm trying to relax. You know the drill, Elena, no? I must return to town. My apologies. Are you OK with taking a taxi back? Good. I'll make sure one's available to you after the show. You may not want to stay too long. Seems bad weather's coming."

McGrath and Elena stood up to say good-bye. McGrath thanked Ramiro again for the evening, relieved to see him go.

"Do you find that odd?' McGrath asked.

"You mean his being called away?"

"Exactly. Why would he be called at this hour?"

"Oh, I don't know. Could be anything. He's a busy man. State security never sleeps. Still, it does seem a little strange, I agree."

Shortly after Ramiro left, a standing ovation brought the first half of the show to a thunderous close. As the dancers wound their way off the stage and orchestra members stood up for a break, McGrath and Elena worked their way over to General Herrera's table. The general stood up, shook hands with McGrath and invited them to sit down.

Herrera, his wife Raquel, and son Alex, made them feel instantly at ease. "We're celebrating Alex's sixteenth birthday," Raquel said.

"He's going into the air force as soon as he finishes high school," the general added proudly. He reached over and patted the well-built, dark-haired, dark-eyed young man on the back.

The five of them shared light conversation, waiters bustling about, Cuban rhythms wafting through the stage area. Herrera said he was delighted to have a chance to chat a little more about McGrath's research and his impressions of Cuba. Attention soon turned to Alex, who explained how he wanted to be a pilot like his dad. Raquel, an attractive, slim woman, hair combed back tight in a French braid, wearing a short sleeve black dress, told them how fearful she was for the two men in her life who insisted on flying. It had been hard enough with the general, she said, and now, Oh Lord, her son was into it.

Elena reminded McGrath about the general's admiration of José Martí. He would be the person to ask about Cuban patriotism.

"But first Elena," Herrera replied, "you must tell me what *you* think Martí would say about today's Cuba."

"I'm not certain what he would say, General. What do you think?" she asked with a coy smile.

"Well, as far as I'm concerned, I think he'd turn over in his grave if he saw what we have come to!" the general responded.

"Julio, *stop* that kind of talk!" Raquel whispered sharply. She looked around to see if anyone could hear them. Don't speak in public that way."

"Mother's right," Alex said, looking over his shoulder

nervously. "We've been over this a thousand times, Pop. This is not the place."

"OK, OK. Let's change the subject. So when do you go back to America, Professor McGrath?"

"Next week. I'm only here for a short stay, sir."

"Well, if you get a chance, you have an open invitation to come visit us again. Maybe we can fine tune your understanding of our *patria*."

"Be delighted, sir," McGrath replied

"Good. Meanwhile, enjoy your stay. Keep your eyes wide open. You will see what I mean about Martí."

"They're getting ready to start the second half," Elena said. "We'll head back to our table now. Great to see you again, General. Señora Herrera, Alex. Happy sixteenth to you."

As they sat down at their table, the dancers rushed onto the stage in a gaggle of blue and white feathers only slightly out of choreographed step—in part because it had started to rain. Elena was about to say something, when the music stopped abruptly. Dancers shuffled to the rear of the stage where they huddled together restlessly, looking upward. Next the lights on the stage went out.

"Ladies and gentlemen," a deep, resonate voice said. "We regret to inform you that the rest of the show must be cancelled because of weather. We apologize for this inconvenience. We hope you have enjoyed yourself and will return for another night's performance. The Tropicana thanks you for coming."

As the voice died off, a thunderclap boomed and rolled away in the distance, and the rain picked up. "Good thing we brought an umbrella," McGrath said, snapping it open as they stood up to leave the darkened theater.

They worked their way out to the front driveway of the crowded Tropicana in the jostling crowd. There in front of the reception desk a heated argument had bro-

ken out between a dozen or so angry patrons and two
Tropicana representatives. The agitated crowd shouted
and demanded their money back for the cancelled performance. The staff insisted it was impossible. The argument heated up and one of the men looked like he was
about to take a swing at the manager just as McGrath
and Elena slipped by and found a waiting cab—a faded
red and white 1955 Chevy that pulled up beside them. It
had a showy silver swan with giant wings mounted on
the hood, ornate silver grillwork up front and dirty tires
that indicated much recent travel. McGrath took a quick
look around to see if he might recognize anybody,
maybe even Kincaid.

"Where to?" asked the eager driver who had waved
them into to his taxi. He looked on the tough side, Mc-
Grath thought. Big, square, unshaven jaw; dark, sunken
eyes, hair slicked back in some kind of gel, like a
Chicago mobster of the 1940s. It worried him, and he
abruptly felt on edge, adrenaline pumping.

As the taxi headed away from the Tropicana, McGrath
looked out the back window. He spotted the second taxi,
a yellow Buick some distance behind. Was it tailing
them? McGrath could not be certain, but he had a strong
hunch it was. Still, was this not to be expected? After all,
they had been dodging tails all week. He glanced out
the back window again.

NINETEEN

Havana = Cojimar

The taxi pulled up across the street from Elena's apartment. It was eleven-thirty P.M. They got out of the cab
there to keep up the pretense of normality, then once in-

side the building, they would go out the back door, down another alley, catch a cab, go to Old Havana, and make their way to Espinosa's apartment, safe haven.

The radio had been announcing storm warnings and a potential hurricane threat from the weather system now stalled an estimated seventy-five miles off Cuba's northeast coast.

"Quién sabe?" the driver said, shrugging his shoulders, when McGrath asked him what he thought about the storm. "It might never hit. Maybe she will go toward the U.S. Happens all the time. As they approached Elena's apartment building from the opposite side of the street, the cab driver had suggested they get out. That way, he claimed, they would avoid the barricades up the street where road repairs apparently were underway.

Elena looked at McGrath quizzically. "I didn't know they were working on Linea. But . . . ahh well, let's get out." McGrath could see she looked concerned. He too was apprehensive, not only from the body language of their driver and his telling them to get out here, but also because of the second cab that McGrath was certain had tailed them. That taxi had swiftly pulled up to the curb about a hundred yards or so behind them. McGrath told himself that he had been in tighter situations than this as he glanced back at the second cab. He fished around in his pocket for his wallet to pay the fare and noticed that the driver nervously kept glancing in the rearview mirror. Not good, he thought. They had to move fast.

Even at this late night hour, a fair amount of traffic cruised up and down the avenue, since it was one of the city's major boulevards. As soon as their cab left, McGrath said, "OK, let's go." He instinctively took Elena's arm to cross the street, looking both ways, stepping off the curb.

Just as they were in the middle of the street, McGrath caught something in his peripheral vision. It might have been the gunned-up engine noise above the normal motor sounds. Maybe it was the erratic blur of motion off to the left that didn't fit the expected flow of traffic. Whatever it was, Elena saw it too, and they both picked up the pace.

"Oh my *God*, Neal, watch out!" she cried, pointing up the street.

The yellow cab in question gunned its engine, bolted out from behind a slower-moving van, and raced straight for them like a predatory shark preparing to strike. The distance between them and the oncoming automobile closed quickly, and McGrath and Elena broke into a fast jog toward the five-foot-wide island dividing the boulevard. Elena cursed her high platform shoes as they raced for the traffic island's safety and made a last minute lunge for the median. She tripped on its concrete curb, pulled McGrath down with her, landing sprawled out on the concrete island. The taxi roared by in a yellow flash and missed them by inches.

McGrath, pulled Elena to her feet. "*Jesus*, that was close. We gotta get out of here. You OK? God, you really scraped your hands."

Elena brushed her hands on her skirt. "Yes. Yes, I think so." McGrath watched as she rubbed her knees, which took a pounding when she hit the island. Her hands were trembling as he picked up the contents of her purse, which flew open when she fell. Her left shoe was off, and McGrath slipped it back on her foot. "Here you go, Cinderella," he said, trying to sound more calm than he felt.

"Thanks . . . we need a fairy godmother, don't you think?"

McGrath glanced down Linea Street in the direction the car had headed, and took Elena's arm. "Ramiro's thugs, for certain. We're running out of time, Elena. Oh shit," he said. "Look down there." He pointed. The yellow taxi had made a U-turn down the block and now was racing back toward them on the other side of the boulevard. "Let's go."

"Oh my *God*," she muttered, staring at the oncoming cab flying at them. "What are we going to do?" The panic in her voice was unmistakable.

"Back across the street." McGrath took her hand. "Bend down when you run, stay low," he yelled as the taxi roard toward them. Like a great white that used the first run to stun its prey, preparing it for the second attack, the car closed rapidly. They ran flat out, dodging trees and signs in the median, then out into the traffic lanes they had just crossed, dodging oncoming traffic, blaring horns. This is nuts, McGrath thought, running alongside Elena, eyes darting around the setting, mind racing wildly, sorting out options. What a sloppy way to knock somebody off, he thought. He felt like he was in a Grade B, 1940s movie. Hardly James Bond material. Sloppy or not, they mean business. Once you're dead, you're dead. Doesn't matter how they get you.

"Faster," he said, pulling Elena along.

The taxi was about 75 feet across the street from them now, and they heard a muffled "pop," followed by a whizzing sound that zipped by McGrath's left ear and then a loud "thud" as a bullet smashed into the telephone pole. Splinters flew, and one caught McGrath just above the eyebrow, which began to bleed. A second "pop" and a bullet whizzed closely over Elena's head. "Oh my *God*!" she gasped, running with him as fast as she could.

"Keep running," McGrath urged, as they raced down the empty sidewalk, looking for a side street or alley for escape. Running flat out, adrenaline pumping, they could see the yellow cab now up Linea, preparing to make yet another U-turn that would bring it speeding back in their direction on their side of the avenue. McGrath thought he had spotted two people in the taxi—a driver and another man doing the shooting. The cab made its turn up the street for the return run. Elena was breathing hard beside him, her left foot bleeding.

Then he saw it. Right next to the grocery store not fifty feet from them—an alley alongside the building. McGrath pointed to it, and Elena managed to gasp, "Right. Goes 'round the back. Leads to another walkway. Too narrow for a car."

They plunged into the tight space and charged down it as fast as they could run, until Elena begged McGrath to stop. "Gotta catch my breath," she gasped, leaning against him. She was shaking, color drained from her face. A glance back down the alley revealed a man getting out of the taxi that had pulled up to the curb in front of the alley under a dim street light.

McGrath just had time to push Elena behind a Dempsey dumpster, putting his index finger to his lips. He crept behind a nearby pile of cardboard boxes and junk that would protect him from being seen. He looked around for something to use and spotted a two-by-four lying by the boxes. He picked it up, visualizing his move as the man approached.

When the figure was about seven feet away, a startled cat let out a howl and bolted right in front of him. A muffled shot went off and McGrath flinched, nearly dropping the two-by-four. A bullet missed his head by inches, lodging in the concrete wall behind him. For a fleeting moment, he was certain he had given away his presence. But the figure creeping toward him, four feet away, obviously had not seen him.

McGrath bent his knees to brace himself, took careful aim where he estimated the head would be, and swung the two-by-four with every ounce of strength in his body. The dull splat told that he had made perfect contact—square in the face. Blood flew everywhere as the man groaned and crumbled to the ground, lying there on his stomach, head to one side, nose flattened against cheeks, eyes glazed. His gun lay in his limp right hand. It was the black guy who had attacked him in the nightclub.

McGrath bent over to check the face, and Elena whispered hoarsely, "Neal! Look! Down the alley!" A second man was running toward him. Two flashes leaped out from his revolver, and bullets instantly whizzed by so close they took McGrath's breath away. By instinct, he removed the pistol from the hand of the the unconscious form beside him. It had a silencer. With one knee on the sandy alleyway, the other bracing for an accurate shot, he pointed the gun at the onrushing figure. Cupping his right gun hand with his left hand to steady it, he took deliberate aim and fired. The silencer muffled the sound. The first shot missed. The second hit the attacker square in the face. His feet came out from under him as if he had been hit behind the knees and he hurtled backward, thudding to the ground like a sack of potatoes.

McGrath raced back to Elena, still crouched behind the Dempsey dumpster. As he pulled her up, she threw her arms around his neck. "You OK?" she asked.

"Fine. I'm fine. Here, put this revolver in your purse. We may need it later."

"What happens now?" Her eyes searched McGrath's, lower lip quivering.

"Back to Espinosa's place," McGrath said, hustling her along the alley. "About your uncle's sailboat," he added, as Elena looked at him quizzically. "It's just moved up in the priority line. We're gonna use it. But we have to hurry."

They hunched over in the drizzle now whipping around in the rising wind, like two sailors trying to find a harbor in an approaching storm.

They stopped their taxi near the deserted Plaza de la Catedral, several blocks from Juan and Martina Espinosa's apartment, then started walking through the back streets in the rain. Only when they were absolutely certain that they had not been followed did they finally step off the slick cobblestone street onto the wet sidewalk and knock on Espinosa's side door.

Juan peered out, gawked, mouth open, pulled them in, looked up and down the street worriedly, then satisfied, shut the door and locked it.

"My God," he said, "what on earth happened to you?" Martina rushed over in a flurry, hugged Elena and asked her if she was all right, then hurried to the bathroom for bandages. Samuels, who had spent the evening with the Espinosas, was dumbfounded and deeply concerned. Juan asked again if they were certain they had not been followed.

In the background the radio announcer detailed the stalled storm system threatening Havana. The National Weather Center was advising everybody to draw a bath tub filled with water and warned that electricity soon would go out. "That comes as no surprise. Power outages are the name of the game here, storm or no storm," Juan said, as he watched Martina attend to Elena's bloodied hands and knees.

McGrath quickly related their story. They listened in shocked disbelief.

When McGrath had finished, Samuels said "We're in Trouble City, my friends, that's trouble with a capital 'T.' We gotta get outta here fast."

"No shit, Sherlock," McGrath answered. "That we do in fact. Not much time at this point. Listen, Elena has come up with an alternate possibility . . ." and he went on to explain the sailboat option.

"Might work," Samuels said. "Yeah, but what about the hurricane?"

"We might be able to beat it, Don. Damn well worth the risk. We don't have a bunch of possibilities here."

"What about Kincaid and the papers and passports?"

"We don't have time. Not after tonight."

"You got a point. OK, what can I do?"

"Nothing much, partner. Just lie low until the storm passes, then catch a plane out of here. They're not after you. Juan . . . can you get us out to Cojimar?"

"*Sí* señor, I can get you to Cojimar," Juan said. "*No problema*."

"Great. Listen, Martina. If I write a note to Mr. Kincaid at our Interest Section here in Havana, do you know anyone who can get it to him?"

"Absolutely," she said. "My best friend works there."

"Great. I've got that packet of cocaine from *El Tesero*. I'd like to get to Kincaid too. It goes with the note. Tie it all together, OK? Kincaid knows all about it."

"*Sí* señor."

"Shouldn't we call him, Neal?' Elena asked.

"No time. The note will explain everything."

"My God, Neal, I almost forgot . . ." Samuels said. He walked over to the living room table and picked up the evening copy of *Granma*. He handed it to McGrath. Look here on the third page. Read that," he said, his finger pointing to a photograph and the article.

McGrath looked . . . and caught his breath. The photo was blurred, but clearly a body lying near a Dempsey dumpster on a dock. The story reported that the man, a so-called Canadian citizen according to his passport, had been found dead on this dock up in Matanzas Harbor early that morning. *Granma* stated that Cuban authorities speculated that the man had died from a drug overdose of cocaine. Several packages of the stuff had been found in his pockets. The man's identity: Larry Diamond.

"Jesus," McGrath whistled. He looked again more closely at the photograph. "I can't believe it." Then he said, "Don, look at the position of Larry's body. Right there, look at the way his head is twisted."

"What are you thinking? "He didn't die from cocaine."

"What do you mean?'

"His neck's broken. From the looks of it, I'd say he was murdered."

"Murdered? By whom?"

"Who knows? Maybe he was dealing in cocaine and got greedy. He spent a lot of time out in Veradero with the tourists. Could have been pushing the stuff there. Maybe he knew too much and had to be put away."

"Read the last paragraph in the article, Neal." McGrath sat down on the sofa for a minute and read. Then he looked up at Samuels and let out a slow whistle. "Jesus Christ," he said. He just sat there for a minute, thinking. Then he said, "You know, I kind of suspected it, and in a way it makes sense. But the reality of it takes a minute to sink in, doesn't it?"

"Yes . . . it does." Samuels looked at Neal in disbelief.

"A spy for the CIA," McGrath murmured.

"That's what the paper says . . ."

"This means Goodwin and Kincaid probably assigned him to protect us from the get go."

"But Jesus, Larry Diamond . . . he sure fooled me," Samuels said. "He put his life on the line for us, especially in the nightclub."

"Listen," McGrath said, "it's sad, but we can't worry now. We got to get going."

"Let me pack some food for your trip," Martina said. "I'll get right to it."

"Thanks Martina. Also, any bottled water you can spare," he added as she walked into the kitchen. "Elena and I can throw some clothes together in my knapsack."

A half hour later they were ready. Neal wore his Levis, a long-sleeved blue cotton shirt, baseball cap, running shoes, and a rain jacket. Elena put on her own Levis, one of Neal's long-sleeved shirts, tennis shoes, a borrowed baseball cap from Samuels, and her raincoat.

"Got your passport?" McGrath asked.

"Right."

"Think now," McGrath said. "What are we forgetting?"

"The boat's pretty well stocked with emergency supplies," Elena said.

"Here's five bottles of *agua pura*," Martina said. "I hope it's enough."

"Thanks. It'll do just fine," McGrath said, smiling at Martina.

They slipped out the back way, and five minutes later they piled into Juan's taxi, Juan at the wheel. They were off.

"You sure you'll be safe in this weather?" Juan asked, peering through the rain-soaked front windshield with the wipers steadily beating back and forth.

"There's a chance the storm won't hit here soon," McGrath said. "Maybe it'll veer away. In any case, we really don't have any alternatives."

"Anybody following us?" Elena asked.

"Hard to tell," Juan said.

"I don't see any headlights close behind us," McGrath replied, cranking his head around to check the back window.

"How about Don? He'll be OK?"

"He's resourceful, Elena. I left the satellite phone with him. He's going to check in with Goodwin and Kincaid, and I know he'll get help from them. He may have to go the route of fake papers, passports, and new airline tickets."

Elena turned to peer out the rearwindow. "You sure that car's not following us? Seems closer now."

Ramiro was livid, yelling into the telephone. "Dead? They what? Missed them? For *Christ's* sake, how could they *miss* them?" He slammed the flat of his hand on the desk with a loud bang. "They were walking right down the middle of the *fucking* street. Like goddamn ducks in a shooting gallery. You *fucking* screw-ups! What the hell's the matter with you! Bullshit! Don't give me that lame excuse! Listen to me, and get this straight!"

He unleashed a litany of scorching words that got the attention of the man at the other end of the line. "Now get this right or there will be *hell* to pay at your end, my friend. I want two men posted in the Florida lobby," he commanded. "Don't do *anything* to alert the hotel staff. Remember, we want *nobody* tracing this back to this office. You got that straight *dickhead?* Put another two men near her apartment entrance. She may try to return. Get two cars combing the streets around her apartment. They can't be far away. Watch McGrath's hotel like a hawk. Send one of your men over here to my office. Yes, right now, you idiot! I've got a list of her friends. Check them out immediately. Keep an eye on her uncle's home. We'll make up a story why we're looking for her. Now get your ass in gear!"

He slammed down the telephone and turned to Victor.

"Those *morons*. They blew it! Christ, I should have done the job myself. Now she's out there somewhere with McGrath, and those *idiot jerk offs* can't find them. She knows we're on to her. Well, they can't go far. We've got all the airports covered. Sure as hell no boat's going out in this weather. Not with this storm coming in. We'll get her," he hissed.

Juan got them to the Cojimar marina fast. The car they thought was following them turned off a ways back, or at least they thought it had turned onto a side road. Its lights disappeared. They pulled into the sandy parking lot and got out. "Can I help you get started?" Juan asked.

"Absolutely," McGrath said loudly, wind overpowering his words.

"This way," Elena shouted, pulling McGrath along. "Boat's over there, at that dock."

A line of boats in slips along the dock extended two hundred feet out into the sea, riding up and down with the waves, halyards slamming against masts like an out-of-tune orchestra, distinctly audible over wind and waves pounding against the dock pilings.

"Which one is it?"

"Out there," Elena pointed excitedly, although in the dark none of them could see it clearly. "That wooden one. The *Aguila*."

They made their way along the creaking, undulating dock that reminded McGrath of a giant concertina. Navigating questions bounced around in his mind like ping pong balls. Wind, speed, and direction? Wave height? Dock conditions? How to maneuver *Aguila* out of her slip to get underway? No picnic, but with a little luck they could depart without getting tangled in dock lines or jammed against the dock itself. Think, he told himself. Don't panic. He hadn't expected the waves to be this high so soon. Storm was supposed to be far away at this hour. He had plenty of experience in dirty weather, but never anything approaching a hurricane. He said a silent prayer for the second time that this hurricane would veer off before it got much closer.

McGrath could just make out the boat under the dim dock lights. "Watch your step." As they worked their way out onto the rocking, weather-beaten dock, McGrath took some consolation when he saw the size of the *Aguila* and its general well-kept condition. "She's a beautiful boat. Hang on here for a minute. Let me check her out."

Elena nodded, grasping a piling to steady herself against the wind. Juan did the same. As McGrath stepped cautiously off the dock into the *Aguila*'s tossing cockpit, Juan suddenly seized Elena's arm. He nodded in the direction of the parking lot where their car was parked. "Elena," he said loudly, so he could be heard over the wind, "Look. A car's pulled up beside ours. Jesus, its lights are off. Somebody's getting out!"

McGrath heard none of this conversation. He was busy inspecting the *Aguila*'s lines, pleased that the boat was secured sternside to the dock of its berth—the bow tied by its lines to battered wooden pilings out in the water, away from the dock and positioned for a straightforward exit. He checked the fuel gauge in the cockpit. Full. Like Elena had predicted. He was absorbed in examining the throttle and gear shift system by the wheel, when he heard Elena's voice saying, "Neal. Neal. Out there. The parking lot. Two guys coming this way. I think they . . ." her voice stopped short when they saw a bright flicker of light and a bullet screamed by the cockpit. Then another flicker and another bullet whizzed by and slammed into a piling.

"Get down. Lie down on the dock," McGrath shouted. He pulled the revolver from his belt and rolled onto the dock beside Elena. "Stay low," he whispered, resting his right elbow on the dock, aiming his revolver with his right hand, bracing his wrist with his left, as the two men crept swiftly toward them. "Elena . . . get the gun out of your purse," McGrath yelled. Loud enough for her to hear, but hopefully not the guys at the end of the dock. But when he turned to look in her direction, he could see her lying prone on the dock, the gun out, aimed in the right direction. What the hell, he thought, seeing her on the dock in that position, gun held just as it should be. He had no idea that she had ever shot a gun before, and there she was looking like Annie Oakley herself. But there wasn't time to give it his full concentration. Things were moving fast.

When they were about thirty feet away, McGrath fired three shots in rapid succession. The first hit one of the men in the left shoulder, forcing him to lurch sideways. The second caught him high on the left side of his chest. He cried out and plunged into the waves. Before the second man could react, McGrath's next bullet entered his throat, and he collapsed like a rag doll on the rocking dock. It was then that McGrath saw the third man, making a beeline back to the car.

McGrath jumped up, shouted to Elena and a visibly shaken Juan to say put, and charged down the dock after him, trying not to fall off the unstable, rolling, planks. But by the time he reached the end of the dock, the assailant had jumped in the car, thrown the gear into first and had started to peel rubber out of the lot. McGrath instantly dropped to his knees, raised the revolver and emptied the chamber into the rear end of the car, hitting the right wheel and the gas tank. The car lurched out of control in a fiery explosion, skidded across the road and slammed head-on into a royal palm on the other side.

Running back up the dock, McGrath embraced a wide-eyed Elena, let a grim Juan shake his hand, and returned to his inspection of the *Aguila*, his adrenaline pumping nonstop. That Elena did not seem more shaken than she might be caught his attention. He was beginning to think he didn't know this woman as well as he thought he did.

He gave the rigging a quick look over, elated to discover that all lines—main and jib sheets, and reefing lines—were rigged for access in the cockpit. The traveler was positioned over the cockpit hatchway, designed for easy use. He reasoned that the *Aguila*'s wooden structure would aid their escape attempt, for it would reduce chances of Cuba's coastal radar detecting them. He was surprised and satisfied at how sturdy *Aguila* appeared.

After he had given the safety lines a quick look over, he tested them for strength and security. Then he walked cautiously forward on the *Aguila*'s swaying deck to examine the anchor system, to make certain the anchor was secured tightly in its bow chest. He checked out the genoa's roller-reefing mechanism and its connection to the bow mount system. As a sailor, McGrath knew that this check out time was vital if they were going to pull off this trip. He needed to know this boat as well as he could *before* they left the dock. But time was precious, and he knew he had to work fast. If some of Ramiro's men could find them, others might not be far behind.

Seems OK, he thought, as he worked his way back to the rising and falling cockpit.

"Looks in terrific shape," he said. "But there's a slight problem. We've got to break into the cabin. Engine's down there. I'm going to try to jump-start it. Lock's pretty old. I've got to find something to jimmy it loose. Got the ignition key in your purse?" he said, smiling, trying to break the tension.

"Sorry," she replied, her voice barely audible in the high wind.

"OK," I'll have to find something else.

"The dock shed," Elena said. "I know the lock combination."

"Let's try it."

Five minutes later they were back at the *Aguila* with a crowbar. McGrath stepped carefully down into the pitching cockpit. He steadied himself, stuck the crowbar into the cabin door lock, and with one powerful yank forced it loose.

"Listen," he shouted. "I'm going below for a minute to check out the engine. Wait here."

He removed the lock, tossed it overboard, pushed back the hatch entranceway and stepped below. He found a flashlight lying on the port berth and shined it around to get a quick fix on the cabin set-up and equipment. He spotted safety harnesses and foul weather gear—bright yellow rain jacket and pants for two—which he tossed on the port berth. He worked feverishly, another possible assault from Ramiro's men playing at the back of his mind. He discovered that the *Aguila* was well maintained and equipped, including ample provisions of bottled water.

The more McGrath saw below, the more certain he became that he could pull off this trip, even if he had to make it up as they went along. The navigation station had everything he needed for a safe crossing. GPS, VHF radio, even radar. Fantastic, he thought.

Grabbing the foul-weather slickers and safety tethers, he climbed back out to the cockpit and motioned Elena to jump aboard, extending his hand. "Hang tight up there, Juan. We're going to need you, OK?"

As soon as they had put on the jacket and pants, he got them into their saftey harnesses and secured Elena's safety line to the base of the mast.

"We can do this," he said. "Now listen, Elena. Do you know how to use the gear shift and throttle?"

"Yes."

"Good. I'm going to put the gear in neutral, OK? Now, I'm going down below to try to jump-start the engine. When the motor's running, I want you to leave it in neutral, but advance the throttle to about twelve hundred rpms, OK?"

"Got it."

"Juan, you just stand by, OK? We're going to really need your help in a couple of minutes, all right?"

"*Si* señor."

"*Bueno*, my friend."

With that, McGrath went back down below and removed the gangway ladder coming down into the cabin. Behind it lay the engine.

"OK," he shouted up, as he removed the crank from its clamps attached to a wall beside the engine, keep your fingers crossed." He braced himself in the small working space around the engine. He grasped the pressure release lever, pulled it up, inserted the crank in its slot and cranked it around vigorously to get the fly wheel turning. On the fourth crank, with the fly wheel whizzing around, he slapped down the pressure release lever and was greeted by the "chug, chug, chug, chug-a-chug" sound of the engine. It had ignited and turned over like a reliable old friend.

"OK, advance the throttle just a little, but not too far," McGrath shouted.

He replaced the crank, put the gangway ladder back and clamped it shut tight. Then he climbed up and joined Elena in the cockpit. "This is one hell of a boat."

Elena nodded. "I know."

"Let's warm her up for a few minutes, then we've got to get underway. Hang on. I'm going to triple reef her. We should be able to sail for awhile after we get out there. We can pick up more speed that way."

"Aren't we going to wreck the sails?" Elena shouted. "The wind's so strong."

"It'll be safe a little longer," he said, as he reefed the mainsail. "We can use the extra power. We won't raise the sail until we're out aways."

"You're the captain."

Ten minutes later, McGrath said, "OK. Now or never." He placed his arm around Elena's shoulders, hugged her reassuringly. "Let's do it!" With the wind blowing against the rolling port side of the *Aguila*, McGrath released the starboard stern dock line and tossed it up on the dock.

"Here's how we're going to leave this place," he shouted. "Can you hear me Juan?"

"Good. OK, here's the deal. I want you to untie the starboard stern line up there on the dock cleat and toss it into the cockpit. When you see me up on the bow, I'm going up there in a minute, I want you to untie the port stern line, but very carefully, keep it wrapped around the cleat, three wraps should do it, so it doesn't get away from you, OK? Then, when I shout to you that I'm ready up on the bow, I want you to quickly unwrap that line and toss it to the cockpit exactly at the moment Elena guns the engine to push us out of the slip. Understand? OK, good, you got it, my friend. Thanks for everything, Juan. I can't thank you and your family enough for all you've done for us. We are eternally grateful," McGrath yelled above the wind.

"Our great pleasure," Juan shouted.

"You've been a true friend. Be careful now, OK? Make sure you and your family lie low for a few days. Take good care of Don. I'll contact you when I get to the States."

"*Sí* señor McGrath. *Buena suerte, mis amigos.*"

"What am I supposed to do?" Elena asked.

"First, I'm going up to the bow to untie the starboard line attached to the piling. Then I'll untie the port line. I'll hold onto it—letting it slip around the bow cleat as you throttle us forward—to keep the bow more or less pointed to the opening between the two pilings. Now your part." As a seasoned sailor, McGrath was highly conscious of the necessity for clear communication on a boat. Everyone had to know exactly what they were doing and why. He confirmed once again that she knew how to use the motor.

She did.

"Good. OK. Now when I shout the word, *Go*, I want you to throttle forward. Give it plenty of juice so we can power our way between the pilings. Juan, that's the moment you toss your line into the cockpit as we pull away, OK?

"All right, I'm going forward now."

McGrath turned, grasped the safety line, and was about to work his way up to the bow, when he stopped dead in his tracks. By a voice. A commanding voice. Heavy accent, sinister, foreboding. McGrath caught sight of Juan staring in disbelief, Elena looking like a piece of petrified wood. McGrath tightened his grip on the safety line.

"Don't move," a deep voice thundered out of the dark.

The voice belonged to a man on the dock, standing about ten feet from them. They had been so absorbed in their departure, they hadn't seen him on the dock's creaking wooden planks. The noise of the rising wind and banging halyards didn't help, and he was black, wearing a torn and singed black T-shirt, ripped, partly burned pants.

McGrath saw instantly that he was the same guy in the car. The same guy in the nightclub restroom. Same guy in the alley. Blood ran down his cheeks from the gash on his forehead, and his left hand was was bloody. How he lived through that crash, God only knew, McGrath thought. He looked like an apparition returned from the dead, from a head-on collision with a royal palm. He stood there on the swaying dock, left arm hooked around a piling. His right hand held a revolver pointed at them.

TWENTY

Cojimar = San Diego

"Get out of the boat," he screamed. "Out! Out!"

McGrath did not notice that Elena still had her purse slung around her shoulder like an infant carrier. As he climbed out, she edged herself behind him, her knees bent slightly to appear smaller. She slipped the revolver from her purse and dropped her hand with the pistol down by her right side, out of view. But only for an instant. Things were happening fast, timing critical.

As McGrath stepped onto the dock, Elena raised her arm and fired point-blank twice. The first bullet smashed into the stunned thug's chest. The second tore into his arm. He yelled in pain, dropped his revolver, stumbled backward off the dock, and plunged into the water.

"My God, Elena," Juan shouted, shocked by what he had just seen, "are you all right?"

"Elena," McGrath said, after climbing back into the cockpit, he tried to think of something to say, come up with: "You *amaze* me. Gun in the purse trick. Nick of time. Listen, sweetheart, why don't you just sail us over to Key West? I'll guard the purse. Waddaya say?"

"Funny man," she shouted. "Let's go!"

"Right. OK, back to work. Wait until I tell you to untie and throttle forward, Elena. I'll go to the bow now." Seconds later he yelled back, barely audible over the wind.

"All set. Heads up, Juan. Unwrap your line. Elena, give it the juice!" He held his line tightly, aware of the danger of hitting another boat or, worse, catching *Aguila*'s shrouds on the pilings as they powered ponderously forward in the side-swiping waves.

Elena nearly lost her balance, but caught herself; she looked at Juan, nodded her head, pressed the gearshift forward, and advanced the throttle.

"Here we go!" she cried, as a wet and soggy dock line came flinging over her head and shoulders, along with Juan shouting, "May God be with you. Good luck." •

The sailboat's stern instantly drifted downwind several feet, but not far enough to offset its angled exit through the two forward pilings. McGrath held the bow piling line, pulling the bow toward the exit area until it was even with the two pilings. Then he reached out and slipped the line up over the piling in order to avoid its snagging the engine shaft and propeller underneath, quickly moving to the downwind side of the boat to fend off the downwind piling. He worked his way along the starboard side of the boat, trying to keep his balance on the rolling topside, pushing against the lee piling. He motioned to Elena to rev up the throttle more to gain momentum against the wind and waves as *Aguila* clawed its way through the watery turmoil.

"More juice," he shouted to Elena. "More juice!"

As *Aguila* sluggishly cleared the two pilings, Elena

braced herself and turned the wheel to port, heading the bow at a forty-five degree angle against the waves. Mc-Grath nearly went overboard. He saved himself by grabbing the safety line with both hands. Bent down, he inched his way back along the slippery deck, and slid into the cockpit with Elena, grabbing the cabin handrail to steady himself.

He signalled to hold this course. But they weren't making much headway, as *Aguila* struggled against the wind and waves like an overloaded ferry on the Amazon. For a fleeting second, McGrath almost panicked when he thought she might veer sideways to the wind and plow back into the marina. What's holding us up? he thought. His mind raced as he checked and rechecked the vessel from bow to stern.

The stern? Something wrong. What was it? The engine was pounding, prop churning. Steering wheel worked. What could it be? Then he saw it, and his heart jumped. The starboard stern line had fallen off into the water and trailed out behind the *Aguila*. Something big was attached to the end of the line, twenty feet back. Something human, large, and writhing in the churning waves. Something ominous that would not let go.

McGrath quickly reached in his pocket for the large boat knife he had found in the cabin. He pulled out the sharp blade and in three strong thrusts cut the line. He leaned out over the stern, shouted at Elena to give it more throttle, and watched as the man's head sank slowly under the waves. The last thing McGrath saw was the whites of the man's eyes, staring transfixed in grim finality.

As they left the marina and headed out to sea, even in the darkness of early morning they could make out the oily gray long rollers steadily marching in from the ominous sea—undulating mountains of water, whitecaps beginning to form, against eerie, deep purple clouds riding in from the northeast. The wind by now was whistling at a high-pitched wail, unrelenting and uninviting. Still, *Aguila* seemed to be taking the waves in stride, rising up one side of a wave, sliding down the back side. "Remember not to take the waves head-on," McGrath yelled, reminding himself and Elena, as he relieved her from the wheel.

A short distance out, he raised the shortened mainsail, then pulled out a small amount of sail on the roller-furling genoa. Setting their course on a close reach, he angled northeast. So far so good, he thought. Put as much distance between us and Cuba—as fast as possible. Try to beat this storm across the Florida Straits. Let it become the barrier to put a stop to anyone thinking about chasing us.

Moreno entered the U.S. on the morning flight from Mexico City to San Diego. His new passport identified him as José Paz, a Mexican television cameraman. His credentials indicated he would be working in Los Angeles for a short time with Universal Studios. The passport number did not bring up anything out of the ordinary on the computer and satisfied the bored U.S. passport control officer. Yes, the picture in the passport matched the man standing in front of him. So he stamped it and handed it back. "Welcome to the States," he said.

"Thank you," Moreno replied curtly.

He spotted his baggage on the conveyor belt, stepped deftly in front of an elderly gentlemen, bumped him slightly, and without apologizing, jerked his bag off the rotating belt, adjusted the knapsack on his shoulder, and headed for customs.

Moreno handed over his customs declaration form to the official and placed his suitcase and knapsack on the table in front of him. He had nothing to declare.

"Nothing to declare?" repeated the customs official

routinely, eyeing the clock, his mind already thinking of what he would do when he got off work in five minutes.

"No sir," said Moreno, flashing a huge grin. "Just happy to be returning to the U.S."

"Aha," came the bored response. "Open your suitcase, please. And the knapsack."

"Certainly," replied Moreno. All charm and courtesy.

The customs official rummaged briefly through the suitcase, then moved to the knapsack.

"That's my own television camera," Moreno said proudly, flashing his Mexican press credentials. "I carry it in the knapsack to protect it."

The customs official showed some interest in the camera, slowly running his finger along the edge of the lens.

"I'm a television cameraman," Moreno said, offhandedly. "Our channel in Mexico City is doing a series on the U.S. movie industry. I'm headed up to L.A., for a visit to Universal Studios. Maybe I'll meet Madonna." Moreno thought he said that pretty well.

"Sounds interesting. Don't let Jaws get you," the customs official smiled back.

"I'll be on my best guard, that's for sure," Moreno replied.

The official nodded indifferently. He asked permission to open Moreno's ditty bag. He rummaged around a second or two more and found nothing of interest. So he stepped back, and said, "OK, you're good to go. Enjoy your stay."

Following the signs for "Ground Transportation," Moreno walked out through the double glass doors and caught a taxi.

"Where to, buddy?"

"I need to buy a used car," replied Moreno. "Take me to the best place. There's an extra twenty in it for you."

"Great. There's one just down the road. My sister just bought a terrific car there."

"Thanks."

Two hours later, Moreno was the owner of a 1998 Toyota Camry, fully loaded, with low mileage. He was careful to buy a car under ten thousand dollars, so that the cash transaction would not be reported. "It's a pleasure to do business with you, Mr. Paz," the salesman said. "We'll have tags and registration ready for you by noon tomorrow. If you need a place to stay for the night, you'll find quality motels right down the road."

Moreno accepted the car dealership ride to the nearest motel, thanked the driver, arranged to be picked up the next day at noon, and went in to register.

By mid-morning in the gray, rain-swept seas, the storm had dramatically increased in intensity—far stronger than McGrath had ever sailed in, and he had been through a number of big blows. When winds reach or exceed 72 miles per hour or 63 knots, a storm is classified as a hurricane in which waves reach 45 feet and higher. They now faced these conditions.

McGrath had to brace his body, hanging onto the helm, leaning into the roaring wind and huge, froth-whipped waves, up which *Aguila* charged at forty-five degree angles into a fury of flying foam and spray, raging rain driven horizontally in painful bullet-like streaks tearing into his face as he struggled with the wheel. He kept checking on his safety line to make sure it was securely in place and did the same for Elena's.

Elena huddled on the cockpit seat up against the outside cabin wall, shivering from exhaustion, her shaking feet bracing her body against the steep incline of the waves, chin tucked down into her foul-weather gear. One hand clutched the cabin entrance handrail and the other the bottom of the cockpit seat. They could not talk to each other without screaming, so overpowering was the wind's roar.

The winds had picked up steadily since Cojimar. They soon had entered a new and fearsome domain, gale forces driving against them, spray like shotgun pellets, impossible to determine where air began and the sea ended. It was a dark, roaring hell made all the more terrifying by forked flashes of exploding lightning, followed by teeth-rattling thunder that could not be heard—but felt—over the hurricane's own overpowering noise.

In the battering maelstrom, McGrath struggled desperately to keep *Aguila* upright. He took the tall waves that towered over them at an angle, avoiding the more perilous direct angle approach. The latter risked having the boat ride up a wave at such a steep angle that the bow could rise straight up vertically—only to fall back over the stern. Or it could ride up and over the crest of a huge roller only to slide down the back side at such a steep angle as to plow the bow into the trough. If this happened, the following wave could flip the stern, pitchpoling it over the bow, end-over-end. Equally fearsome was the prospect of surfing down the backside at such a speed and steepness that the rudder could lose its grip, causing the boat to go broadside to the wave and take a knockdown, winding up rolled over and over— totally out of control.

Sails had long ago been taken in, mainsail wrapped securely on the boom, the roller-furling genoa pulled in completely. The wind was so fierce and unrelenting that even a shred of sail was out of the question. Under bare poles, McGrath was trying to exploit *Aguila*'s buoyancy as their one hope for survival. As he struggled, words in a Joseph Conrad novel came to him. One of Conrad's captains had said in such a storm that it was imperative to, "Keep her facing it . . . Facing it—always facing it— that's the way to get through . . . and keep a cool head." Keep a cool head, he thought. Easier said than done in hurricane conditions like this.

Just after sunrise, in an effort to stabilize the bow and keep it pointing into the wind, to prevent the *Aguila* from being swept backwards out of control and risking a breach, McGrath rigged a sea anchor to the bow. Leaving Elena at the wheel, he had gone below, gathered the two mattresses off the bunks, slit them with a knife so that water could get through and make them work like a giant sponge, and tied them together. Next he stuffed several cabin cushions into a large sail bag and tied the two mattresses and stuffed sail bag together, hauled the stuff out the cabin, dragged it down the writhing foredeck on his hands and knees, grasping safety lines, out to the wildly pitching bow.

There, barely able to see what he was doing in the torrential driving rain and stinging spray, head turned away from the gale, he secured the cabin cushions and cabin mattresses to *Aguila's* anchor. He released the whole mass overboard, using the anchor, chain, and anchor line as the main line for everything, and began to let it slide down off the bow. He remembered to run his "sea anchor" line through the bow chock and tied rags around the line where it ran through the chock in order to try to prevent friction and fraying of the line. As the *Aguila* moved backward under the wave action faster than the "anchor," he soon was able to let out 300 feet or so in order to increase the drag and slow the vessel's retreat with the wind and onrushing giant crashing waves.

Elena's hands shook so much from fatigue and cold that she could hardly hang onto the helm. She told McGrath more than once that she was fearful that at any moment she would see him pitched off the bow into the roiling sea. Then, she asked, God knows, what would I do?

Giant waves now reached fifty feet, some higher— monstrous walls of green water, heaving, rolling, tumbling, mountains and valleys that the tiny boat climbed, then rode down, slowed somewhat by the sea anchor trailing forward off the bow. Weather obscured the horizon from the sky, and McGrath could see only flying froth and foam as tops of waves blew off like a roof separating from a tall building in a storm-whipped tornado. His heart was beating at a fearful pace, adrenaline rushing through every pore of his body, eyes squinting into the tumult to try to gain even a slim glimmer of the direction he hoped to steer. He looked from time to time at Elena, crouched down, white-knuckled. He gave her a half-hearted smile of encouragement now and then, but smiles were short and infrequent.

As best McGrath could make out from reading his compass and angle of the gale, the hurricane seemed to be moving in a west or northwest direction. The wind was coming out of the north, northeast—consistent with the counterclockwise wind direction of hurricanes. He suspected the gale was blowing them back in the direction of Cuba—how close they were to the island he did not know. But in the back of his mind was the gnawing ugly thought that they could wind up back in Cuba, maybe even crash somewhere on the island's north shore. He tried to repress such darkly unwelcome thoughts.

No one could have predicted what came next. No one could have seen it under such frightening conditions. Amidst the sound and fury, it was all he could do to keep the *Aguila* rising up the roiling green mountain-waves, trying to discern some sense of direction through roaring froth and foam. Suddenly, there it was—a rogue wave perhaps sixty feet high, a gigantic wall of water coming at them like a runaway freight train. McGrath only had time to estimate that they were at least thirty feet up the side of this towering, howling massive body of water and still climbing, when the top of the killer wave suddenly crested, breaking apart and sending tons of water thundering down on *Aguila*.

He clutched the helm with a death grip and screamed at Elena to hold on tight. His cries were muffled by the wall of water that surged completely over the boat and burst into a giant explosion. Just before the wave engulfed him, he thought he heard a distinct "crack" over the fury that raged about them, but he was not certain. He looked wildly at Elena, who did not see it coming, and may not even have heard him, so great was the din about them, her face buried in her foul-weather jacket. The wave crashed down with a force that wrenched his hands from the wheel, lifting and sweeping him away, his fingers pulled from their tight grip, body tumbling end-over-end in the confused sea around him, heart pumping, eyes open wide to the stinging salt water, his body floating free in the swirling melee about him.

He did not know how long he was under, but remembered gulping a huge gasp of air, when he saw the sea wall pouring down upon him. Under the water, he thrashed frantically for the surface, his heart pounding as if it would burst. But which way was up? He didn't know. He had never been as scared, petrified, in all his life. Alive in this wildly churning grave in the sea, he believed it quite possibly was over for him. This was it. Rebecca swam into his mind's eye, then Elena, who was somewhere out there. "So this is how they said it would be," he thought. He could hold his breath no longer. He felt his lungs would surely break.

Suddenly, he broke the surface. Air! He heaved in a giant gulp of air, but within the wild environment above water it was hard to believe the bellowing gasp that came from his own lungs. Floundering, convulsively gasping, he realized he was being pulled along in the water. He went under again, then popped up and grabbed another gulp of air. Was he dreaming?

The *Aguila*. Where was the boat? There. Down in front of him—not fifteen feet away below him in the trough of the wave. Then he remembered. His safety line. Yes. Still attached, he thought excitedly. He was being pulled along in the water by his safety line still somehow tied to the boat. He gulped in more air, along with sea water, which he choked on, vomited for a minute, then got hold of himself as another bolt of lightening lit the horror scene around him. He grabbed the safety line and pulled himself arduously forward. As he gained way, inch by inch, he thought of the danger of the unsteered boat hitting a wave at the wrong angle and flipping, sending him and Elena spinning under with it. He grit his teeth and even more fiercely fought his way hand over hand forward toward the stern.

"Neal, Neal," came a distant petrified voice. "Where are you?" He heard Elena's choked and muffled scream off to his right—not from the boat, but in the storm-driven waters.

"Here! Here! Hold on, Elena!" McGrath screamed through the churning sea, as he swallowed another gulp of salt water. "Hold on," he yelled as loudly as he could.

As the boat surged ahead, McGrath pulled himself hand over hand through the green foam, struggling, fighting, inching his way closer and closer to the stern, which now began to ride up the side of the next incoming roller, trailing McGrath and Elena along behind. Under normal circumstances hauling a person back on board a sailboat can be a major problem. Unless the vessel has a boarding ladder, a permanent stern transom ladder, or lifting tackle of some type—assuming someone were in the boat to assist. Riding along beside the vessel, he knew he faced a major chore ahead, getting himself aboard and pulling Elena back into the cockpit.

Clinging tightly to his safety line as the boat rode up the next giant 40 foot wave, he suddenly realized all was not lost—at least not yet. In one great surge of energy, he managed to scramble aboard as the vessel crested over the top and started on its down-wave trajectory—stern low in the sea because the cockpit had filled with water.

Fortunately, he had remembered to close the cockpit door tightly.

Tumbling hip-deep into the cockpit water, he sloshed around, got his balance, located Elena's safety line and began to pull her in. It took every ounce of energy he had to shorten the distance between her and the boat. Following the same routine on the next down-wave run that he had used, he shouted, "In you come," as he hauled her in, sputtering and spitting water, her eyes wide open with fear and trepidation. She too tumbled into the sloshing cockpit, going under for a second. McGrath clutched her clothing behind the nape of her neck and pulled her up. As she fought for her balance in the heaving, water-filled cockpit, he clutched her close to him.

"Elena. Elena," he cried. "Are you all right? Are you hurt?" he said, hugging her.

"No, I'm not," she moaned, terrified. "No," she shouted, her soaked hair streaming down in her face, wiping the salt from her eyes with the back of her right arm. "I think ... I think ... I'm OK. ... God I was so scared."

"Me too," he shouted. "We've got to try to get some of this water out," he yelled.

He let go of her and grabbed the wheel, yelling over the howling confusion. "Untie the bucket under the cockpit seat. Use it to bail out the water."

She nodded her head in agreement.

"Good God," McGrath then shouted. "Look at the mast!"

They stared in disbelief at the horrible mess and damage done by the killer wave. The mast had cracked completely in two and now one section floated half in the frothy sea, rigging entangled in a mess over the boat and overboard. The forestay had snapped free, dragging the roller-furling genoa in the churning sea, its top still attached to the head of the severed mast. The cabin top, however, remained intact, and McGrath could see no visible holes in the deck or hull. But the cabin compass had been ripped from its floor base and now was sinking to the bottom of the sea. Their safety harnesses were still snapped in place

Elena, regaining her breath, feverishly started pitching overboard one bucket of water after another. McGrath lashed down the wheel, trying to get control of *Aguila* to aim her on the required 30–45 degree angle up the wave heads. Doggedly he began the hellishly difficult task of trying to get loose lines out of the water, while thinking frantically how to secure the mast so that it did not gash into the boat's hull.

"Keep bailing," McGrath shouted.

It was shortly after mid-day. Just an hour before, the storm had raged at its highest wind-lashing, foam-flying, wave-crashing, howling velocity. Elena, exhausted, worked feverishly, tossing buckets of water overboard, trying to reduce the water level in the cockpit. McGrath, worn down by steering the boat up one perilous wave and down its back side, was certain he could not hold together much longer. Hour after hour, in conditions so fierce that he could see no reference point of sky and sea—only turmoil and boiling monstrous ocean about him—he battled the fury, trying to keep mind and body in some semblance of control, as fragile as that control might be.

But now something absolutely remarkable happened with the weather. Numb to the fury of roaring wind and driving rain, they saw the nightmare of a storm suddenly recede. Fading into the distance, the thunder's echo moved farther and farther away. Shortly they found themselves in an unnatural quiet, as wind died to ten miles per hour and the heavy rain stopped, except for a steady drizzle. At once the sky cleared, and they caught glimpses of the sun through cloud fragments hanging overhead—as if they had entered a giant amphitheater of dark cloud walls.

In effect they were inside and at the bottom of a giant well—a low pressure area, the hub of the hurricane outside of which thousands of square miles of this gigantic engine of destruction swirled about them. Yet it was quiet where they bobbed around, although the seas were still wild and churning. The air had become sultry, an oppressive feeling as the temperature began to rise.

Elena wanted to remove her foul-weather gear, but McGrath warned against it. "But it looks like the storm has blown itself out," she said.

"No." McGrath replied. He pointed up at the score of birds flying around overhead. Sea gulls started to land on *Aguila*'s bow, gathering in growing numbers. Others tried to land, but it had become too crowded. "Listen," he said, "we've got about twenty minutes, maybe a half hour at best, before the wind hits again."

"What do you mean?"

"We're in the eye of the hurricane, Elena. In just a few minutes, we'll be struck by the other side—and the wind will come from the opposite direction."

"Oh, *my God*," she gasped.

"But one thing will be working for us. When the winds return, they'll be blowing us toward Key West—north, not south toward Cuba, which is the direction we've been travelling."

Elena smiled wanly back at him, a quizzical look on her face. "I guess we should be happy," she managed to get out.

"Look, we've got to ditch this mess of lines and sails and get rid of the broken mast. This stuff is going to do us serious damage unless we cut it loose. We'll float better if we can shove the whole load overboard. I'll work on that problem. You keep bailing, OK?"

"Right." She reached out for his hand, and as he did

so, he waded over the remaining water in the cockpit to her to hug her again.

He knew they had to work fast. If they were to be even remotely prepared for the hurricane force that lay poised to smash them, now only a short distance away, they must get a move on. Looking across the eye at the solid wall of violent wind and dark clouds boiling in the distance, a black tempest looming on the horizon, he frantically set to work.

Water in the cockpit now was below the entryway into the cabin, so McGrath was able to unsnap the cabin door without sending a rush of water down. He had secured it earlier to prevent water in the cockpit from pouring down into the cabin, so now it was possible to go below. He stumbled down the steps, found the toolbox, removed the wire cutters and climbed back out as swiftly as he could.

He went forward to the bow amongst the weary seagulls, most too exhausted to move away from his invasion of their territory, cut loose the roller-furling gear assembly from its bow connection, and tossed the whole mess overboard. He began working furiously on the shrouds. Got to keep moving, he thought. He urged himself on, aware of the distant thunder and wail of the approaching wall of storm growing louder.

After he had cut the port and starboard shrouds loose, he moved to the stern of the *Aguila* and snapped free the back stay. "Elena," he shouted, "I'm going to toss all this stuff overboard. It's better in the sea . . . less chance of the mast putting a hole in the boat! Can you give me a hand here." They heaved the whole tangled collection of stays, shrouds, mast, boom, sails, and most of the lines overboard, saving some of the line for future use.

"Keep bailing," McGrath said. "I'm going below to put the wire cutters away. He ducked his head, stooped low, and went into the cabin. It was only then that he noticed something he had not paid attention to before—

the cabin floor was under about four inches of water. "Oh my God, major leak. Shit. Shit. Shit," he muttered. He grabbed a flashlight from the tool box and began to look for the leak.

It was not hard to find. He saw the water running out from under the cupboard by the sink into the cabin. Opening the cupboard door, his flashlight beam found the hole punctured in the hull by God knows what. He grabbed a piece of sheet lying near the starboard bunk, ripped it into smaller pieces, which he stuffed into the hole. As the water seemed to have stopped coming in, he closed the cupboard door as tightly as he could and climbed back up the cabin stairs to the cockpit, securing the hatch. Next he tried to jump-start the engine, but to no avail.

The wall of violent winds from the other side of the hurricane was closer now. The seas began to rise, and in the near distance they could see the dark clouds and jagged lightning and hear the roar of whirling gales growing louder like some predatory beast. The birds, at first cocking their heads, grew restless, ruffling their feathers, and then lifted off into flight. They took off low and away from the approaching wall of violent storm and toward the center of the eye. McGrath remembered reading somewhere that sea birds have been carried from the lesser Antilles to New England in a hurricane's eye.

"Oh shit!" cried McGrath, as the storm bore down upon them.

"What's the matter?" Elena looked up, her eyes terror-stricken.

"We're lying broadside to the wind!" He shouted. "Got to get the bow into the wind! Otherwise we'll take a knockdown!"

"You mean we're going to turn over sideways?" she screamed.

"Yes . . . the boat will right itself, but we're gonna ship lots of water in the cockpit."

The seas were rising fast, and in a matter of seconds the hurricane and its awesome dark purple violent gusts would swoop down upon them. The outer edge of the fury was a stone's throw away.

"Check your safety line! Quickly!"

"Oh *God*," cried Elena.

"Hang on!" McGrath shouted, "we can ride this out!"

TWENTY-ONE

Atlantic Ocean = San Diego = Havana = Key West

The second half of the storm virtually duplicated the first. They took a vicious knockdown when the the eye of the storm passed and again the hurricane crashed down on them with a vengeance. The blow flung McGrath into the boiling sea, leaving Elena to thrash about with the *Aguila*. Miraculously, their safety lines held fast, and in an incredible twist of fate the bow came round into the wind, owing to the sea anchor.

McGrath, gulping for air, pulled himself through the sea by his safety line back toward the stern. Elena helped him aboard, and they got to work bailing out the cockpit. The leak McGrath had fixed stayed fixed, much to his surprise, so the cabin did not fill with water. About half way through their nightmare, another rogue wave rolled them, but they came 'round, and the two of them hung on to avoid being washed overboard.

The last remnants of the storm faded in the early morning and there they were—dismasted, dead motor, no radio. The hurricane moved slowly but steadily beyond their small craft on up the U.S. East Coast, pounding into North Carolina. Seas remained high, carrying the *Aguila* up and down 15–20 feet waves, but the sea anchor kept them facing into the wind. As the storm subsided, McGrath helped Elena down into the cabin. Elena found a couple of towels and some clothes in one of the overhead lockers in a waterproof sea bag. They stripped, slipped on dry T-shirts and pants and tumbled into bed, where they wrapped themselves around each other after sharing a bottle of water. There they drifted in and out of sleep.

McGrath was in love with Elena. Not the deep, soulful love he had with Rebecca, the love that develops over years, tested and true, shaped by the sharing of mutual events through time. This love was new and fresh, exciting, spawned by braving the elements together and, so far, by near misses from death itself.

Back out in the cockpit, the sun had started to rise on the horizon, when a vessel appeared in the distance, steaming rapidly over the waves toward them. At first, they panicked, thinking it might be Cuba's Coast Guard, but a binocular check laid that fear to rest, because McGrath could make out an American flag flying off the stern. It was a fishing boat, riding authoritatively up the waves and down into the troughs, drawing closer by the minute. When it was a hundred yards off, its crew members had gathered at the starboard side, waving and shouting at them. Moments later its captain asked them to identify themselves and if they were OK.

"Yes." McGrath gave his nationality and said they had lost radio and GPS. Nobody injured but they needed food and water.

He told the captain that he was with the U.S. government—that Elena had information that needed to be reported. He gave him Sam Goodwin's name and number where he could be reached. They needed to get to Washington, D.C. as quickly as possible. Could they get that information to the coast guard?

Yes, came the reply. They were about thirty nautical miles southeast of Key West. He would inform the coast guard. They should be here under two hours. McGrath and Elena caught the sandwiches and fruit tossed aboard.

As they faded off into the gray, cloud-streaked, horizon, Elena snuggled back into McGrath's arms in the cockpit, sharing food and water. Things were looking up, they agreed. But Ramiro remained of dark concern. Would they be safe in South Florida?

Moreno awoke at seven-thirty in the morning and went immediately into his disciplined exercise routine. He completed one hundred push-ups, an equal number of sit-ups and a fifteen minute karate workout, practicing several kicks at which he excelled.

His exercise finished, he took an ice-cold shower that left him invigorated. As he dried himself off, he looked into the full-length mirror and smiled as he flexed his shoulder muscles. Dropping the towel, he pounded his rock-hard stomach several times in a karate hand-chopping motion to get the blood circulating. He got dressed—Levis, dark blue polo shirt, running shoes— combed back his dark black hair in its ponytail, placed a bright red tie band around it, and went out for breakfast.

He returned a short time later and removed the television camera from the knapsack. He carefully took it apart piece by piece, firing mechanism in its various components, each of which he laid on a clean towel on the bed. With the pieces spread before him, he oiled and cleaned the calibrated barrel, firing assembly, and metal device used for the trigger mechanism. He cleaned the photo site—the camera lens—and looked through it to practice how to fix his target when the right time came.

Satisfied, he carefully put the "camera" back together, piece by piece in precisely the correct sequence. His work was that of a professional, a man completely at home and in charge of his weapon. It calmed him to work with the weapon. Finally, he wrapped the camera in felt material and packed it in his knapsack.

He returned to the used car dealer in the early afternoon and picked up his Toyota Camry. From there he headed for the shopping mall down the highway, pulled in and used the public telephone to place a call to Cuba. After two disconnects, his third attempt made it.

"Hello?" came the answer at the Cuban end of the line. In their coded language, Moreno explained to Ramiro that he now had wheels and would begin his trip East this afternoon. He said that he would call again in two days. Ramiro in turn told Moreno about the hurricane that had probably eliminated Elena and her professor friend.

By two-thirty in the afternoon, Moreno was on Route 10, headed east for Phoenix. So far, so good, he thought, the car ran smoothly. He had carefully studied the maps for this trip He glanced at himself in the rearview mirror to check his slicked-back ponytail. He grinned and returned his dark eyes to the road ahead, a firmly confident smile on his face. All in all, he was satisfied this trip would prove historic.

Army General Carlos Céspedes, Castro's chief of staff, was an imposing six foot two, athletic build, dressed in a crisp olive green military uniform. He sat at the head of the table in the situation room of Cuba's Central Committee Headquarters at the Plaza de la Revolución. He had dark bushy eyebrows, deep set dark eyes, large ears that stuck out like those of an alert Doberman pinscher, and short-cropped wavy black hair. His assistant, Manuel Rincón, smaller in stature, slouched shoulders, half-closed eyes with a little moustache perched above his upper lip, sat languidly next to him. The two had been together since the days they fought against Batista, closely allied with Castro and his brother, the two top leaders of the country. Céspedes and Rincón in many ways served as alter egos to the Castro brothers in running Cuba. Rincón, however, lacked Céspedes' charismatic personality, political clout, and physical presence, despite his high ranking political role.

Outside the Situation Room, in which high-level officials regularly gathered for key policy meetings, they could hear the subsiding wind whistling softly around the closed window edges. Paper and debris lay strewn across the plaza below. Restlessly awaiting people to seat themselves, Céspedes shifted his weight in his chair. He casually looked at his watch, which he wore with its face on the inside of his wrist, scrutinizing and greeting each person who entered.

Whenever Ramiro saw Céspedes in sessions like these, he was reminded of a giant Komodo dragon—a big lizard peering out of his hole waiting to devour some unfortunate prey that happened to stray into his territory. A wary lizard whose job was to represent the interests of his boss, Cuba's supreme leader, *el líder máximo* as they called him, and that made him dangerous. Ramiro always reminded himself to be on the alert around this guy.

"Good morning, General Ramiro," Céspedes said, when Ramiro entered the room. "You look quite well today."

"Good morning," Ramiro answered in his best deep-toned voice, his face a mask of respect and deference. He smiled amicably, hiding the rising tension he felt in his stomach in the presence of this once long-time friend.

Today was an unscheduled Tuesday morning meeting of the Political Bureau, Cuba's top political elite, summoned for post-hurricane reports and, yet again, to go over some details for the upcoming Territorial Troop Militia exercises. On the table before the group were bottles of mineral water and a variety of American brand soft drinks, Coca-Cola the favored drink, imported through Mexico.

Around the table sat Ramiro's boss, Division General Miguel Santos, chief of the Ministry of Interior; three of the five vice-presidents of the Council of State, who held posts in the Council of Ministers; two more division generals of the Revolutionary Armed Forces (FAR), who were members of Cuba's Council of State and first vice ministers in the Revolutionary Armed Forces. Well, Ramiro thought, we've got the whole fucking power group here. Castro still insists nothing gets done unless he personally supervises every fucking detail, and there sits Céspedes his toady. What a colossal waste of time. Céspedes sticks his fucking fingers into everything and typically fouls it up big time. Ramiro's lips tensed for a fleeting moment, then he forced himself to relax. He was painfully aware he had to watch himself. He knew, as did everyone here at the table, that neither Castro or Céspedes took criticism lightly. Several of his guerrilla *compañeros* had "disappeared" after publicly disagreeing with him in the early days of the revolution. So he would have to treat Céspedes with kid gloves. Send no negative signals back to the top dog.

Céspedes, as Fidel wanted, dominated these meetings. He and he alone orchestrated the line of thought. He set the agenda, formulated responses to all issues raised. To try to shift the direction of inquiry, raise questions, or suggest alternate policy guidelines would be folly. To push one's point beyond his tolerance level would be insane. You did not challenge him. Not even those in the inner circle. You basically sat and listened, Ramiro thought. He could play this game with the best of them.

Céspedes opened the meeting by reading aloud from the most recent weather report handed him by Cuba's National Weather Service. In barely audible words he read that the hurricane had passed, and the barometer was rising rapidly.

After the post-hurricane reports, Céspedes shifted gears. "This storm is ... is ... may be ... symbolic ... of our current time of troubles, my friends," he intoned. Scratching his chin, he shifted his weight to one side in his chair, raised his left arm and waved his hand across the air as he spoke, heavy perspiration darkening his olive green fatigues. You could hear the starch creak in the newly pressed uniform as he shifted his weight yet again, cocked his left eyebrow, and pointed his left arm and index finger above his head in one swift circular motion. "I do not have to remind you that we are in a period of turbulence and face threats to our revolution ... most certainly ... to our future," he added defiantly.

They all knew he was referring to all the buzz about a possible U.S. invasion under Washington's right-wing leadership.

"The U.S. has never been more threatening than now, in these times of trouble," Céspedes went on. Never has any U.S. administration been more insolent and threatening than this one," he blasted. His eyes opened wide as he squirmed in his chair, both hands now waving in the air.

Ramiro stiffled a yawn.

"We got to tighten our national security. General Santos ..." he said, at which point Division General Santos straightened up in his chair, neck muscles tightening as he bit down hard on his back teeth, his face reddening. Céspedes had his attention. "You must, I repeat, *must* root out all signs of internal corruption in the Interior Ministry. You and I both know what we are talking about. We have discussed this matter before. I can tell you honestly that Fidel's patience is wearing thin. Do I make myself understood?" His voice had increased in volume.

"*Sí General*. Absolutely clear." Santos was sitting ramrod straight, smiling broadly at Céspedes. "I will deal with these problems with a firm hand. Rest assured, sir." It was normal for Céspedes to use a public forum to embarrass staff.

Still, Santos took to heart the thrust of this criticism. Recent weeks had seen at least three defections by highly placed Cuban officials, who wound up in Madrid or Washington, loaded with incriminating evidence of corruption in high places. This was vigorously publicized in U.S. newsprint and electronic media. The General did not have to be reminded that he himself, as well as his wife and children, had been identified in the U.S. and Western European press as leading *la dolce vita* when they travelled abroad. Others in his Ministry had been cited by defectors as skimming hard-to-get consumer goods imported from Mexico and Panama.

"General Morales," Céspedes barked, "We are promoting you from alternate member to full member of the politburo, and appointing you head of the Committees for the Defense of the Revolution. We owe you a round of applause for this well-earned promotion." They applauded vigorously, as General Morales's shoulders stiffened and his back became ramrod straight. His face flushed with pride.

This new promotion, each politburo member knew, signalled a tightening of political repression. By placing a military leader behind the CDRs those old grassroots neighborhood watchdog committees, whose duty was to check on anything suspicious going on in their blocks, became strengthened. Long noted for their prying eyes, the committees now would act with military-backed clout against anyone acting suspiciously.

Castro was tightening national security, no doubt about it.

"General," Céspedes said, cocking his head sideways again, narrowing his eyes in Morales' direction and waving his right hand across his chest, "I have one other point to raise at this meeting. A small point. Nevertheless significant." His acid tone of voice indicated a distinct mood shift.

"Yes sir?" Morales replied quickly and nervously.

"You know, General—better than anyone else—that military unity and loyalty is absolutely required during this difficult period."

The general nodded yes, but they could tell from his nervous body language and twitch in his left eye that Morales was apprehensive of this attention.

"Good. Now then, I have reports that some general staff officers lately have expressed personal opinions about the direction of our revolution—particularly about our reform process, which they see as not moving as swiftly as they would prefer. From my reports," one of which he picked up and glanced at, ". . . some have attracted public attention. They have set themselves up as special problem-solvers The question is: how must we react to such activities?"

They soon reached a unanimous decision. They voted to instruct General Morales to take necessary steps to end the matter immediately. On that note the meeting adjourned.

Ramiro's pulse raced. General Herrera's name was not mentioned, but it was clear that Fidel was displeased with Herrera's popularity and public adulation. Displeased? Furious was more likely. Herrera's popularity threatened Fidel's. That vain sonofabitch, Ramiro thought. What if they arrest Herrera? Would Herrera talk? Ramiro's mind leaped to Internet speed, calculating odds that Fidel might nail Herrera before the coup.

Ramiro wiped his sweaty palms on his pants under the table. Jesus, he thought, I'm starting to act like Victor. That thought disturbed him nearly as much as Herrera's situation with Fidel.

They arrived at the coast guard station in Key West, Florida, in the early afternoon. McGrath and Elena, wearing clothes from the coast guard cutter, were escorted to a debriefing room after they berthed the *Aguila* at a temporary docking area. Processing went smoothly, just as McGrath had expected. Goodwin confirmed McGrath's story and was sending someone down to pick them up. The coast guard simply needed to pick up some odds and ends at this point, including a check of McGrath's battered passport to confirm his identity.

At the outset of their debriefing, the coast guard debriefing team looked at McGrath and Elena in stunned disbelief when McGrath described the hurricane and demasting. "But why would you leave Cojimar in a storm?" they asked him. "Didn't you hear the weather reports?"

"Yes, we followed the weather reports, but Havana believed the storm had stalled some distance away and in all likelihood would veer off to the northwest—away from Cuba."

"The boat belongs to a friend of yours, Elena?"

"Actually it's my uncle's boat. So we decided it was now or never and just sailed away."

The officers sat there, leaning forward in enthralled interest, slack-jawed, as McGrath described their experience in the eye of the hurricane, and they peppered him with one question after another about their harrowing voyage.

After he answered all the questions and explained what it was like when the *other* side of the storm capsized them, Chief Petty Officer Alastair O'Sullivan said to him, "Listen, McGrath, if you ever want to join the

coast guard, come see me. I'll sign you up on the spot."
More questions and medical exams for both of them and
the processing wound down.

Finally, they were in the coast guard guest house.

"Enjoy your hot shower and rest," their escort said as
he left them in their suite.

As their escort closed the door behind him, Elena
looked at McGrath with worry in her eyes. "You think
we're safe here?" she asked. "I mean, you know, here we
are in the security of the U.S. Coast Guard, but what
happens when Ramiro finds out we're still alive? He has
agents everywhere, right here in Key West, I'm sure."

"I've been thinking about that problem, too," Mc-
Grath said, as he pulled her close to him. "One thing's
for sure," he said softly. "Goodwin no doubt has given
the coast guard specific instructions that no word of our
arrival should get out. The bigger question is the fishing
vessel that helped us. Did they say anything to anybody?" He tried to sound confident, but yes, they still
were in deep danger. If the The *Miami Herald* hit the
streets with their hurricane adventure, it would be aired
clear across the Straits of Florida to radio and television
in Havana. Ramiro would know exactly where they
were and what he must do.

Ramiro called the meeting to order at 10 P.M. Victor, all
ears and ever alert, was there along with two other generals in on the coup.

Quintero had returned from Colombia and would
now report to Ramiro on his meeting with Esteban. The
group had gathered for dinner, drinking beer while they
waited to be served, the aroma of black beans, rice, and
fried plantains wafted out from the kitchen down the
hall. Ramiro had put on Cuban music as background to
mask their conversation. They were all dressed in civilian clothes, light linen trousers and colorful flower-
printed *guayaberas*, and each smoked a dark black

Cuban cigar, rich tobacco smoke mixing with the aroma of garlic and oil.

"So how did the trip go?" asked Ramiro. "Hope you didn't spend all your time chasing women."

"No, sir," replied Quintero, self-importantly, smiling under his thin little moustache, trying to put his shoulders back and stretch up taller. "This trip was all business."

"Good," Ramiro responded, taking a drag on his cigar.

"You should have seen Esteban's safe house, sir," Quintero said. "A palace, but guarded like nothing I've seen before. They jammed me into a car, blindfolded. When we reached Esteban's place, you could trip over the guards just getting to the front door."

"Interesting," answered Ramiro, watching Quintero like a hawk.

"Of course, in his business, he's got to be protected. After all, he's the *Numero Uno* drug dealer in Colombia. The Colombian government's really after his ass. So are other Colombian drug dealers who say he's cut into their territory. I'd have my carcass covered with guards too."

"What was it like inside?"

"Well, I can say he gave me the red carpet treatment. You know, like we give the dealers when they come here. He had a cook fry me up a bunch of steaks and pork chops, good beer, and they even served chorizos and eggs for breakfast! Quite a feast."

Ramiro did not smile.

"Anyway," Quintero went on, "I negotiated with him *precisely* as you instructed." Quintero was at his greasy best in this type of situation, when he had information he knew his boss valued.

"Yes?"

"Basically speaking, it comes down to this," Quintero said, affecting a posture of authority, toying with his words ever so slightly to lend them even more credibility. "Esteban himself wants to come over to take a look at our operation at this end. You know, satisfy himself we can handle the increase. He's set to go if he's pleased with things at this end."

"Good," replied Ramiro. "What else?"

At this moment the two waiters brought in the hot plates of food and conversation switched to baseball and fishing, then resumed when the waiter had returned to the kitchen.

"Esteban's impressed with our operations," Quintero said. "Likes doing business with us. Says we are reliable and efficient."

"Doing business with someone who knows your product makes life so much easier, no?" Victor said, pouring himself another beer.

"I gave him a good sales pitch," said Quintero. "But he did have some questions."

"Oh?" Such as?" asked Ramiro.

"Well, essentially," Quintero said. "Esteban asked if this drug expansion was OK with our top guys. Well, more bluntly, he wanted to know how high up this business was cleared."

"So what did you tell him?"

"I told him what we agreed to say," answered Quintero. "That our operations were cleared straight to the top—approval at the highest level. I asked Esteban how he thought all those planes could come into our restricted air space—even in broad daylight—if they weren't cleared at the top. I assured him that the Ministry of Armed Forces, directed by our commander-in-chief's brother, gave the direct orders for Colombian planes to fly into our air space, and that we could hardly do this business without the knowledge of Castro himself."

"Good," responded Ramiro. "That's what we want him to think. If he's so confident about our capability to transship his drugs, did he say how much he is willing to supply?"

"As much as we can take," Quintero answered. "He's

just a little concerned that the feeder boats from Key West and Miami will have a safe haven here—and he'd like to look over security arrangements for his planes. Said he'd talk money when he arrives."

They discussed the drug operation for another hour, then turned to the next subject foremost on their minds.

Ramiro introduced it. "I've got bad and good news about Elena and McGrath," he said. "First, the bad news. It looks like they got off the island by way of Cojimar. No doubt used Elena's uncle's sailboat. It's missing from the Cojimar marina. Two of our men were killed right there at the marina, and one of our motor pool cars is wrapped around a palm tree and burnt to a core. Another man is missing. It all adds up. Missing sailboat. Dead bodies at the marina. Let's hope Elena and McGrath drowned in the hurricane," he added darkly.

A knock at the door sent Victor to it, where someone handed him a note. He read it, looked surprised, smiled, and came back to the table.

"What is it?" Ramiro said tersely.

"New development," Victor said.

"Well . . . don't just stand there, dammit. What is it?" Ramiro snapped.

"Elena and McGrath were not drowned in the hurricane," Victor said. "They've turned up in Key West. Alive and well. Rescued by the coast guard. This just came through from our contact there. It's the big news in Key West today."

"Well, well, well," Ramiro said, eyes gleaming, taking a long draw on his cigar, drumming his fingers on the table. "So we go to our backup plan."

"Right," Victor replied.

"Telephone Miguel immediately. He'll give our friends a proper welcome."

"Take them alive?" Victor asked. "We need to know what they've told the CIA before we kill them, no?"

"Obviously," Ramiro said sarcastically. "But that may not be possible. Besides, maybe they haven't contacted CIA yet. If that's the case, we can eliminate them."

"What about McGrath's friend?" Victor asked. "He may still be here in Havana. Our report from Key West mentions only two survivors, unless he went overboard in the storm."

"The lawyer's checked out of his hotel. He's not all that important. Still, let's keep an eye on the airports for him. Our main objective now is to eliminate Elena and McGrath. Go ahead, Victor. Call Miguel."

TWENTY-TWO

Key West-Flagstaff-Havana-Washington, D.C.

It had been a sensuous night for McGrath and Elena, a Key West kind of night that Mr. Ernest Hemingway himself would have liked. They shared long caresses and intoxicating kisses, lay wrapped in each other's arms, contented, talking, laughing, drifting off, awaking to the wonder of it all over again. McGrath awoke now and again to gaze at her as she slept peacefully, inhaling her scent, trailing his fingers along the lines of her body, relishing every moment of intimacy. He could scarcely believe this enchantment of her coming into his life.

It was difficult to leave the bed when they awoke at sunrise. Still, McGrath was restless that their CIA escort would not arrive until later in the morning today. It was critical that they talk to Goodwin as soon as possible. As he and Elena headed for the shower, he found himself preoccupied with Don. Had he gotten out of Cuba yet? He wanted to let Don know that they were alive and well.

They checked in with the security officer at coast guard headquarters and walked down the palm tree-lined street to the House of Pancakes. The minute they entered the half-filled dining room, they saw the headlines blazoned in The *Miami Herald* laid out on the counter: "Couple Survive Hurricane in Escape from Cuba."

"Neal, look at this," Elena whispered. The story detailed how a gutsy man and woman had managed to live through the storm in a dismasted sailboat without motor or radio. Names withheld pending further investigation.

"The fishing boat," McGrath said. "They must have leaked this stuff."

"You know what this means," Elena said in a whisper, looking around the busy dining area.

"Ramiro knows we're here. Radio and TV Martí will jump on this like hogs at the feeder. Broadcasts to Havana all day long."

"A story everybody loves in Miami," Elena murmured, leaning close to McGrath. "American man meets Cuban woman. Delivers her from Cuba's communist grip."

"*Beautiful* Cuban woman," McGrath interrupted, smiling.

"No, wait," Elena interrupted. "A Cuban woman who works for Havana's highest security agency. They fall in love. They borrow a sailboat, flee the island . . . and . . . well, maybe *escape* is a better word. So Ramiro now knows," her eyebrows arched in concern, her arm in McGrath's as they followed a waitress to an open booth.

"Ramiro for damn sure has connections here in Florida."

"Dead on," she said, as she glanced nervously around the dining room. "Makes sense. Drugs flow in from Colombia, transshipped to the U.S., arrive right here in

Key West or somewhere up the Keys, maybe Miami. That would mean . . ."

"That Ramiro has contacts here in Key West, certainly in Miami," McGrath said, completing her sentence.

Later, as they finished a hefty round of pancakes, orange juice, and two cups of coffee each, exploring alternate possibilities about Ramiro, they heard the thudding of an incoming helicopter. The heavy pounding engine noise grew louder, and just then a coast guard-enlisted man appeared inside the restaurant entrance, spotted them, and walked over smartly.

"Morning folks. Your ride to Miami's here," he said, smiling, extending his hand. He opened the door for them, and they could see the SH-60F Sea Hawk helicopter settle onto the giant bull's-eye landing pad two blocks away, kicking up a sandy windstorm.

McGrath knew enough about helicopters from his stint at CIA to recognize this one as the standard carrier-based, anti-submarine warfare model now used not only for ASW work but for search and rescue missions. The man in a light tan suit who stepped out of the helicopter carrying a briefcase ducked low under the still slowly turning giant blades. He walked toward the coast guard headquarter's building.

Across the street, at an angle neither McGrath nor Elena could see plainly, a short, dark haired, middle-aged Latino sat casually reading a newspaper on a steel black park bench. Built like a bulldozer, he wore chinos and a dark blue *guayabera*, Ray-Ban sunglasses perched over a thick black moustache. When McGrath and Elena headed for the coast guard buildings, he folded his newspaper, stood up and walked calmly to the flashy black Chevy Suburban parked across the street in front of the coast guard headquarters not more than a hundred yards from the helicopter pad. He opened the car door, climbed in, pulled a cell phone from the glove compartment and made his third telephone call in the past three hours since he first drove up to begin his watch. His eyes were fixed on McGrath and Elena as they entered the headquarters building.

By 11:00 A.M. their CIA escort, Phillip Shepard, had made arrangements with the coast guard and Bureau of Naturalization and Immigration to release McGrath and Elena so they could fly up to Miami with him, and from there to Washington, D.C. They came out of the two story gray building and walked toward the waiting helicopter, ducked low, and hunched over from the wind churned up by the rotating blades.

Across the street, the man in sunglasses slouched in the driver's seat, was back on the cell phone, speaking rapidly in Spanish, eyes locked on the coast guard helicopter lifting in a cloud of sand. In his phone conversation, he mentioned the name, "Miguel," more than once.

Minutes later, McGrath and Elena were 3,000 feet over the Florida Keys, looking down on the breathtaking view, seated just behind the pilot and co-pilot. They could see, through the large wraparound front window in the cockpit, the sun glistening off shimmering crystal green water below, dotted with fishing and sailing boats.

The Key West to Miami causeway cut through the diamond-sparkling sea below and stretched in a thin line miles into the distance. McGrath thought about the *Aguila*, left in coast guard custody pending further notice, wondering what would happen to her. With the thudding of rotor blades pounding the cabin interior, Shepard did not pester the two passengers with a bunch of sensitive questions. It was understood that Sam Goodwin would debrief them when they reached Washington. But Shepard, like the others, *was* intrigued by their story of the storm, because he too owned a sailboat, moored in a local harbor near Miami.

He was fascinated by their experience in bringing a

sailboat through a hurricane, especially what it was like trapped in the eye of the storm. "So birds are really trapped inside?" he yelled over the noise. "You must have been terrified. I know for certain I would have been numb." Two comments later and a question formed on his lips, Shepard suddenly sat up straight, staring in disbelief at the window next to Elena.

McGrath caught the look of alarm on Shepard's face, and his own heart unexpectedly jumped. He grabbed Elena's arm, turned to see what had transfixed Shepard, and sensed Elena's body stiffen. They both swiveled in their seats and looked out the window.

"Oh my Lord," Elena gasped.

McGrath murmured, "Jesus . . . what the hell . . . ?" Then it came to him instantly. He knew exactly what it was. A V-22 Osprey. Approaching with the speed of a rocket on what looked like a collision course.

They stared at the giant plane, with its helicopter-shaped body, racing toward them, now about five hundred yards away. Instead of huge rotor blades like a helicopter, it had one big black wing across the top of the body with tilt-rotor engines attached at the wingtips.

"It can fly straight ahead, do vertical takeoffs, or hover like a helicopter," Shepard shouted. "Depends on which way the engines are pointed. Flies a lot faster than this Sea Hawk."

"It's coming straight at us," Elena yelled.

"I don't like the looks of this . . . do you think . . ." McGrath shouted at Shepard, his words interrupted by the pilot, who also had spotted the incoming plane. "Hold on everybody," he yelled over his shoulder.

The helicopter pitched suddenly into a steep bank to starboard and down, diving just as the ominous black Osprey opened fire with its fifty millimeter machine guns. Evasive action came too late. Bullets ripped through the cockpit window, exploding plexiglas, pieces

flying everywhere, everyone ducking low, arms shielding eyes in all the noise and confusion. The next seconds,
McGrath would remember, his mind trying to figure out
what to do, were a wild blur of action. Incoming rounds
pierced the helicopter cockpit and struck the pilot in the
head and chest.

Blood splattered across the instrument panel and controls as the pilot slumped forward. The co-pilot was hit
on the left side of his body, and he passed out in his seat.
In the melee, Shepard, who barked out, "I'm a pilot,"
and McGrath unstrapped themselves and wrestled the
pilot from his seat. They parked his body in the space
between the front seats, while McGrath helped Shepard
wedge himself into the pilot's place, where he began to
struggle with the controls. McGrath looked over his
shoulder and shouted to Elena, "Hold on."

As Shepard fought the controls, trying to stabilize the
helicopter with all the racket and wild buffeting wind
ripping through the shattered cockpit window, they
heard, then saw, a flaming explosion and fireball off to
their port side and up above them. The impact rocked
the helicopter, and flying pieces of metal whizzed by
them, narrowly missing the helicopter, in what McGrath
thought looked like some kind of action-packed sci-fi
video war game. They watched, mesmerized, while the
rest of what remained of the the V-22 Osprey, twisting
pieces of smoking metal and debris, plunged through
the sky to the sea below leaving a wake of black smoke
trailing behind.

"My God!" Elena yelled, panic in her voice . . . what
the hell's going on?"

"Whatever it is, it isn't a welcoming party," McGrath
shouted back in the wind whistling through the cockpit.
Look," he said, "look there . . . off to starboard." It was
then they caught sight of two jets, which they later
learned were S-3B Viking tactical jets scrambled out of
Jacksonville Naval Air Station. They were faster than

than the V-22, fully geared up for electronic warfare and over-the-horizon targeting. They made two flybys, wagging their wings, close enough that they could see the pilots salute them from inside their cockpits.

"But how did they know where we were or that the Osprey was going to attack?" Elena asked.

"Long story," Shepard shouted back. "We've been tracking one of the top drug dealers in Key West for several months now. Guy named Miguel Contreras. Got onto him by fluke. Coast guard picked up one of those speed boat drug traffickers a few days ago, fellow named Orlando Sánchez. Bad luck for him . . . his boat broke down not far out from Key West. Coast guard plucked him and his contraband from the sea . . . got some solid information out of him. He put the finger on this guy Miguel Contreras. Not a big jump from there to electronic surveillance . . . found out about the Osprey they'd hidden away off on one of the cays. Drug money buys toys, y'know."

"This guy Miguel's gonna be pissed he lost his plane," McGrath shouted.

"You got that straight, buddy," Shepard shouted back. Now I gotta concentrate on flying this baby. We can talk more later. Hang on tight."

Moreno left Flagstaff early in the morning, taking care to settle his bill with cash, and now, having just checked his fuel gauge, knew it was time to stop and fill up. The trip was going well enough, he thought, highways what he had expected—wide, no potholes, with plenty of well-marked road signs. In Joseph City he spotted what he was looking for: a small, isolated station on the outskirts of town. He pulled up to the self-service pumps, filled the tank, and handed a hundred dollar bill to the attendant who came sauntering up to him.

"Gee, that's an awfully big bill, Mister," the suspicious redneck gasoline attendant said looking at

Moreno's ponytail and out-of-state license plates.

"What?" Moreno said. "What do you mean?"

"This bill's too big, Mister. I'm not supposed to take anything larger than a twenty. You probably don't have a credit card, I guess."

"No," replied Moreno. He was surprised that here in the land of the *Yanqui* capitalists they could not change a hundred dollar note. He looked the attendant hard in the eye to challenge him to get on with it. Moreno's temper was rising, but he knew he could not afford to make a scene. He wanted to get going.

"Well, I gotta check on this. I don't wanna get inta trouble." As the attendant walked away, Moreno heard him utter "stupid Mexican" under his breath.

On hearing that bigoted remark, Moreno was on the verge of jumping him, when he saw a second man standing outside by the door of the service station. He could hear the attendant walking away from him now talking out loud to the second man. Something about those "pushy fucking Mexicans." Then, "Jesus Christ, this guy's got some nerve. Puts a few gallons of gas in his goddamn car and shoves this hundred bill in my face. It's gonna take damn near all the change we got left. Look at that ponytail the guy's wearing. Probably doesn't know whether he's a girl or a boy."

Moreno got into his car and drove away, peeling rubber as he hit the highway.

As he sped away, it occurred to Moreno that this kind of bigotry no doubt was common in this part of the U.S., an attitude he was going to run into in his eastern/southern route across the country. Should he change routes and go up north and then east? No, he thought. Sure, it might mean less trouble, but he'd stand out more as a Latino male and it would take longer to reach his destination. No, he would stick with this southern route and be prepared to run into this kind of bullshit as he went along. He reminded himself keep his temper in check.

* * *

Samuels hurried across the hotel lobby toward the registration desk with his bags, eager to check out and leave. It was all over the radio that a couple had miraculously survived the hurricane in one piece in a sailboat from Cuba. Time for him to bust a move out of here. The hurricane had kept him restricted to the Espinosas longer than he wanted. He had spent most of day after the storm down at the Cubana Airlines office, not far away, trying to rearrange his flight back to Miami. By luck he nailed a seat.

Riding out to the airport with Juan, it was clear to Samuels that Havana had been hard hit by the hurricane. Broken electrical and telephone utility poles. Debris everywhere. He worried about his flight, but Martina had telephoned ahead, assuring Samuels that some flights *were* operating this morning—a least the one to Miami. He bounced along in the cab, in and out of potholes, down the main boulevard running off the Plaza de la Revolución, thinking about McGrath and Elena. He hadn't slept a wink after they departed. Now he needed to get off the island himself, but he was apprehensive he might be held on some trumped-up charge.

He snapped off some photographs, including three blown down billboards crumpled by the road and finished off his last roll of film. When the Jose Martí Airport came into view, he could see that a section of the roof of one of the airport's hangars lay broken in the branches of a large uprooted palm tree. Bushes and sections of tin sheets had been tossed up against building walls.

When they stopped in front of the terminal, Don thanked his friend profusely for all his great help and slipped him a hundred dollar bill. "Listen Juan, don't get out of the cab. Act like a normal taxi driver, OK? Watch out for yourself and Martina now. I'll try to get in touch with you. You have the satellite phone, right?"

"*Sí mi* amigo. Right there in the glove compartment."

'Good. Now later today I'd like you to contact Señor Kincaid and tell him I got out, OK? You have his telephone number, right?"

"*Sí*. I will call. Go with God." He reached over and shook Don's hand.

Don got out of the cab, grabbed his suitcase from the backseat, slammed the door and went into the airport terminal jammed with tourists eager to depart Havana.

When they called his flight, he joined the other excited passengers who quickly lined up in front of the door. His heart beat rapidly. He wanted on this plane. It was then that two Cubans in plain clothes stepped up to him, flashed their badges—which he did not have time to read—and asked his name.

"What can I do for you," he replied, his heart racing.

"You are travelling alone?"

"Correct." He sized up the two men, gave no ground and tried to stay calm. He smiled diplomatically. "That's correct. I'm returning to San Diego."

"*Aha*, I see," replied the larger man. "May we see your passport? And may we ask, where *is* your travelling companion, Señor McGrath, this morning? He is not returning with you?"

"That's right," Don replied. He shifted his knapsack on his right shoulder. "Unfortunately, I have to leave. Family situation in San Diego." What the hell kind of game is this, he thought. They had to know that Neal and Elena by now were in the U.S. He had heard the news himself on Radio Martí.

"Oh? And Mr. McGrath is still here?"

"Yes. Of course. As far as I know. I haven't seen him in the last few days. Apparently he has fallen in love. You know how that goes," Samuels said, winking at them, trying to appear as calm as possible.

They took what seemed to him an eternity. First, they checked his documents, slowly turning the pages. Ran a finger down the stamps. Looked him up and down. Ex-

amined his visa again. Thumbed through the passport a
third time. Clearly stalling for time. What were they
waiting for? The line inched forward. Some of the people stared inquisitively at Samuels. Others studiously
avoided eye contact. This was an all too familiar and uncomfortable scene.

"We will wait here," said the shorter man, while the
other shuffled over to the ticket desk. There he huddled
in muffled conversation with one of the ticket agents.
Don looked at the clock. His flight was about to depart.
He shifted his knapsack again and casually looked over
at the Cuban security agent. Perspiration ran down his
back. He was certain they could hear his heart beating.

Most of the passengers were now comfortably in their
seats aboard the plane. Finally, just when an agent prepared to close the door leading out to the aircraft, the security man returned and handed Don his papers.

"You are free to go." He gave Don a thin smile, stood
there and watched him hustle to the gate agent to have
his ticket pulled.

You bastards, he thought, racing for the plane. He ran
up the ramp, just as they were about to pull it away. At
the plane's doorway, he stopped for a minute to look up
at the viewing balcony. He could swear he saw Juan
waving.

Sam Goodwin was there when they entered the waiting
lobby at Andrews Air Force Base outside Washington,
D.C. McGrath recognized him immediately in his blue
polka–dot bow tie, white shirt, gray trousers and dark
blue blazer. Goodwin came over, held out his hand and
introduced himself to Elena.

"So this is the unidentified couple in The *Miami Herald*," he said, grinning.

It took over an hour to get back into Washington, using Route 4, and they made good time, because at this
hour of day most of the traffic was outbound, Washing-

ton's worker bees returning home to Maryland suburbs. As soon as they were in the car and driving, windows up, air-condition on, Goodwin said, "I got your message and package from the U.S. Interest Section, Neal. Quick thinking on your part, especially given the circumstances. Kincaid sent it up by diplomatic pouch. He's a good man. We knew right away from him that you had wound up in prison your first full day in Havana. We're going to want to hear all about that little incident," he said with a broad smile. Then a dark shadow suddenly crossed his face. "Terrible news about Larry Diamond. One of our best men."

"We liked him," McGrath said. "We were shocked to learn of his death."

"That sonofabitch Ramiro got to him," Goodwin said.

The Pig's Foot restaurant was jam packed as usual, noisy, but, again as usual, the waiters found a table for three. Goodwin, smiling, his ever-chipper self, turned the conversation to a nonsensitive issue. How in God's name did they make it in the hurricane? Were they OK? Any injuries? They *must* feel supremely lucky to be alive. They had to talk loud enough to be heard, but in "The Pig" nobody paid much attention to other conversations, because so many people were talking at once. McGrath was describing the eye of the storm when the waiter sidled up to take their orders: giant hamburgers with all the trimmings, oversized french fries, tossed salad, and three Sam Adams beers. Elena seemed, or at least McGrath thought, to be letting Goodwin and him carry the weight of the conversation. She understandably must be nervous and unsure, McGrath surmised, going on with his story of the hurricane.

They finished dinner and walked out onto the sidewalk in front of the restaurant. Goodwin looked quizzically at McGrath. "So what are your plans?"

"We're headed back to my place."

"I'll give you a lift?"

"Terrific. Thanks."

"Look, we don't want you hanging out at your house without protection. We aren't about to take any chances now. Ramiro undoubtedly has contacts here in D.C. I've requested two secret service agents to keep an eye out around your house. Don't be surprised, too, if you find yourself being tailed. We're gonna watch like hawks for awhile," he smiled. "With all that in mind, are you up to more conversation now at your apartment? Tomorrow morning of course we'd like you and Elena to come out to Langley for a debriefing."

McGrath looked at Elena. She nodded in agreement.

When they reached his townhouse, McGrath was pleasantly surprised to find his door key in its little box behind the shrubs and doubly pleased to experience no trace of that old melancholy when he opened the door. Elena, on the other hand, seemed ill at ease and hesitant. McGrath, sensing her discomfort, guided her in with a "Here we are. Make yourself at home."

McGrath asked Sam and Elena to go on into the living room and have a seat, while he went upstairs to open some windows to air out the place. In the bedroom he had a momentary pang of heartache when he saw Rebecca's photograph on the bureau, but removed it and put it in the top drawer behind his socks.

Back down in the living room, they resumed their conversation, which now had turned into a mini debriefing.

Goodwin looked at the two of them with a wry grin, ran his hand through his hair, and shifted his weight on the dark blue sofa. "I won't try to be coy," he said. "Like I said, Neal, we received your message from Kincaid. Great move on your part, good thinking, especially given the pressure you must have been under. So we knew that you were in that damned hurricane. You near scared us to death."

"Makes three of us," McGrath replied.

"So let's talk more about Ramiro. Elena, we can help you if you cooperate."

Elena seemed reluctant at first, but she gave in, as she realized that she had to deal with CIA, like it or not.

She quietly explained to Goodwin exactly what had happened the day she found the file cabinet lock open, how Ramiro had nearly caught her, and how he most certainly suspected it was she who had been into the files—which would explain why it had to be *Ramiro* who had tried to have them killed.

At that point, McGrath jumped into the conversation. He'd been waiting a long time for this opportunity. "Sam," he said, making a split second decision that now was the time to pounce, "you remember our initial meeting about my going down to Havana to contact Elena?"

"Sure."

"Well, after all we've been through, you owe me one. You told me then that Elena might be in trouble."

"Yes, sure, I did."

"Simple question. How did you have that information?" Elena looked on, and McGrath could not read a thing from her poker face, but she had a look in her eye that suggested that she'd be interested in hearing the answer to that question too.

"Elementary, Neal. It's just like I said then. We had an informant that knew Elena's uncle. Our informant told us that the uncle had alluded to the fact that his niece might be in some kind of jam over at MININT. Since we knew that MININT is a snake pit of infighting, we believed him. Turns out we were right—and a damn good thing you showed up when you did for Elena's sake. Right Elena?"

Elena smiled demurely and nodded agreement. Then she said, "He's right, Neal. I could be dead by now."

With that, McGrath accepted this original version of the truth.

Goodwin wanted to know more about the assassination attempt after the Tropicana. He leaned forward attentively as McGrath related the events.

"*Jesus*," Goodwin said, "what a *hell* of a story. You two must have guardian angels. Or else you are the luckiest people alive. I've seen a lot in my business, but this one takes the cake." He reached over to shake McGrath's hand and grinned broadly at Elena. "I just can't believe you made it, and here you sit, alive to tell the tale."

"It was *really* close, Sam." McGrath said. "But the freighter had us going too. Still, it paid off. We got the goods on that bastard, Ramiro."

In recounting the freighter event, the subject naturally turned back to Elena's discoveries in Ramiro's file cabinet. McGrath leaned forward and said, "Tell Sam about the file on Mexico. The one with that guy Moreno you told me about."

"Right. Umm, here's the thing . . ." and she went on to recount what she had found in the file cabinet's folders.

Sam looked at her. "Strange. What do you make of it?"

"It's curious, for sure. Now here's something else. I don't know for certain what it means, but as I told Neal, I saw a man with Ramiro, out on the plaza in front of our Ministry of Interior, the day after the file cabinet incident, who is a *known assassin*."

"So . . . and that means . . ." Goodwin replied, dark eyebrows arched.

"Just this. I saw a photograph of a man who is a well-known assassin. A Mexican. Name's Carlos Moreno. He's got a long dossier that explains his background. It was all in the files. He's the same man I saw with Ramiro."

"I still don't see what . . ." Goodwin said. "So what's the point?"

"About that same time, I had dinner with one of Ramiro's top assistants, a man named Quintero . . ." She paused for a moment. ". . . A disgustingly greasy little worm who brags a lot. Anyway, he tried to impress me and kept talking about this Moreno fellow, the *assassin*, the very words he used, who was visiting Ramiro. Quintero had been drinking a lot when he told me all this. I must confess I pumped him for information. He said Moreno was a Mexican. That checks with his dossier. Moreno's photograph was in the file that contained information about Mexico's president, and several newspaper clippings about his upcoming trip to the U.S."

"Interesting point," Goodwin interjected. "The Mexican president in fact *is* flying in to meet with our president."

"Quintero alluded to something big Moreno was going to do," Elena said, "something connected with Mexico's president. He said that Moreno's action would mean great things for Cuba and for his boss, General Ramiro. Said his action would have a huge impact on Mexico too."

"What kind of *action* do you think this Quintero meant?" Goodwin asked.

"I think he meant *assassination*. Makes sense, no?" Elena said.

"Assassinate?" Goodwin asked.

"Precisely," Elena responded.

"Assassinate who?" Goodwin asked.

"Mexico's president." McGrath said.

"Exactly," Elena said.

TWENTY-THREE

Caribbean Sea = Havana = Washington, D.C.

The sea's undulating swells gently lifted the fishing cruiser up and down to ancient rhythms, as seagulls circled in hopes of something tempting to make a dive.

Perfect day for fishing and swimming, a time to enjoy the more placid side of Poseidon's moods. People relish a days like this, with uniquely clear tropical skies after a hurricane. Unless you were the victim awaiting a horrible fate.

Two men stood on the stern, sun beating down, beads of perspiration on their foreheads, legs apart as they braced themselves to roll with the swell. Each man had one hand under the armpits of the third man dressed in bright orange coveralls, gripping him tightly so he could not escape. He was barefoot. What was remarkable about him was his composure under the circumstances. Despite what they were doing to him and the obvious thing that was about to happen, he remained in control of himself and in an odd sort of way acted as if he were in control of the others.

"This is a colossally stupid move on your part," he said through tight lips. "No way you'll get away with it. Think before you act. You're about to bring a ton of trouble to your country, gentlemen. Think of the repercussions. For Christ's sake, use your goddamn heads," he said. They all just stared at him and grinned menacingly.

Another man braced himself at the stern railing, trolling a thick line about a hundred and fifty feet out in the wake made by the boat's slow passage. He watched intently as the one foot long bright orange artificial bait attached to the end of the line splashed through the sea with an erratic motion he hoped would agitate the type of fish he was after. While trolling, he continued to chum the water by throwing out handfuls of meat chunks. Soon he turned to the others and announced in an excited voice.

"They are here."

The others turned to look at him as he pointed to the attack on the artificial lure, "I make it around five of them, sir."

The fish savaged the lure, clearly visible through the

translucent green Caribbean waters. It was a sleek, pike-looking predator about three and a half feet long, razor sharp fangs in the jutting lower jaw glistening as it mauled the lure.

"Barracuda?" asked the man in obvious command.

"Yes, General, big ones this time."

"Well done." Ramiro stood before the man in the outrageous orange get up, held by the two larger men. "You been fucking with us for a long time, señor. *Sí, por mucho tiempo.* Now we will show you why nobody . . . I mean *nobody* . . . fucks with General Ramiro. You were warned, no? You saw what happened to Señor Diamond, no? That, my friend, was a signal you refused to see. So? So now you pay the big penalty." Ramiro smiled. He placed one hand on the man's shoulder, as if in friendship. Then he spit in the man's face. "When they read your suicide note, *chico*, nobody's gonna for certain know what happened to you. You just . . . disappeared . . . into thin air . . . with no trail to follow." He smiled at the man who stared back at him with ice-cold eyes.

The victim suddenly lurched, tried to jerk away, like a bait fish attempting to shake the hook under its dorsal fin. As he struggled to pull free, his two guards dragged him to the stern railing. The man who had been trolling set the brake on the reel and secured the fishing rod. He reached down and picked up the bucket of days old fish guts and poured it over the man's head and body. The stench was overpowering as they lifted the bright-colored victim and hung him over the stern of the boat, then dropped him.

Somehow, his hands managed to catch the gunwale, and he kicked his legs in the air, staring up at Ramiro, trying to climb back aboard. One of the guards pulled his marlin spike from its holster on his belt, bent down and stabbed again and again on the dangling man's fingers. The victim let go, splashed into the water, and floated away from the boat, flailing frantically in his bright coveralls, as the trolling lure approached—with its great barracuda assailants.

The general stood at the stern and watched the barracudas put in a show worthy of their reputation as a danger to humans when provoked. The victim's erratic efforts to escape only infuriated the attackers more, the violence of their kill intensified by bright color and fish guts. Fangs went first for his thrashing legs and arms. Only seconds later they slashed at his head. The general, grinning, nudged the man next to him and pointed to an ear floating away from the watery war zone of mangled clothing, pieces of ripped flesh and churned up blood-red sea.

"They missed something," he said, chuckling. "But they will go back for it. They miss nothing. Attack like a well-drilled army. Such precision. Their mission is clear. No mistakes." He smiled broadly.

Soon the boat's engines revved up and they headed back to port. General Ramiro pulled out a cigar, walked over to a seat, sat down, and casually clipped off the end. He put it in his mouth to moisten it, lit up, and exhaled a trail of rich blue smoke. Gazing out to sea, giving in to the pleasure he sensed from what he had just witnessed, he was looking forward to getting back to "The Mansion," where two stunningly attractive young dancers from the cabaret show at the Riviera Hotel awaited him. And the best part of this, he mused . . . no more Señor Kincaid.

Ramiro needed the women. Getting rid of Kincaid helped, because when he learned that Miguel's Osprey attack on Elena and McGrath had failed, he flew into a rage and screamed about another fuck-up, as Victor stared back in controlled objectivity.

"OK, OK" he said after he had flung the chair across the room, nearly hitting Victor. "We can still nail them."

"How's that?" Victor asked.

"We let Moreno know. Give him another assignment when he's in Washington."

"Another assignment?"

"Elena and that sonofabitch McGrath. Let Moreno get rid of them."

"Tall order for one man," Victor said. "Even for Moreno."

"Maybe so, maybe not," Ramiro said in his low, now controlled voice. But our friend Moreno will have plenty of assistance."

"Oh?"

"Miguel and Bernardo. They will be in Washington with Moreno. Miguel has friends there too. I will call Miguel immediately." Smiling darkly, Ramiro had brushed by Victor, gone to his desk, sat down, and picked up his secure telephone. He dialed the number in Key West.

Toward evening Herrera pulled his Lada into the cramped parking space on a back street in Old Havana, got out, locked his door, and started walking down the narrow, dirty, cracked concrete sidewalk. His destination was about a block away, second floor of a rundown apartment building, home of Alberto Rivero—head the Yoruba Cultural Association of Cuba, the island's largest Santería group. This was not the first time Herrera had paid a visit to Rivero, a small, wizened old man with pale blue rheumy eyes, trembling hands, a well-known *babalawo*, a high priest of the Santería religion. The two men had met five times in the last month, because they shared a common interest: ridding the country of the Castro brothers.

Herrera, one of many Cubans who considered themselves good Catholics, but also practiced Santería and saw it as a vital part of the *patria's* identity, had good reason to meet with Rivero. Herrera had made it a point to establish a relationship with Rivero, because he had known for some time that Santería priests like him were angry with Castro for his shift toward favoring Cuban

Catholicism, underscored by Castro's sponsoring of two visits by the pope to Cuba. There had always been tension between the Catholic Church and Afro-Cuban Santería worshippers, stemming from Castro's playing each off against the other as a way to consolidate his support and undermine potential opposition. Inviting the pope meant for Santería leaders that Castro no longer honored their role in society and was returning the Catholic Church to its historic powerful role once played before the revolution.

Herrera knew that Castro had been a sharp *político* in dealing with religion since the early days of the revolution. Once Batista was overthrown, the fiery Cuban leader began to protect and encourage Santería, given its preexisting, powerful roots in a society with strong ties to Africa and its slave trade links with Cuba. Knowing that polytheistic African faiths resided in the Cuban soul, where Santería's specialized gods were hidden behind Roman Catholic saints, Castro allowed Santería cermonies to flourish. In return, Santería priests let it be known to followers that Fidel rode the horse of *Shangó*, lord of lightning, fire, thunder, and the dance—a unique and dramatic source for legitmizing Castro's power.

Herrera knew something else. *Shangó* arguably was the most popular orisha, or specialized god among Santería worshippers, owing to his romantic and flamboyant nature, his embodiment of passion, virility, and power. Hard-core Catholics were not at all pleased with Castro's pronounced support of Santería. They decried its widespread practice in private homes rather than churches, while the government denied Catholics their requests to take their religious processions out of the churches and into the streets.

Now Castro was turning back to the Catholics, and the *santeros* were prepared to withdraw their support of him. He would no longer ride the horse of *Shangó*. All this made Rivero a key player in Herrera's coup strategy. Bring Rivero aboard, the unofficial *santero* leader—and Herrera's men would have the support of Santería worshippers all across Cuba.

"Ahh, Julio . . . so good to see you," Rivero said, when he recognized who had knocked on his door. "Come in. Come in, my friend."

The apartment reflected what you would expect of Cuba's leading *santero*. Herrera glanced at the glasses filled with water, offered as appeasements to the spirits of the dead. He saw colorful statues of Santería orishas, one of Saint Barbara, in reality *Shangó*, standing on a mantel. On a table near where they sat lay a *tablero*, a circular board on which key items were cast, lying beside a *cadeneta*, a metallic necklace with dangling objects.

They exchanged formalities. They saluted the health of each other's families. They swapped a story or two about nieces and nephews, how the wives were doing, and the difficulties each faced in their occupations. Rivero complained that his biggest problem was lack of money by his followers to buy the animals needed for the sacrifices so critical to their faith. After all this, they got down to business. "The day of our deliverance is still the same?" he asked.

"Yes. Next Tuesday," Herrera said, confidently. You will hear about it on the radio and television. You are ready to go?"

"Julio, I can tell you this," Rivero said solemnly. "The moment the news breaks, our *babalawos* will be instructed exactly what to do. General Julio Herrera, Cuba's new president, will be the new rider of *Shangó*'s horse. You will inherit the mantle of leadership, Julio. Fidel and *Shangó* and no longer united. Afro-Cubans will support you, my friend, one hundred percent. You have our blessing."

As Herrera walked back to his car, he looked furtively up and down the street to make sure nobody had spotted him. When he reached his car and pulled out his keys to unlock the door, a terrifying thought suddenly struck him out of the blue. What if the Santería orisha, *Shangó*, had a fickle change of heart in the near future? What if *Shangó* decided to allow Castro to ride him again? That would be a terrible shift in fortune for Herrera and his conspirators, a catastrophic event. Herrera stopped dead in his tracks. He stared at his hand trembling on the door handle, riveted in place, deep in thought. It had happened before. *Shangó was unpredictable.*

Goodwin put down the telephone at 6:30 A.M. He sighed and took another sip of coffee. He pushed back his green office chair, stood up, and walked out of his office. It was located at the end of a main inner corridor with a string of offices, toward the last one at the end of the corridor occupied by his colleague, Kim McGinnis—specialist in Latin American politics, Goodwin's old friend, trusted ally inside the combative intelligence community, somebody he could trust. In the intelligence labyrinth, Goodwin knew one important rule: develop confidants to stay sane. He walked into McGinnis' office and shut the door behind him.

"Got a minute?" he asked.

"Sure thing," she said. She turned in her chair to face him. "Hey, you don't look so hot. How'd it go with Mc-Grath yesterday?"

"Great. He's all in one piece. A miracle he made it with Elena through that hurricane. Looks like he has hooked up with her. There's definitely something going on between them. She spent last night at his place."

"Oh? The whole thing's just unbelievable, isn't it?" McGinnis replied. "So what happens now?"

"Before we get into that," Goodwin said soberly, "I'm afraid I've got some bad news."

"Oh," McGinnis said, "Sounds bad. I knew it when you walked in the door."

"It is. Really bad. Kincaid's missing down in Havana."

"What do you mean . . . missing?"

"Just that. Hasn't shown up for work. They sent some-one over to his apartment, thinking he might be seriously ill or something . . . and they found . . . a suicide note."

"Suicide? Jesus, Sam. Why? How?"

"That's just it. He's not the kind of guy who would do something like that. Physically fit. Mentally balanced. No financial or personal problems we knew of, no nasty habits, great scores on his last polygraph. Damn strange. I don't buy the suicide for a minute. I think the note's a fake. Something else has happened."

"You mean something like what happened to Larry Diamond?"

"Exactly. I'll tell you this. If his disappearance leads back to Ramiro, then that guy's in for a real surprise. If it's internal war he wants, two can play that game."

"What's our Interest Section in Havana doing?"

"They've launched a full scale investigation. Oh, we'll get to the bottom of it, never fear, and when we do . . . someone's going to have hell to pay." Goodwin slumped down in the chair across from McGinnis' desk.

"We have our informants," McGinnis said. "Maybe they know something."

"We're already on that trail," Goodwin said.

The phone rang, and McGinnis picked it up. "Yes, he's here. Sure, you want to talk to him? . . . OK, here he is." She held her hand over the receiver.

"It's your secretary. She's on the line with one of your folks in Miami. They got a call from somebody in Ha-vana who wants to talk to you. They're going to patch it through." She handed the phone to Goodwin's out-stretched hand.

"Hello?" he said, then listened for two or three min-utes. "Uh-huh . . . I see . . . yes . . . yes . . . OK my friend . . . yes, I'm more than grateful for your call. Thank you very much. Yes . . . yes . . . I will let McGrath know. OK, *hasta luego*." He handed the phone back to McGinnis who replaced it.

"So?" McGinnis said.

"That was Juan Espinosa. You know, the guy that helped us so much in Havana. He called for two reasons. First, he saw McGrath's friend get on the plane and depart Havana. So that wraps up one loose end. Neal should hear from him soon."

"And the second reason?" McGinnis asked.

"Kincaid. Espinosa said he and his wife have a contact at our Interest Section. The place is buzzing with the mystery of Kincaid's whereabouts. Espinsosa says nobody understands how he disappeared."

"Jesus," McGinnis said.

They discussed Kincaid for another five minutes, then Goodwin said, "OK, let's get back to McGrath and Elena. Here's what we know." He related McGrath and Elena's story, all about Ramiro and the drug links, the freighter, attempt on their lives in Havana, and the part about a Mexican assassin that Elena was certain she had seen with Ramiro. "This man in Ramiro's office, Quintero," Goodwin said, looking at the report he held in his hand, "confirmed to Elena that Moreno was about to do something that will impact Mexico spectacularly and affect the fortunes of Ramiro and his office."

"So what do you make of it?" McGinnis asked.

"Hard to say. She did mention that Ramiro's file had several newspaper clippings about the Mexican president's upcoming summit meeting with our president. I want to explore the possibility that this Moreno really is who she thinks he is. She and Neal are coming over this morning. We have a full-scale debriefing laid out. I'm going to have her look at some photographs. Let's pull that file on terrorists in Mexico. Maybe Moreno will show up."

"You don't trust her memory or reasoning on this Moreno character?"

"No, no. It isn't that. I'd just like her to see the photo we have of Moreno. I want to be certain that the Moreno we have on file is the same man she saw. It would confirm his identity for all of us."

"Wouldn't it be interesting if Ramiro and this so-called assassin Elena thinks she saw is tied up with the rumored coup in Cuba we've been tracking?"

"Who knows? Anything's possible. It's not unthinkable that Ramiro's in on it. He's got a lot of political clout. He's an operator who can pull the strings. But we can't jump to conclusions. Makes you wonder, though, what kind of sideshow that sonofabitch Ramiro's running down there. Whatever he's got going makes you question how he's going to react to Elena's escape. That is, assuming he suspects she knows about his drug operation and Moreno, and we have to assume he does. You know, this could throw a giant wrench in the works. If he's in on the coup, and has the power, maybe he'd call the whole thing off, thinking Elena could somehow implicate him. But, y'know, I doubt it. The coup looks like a stand-alone operation. Elena saw nothing in the file suggesting a coup. Only evidence of a drug operation. So it would appear that Moreno may have more to do with a Cuba-Mexico drug connection than a coup in Cuba. Make sense?"

"Makes sense to me. Logic's sound."

"Moreno is our number one worry. Dig up everything you can find on terrorists in Mexico, OK? Call your buddies in the Leadership Division and see what they've got down there. Give your friend, Robert Pranz a call. He loves grubbing around the gory details on these types. Call Ben Hardy at the Mexico desk. Find out everything you can on Moreno. I want a complete profile. Think you can get back to me by tomorrow morning?"

"Sure thing. What an incredible turn of events," she said, picking up the telephone to start her calls.

Goodwin left McGinnis's office. He stepped into the inner corridor connecting the string of offices lying within his domain, opened the door to the outside hallway corridor, and then exited, excited they might be onto something. He walked swiftly down the hall to speak to a couple of his colleagues in the Directorate of Operations—hands-on types with covert contacts in Mexico. The thought that kept turning in the back of his mind was that Moreno might be headed for Washington—for a rendezvous with the president of Mexico. We've got to move fast, he thought to himself. How could they stop him . . . assuming he was going to try to do what he was starting to suspect?

When McGrath and Elena came out the door of the town house at 7:15 A.M. that morning, two Latinos waited for them in a parked gray Toyota Camry five town houses down across the street from McGrath's. Their car was but one in the long line of bumper-to-bumper cars parked along the street. So there was nothing to distinguish that particular automobile from all the other late models. Both men looked in their late thirties, athletic, just over six feet, clean-shaven, thick black hair combed straight back. They wore workout sweatshirts and pants, as if prepared for a jog or game of tennis. The name "Georgetown" was emblazoned on the blue sweatshirts. The ashtray near the glove compartment was out, filled with cigarette butts.

"Here they come," the driver, the larger of the two men, said in a low voice.

"Your sure that's them?" asked the other in a hushed voice.

"Got to be. That's McGrath's address. Here're the photographs. Check them out." He handed over the binoculars.

"Yeah, that's them all right." He put the binoculars back in the glove compartment and unzipped his tennis jacket. "Looks like they're headed for the university. Let's go. Let's get this thing done. We don't have much time."

They got out of the car, the shorter of the two men carrying what looked like a dark green and white tennis bag, the handle plainly visible. They stayed on their side of the street, following McGrath and Elena at a safe distance.

They reached the Georgetown University parking lot ten minutes later. McGrath stopped for a minute at the entrance to chat with Bill Stimson, the parking lot attendant whom he knew well. It was at that moment that something clicked with him. Exchanging pleasantries with Stimson, McGrath glanced out of the corner of his eye. Two men wearing warm-up suits across the street. Same two guys he first noticed not far from his town house, when he stopped with Elena to pat that golden retriever.

The *one* tennis bag grabbed McGrath's attention. Odd, he thought offhandedly at the time. Tennis players typically carry their own bag with racket. Why only one racket? Out of place. He also thought it too hot for anyone heading for the tennis court to be in those warm-ups. The scene just was not right.

Second, what were they doing on McGrath's street, then winding up over here? There were no tennis courts near his town house, so they couldn't be coming *from* a game of tennis. The university tennis courts were not near here. So what were they doing over here near the parking lot? His pulse picked up rapidly as the adrenaline rush escalated with each question he asked himself. In seconds, he knew that he and Elena were in danger. He had to do something fast.

"Bill," McGrath said quietly and calmly, "don't look

too directly, but there're two men across the street dressed in warm-ups. One's carrying a tennis bag. It's a long story, but I think they may be following us. I'll tell you all about it later."

"Yeah, I see them," Stimson replied. A retired D.C. cop, he knew how to look discreetly. "Anything you'd like me to do, Professor McGrath?"

"If they come into this lot after I head for my car . . . it's parked way back . . . over there," McGrath nodded imperceptively with his head, ". . . and continue in our direction, call the university police immediately, OK? Tell them to put on their siren. It will be an emergency."

"Consider it done. I could call them right now, if you want."

"Even better."

"Gotcha."

"One other thing . . . we do have more help here. There're two men walking behind the tennis players. They're the good guys. See if you can get their attention . . . let them know what's going on. They're secret service."

On the way to his car, McGrath explained to Elena that they were being tailed. "Elena, do you have a mirror in your purse?" he asked, as they walked through the parking lot. She did.

"Take it out casually and check your makeup. See if those two men are still back there. I don't want to turn around and look."

Elena did as she was asked. "Oh God," she murmured, "they're right behind us. Maybe seventy or eighty feet. What's going on here?" Her hushed whisper was laced with fear.

"Look, I don't like the smell of this. Something's definitely out of whack. We need to move fast. See that maroon Chrysler PT Cruiser over there, next to that red car? That's mine. Get ready to make a run for it, OK?"

"My God," Elena murmured, "not again."

"Stay cool," McGrath said, as he dug into his right pants pocket and pulled out his tiny black remote starter and door lock attached to the key chain. He pressed the small red button to start the engine. The engine fired up ahead. Next, his finger found the green button that unlocked the doors. "OK," McGrath said. "Ready?"

"Yes," she replied, as McGrath took her hand.

"OK," he said, "run." They dashed for his car like two Olympic sprinters off the starting blocks, just as the university police patrol car came screaming into the parking lot entrance about two blocks away. The two "tennis players" gave chase, as the larger man unzipped his bag, reached into it, and groped around. As he got closer to McGrath's car, he pulled out what he was looking for. A grenade. An old-fashioned hand grenade. Running, he pulled the pin, but held the clamp tight. Then, not more than ten feet from McGrath's car, he let go the safety clamp, took careful aim, and pitched it under the rear end of McGrath's Cruiser. Then he turned and darted between two parked cars. "This way," he hissed to his partner, "over there, run your ass off, man."

McGrath and Elena jumped in, and Elena had not yet closed her door before McGrath had the car in first gear and peeled out in a fishtail wake of flying pebbles, stinging grit, and hot scorching rubber. The booming explosion and flying shrapnel erupted like a WWII field combat scene just seconds after the Cruiser flew out from the parking space. McGrath and Elena hunched forward, low in their seats, and sucked in their breath, half expecting bullets to rip through the windows. They felt the concussion and heard the dull thud of an explosion behind them. They saw pale blue smoke in the rearview mirror and heard metal fragments ping off the back of the car.

The university police, after pausing in the squad car to speak for a moment with Stimson, raced off in the direction where the two Latinos had headed, with the two secret service agents in hot pursuit. McGrath roared up to the parking lot entrance, slammed on the brakes and skidded to a stop. He thanked Stimson, told him he'd be back later to explain the whole thing, but had to get going. Stimson stood by the Cruiser and shook McGrath's hand. "Glad to help," he said. "sounds like one helluva story."

"It is," McGrath yelled, peeling rubber and heading for Key Bridge and the George Washington Memorial Parkway, which would take them to Langley. Elena reached into her purse for a handkerchief, leaned over, and mopped McGrath's brow.

"That was close," she sighed, rolling down the window for fresh air.

McGrath could see that her hand was shaking, as she said, "Those bastards just don't give up, do they? Must have been Ramiro operatives, right?"

"Smells of Ramiro, that's for sure," McGrath said, rubbing the back of his neck, a worried look on his face.

"So his goons found us. What do we do now?"

"One thing's for certain. We can't stay at the town house. It's no longer safe, even with the Secret Service guarding us."

The ominous question marks in this dark situation were Ramiro and Moreno. When would Ramiro strike next? Where? How? And what about this Moreno character? He wondered what he would do if he met this killer face-to-face. Then, for some reason, he remembered that old U.S. Marine axiom, "Superior thinking has always defeated superior force." It occurred to him that it was time to engage in some mighty sharp superior thinking himself if they were going to come out of this thing alive.

TWENTY-FOUR

Washington, D.C. = Havana = Bearden, Oklahoma

The CIA speaker box sat on a pole in the open near the giant shade trees. McGrath leaned out the car window and listened to the metallic voice asking him to state his business. He said he had a meeting with Sam Goodwin.

"Just a moment please." A minute later the voice said, "Please drive forward and come into the security office. Park in the indicated spaces."

Fifteen minutes later they had permission to pass into the gigantic Langley compound, found their designated Visitors' parking space, and made their way across the short distance to the main entrance with its huge glass doors.

"At least we're safe here," Elena said, as they walked up the outside stairs into the huge glass-enclosed foyer onto its spacious polished floors displaying the official intelligence agency emblem. "Impressive," she added.

When they entered the foyer a security guard instructed them to go to the large busy security check-in office off to the left, with its bank of receptionists, all business. A human holding pen for those who awaited their contacts to come and fetch them. In ten minutes they had their visitor badges. They waited for Goodwin to come down on the elevator to meet them.

"Good to see you," he said crisply, big smile on his face. "Let's go."

"You won't believe what just happened," McGrath said, as he and Elena stood up to greet him.

"I think I do," he said, a worried expression on his

face. "Secret Service just checked in and told us all about it. You folks OK? Elena, how are you doing?"

"Shaken but not broken," she replied.

"Good . . . so Ramiro has made his presence known right here in D.C.," Goodwin said. "Those two characters got away. We're still looking for them. Meanwhile, we have to find you two a safer place to stay until things quiet down."

"And when do you think that might be?" McGrath asked, painfully aware that Goodwin had dragged him into this whole thing in the first place. Of course, had it not been for Goodwin, he might not have contacted Elena.

"Can't say for sure, Neal, but I got a feeling all this is about to come to a head soon. Be patient, OK?" He walked swiftly across the lobby, obvious that he wanted to get going with the debriefing. He escorted them through the main lobby security gates, over to the bank of posh elevators down the glossy wide hall, and up to his office on the fifth floor. Elena was quiet, taking it all in.

When they reached Goodwin's office, he casually asked if they would like something to drink. "Coffee? Soft drink?" Both declined, and Goodwin got down to business.

"Elena," he said. "We have photographs we'd like you to look at. We're trying to see if the Moreno we have on file is the same guy you saw with Ramiro."

"Sure. Whatever I can do."

"Good. OK. If you would come over here to the computer, please, we've got a hefty set of photos on our database. Pull up a chair. Why don't you sit here, use the mouse, and click at your leisure. Tell me if you recognize the person." Elena began clicking the mouse, and with each click a clear color photo came up on the computer monitor. Sam chatted quietly with McGrath, while she studied the photos.

Elena looked at the first seven photographs and found nobody she recognized. At the eighth photo, she stopped, paused, then said excitedly, "Wait just a minute . . . here's the guy."

"Are you sure?" McGrath asked, as Elena leaned back in her chair and let out an audible sigh. The photo showed a man sitting by a jungle campsite in a clearing, clearly taken with a telephoto lens.

"Absolutely. I'd recognize that face anywhere. Gives me the creeps. It's Moreno," she said. "Same man I saw in Ramiro's files on Mexico. Same guy I saw Ramiro with in Havana. It's him all right."

Goodwin stared at the photograph on the screen and clicked the mouse to bring up a report, part of which he read aloud. "Carlos Moreno Gutierrez." What he did not read aloud was that the photo was taken in Mexico by a CIA operative.

"Who does he work for?" McGrath asked.

"As far as we know, he's with Mexico's Zapatista Revolutionary Front," Goodwin said. "Out of Chiapas. Been seen a lot around San Cristóbal de las Casas, a small town up in the mountains."

"How old is he?" McGrath asked.

"Well," Goodwin said, reading from the report that went with the photo, "he's forty-two."

"Tough guy?" McGrath asked.

"Tough? Are you kidding? Moreno's a martial arts specialist. Skilled in small arms and explosives. Trained for assassination. Elena, didn't you say the file you saw had lots of clippings about the Mexican president in it, along with information on Moreno?"

"Right."

"OK. Look, Elena, we need a full debriefing from you and Neal. One of our staff will be here in a minute to walk you down the hall. We'll talk to you separately . . . protocol y'know. Meanwhile, I'm going to arrange a safe place for you to stay."

* * *

Castro stood at the podium on the giant stage in the Palace of Conventions in Havana. He leaned forward over his notes on the lectern, waved his hands, and spoke into the five microphones lined up before him on short stubby stands. The mikes tilted toward him like obedient servants, ready to receive his words and send them on their way. In front of the stage long rows of official Communist Party delegates sat obediently, taking it all in.

Castro's central message was his absolute certainty that the U.S. was on the verge of launching an attack on Cuba. Cuba must prepare for this inevitability, he insisted, for it was written all over the U.S. president's actions—coupled with his doctrine of preemptive attack on perceived enemies, already used against Iraq. Everyone knew that Cuba ranked high on the U.S. enemy list as the president frequently made clear.

Four hours later, standard for a Castro speech, he ended with his usual "socialism or death," victory slogan for *la patria.* Delegates filed out of the Palace of Conventions, some inspired, others walking shoulder to shoulder, heads tilted toward each other, whispering, knowing Castro could be right. War might well be on the horizon.

Castro shook hands with officials on the stage and walked to one of the back rooms with his brother and two highly trusted staff officers, one of whom was General Ramiro. They went in and sat down so Castro might rest before returning to the Situation Room. He slouched into a chair, leaned back, scratched his beard, and shot his left arm in the air in a gesture of intense frustration. "I tell you, *compañeros*, we absolutely must prepare for the worst. We do not have much time. General Ramiro, your job is counterespionage, I want you to add more operatives, understood? We may have more than one mole in our ranks."

Before Ramiro could respond, someone knocked at the door.

Ramiro walked briskly across the room.

One of Fidel's aides stepped smartly inside and said, "I thought you might want to see this immediately, sir." He handed Castro a bulletin from the Situation Room.

Castro scanned it and suddenly exploded, slamming the table with the palm of his hand. "That bastard," he roared, almost choking as he spoke, flecks of spittle flying from his mouth. He got up from his chair and slammed the wall with his fist.

"What happened?" one of the officers asked.

"Enrique Ventura. Defected to the United States. Flew out in a single engine plane. Took his family. Straight to Key West."

They all knew Ventura—a high ranking officer with close personal ties to Ramiro, the tenth high-ranking defector in as many months. Everyone looked at Ramiro, who tried to look calmly professional, but they could see his face blanch, jaw muscles tighten, eyes fixed and staring straight ahead. They knew he would be held guilty for Ventura's defection. Somebody *always* had to be held guilty for a screw up of this magnitude. The plane that Ventura had used was one of the planes he had used for drug trafficking, and it was Ventura with whom he had just had a conversation about expanding the drug trade.

Ramiro groaned inwardly. His heart raced. Yet he remained coolly confident. He knew he had a strong hold over most of the people gathered in the room and was supremely confident in that control. But he was furious that he hadn't learned of this defection first from his people before Castro got wind of it. He was seething inside over the recent blows to his plans—Elena escaping with McGrath and now Ventura—but he vowed to get rid of these obstacles in short order. Ventura? That fucking bastard. He suddenly wished he knew where CIA would keep him. Surely he would wind up in a safe house somewhere. He would telephone Miguel immediately. Maybe he could do something.

Moreno pulled off Highway 40 into the dirt parking lot just after sunset. The ruby red neon sign blinked on and off, "Jay's Tavern," advertising cheap beer and home-cooked meals. He pulled his car in between two pickup trucks, which had seen better days, one with a broken taillight, the other with a huge dent in its left side. He could hear the music inside playing what he knew Americans called country western. He turned off the ignition, stretched his neck and head back, rolled his head around on his shoulders, and rubbed his temples with the palms of his hands. He watched a middle-aged man and younger woman stumble out of the bar, arms around waists, giggling as they made their way through the parked cars to an old red Chevy on the other side of one of the pickups. The man slapped the woman playfully on her backside, in return for which he received a friendly shove. He sat there until they drove away.

Moreno had been driving hard all day, planning to make Little Rock, Arkansas, before calling it quits on this leg of his journey. For now, he needed food and drink, and he had to make a phone call to Havana. He opened the door, stepped out, shook one leg, then the other to stimulate circulation, checked to make certain the car doors were locked, and looked again at the backseat where he kept his gear, especially the television camera. Then he cracked the knuckles of each hand, patted the left side of his backside to make sure he had his wallet, and walked toward the entrance. Stiff from driving, it would be good to grab a beer and some food.

As he pushed through the creaking wooden door to Jay's, it took a minute or two for his eyes to adjust to the dim light, but muffled conversations and tinkling glasses indicated the place was crowded. Once he adjusted to the darkness, he walked to an empty seat at the bar, preferring it to a crowded table, where he might be forced into conversation. He pulled out a bar stool and slipped onto the seat. In a second or two, one of the two young bartenders came over and asked him what he wanted to drink. "I will have a beer—a Budweiser or Coors," he said.

The bar tender gave Moreno a matter of fact look. "Right. One Bud coming up."

The large heavy set man next to Moreno, who had caught sight of his Latino features and immediately pegged him as a wetback, slugged down a shot of bourbon and said, "Hell, give him anything. He won't know the difference." The man had a huge barrel chest, and wore a dirty T-shirt stretched over his protruding beer belly. He nudged his friend on his right, and whispered, loud enough for Moreno to hear. "Get a load of this dude sitting next to me. Looks like he just swum across the river from Mexico. Bet you five bucks, he's still wet from the swim." Then he snickered and ordered more bourbon. What really burned him was that Mexicans were taking all the factory jobs in the area, and he had just been laid off. They had actually fired him for coming to work hungover too many times, but with all the Mexicans at the factory, they had become his scapegoat.

His friend, equally hefty, wearing a sheathed hunting knife strapped to his belt, also had been fired recently for absenteeism, bent forward over the bar to give Moreno a hard stare. He followed it with a cold smile and laughter and finished his inspection of Moreno with a long swig of his beer and a belch for the enjoyment of those around him. Then he said loudly, "you cain't tell if'n he's a girl or boy!"

The bartender returned to Moreno, placed his bottle of beer and a tall, cold beer glass before him. Moreno pulled the beer bottle and glass toward him with steady hands, trying to ignore the two men next to him he calmly asked, "Where's your telephone?"

"Down that hallway over there, Mister. Next to the men's room," the bartender said, pointing in the direction of the hallway.

Moreno finished the beer and as he pushed back from the bar to make his way to the telephone, the huge man sitting next to him said to the bartender, "Hey, make sure this guy pays—you never know with these wetbacks." He grinned and nudged his friend.

As Moreno started to step away from the bar, the huge man to his right shifted his weight slightly as to make it more difficult for Moreno to move. Moreno's temper was rising fast, but he did not bat an eyelash. He slipped through the narrow opening without so much as touching the man and strolled toward the telephone.

Reaching the phone, Moreno punched in the numbers for his credit card and then the numbers for Havana. After five rings, Ramiro picked up the receiver in his office at "The Mansion."

Moreno followed the same procedure as before, and told Ramiro that his trip east was on schedule. He expected to be in Little Rock by tonight.

"Good, good," replied the voice at the other end. Then Moreno described his trip thus far, stating that nothing spectacular had happened. He foresaw no difficulties in completing his trip on schedule.

After two minutes into the conversation, Ramiro interjected, "Listen, I have news that may be of interest to you."

"Yes?"

"Do you remember the lovely young woman who worked in my office here?"

"*Como no*, certainly. As I recall you were having difficulty with her work habits and planned to, ahh, get rid of her."

"Yeah, that's the one," came the terse reply. Well, she's now in the U.S. In Washington, D.C."

"What happened?"

"Somebody fucked up."

"And you know who it was?"

"*Sí* señor. He is no longer with us." When Ramiro finished, Moreno had a clear picture of the situation in Washington. He knew what he would have to do.

Moreno went back to the bar, cursing this new development, trying to calm himself, wondering what the hell this Elena and McGrath knew for certain anyway? Still, he was angry about this wrinkle in his airtight plan. She and McGrath were loose cannons. He didn't like it. He returned to his place at the bar and asked for a menu.

"Here you go amigo," the bartender said, reaching to the counter behind him. He wheeled back to drop it in front of Moreno, who opened the first page and looked it over.

"I wonder if your amigo can read English," said the hulk to Moreno's right, which produced snickering from two or three men along the bar.

"C'mon, Hank," said the bartender, wiping the counter, "give it a rest, OK?"

Moreno could feel his anger rising dangerously high. Insults to his face always got his adrenaline going, especially from such ignorance. But he held himself in check. The last thing he needed was an incident to complicate his mission.

He tried to ignore the comments, studied the menu, breathing evenly to put his emotions to rest. Stay calm, he thought. But his rapid pulse would not slow, and the tension mounted.

"Here, lemme hep you," said Hank, hoping to have a little fun with Moreno. Snatching the menu away from him, he began to read in a loud voice for his friends to hear.

"It says here . . . tamales, five cents a piece . . . fried rice, ten cents . . . refried beans, fifteen cents, and dog meat, thirty cents a helping." He laughed at his joke, along with two other men. "And for a half-buck you can git all the cat you can eat," he said, laughing so hard, he had to wipe the spittle off his chin with the back of his hand. Then he slapped the menu back down in front of Moreno and thumped him hard on the back. "And for drink, you can get yoursef a big glass of cow piss," he added. More laughter all around. The two bartenders, seeing the expression on Moreno's face, his intent eyes, jaw muscles tensed, moved away, busying themselves drying glasses.

Moreno knew he had to avoid a scene, had to get out of there fast and try for something to eat further up the line. He calmly drank down the last of his beer, put a five dollar bill on the counter, and without a word, started to get up off the bar stool to leave.

The bar went suddenly quiet. All eyes were on Moreno, the tension near him so tense you could cut it with a knife. Moreno turned to put his right foot down on the floor, when he felt a hand tug at his ponytail.

"Ain't that purty . . . all tied up in a fancy red ribbon 'jes like a little girl."

Hank Clemens had no idea what happened next. Moreno raised his right arm slowly, as if to press the back of his hand to his forehead in a gesture of befuddlement and confusion. Glancing into the eyes of his antagonist, he twisted his body slightly on the bar stool, brought up his left arm and drove his left thumb and forefinger straight into Clemens' eyes with a powerful blow. To Moreno it felt wonderfully like two ripe grapes as his fingers sunk in.

When Clemens cried out in excruciating pain, Moreno pulled his left arm away from his eyes, and smashed his windpipe with a right hand karate chop, which brought an audible crunch, heard by those sitting close by. It was over in seconds. The cries of pain stopped as suddenly as they had begun. The huge, lifeless, upper torso slumped over on the bar, his head knocking over the bourbon glass as it came down. Liquor trickled out from under Clemens' inert head, mixing with the drool from his open mouth.

As Clemens' body fell forward, Moreno stepped around it—faster than anyone could understand—and smashed the second adversary with the heel of his right hand in an uppercut motion, driving his nose bones into his brain. Then he moved in and broke his neck. The hold, which no one later could adequately describe, because it all happened so fast, produced another loud *crack* in Jay's Tavern. Everyone stood completely motionless, stunned in paralyzed silence.

Moreno walked silently and purposely across the room and out the door. Everyone else stood there gawking. Nobody made an effort to stop him. They were frozen in their tracks.

Outside, he broke into a trot, heading for his car, pulling the keys out of his pocket, jogging across the darkened parking lot. He opened the driver's side of his car, jumped in, started the engine, slammed into first gear, released the clutch, and peeled out at high speed. He left a trail of flying gravel behind him, as he checked in the rearview mirror to see if anybody was after him. Moreno let out a long sigh, because no headlights were behind him.

As he shifted gears and picked up speed down the highway, Moreno muttered to himself. "*Calm* yourself. Don't drive over the speed limit. Don't attract attention." He wiped the palm of his left hand on his pants leg. Shit. He had screwed up royally. Still, his bloodlust was up, adrenaline pumping. He had to admit that he had enjoyed the recent scene in the bar, but knew he now would really have to be on guard. This was going to be no picnic, he told himself, although he remained supremely confident he could pull it off.

* * *

But he had attracted attention. Two teenagers making out in the field next to Jay's parking lot saw Moreno when he had come out the front door. About an hour had elapsed before they admitted having been in the field.

"Did you see the car?" the state police officer asked, notebook and pen in hand.

"It was kinda darkish," said Mary Nelsworth, "hard to see much."

"He lit outta there like greased lightnin'," said John Blakesmore. "But I'm sure this is part of the license number. Here, I wrote it down."

"Thanks much," replied the state trooper. "This isn't a lot to go on, but it will get the ball rolling," he said, smiling at the two youngsters. "If you think of anything else, let us know, OK?"

Once the trooper interviewed witnesses in Jay's Tavern, he had a sketch artist come in to get a rough idea of what the guy looked like. The state trooper reported this information to his chief, who in turn passed the drawing and information up the chain on what appeared most likely to be a Latino assailant, probably Mexican. Because of the nature of the incident, and the fact that a foreign national may have been involved, the state police in Oklahoma City in turn passed it on to the FBI field office, which routinely checked Moreno's description against recent incoming "Wanted" lists. Nothing came up at this point, but they knew from a description of the license plates that the car was from California.

Moreno drove another few miles on Route 40 after leaving Jay's Tavern, then turned north onto Route 56. He knew that the state police likely would be watching the main highway east and west. At the first shopping mall he passed he pulled in, parked, and entered a Circuit City store. There he bought a Bearcat radio scanner and picked up a manual of frequencies that he would program to monitor police reports. He drove on for a short time, pulled into a secluded dirt road, stopped, and with a flashlight hooked up the scanner. He would now use secondary roads and drive straight through to D.C.

•

Herrera and his coconspirators frequently met at La Terraza, a restaurant in Cojimar, a local favorite of Hemingway fame, now owned by one of Herrera's friends. By now they had met a number of times—Generals Herrera, Gómez, Domínguez and Campos—typically late at night around ten o'clock. Tonight the doctor was present. He would play a key role in the conspiracy. The restaurant's owner would have one of his chefs cook up something for the officers. They took their meal in a special private room out back away from the crowd. There they talked in private.

Tonight, with five days to go, they were all on edge, nervous energy running high. They were acutely aware of possible information leaks as more and more people had been brought into the loop of this impending coup. They knew the danger of denunciation, of possible betrayal. Herrera could see that hint of anxiety in Gómez's eyes, in Campos' restless body movements, and Domínguez's controlled tone of voice as he toyed with his ring. Herrera felt the tension too.

"So, gentlemen," Herrera said, washing down a bite of chicken and rice with his beer. "Our teams are ready to go. It will be a day to remember." By now they had been over strategy and tactics again and again, everything from eliminating Castro and his brother to all the subsequent set of events. They had planned this thing from beginning to end, down to the last detail. Neutralizing the state's defenses. Selecting targets. How to manage the security forces and infiltrate the army and police. All in place. How and when to strike. Communication and transportation links to be shut down. Leading personalities and potential opponents to arrest. What to do with hard-core loyalist forces resisting the coup. Essentially they were set.

"Dr. Torres, you're certain Castro will not die?" Campos asked. "Yet he will still remain incapacitated?"

"No," the doctor replied. "It's foolproof, my friends. Castro will not die. Yes, he will suffer a terrible stroke. So we preserve the icon of the *patria*. But an icon who no longer leads. That's the beauty of it. A coup without the appearance of a conspiracy. Simply a normal course of events."

Herrera jumped in. "And with Castro on the sidelines, we can chart a new course for the country with the full support of the nation. Except for Ramiro and his faction, that is. But we will take them out of the picture soon after Castro is incapacitated. And of course Castro's brother. He, of course, will be arrested and charged with drug trafficking."

"His use of Viagra will be ironic, no?" Campos chuckled. "Viagra's not supposed to work that way, y'know."

"I know. I know," Herrera responded, smiling. "But Castro's getting older. He can't get it up the way he used to."

"That's where Viagra comes in, no?" Gómez asked. "Explain it to me again, Doctor."

"It's relatively simple," the doctor said, smiling. "I've had Castro on blood pressure medication for three years now. He takes nitrates for it. One thing you do not want to mix with nitrates is something like Viagra, because it will produce a terrible side effect."

"Like a stroke," Herrera said.

"Exactly," the doctor replied. "Now we all know that Castro enjoys a late morning delight, right? And," he chuckled, "we know for certain that he wants to get together with a certain young army lieutenant just as soon as his helicopter lands for the upcoming Territorial Troops inspection. So they've laid on a one hour break after the helicopter lands, before he begins the actual inspection."

"He will need Viagra to be ready?" Campos asked.

"Precisely," the doctor said. "I will give it to him just before he begins his flight early Tuesday morning from Antonio de los Baños. He will be handed his blue fifty mg tablet as he boards the helicopter. I shall not," he smiled, "remind him of its possible consequences when he's on high blood pressure medication."

"How long does the Viagra last, you know, in terms of doing its job?" Gómez asked.

"Two or three hours."

"When will the stroke occur?"

"Within two or three hours," the doctor replied.

"What exactly will happen?" Gómez asked.

"He simply will collapse."

"That will be the stroke?"

"Exactly," replied the doctor.

"At that point we will be ready to step in. Smooth as silk. It will look like a natural event," Herrera said.

"Anything else?" Campos wanted to know, taking a long drink of his beer.

"Well," Dr. Torres smiled. "If he fantasizes about sex on the helicopter ride, he will greet the awaiting brass with one big erection when he lands."

"Brilliant," Campos said. He lit up a cigar. "It's a splendid plan, Julio. Timed to correspond with his Tuesday review of the Territorial Militia."

"Right," Herrera said. "We won't know the precise hour of his stroke, but it'll certainly be within the time he departs Antonio de los Baños in his private helicopter and his observation of the Militia maneuvers. We will have our teams on full alert during this period, ready to go when his stroke occurs. Everyone will be ready to go into action immediately."

"Ramiro wanted to use that explosive device on Castro's helicopter, remember?" Domínguez said. "But I agree with you, Julio, an explosion would have been too obvious. This Viagra stroke idea is far more professional. More sophisticated. Much better for our purposes."

"Still convinced it was a good idea to bring that *santero* Rivero into the loop?" Gómez questioned, a frown on his face.

"Absolutely," Herrera snapped. "He's our guarantee of Santería religious support. A vital element of our strategy. We've got to have that religious group on our side. Now let's go over our timing once again. Remember, we start our countdown with our teams precisely ten hours before the explosion. That means that if *el Comandante's* schedule holds, our countdown starts at ninethirty at night next Monday. That gives us ten hours before he's scheduled to depart Antonio de Los Baños on his helicopter at seven in the morning on Tuesday. Everybody understand?"

Of course it was clear. They had been over it a hundred times.

"But there is that problem of Ventura's defection," Campos said.

"I know . . . I know," Herrera replied. "Ventura was one of Ramiro's men, that's true. But Ramiro assures me that Ventura was not in the loop on this thing. Ramiro says he knew nothing about our plans . . . I hope he's right. At this point, we proceed as if Ramiro is absolutely correct."

But in the back of Herrera's mind, he worried about *Shangó*. He could not shake that eerie question that had begun to haunt all his planning . . . would *Shangó* betray him?

TWENTY-FIVE

Washington, D.C. = Havana = West Virginia

Goodwin's meeting in his CIA office started at 7:00 A.M., with key players seated around the conference table—McGinnis; Bob Pranz, specialist on guerrilla leaders in Central America and Mexico; Ben Hardy, Mexico desk; and Fred Bench, Cuba section. Each knew the situation.

Goodwin recounted Elena's story about her discovery in Ramiro's file cabinet—the information on Moreno, news clippings on Mexico's president, and money stashed in a brown paper bag. He described the *El Tesero* findings, assassination attempt on both of them in downtown Havana, and the harrowing escape in the hurricane. He reminded them of Larry Diamond's murder and Robert Kincaid's likely murder.

"We believe General Ramiro tried to kill McGrath and Elena, probably because she had stumbled onto classified information that could compromise his drug operations," Goodwin said. "McGrath was on the scene at that time. Ramiro would have to be one dumb sonofabitch, which he is not, to think that McGrath was not privy to Elena's information after they started seeing each other. He no doubt assumed McGrath was one of our agents."

"Where're McGrath and Elena now?" Hardy asked.

"In a safe house downtown."

"How long do you intend to keep them there?" McGinnis asked.

"Don't know," Goodwin replied. "We'll let them use it as home for awhile, at least until the president of Mexico comes and goes. But I'll be getting to that issue shortly . . . anything else? No? OK, let's move on. Beyond Ramiro's drug operation, we have a rumored coup that our defectors have been mentioning. Our Operations Team will be debriefing Elena on anything she might know. Maybe she's got something new she can tell us."

"That's assuming her ex-boss, Ramiro, is implicated and Elena has relevant information," Pranz said.

"Enrique Ventura worked for Ramiro," Goodwin said. "Maybe he knows something. They're still debriefing him."

"A coup would be absolutely incredible," Bench said. "Hard to imagine it with all the power Castro exerts."

"You never know," McGinnis said.

"Issue number three," Goodwin continued. "This guy Moreno . . . who Elena saw with Ramiro outside MININT offices in Havana and identified as the Moreno in our files. He remains somewhat of a mystery. I sent a message down to our folks in the embassy in Mexico City, requesting a background check on him."

"Anything come up?" Ben Hardy asked.

"You know," Goodwin responded, "I am forever amazed at how things work out sometimes in this business. To answer your question, yes, it did . . . in a most bizarre way."

"What do you mean, Sam?" McGinnis asked.

"OK, get this. Our CIA guy goes fishing around down there and makes his usual call to Mexico's Federal Security Directorate, DFS, in Mexico City."

Hardy said, "Those guys can be efficient, despite all the talk of corruption."

"Right. Well, here's the story. Turns out, DFS tells him to come over and read a report that had come in a couple of days earlier. So he goes over there and finds out the mother of a Mexico City policeman had visited a shoe repair shop down near the Zocalo with her granddaughter several days before. While she's in the shoe shop, she observes something she thought out of the ordinary. So she tells her son, the policeman, who works that area of the city."

"What do you mean, *out of the ordinary?*" Pranz asked, stirring his coffee, staring at Goodwin.

"Just this. The woman visits this shop frequently, so she pretty much knows the place. Well, while she's in there with her granddaughter, a man comes in, no one she recognizes. She remembers him, because he had this long ponytail and a scar on his face. Not your average looking guy. She said the guy was not friendly looking."

"That and a dime will get you a cup of coffee. Doesn't get us very far," Hardy said.

"Right. But it was his request that startled the woman. This guy orders a special pair of riding boots to be made for him. When he says this, the proprietor drops everything, as if on cue, tells his daughter to come out and mind the store, and then invites the stranger into the back room to get measured for the boots. Now this woman told her policeman son that the proprietor is a gruff kind of fellow with zero interpersonal skills— except for the grandmother whom he likes. Yet there he is, slavishly catering to this stranger. The woman said that in all the days she has been going into that store, no one has ever ordered riding boots or been invited to the back room to be measured."

"So what happened?" asked McGinnis.

"Turns out the policeman reported it to his boss and he passed it on up to the DFS. What's interesting here is that the woman's description of the man who went into the shoe repair shop fits Moreno's description."

"But why would the DFS get involved?" Kim asked, looking skeptical.

"Good question. Because they have suspected for some time that this particular shoe shop might be a place Mexican guerrilla leaders frequent to have special types of guns made. DFS has never gotten anything solid on it, but they suspect the shoemaker is in fact a gunsmith and his shoe repair shop a front for weapons deals. Remember, the Mexican government generally allows guerrilla leaders safe haven in Mexico. So nobody at DFS wants to do anything to disrupt these visits. You know, better to let the visitors come and go. One way to keep tabs on their whereabouts."

"This is getting more and more interesting, Sam," Bench observed, making a note to himself on a pad of lined yellow notepaper.

"There's more," Sam said. "The DFS report indicates that two days later, this guy returns to the shoe shop, stays awhile and comes out carrying a large box, wrapped in plain brown paper—could have been anything. They don't know what it was. Maybe boots. But it's clear that this guy bought something there, and DFS don't think it was riding boots."

"And you believe it was Moreno?" Kim asked, smiling at Goodwin.

"Could be," Sam said. "One last thing regarding this DFS report. Our CIA man in Mexico City says the DFS told him that they have heard rumors from their informants that sometime around the time the suspect was doing business with the shoemaker, Zapatista guerrilla leaders close to Moreno held a secret meeting. Moreno might have attended himself. That meeting, if DFS sources are accurate, appears to have generated much excitement about something big that's supposed to occur, maybe as early as next week. They have not yet discovered exactly what is supposed to happen, but they suspect that it's supposed to be dramatic. Anyway, that's the information I have. Kim tells me you've been looking into this Moreno matter, Bob. Let's start with you. What do you have?" Goodwin set aside the DFS report and looked at Pranz.

"Right. Moreno is one of the top terrorists in Mexico. He has an upper-class, university-trained background, not uncommon for guerrilla leaders in that part of the world. Joined the leftist insurgents at an early age. Trained hard. Worked diligently within the ranks, and rose swiftly—eventually becoming a Zapatista leader. Known to take on daring assignments. Ice water in his veins. Killed at least three members of the Mexican government with his bare hands—not the sort of fellow you'd want to meet in a dark alley. Moreno is driven by "true believer" sentiments. A revolutionary to the core. Violently anti-American and will stop at nothing to overthrow the government of his country. Oh, and one other thing. It's true. He has been on training assignments twice in Cuba. Get this. Arranged by Ramiro himself. Those two probably know each other well. Finally, he's got a hell of an ego. Likes to pull off daring stunts, you know, push the envelope."

"Any idea where he is now?" Goodwin asked.

"Unfortunately, no. We've got feelers out . . . maybe something will come in later today from one of our field offices. I'd like to know what Elena thinks. After all, she saw that Mexico file in Ramiro's office, the one you said had Moreno's photograph in it. Then, too, you said Elena had a conversation with . . . with . . ." he said, looking at his notes.

"Quintero," McGinnis said.

"Correct. Quintero."

"Elena thinks, to put it bluntly, and remember that we have no direct evidence of this, that Moreno may intend to assassinate the Mexican president . . . right here in Washington, D.C. when he comes in for the meeting with our president."

"Holy Christ," Pranz gasped.

"Holy Christ is just about right," Goodwin said sardonically. "Ben, what can you add to the story—Elena's theory?"

"First, I agree with Bob. Moreno is the number one star when it comes to violence in Mexico. He's responsible not only for the killings Bob mentioned, but also for a number of bomb incidents on public streets, with a number of fatalities. He has orchestrated the explosion of at least three electric power plants in Chiapas. He's absolutely the *Numero Uno* ranking terrorist in Mexico, certainly the most violent of all the insurgents we track. Other guerrilla leaders fear him because of his explosive temper. They never know what he's going to do next."

"So nobody has a clue at this point where he is now or what he's up to?"

"Right. But we do know that the president of Mexico will be here early next week, for what that's worth."

"Kim, any thoughts?" Goodwin glanced at McGinnis.

"Could you run over Elena's line of logic for us once again, Sam?"

"Sure. The files on Moreno and the Mexican president were close together, with some of the president's newspaper clippings mixed in with Moreno's files. Because Ramiro knew Elena had been into these files and probably saw the money, he was agitated enough to want to eliminate her, and quickly."

"The drug operation would be reason enough for Ramiro to go after her." McGinnis said.

"Yes. But look, there were those two files, combined with Moreno's presence in Cuba and his intense discussions with Ramiro, that Ramiro and Moreno knew Elena had observed . . . all that gave Ramiro still more reasons to go after her."

"The implication being that Ramiro and Moreno are in on a plot to assassinate the president of Mexico?" Bench asked. "Here in D.C.? That's what Elena thinks?"

"Yes," Goodwin said.

"In D.C.?" Hardy said skeptically, a distinct smirk on his face. "Don't be silly. If anyone were going to assassinate the Mexican president—admittedly he'd be a prime target for a guy like Moreno—they would do it in Mexico."

"No. Not necessarily," replied Bench. "Think about it.

It makes sense. The Mexican president feels safer here. In Mexico he has to be on guard every minute. Here he's on safe territory, or so he thinks. So Moreno slips into the U.S., shows up in D.C., and assassinates the president."

"You believe Moreno would think it would be easier here?" McGinnis asked.

"In some respects, yes," Bench said. "Moreno's got the balls to do it. He comes in undercover, gets into D.C., makes the hit, then in the confusion, he disappears. He's an expert in assassinations and getaways, right? If he makes it out of here undetected, no one could pin the assassination on the Mexican guerrillas. So D.C. becomes a natural place for a go-for-broke terrorist like Moreno."

"What's in it for Ramiro?" McGinnis asked.

"That's not clear," Goodwin replied, sipping his black coffee

Bench interrupted "Wait a minute. Suppose the president of Mexico *were* shot here in Washington. What would happen back home?"

"We're quite familiar with that scenario," Hardy replied. "Given the turmoil in Mexican politics, we factored in that possibility long ago. Here's the scenario. If Mexico's president is suddenly out of the picture, the vice-president becomes president. The vice-president does not command the respect of the president. Political infighting ensues. The military intervenes to impose law and order."

"How do you think Mexico's population would react to military rule?" McGinnis asked, "especially after a popular president has just been killed?"

"They'd be pissed," replied Hardy.

"What effect do you believe it would have on Mexico's left-wing movements like Moreno's?" Bench asked.

"They'd be sitting pretty," Hardy said. "Much of the population might turn to them as the only way out. Their ranks could swell. The revolutionary movement would have a new cause. Moreno would be in fat city. He'd press his socialist agenda with all energy at his disposal," answered Hardy.

Goodwin leaned back in his chair, coffee cup in hand, twirling a yellow number two pencil in his fingers, looking doubtful.

"Interesting thesis," interjected McGinnis, "particularly as Moreno and Ramiro might see it. Moreno's future could be brightened. And for Ramiro, a man who backs revolutionary causes in Central America, his organization in Cuba would be in great shape with a revived leftist, insurgent movement in Mexico. High in morale and committed to use weapons provided by Ramiro's MININT. Hell, even Castro couldn't quibble with that scenario."

"Absolutely," replied Bench, "it all fits."

"It jibes with Elena's thinking. It just might explain another reason why they were trying to kill Elena and McGrath here in Washington. Given the high profile nature of the operation and time factor, Ramiro would be climbing the tree lest Elena spills the beans. Let's see, anybody know the Mexican president's itinerary?"

"He arrives this Sunday," Hardy said, reading from a folder of memos he had brought along. "He'll address Congress and the National Press Club on Monday."

"OK, look, even though all this is pretty much conjecture," Goodwin said. "I'll go ahead and ask the FBI to try to find out if one Carlos Moreno Gutierrez has entered the country. Meanwhile, keep digging. We still don't know how all this might impact the possible coup in Cuba, assuming our intelligence is accurate. In any case, let's concentrate on Moreno for now. Robert, put your guys to work on this full-time, flat out, starting now. We're going to need all the information on Moreno we can get as soon as possible. Call me if you come up with anything that looks promising. Let's meet again this afternoon. How about three-thirty P.M.?"

Goodwin closed the door to his office, went to his desk, and used the secure line to place three telephone calls—first, William Magstadt, Director of Operations in his building, second, Gary McShane, National Security Advisor at the White House, who reported directly to the president, and third, Phil Meyers, an agent with the FBI in downtown D.C., and a close friend. Without wasting time on pleasantries, he explained the Moreno situation to each of them.

Ramiro parked his car in the lot next to hangar 4747, which housed Castro's private helicopter—more precisely, the one he and his brother would use to monitor the Territorial Troop Militia exercises next Tuesday. Nobody else was near the helicopter, except one man in oil coveralls.

"*Hola!* Ricardo, how goes it?" The officer queried in his typically affable voice that Ricardo Agramonte, Castro's chief mechanic had come to recognize.

Agramonte looked up from his greasy worktable, covered with oily engine parts, wiped his hands on an old brown rag, and replied, "General Ramiro, what an honor."

The general picked up one of the airplane parts, acted as if he were showing it to Agramonte, lowered his voice, and said, "How's the device coming?"

The mechanic looked over the part held in the general's left hand and whispered back, "All complete, sir. Ready to go."

"You are certain it will work?"

"Absolutely. Guaranteed. Without a doubt, sir."

"You are clear on the timing?"

"Yes sir. It will be rigged to go off twenty minutes after take off."

"*Excelente.* Now let's briefly go over the plan again."

Five minutes later, after listening to the mechanic go through the rehearsal, Ramiro said, "*Perfecto.* You've got it, my boy. Look, let's set the timer for thirty minutes, assuming the fire will delay take off.

"*Sí, mi General.*"

"As for Castro, you know how impatient he is. He likes to whip onto the scene, jump into his helicopter, and whisk off to yet another heroic exploit. In fact, just to be on the safe side, we will have someone posted down the road from here, who can call one of our guys on radio-phone, indicating when he's just minutes away."

"Sounds solid to me, sir."

"It is. As the Americans like to say, it's locked in concrete." The general gave the mechanic a huge grin. "OK *chico*. Stay calm. We are on the precipice of a glorious new future for Cuba. You can be proud of your part in this drama." They saluted each other, and the general strolled calmly out the hangar.

Driving through West Virginia, Moreno used secondary roads and checked his map regularly. He slept an hour or two at night, parked on dirt roads out of sight. Tired and grubby, the APB reports of his description that he picked up hourly on the scanner since the incident in Oklahoma had led him to grow a thick black beard and moustache. He cut his hair short, so he no longer fit the APB reports on police frequencies.

He changed frequencies constantly to monitor police reports from one region to the next and eventually pulled off the road into a dilapidated wooden service station. He rolled up to the gas pump, turned off the ignition, and stretched. A thin, slump-shouldered old man dragged his body off the porch with its faded "Drink Coca-Cola" sign hanging off the shingled roof, and shuffled over the gravel up to Moreno's open window. Moreno, with his heavily accented voice, indicated that the tank should be filled.

He got out and headed for the rusting phone booth at the south side of the sagging porch and removed a small, dirty white card with a telephone number on it from his wallet. When the operator came on, he said this was a collect call to a Mr. Miguel Espinosa.

"Who is calling, please?"

"José Paz," replied Moreno.

"Thank you, Mr. Paz," said the operator. "One moment please."

Miguel's voice came on the line. He accepted the charges.

"Mr. Paz," he said, "How good of you to call."

"I thought you would be pleased," Moreno replied. "Any problems coming up from Miami?"

"None at all. Where are you now?" came Miguel's voice.

"West Virginia. I will arrive in Washington soon. Everything set?"

"Yes. Your automobile is ready, and we have a place for you to stay."

Before Miguel could finish his sentence, Moreno interrupted him. "Listen. We have major difficulties with my original arrival plans, so we will change to the alternate arrangement."

"I see," replied Miguel. "Yes, I see. So it would be best for me to meet you in the alternate location?"

"Correct."

"About what time?"

"Let's say sometime tomorrow morning."

"That's fine. I'll be ready and waiting."

"OK, I look forward to seeing you shortly, then. We have much to discuss."

"Yes we do," replied Miguel. "I've completed the work we talked about."

As Moreno walked back to the car, he felt better, learning that Miguel had completed his part of his assignment. It meant that a stolen a car with switched plates awaited him. He also knew that Miguel had additional stolen plates in the trunk of that car. Moreno would put these plates on his rented car, which he could then park with less worry. That should do it, he thought. He stepped out of the booth, walked slowly back to his car and paid for the gas with a twenty dollar bill. He had learned his lesson about larger bills. The attendant languidly accepted the money, shuffled back to the porch and slumped in his rocking chair.

Before leaving the station, Moreno checked his map. He looked for Reedville, Virginia, a small town at the mouth of the Potomac River. He started the engine, shifted through the gears and sped off down the highway. At this point he was driving on pure adrenaline, totally focused on his assignment ahead. Yet in the back of his mind, he wondered what he might encounter in the final chapter of his mission.

TWENTY-SIX

Reedville, Virginia = Washington, D.C.

The sun was just rising when Moreno drove cautiously into the sleepy little town of Reedville, Virginia. He followed his town map and went to the public marina he and Miguel had agreed on. He turned onto the gravel road running alongside the creek that emptied into the main river and followed it to the marina. There he spotted the parked red Ford sedan. Dead tired, he pulled in behind it, and watched Miguel get out, shutting the door quietly behind him.

Moreno could feel it was going to be a humid summer day on the Chesapeake Bay, as he put his head back wearily on the headrest. He eyed Miguel through the half-open lids of a rattlesnake as the drug kingpin approached his car, footsteps crunching closer and closer on the gravel. The marina looked deserted. Miguel had chosen a meeting place where only a few sail and power boats floated in their slips.

"*Hola*," Miguel said quietly. He stuck his hand cautiously inside the car window to shake Moreno's hand. "You made it. You know the FBI is on your tail, man. Big time. You're lucky as hell you didn't get caught."

Moreno stared back blandly, blinking his eyes a couple of times, trying to stay awake, then slowly, as if he were entering a karate ring, opened the door to get out. Standing by the car, he stretched for a minute, yawned, and, tired and red-eyed, started to exercise his arms lightly to get his circulation going. He could feel the lack of exercise in his body and was not at all happy about it. He looked at Miguel, taking his measure, and wondered if he could be trusted.

"Look," Miguel said, "we should get going."

"Right," Moreno replied, opening the car's back door to remove his gear. "Just a minute, while I unhook the scanner."

"I've got food and drinks already stowed aboard the boat. We're tied up down the way . . . over there," he continued, pointing toward a dock about 200 yards down the road. "We can park your car in the public parking lot here. I got a pair of plates we can switch with your California plates. We have to change them before we go. The cars will be safe. Boat people leave cars here all the time. Nobody pays attention. And our boat belongs to one of our local contacts. It's properly registered in case we are stopped. Papers all in order. OK, my friend, what do you say? Let's get going. You can sleep on the trip up to Washington."

They parked the cars in the marina parking lot, changed license plates, walked to the slip with Moreno's gear, and boarded the 38-foot Bayliner cabin cruiser, with its T175 Hino diesels and two staterooms below. Once aboard, Miguel showed Moreno his stateroom. He introduced him to Bernardo Alguero, who would be their captain for this cruise up to D.C. and to the three other thuggish men, one of whom would pay a critical role in this operation.

Bernardo tried to start a conversation with Moreno, but Moreno had written him off as of no use other than to get him up and back from D.C. Bernardo took an instant dislike to Moreno, found him aloof and creepy. He made a mental note to stay as far from him as he could while they were in the close quarters of the boat. He sure as hell would not try to initiate another conversation with the bastard.

Miguel and Bernardo busied themselves preparing the boat to depart. He and Bernardo had made this run to the Washington marina more than once, although these days he had to exercise extreme care in view of the DEA's operations in Reedville. The place had attracted attention for drug enforcement activities in view of the Potomac's access to Washington's thriving drug bazaar, but at times, like today, nothing much was happening. Once they had cast off the dock lines, Bernardo backed the Bayliner slowly and smoothly out of its slip, engine murmuring softly in the quiet water. He shifted into forward, throttled up, and headed for Cockrell Creek, which feeds into the Great Wicomico River, and from there out into the Chesapeake Bay. From the Bay, their route would take him north to the mouth of the Potomac and an estimated five hour trip to D.C.

Bernardo smiled to himself as he confidently guided the Bayliner effortlessly forward over the flat surface water, leaving its glistening, white-crested wake behind. He had waited a long time for this particular trip—with Miguel and his mysterious stranger on board.

Goodwin picked up the ringing telephone at 7:30 A.M. Phil Meyers calling from FBI Headquarters. McGrath and Elena were with him at his small conference table this morning. Goodwin had brought them in to help monitor breaking events and ask for their input as the day unfolded. He motioned to McGrath to have another cup of coffee and pushed the sugar toward Elena, smiling.

"Phil, any news?

Five minutes later Goodman hung up and turned to McGrath and Elena. "Here's the latest. FBI has a National Crime Information Center APB on your friend Moreno. They've heard back from Oklahoma City with a report on a bizarre double killing out in Bearden, Oklahoma. Suspect fits Moreno's description. They think Moreno may have come across from Mexico into San Diego and is working his way east by car. FBI's launched a full-scale search. They're operating on the assumption that Moreno intends to assassinate Mexico's President Fox here in D.C.

Elena remained quiet, although the look on her face registered understanding, as she nodded in agreement with Goodwin's statement. McGrath thought she had become rather composed since their first debriefing here at the agency. That, in and of itself, was no great surprise, he told himself. After all, it would not be all that odd to see her comfortable in this setting when Elena worked for Cuban intelligence. What Sam's people were doing was similar to what Ramiro's office did.

"But no sign of Moreno?" McGrath asked.

"Unfortunately, no. But the net's drawing tighter by the hour."

"Somebody's got to spot him," Elena said, a note of tentativeness in her voice. "That computer photo you showed us yesterday was really clear. He ought to be easy to identify."

"Oh yeah," Goodwin said, thoughtfully, stroking his combed-back hair. "Of course, by now Moreno almost certainly has disguised himself."

"What about the Mexican president?" Elena asked.

"The secret service will be all over him during his stay.

President Fox's going to deliver an address to Congress on Monday. After that, he's going down to the National Press Club to brief reporters. The secret service will be there along with the D.C. police."

"Sam, what's the chance that Elena and I could attend President Fox's Congressional speech and his talk at the National Press Club? Wouldn't it make sense to have Elena down there at the talks to ID Moreno? She's your best source of information."

They kicked it around for another five minutes and finally Goodwin gave in. "OK, OK," he said grudgingly, "it does make sense, I got to admit it. But I'm going to insist that you have an escort detail as security."

"Think of me as part of that escort service," McGrath said. "Thanks Sam."

"I'll get you cell phones with secret service numbers. Anyway, you both need to get out of the safe house for a little exercise," he chuckled.

Moreno, Miguel, three henchmen, and Bernardo arrived at the marina off Maine Avenue in Washington, D.C. at two forty-five early Sunday morning. They had cruised cautiously up the Potomac, 105 nautical miles to Washington. This gave Moreno plenty of time to rest and catch up on his sleep before they hit D.C. The marina was all quiet now, basking serenely in the moon glow. As they motored quietly into their berth, Bernardo picked up a distinctive fishy odor, unsurprising, for the marina lay within spitting distance of the busy fish market's floating barges and upscale restaurants.

Miguel had secured a visitor's slip through one of his Washington contacts who worked the city's lucrative drug trade. With the boat in slip, they went over last minute plans with Miguel. Bernardo would wait on the boat, keep an eye on things, and be ready to move out when Moreno, Miguel, and the others returned on Monday after the assassination.

"OK," Miguel said, "let's go." It was only a short distance to the apartment Miguel had set up on 2nd Street in a run-down section of the Capitol Hill area in southeast Washington. Not far from the nation's Capitol building, with residents always on the go and seedy neighbors not stopping to ask questions—nobody would pay much attention to men like Moreno and Miguel and his buddies. They arrived at the dingy three room apartment and hit the sack for the remainder of the night. Miguel was just as pleased to go to bed rather than talk with Moreno, because he had decided within the first few minutes after meeting him that he did not like him. He sensed the feeling was mutual, and the result was a distinctly sharp tension between the two killers.

They took their places at the conference table, and Goodwin kicked off the session. "First, let me bring you up to date. The FBI is working on the assumption that Moreno is either near D.C. by now or has already entered the city and is hiding out, laying low. They suspect that sometime during the next three days he will attempt to assassinate Fox. This belief of course hangs on strictly circumstantial evidence of his whereabouts and motives. I mean, who knows? This whole thing could be one gigantic goose chase, with Moreno now down south somewhere in Chiapas eating a stolen chicken."

"One thing we do know," Hardy said. "President Fox arrives in town this afternoon, and the security and manhunt have been dramatically intensified."

"Right. OK, on to other matters. We've completed our debriefing of Enrique Ventura. He's an interesting guy, gave us good information. I can summarize what he told us, or read part of the questions and answers to you. Bottom line . . . Ventura confirms that Havana's drug trafficking goes straight to the top of the decision-making pyramid."

"Castro himself?" asked McGinnis.

"Yes and no," Goodwin said. "Here, let me read the that section of the Q and A." The rest of them gave Goodwin their undivided attention.

"*Question*: Does Fidel know about Ramiro's drug trafficking operation out of the MININT?

"*Ventura*: Nothing of importance happens on the island without his knowledge. He has a *tremendous* intelligence gathering organization in Havana's DGI, and he receives regular briefings from Russian intelligence, which I know for certain has penetrated the Cuban military and security services.

"*Question*: Does Castro call the shots on drug trafficking?

"*Ventura*: I do not know for certain. He knows about the drug trafficking, but may not call the shots.

"*Question*: Then who does?

"*Ventura*: Probably Fidel's brother, Raúl."

"Raúl?" asked Bob Pranz, a distinct note of disbelief in his voice. "He *never* has stood out as a decisive player. Without Fidel, Raúl would be nothing."

"Right," Goodwin agreed. "But according to Ventura, Raúl is up to his neck in this thing, backed by the head of MININT, General Miguel Luís Santos, and, of course, the brains behind the whole business, our good friend, General Manuel Ramiro."

"Raúl? Very, very interesting," McGinnis jumped in. "So it's the brother that pushes the trafficking?"

"That's what Ventura tells us," said Goodwin. "Furthermore, Raúl, Ramiro, and his cousin Victor, according to Ventura's testimony have launched a whole new expanded operation lined up with Colombia's biggest drug dealer, Pedro Esteban of Colombia."

"Not *the* one and only Pedro Esteban?" uttered Ben Hardy.

"You got it."

"Holy Christ," Hardy muttered. "If Ventura is right,

Cuba is about to go *ballistic*. Havana will be *the* drug capital of the Caribbean. Maybe already *is*."

"Cuba could put the Dominican Republic and Puerto Rico to shame when it comes to the biggest drug kid on the block," McGinnis said wryly.

"Right. Ventura was so worked up about this Esteban connection that he says it's what broke the camel's back for him. He wanted no part of it. Up to now he says he had been able to remain on the periphery of the drug loop, but was afraid he would be drawn into it with this new Esteban link. In Cuban politics, you don't have the luxury of saying no to being involved in this sort of thing. If you're in the military, you get sucked into playing the game. He also says there's incredible infighting among the military big guys about the pros and cons of mounting this huge drug operation, and—get this— about the quality of Fidel's leadership. Says he's never seen such disenchantment among high ranking officers in terms of where the country's headed. Lots of disillusionment. Colossal dissent in the ranks."

"I suppose the State Department's going to use this information against the Cuban government," offered Bench.

"What do you think? *Hell yes*, they're going to use it," Goodwin said. "One huge publicity campaign. Y'know how Castro makes a big deal out of his revolution's morality. When Ventura's testimony hits the press, Castro and his brother will be dead jellyfish baking on the beach."

"I wonder how Castro's reacting to Ventura's defection," mused McGinnis.

"I'll tell you what," replied Bench. "Fidel won't sit back and let this happen again."

"You're probably right," Goodwin said. "He'll launch a huge propaganda blitz like last year. Something to debunk the defectors. He'll say the defectors are double agents like he did before, remember?"

"When will Ventura's testimony hit the press . . . later this week?" Bench asked.

"Probably," responded Goodwin, "I wouldn't be surprised to see it on the front page of The *Washington Post* by Thursday, Friday at the latest. U.S.–Cuba frictions are gonna heat up real fast. We're going to have a Caribbean Cold War in the next day or two. Maybe a hot war."

Miguel and Alejandro, the shooter, awoke around nine o'clock Sunday morning. They went out for coffee and donuts and returned within fifteen minutes. Ten minutes after they returned, Miguel and Moreno were in a heated dispute over where to make the hit.

"No," Miguel replied emphatically to Moreno's plan. The two men faced each other on the old stuffed chairs. They spoke in subdued voices, even though Miguel had spotted no one around, when he came in through the back entrance and climbed the stairs to their second floor room. "You can't make the hit on the Capitol grounds. That'll be impossible." His voice was laced with sarcasm, as if Moreno were some ignorant peasant.

"But that's how we planned it," Moreno hissed. "I don't intend to change plans this far into the operation," he added, staring hard at Miguel, taking another bite of donut.

"Listen!" Miguel shot back, dark sunken eyes fixed on Moreno's. The prominent blood vessel on the right side of his forehead arched from his right eyebrow up to his hairline like a wandering river on barren plains. His voice was terse and authoritative. He was a drug lord with a national reputation and not about to accept Moreno's goddamn imperious attitude. He frankly didn't give a damn who Moreno was or what he claimed to be. He had worked his ass off in setting up this operation, down to the final detail. Besides, Ramiro had promised him a huge stake in his expanded drug operation for his role in the assassination. He could afford no screw ups. They were on Miguel's turf now. He would call the shots.

"Goddammit," Miguel said sharply, "security on Capitol Hill is intense. They always have FBI guys, Capitol Hill police patrols, and Secret Service men covering the place when Congress is in session and even more when dignitaries are speaking. With the manhunt they've got on you, you know damn well they're going to be checking everyone twice as much. You'll have to go through their security guys just to get onto the grounds. It's going to be bad enough with security at the press club, even worse up on the Hill. You'd need a special photo identification with just the right kind of photo and right color, and to get that we'd have to write for permission. It's too late in the game to secure those kinds of identification papers. I had to pull all kinds of strings to get the IDs for the press club. You got no idea, so cool your engine, *chico*." His tone was snappish, laced with annoyance.

"A fine *fucking* time to tell me this," Moreno snapped. Still, while he kept eating, his chewing slowed as he started to listen more carefully, despite the outburst. He too wanted the job done right, and he needed Miguel to blow this place when he made the hit. So he grudingly listened.

"Also," Miguel continued, sensing he was on a roll, "we don't think it likely the Secret Service is going to allow President Fox to make speeches to the public while he's at Capitol Hill. I know we planned to make the hit when we thought he would be coming outside for a press interview. It seemed natural, no? Senators and congressmen do go outside to make statements and conduct interviews, so why not foreigners? But since we planned this operation, I've found out that the U.S. government doesn't like foreign spokesmen giving public interviews up there. They don't want anyone's remarks suggesting U.S. support by associating Capitol Hill with whatever some spokesman might say."

"Get to the point," Moreno sneered. He restrained an impulse to grab Miguel and shake the shit out of him.

"So," Miguel said, "he's not going to make an appearance on the Capitol Hill grounds. Anyway," his words mocking, "your camera would be checked and double checked before they'd let us in. They'd want to see if the camera's working. What the hell would we do if the camera was examined? Huh? Answer me that?"

Moreno swallowed his food and took a sip of coffee. Wiping the corner of his mouth with the sleeve of his shirt, he said, "Then where the *hell* do you suppose we're going to pull off this operation? While he's on the can at the Mexican Embassy?"

Miguel pretended he did not hear Moreno's baiting tone of voice.

"No. I've checked and double checked the Mexican Embassy. He'll probably visit it, that's for certain. But he's not going to stay there while he's in town. More likely he'll stay in one of the hotels downtown. Probably somewhere like the Willard, near the White House. So there's no point in our hanging around the embassy. No, like I told you, we make the hit at the National Press Club. It's on 14th Street. Fox goes there tomorrow after his address to Congress. We sure as hell won't be able to get in, but with our media IDs we can get into the press area outside the club.

"We make our move when Fox comes out. We won't be noticed, because of the crowd. Lots of cameramen around the entrance. We'll fit right in. Each of us will have a press ID. See," he said, taking a cardboard box out of his knapsack and showing Moreno the press IDs on chains they would wear around their necks. "Had to pay big bucks for these," he said. We won't be setting up for an interview, only trying to get some footage of the president as he comes out of the club, like everybody else."

"You think that's our best bet?" Moreno asked.

"Right. And the press club's located not far from the fish market marina and our boat. It's perfect. Make sure the silencer works. Let's hope we don't have a lot of blue smoke coming out of the muzzle when Alejando pulls the trigger." Long ago they had decided to bring in the best sharpshooter they could find. Moreno had insisted that he bring in the camera. He trusted no one else to do the job. Even more he wanted to be on the scene to help orchestrate it and to watch Mexico's president die.

"Might work," Moreno admitted resentfully.

"Damn right it'll work. No magnetometer to go through. And with your disguise, hell, I didn't even recognize you when you drove into Reedville yesterday, and our disguises, we should be golden. We'll appear as a team representing an ABC news affiliate in San Diego."

Moreno nodded his head in agreement.

"Don't get me wrong," Miguel said. "Security will be airtight. The press club and streets that run around will be blocked off to traffic. They always do that. There'll be a roped off area to separate the president from the press on the scene, roughly twenty or thirty feet of open space between the cameras and the main man. 'Course, he'll be standing in front of a battery of microphones."

"Lots of police and security types in the area?" Alejandro asked.

"Right," Miguel said. "The blocked off area will be swarming with D.C. police, Secret Service and FBI. This is big, and with this manhunt for Moreno they won't take chances."

"We got to stay cool," Moreno said, looking around at the other men. "Don't panic after Fox goes down."

"Remember, Alejandro, I pose as your assistant. I wear an audio bag with a tape machine, an extra microphone, some cables. We'll look authentic, amigo. I guarantee we will fit in. When you make the hit, nobody's gonna know it was your camera that fired the shot. It will be mass confusion. That's when we walk away, as if we're going to file a report. You guys," Miguel said, looking at the other two men, "go the other way around the building. We'll pick you up two blocks away, remember?" He pointed his finger to the D.C. map, "Right here." They nodded in agreement.

"I stand toward the rear of the press corps to get an overview of the scene," Moreno said.

"Exactly," Miguel said.

"And our pick-up car?" asked Moreno.

"It waits right . . . here." He ran his finger along the D.C. street map to a street corner outside the blocked off area around the press club. The driver takes us straight to the marina. From there we cruise down the Potomac to Reedville. I've arranged a twin-engine Cessna King Air plane to fly us back to Havana. We filed a flight plan for Ft. Lauderdale. We're golden until there. At that point, we just go right across the Straits. Ramiro's men await us. No sweat, my friend. It will work like a charm. To be on the safe side, we can take out anyone standing near us if we need to, when Alejandro fires the shot. The camera's got a silencer, but it's possible someone standing right next to you might hear the shot or see the smoke. Of course, with all the confusion at the club, those protesters bitching about NAFTA and the latest U.S. bail out of Mexico, we got lots of diversion. All to our advantage."

"The more confusion the better," Moreno agreed.

"I've arranged a special distraction at the press club entrance to create more confusion. Some of our people here in D.C. will be in the crowd. They'll start screaming and yelling about Fox having blood on his hands from the recent clamp down in Chiapas. They'll throw balloons filled with red ink at the press club walls. That's when, Alejandro, you make the hit. In the confusion, nobody will be aware, at least for a couple of seconds, what's happened to the president. In the confusion, we make our exit like we're gonna make a report. Alejandro, you pretend to cover the scene with your camera as you back out of the crowd."

"Sounds good," Alejandro said.

"I have a question," Moreno said.

Miguel looked at him.

"What happens if you don't make it to the car with me?"

"I knew you would ask. The answer? Simple. You're going to meet the driver today so he can recognize you. He will take you guys to the fish market marina and the boat without me. Same plan. Same place. Same timing. Instead of six passengers, the plane will have five. No sweat. We visit the press club today to check it out and make a practice run to the marina."

At CIA headquarters in Langley, Goodwin brought McGrath and Elena up to date on the search for Moreno. His report was short. In essence, the FBI manhunt had turned up a trail of eye-witness accounts that extended from Bearden, Oklahoma, to just west of Washington, D.C. But it was all circumstantial evidence. Gas station attendants looked at Moreno's picture and thought they had served a man who fit his description. No one could be certain.

"So not much direct evidence to go on, but lots of conjecture," Goodwin summed up. "The FBI surmises that if eyewitness accounts *are* accurate, then it means Moreno is somewhere in or near D.C. They got a tight search going on for him now inside D.C. itself. But so far, nothing specific has turned up."

"Any idea when or where he might try to make a move?" Neal asked.

"That's the question of the hour," replied Goodwin. "If he's as good as his reputation, then he's capable of pulling off a hit in any number of locations. That's why this place's swarming with Secret Service types. Still, it won't be easy, even for Moreno. FBI's making it as difficult as possible. Anyway, they think the most likely place for Moreno to strike would be at the press conference outside the National Press Club. Secret Service will be there like ants at the honey pot. Elena, you convinced me earlier that you could be of use if you were there, but it will be dangerous. You sure you want to do it?"

"Absolutely."

"OK, good. Your job is to try to identify Moreno. Fox is scheduled to speak at the National Press Club at two o'clock. These speeches last about an hour, when you add questions and answers. Then he's scheduled to give his press interview outside the club after his inside formal address. I think it's a dumb ass idea, one of the worst I've heard in years. I argued against it. No luck. Apparently Fox wants to be seen outside on the sidewalk. Thinks it will build better relations with Americans. He should be out of the press club at three o'clock. You still have those phones I gave you? OK," he said, looking at his watch. "Now listen you two. I know I don't have to tell you to be careful down there. But . . ." he smiled, "Be damn careful. From what you've told us, Elena, Moreno can recognize you."

"Don't worry about us, Sam, By now *careful* is our middle name," McGrath said.

"Right." Goodwin looked dubious. "OK, gotta run."

When Goodwin had departed, McGrath and Elena left his office and headed to the elevator to go down to the CIA lobby, where they would meet the secret service escorts. As they walked down the hall, McGrath stole a glance at Elena. Sam was right. Elena could recognize Moreno. But what if he spotted her first?

The car circled three times slowly in front of the National Press Club on 14th Street, not far from the White House, discussing how they would position themselves for the hit. They agreed that when President Fox appeared in the door leading outside the club to the sidewalk abutting 14th street, Alejandro would have the camera focused on Miguel, posing as a Spanish-speaking correspondent from a Los Angeles affiliate of ABC.

Then, when the "diversion" they had arranged erupted, Alejandro would aim for Fox's head. In the ensuing confusion after the assassination, Miguel, Moreno, and Alejandro would walk swiftly down the street, out of the blocked off street perimeter, and to the corner to the waiting car. They drove to that corner, and then to the next street corner on the other side of the building where the other two henchmen would be waiting for the pick-up.

Once they had familiarized themselves with the pivotal street points, Miguel's driver followed the route they would use to get to their boat. They took 14th Street across Constitution Avenue, continued past the Washington Monument on their right, and turned left on Independence Avenue. There they went to the vast science fiction-looking L'Enfant Plaza and turned right into the plaza, with its ultra-modern street lamps—four huge clear balls stacked on double stanchions every 20 feet or so—and drove to the end of the plaza. At that point, the road looped down and around to the left and emptied onto 9th Street. At 9th Street, the car turned right, crossed Maine Avenue, turned right on Water Street, and drove past Phillips restaurant toward the fish market.

The driver drove slowly by the marina where they

could see their boat still safe and secure. He turned the car around in the circular parking lot on the left and headed back to the apartment. "We don't get out now," Miguel said, as they drove back down Water Street. "We'll come down here later tonight after it's dark. Then I can brief you on the boat, show you the charts, and all that jazz. Even though Bernardo does the driving, you all should still know the layout in case you wind up on your own. By the way," he said, "know what's down there at the end of Water Street?"

"Not a clue," replied an indifferent Moreno.

"The Washington Harbor police branch, about a half mile down," he said, turning off Water Street onto Maine Avenue, "...complete with high speed chase boats."

Moreno nodded in understanding, riding along, slumped in his seat. It would give him full and complete satisfaction to see President Fox eliminated. He gazed at Miguel through hooded eyes. It occurred to him that sometime later down the road, he might want to leave a calling card with him after this operation was over.

The thought of Elena Rodríguez drifted momentarily through Moreno's mind. His animosity toward her had been mounting. She no doubt had revealed his identity to the authorities and created this goddamn manhunt. She would be responsible for trying to pin the Fox assassination on him and increasing security around Fox.

If they did not catch him, then these was no way they would know for certain that it was him who had planned the kill. Still, all this bitter speculation reenforced his wish that somehow, some way, this *Señorita Elena Rodríguez* would slip within his grasp. He would complete what Miguel failed to do—and he would do it with style, he smiled to himself.

TWENTY-SEVEN

Washington, D.C. = Havana

Moreno laid each piece of the weapon with care on the flattened newspaper on the sagging bed. He explained to Alejandro in precise detail how the parts worked. Alejandro admired the workmanship, how the pieces fit together, how they would enable him to fire with accuracy. Moreno had Alejandro oil the pieces and put them carefully back together.

At Antonio de los Baños Airport, work crews feverishly rearranged planes in a more uniform and military order, anticipating Castro's arrival the next day. Inside the hangars they worked around the clock repositioning aircraft under repair, sweeping, dusting, and cleaning everything that needed attention, all in a herculean effort to impress the high command.

Top ranking officers paced around, barking at subordinates to move lively, look sharp and keep working—harder and faster. A golden opportunity to impress the brass, and Antonio de los Baños officers were not going to allow it to slip by. Some of them might snag a promotion if they could gain Castro's attention. When he appeared on the scene, it was always like this—a flurry of activity, high anticipation, adrenaline pumping, a kind of exhilarated fixation on the moment.

General Herrera walked smartly through the crowd of workers mopping and cleaning in the hangar where Castro's private helicopter rested. It was huge—one of Cuba's few Mi-24 *Hind-Ds*. He returned the salutes that greeted his arrival on the scene. Castro's helicopter was itself under intense attention. A swarm of mechanics checked, double-checked, cleaned, oiled, measured, and conducted countless other tasks on the checklist—engine elements, blades, and internal control and communication system. He greeted several lower ranking enlisted men who recognized him instantly.

Herrera made his way through flying mops and brooms, past mechanics going to and from tool boxes, stepped over men down on hands and knees scrubbing grease spots, working to produce a spotless hangar ready for Fidel's arrival. He drew near where Ricardo was busy.

"*Hola!* General Herrera," Ricardo said, saluting, then standing next to the general observing the scene of mass clean-up underway around them.

"Looks like they'll have this hangar ready," said Herrera, half smiling with his hands locked behind his back. "This place hasn't had such a cleaning in months. It would improve this place if Fidel came here more often," he said, smiling.

Herrera and Ricardo were long-time friends, and so, when Ricardo seemed a little pale, Herrera asked him, "Ricardo, *chico*, you feeling OK. You don't look so good, my friend."

"Oh, I'm fine, *mi General*, just fine." Ricardo longed to seek Herrera's advice on this conspiracy Ramiro had dragged him into, but he dared not raise the subject even though he suspected Herrera might be sympathetic. Potential adverse consequences were too great a risk. So General Herrera simply strolled out of the hangar without a clue about Ricardo's little project and his personal relationship with Ramiro.

When Moreno, Miguel, Alejandro, and Miguel's two henchmen arrived in the blue Pontiac, a crowd had gathered outside the National Press Club on 14th Street. They stopped down the street away from the club and got out. Alejando hefted his television camera up to his shoulder. Dressed in comfortable pants, long sleeve shirts, and ties, they all looked the parts they wanted to portray in this drama, professional newsmen. Miguel wore a thick gold chain around his neck, appropriate for a reporter at a Mexican news affiliate.

With their press credentials dangling on chains around their necks, gaining admittance into the blocked off area around the press club posed no major problem. They arrived at the busy club entrance where Fox would appear, and Miguel and Alejandro made their way up to the front of the crowd just inside the ropes with the press corps. Miguel's other two men stood not far behind. They too had cameras and notepads, their job primarily focused on helping in the getaway. Moreno took a place toward the back of the crowd, with all the others wearing official badges, in position to observe. By now television news cameramen were positioning themselves to get footage of President Fox. Miguel spoke in English, doing most of the talking, and Alejandro fussed with his camera and looked in the sighting lens. He pretended to be aligning Miguel to cover his report on the day's event.

McGrath, Elena, and the two Secret Service men appeared on the jam-packed scene five minutes later. McGrath pushed his way through the noisy, restless throng, holding Elena's hand firmly. Good place for an assassination attempt, he thought. "Think you can recognize Moreno?" he asked. They had discussed how he would be disguised.

"With this crowd, it's anybody's guess," Elena said. McGrath thought her voice sounded tense, strained. But he could understand why, he thought. After all, she had seen this Moreno's photograph in Ramiro's file and witnessed him in conversation with Ramiro. Hell, she had looked into this psychopath's eyes. No wonder she's edgy, he reasoned. Who wouldn't be?

They chatted nervously, scanned the crowd and checked in with Goodwin inside the press club building with Fox. Three o'clock came and went. No sign of Fox. At ten minutes past the start time, the crowd grew restless. What they did not know was that Goodwin had arranged for Fox's sidewalk talk to be delayed fifteen minutes. The idea was to throw a wrench in the engine of anybody in the audience planning to take a shot at the president. Goodwin knew from his experience with the FBI that criminals engaged in assassination attempts act with incredible precision. A delay of minutes might throw them off, raise suspicions, maybe call it off. Worth a try.

It was Miguel, not Moreno, who was first to show signs of nervousness when Fox failed to appear on schedule. At ten minutes past three, Miguel glanced back at Moreno. His face wore an inquiring expression. Abort? Moreno shook his head. He would give it another ten minutes. Besides, Moreno thought, it would be too obvious if the three of them walked away just before Fox appeared. Miguel went back to chatting with Alejandro, though it was obvious from his body language that he was definitely antsy. It wasn't going the way he planned.

"Oh look," Elena said, nudging McGrath, "people are starting to come out the entrance. There, Neal, the third guy back, isn't that Fox?"

"Yeah," McGrath said. "Yep, that's him."

Miguel and Alejandro stopped talking and focused total attention on the Mexican president. Moreno's camera began its work along with all the other cameras pointed at the president.

"Neal," Elena said, "if Moreno's here, where the hell is he?"

She looked almost frantic, McGrath thought. He whispered close to her ear, "Remember what Sam said. Pay close attention to the cameramen and press corps up front. If he's here, he'd likely be up front." McGrath had already concentrated up and down the line on the cameramen and women. Now he was scanning the crowd.

It was another four or five minutes before Fox began to speak. They had to get everybody in his entourage out of the building, line them up around him, double-check the microphones. Finally, the crowd hushed, and he began. "Ladies and gentlemen, it is my great pleasure to be here today . . ." It was then that Elena nudged McGrath and said, "My God, Neal . . . I think . . ."

A second later a disturbance erupted about thirty feet down the sidewalk from the president. Two or three people in the crowd had pulled out balloons with red paint and tossed them at the wall, simultaneously shouting anti-NAFTA slogans and holding up anti-Fox signs—to the point of creating panic and confusion all around them. Everyone, including President Fox, stopped to see what was happening.

Even Elena was distracted momentarily as eyes focused in the direction of balloon throwing and shouting.

Nobody paid attention to the cameraman who steadied his focus on the president. Alejandro, despite the jostling and shouting around him, remained calm as he lined up President Fox in his sights.

Moreno, at the back of the crowd, away from all the commotion, watched the unfolding events and counted down the seconds, then said to himself . . . now, man . . . do it.

Alejandro inhaled slowly and aimed for the center of Fox's head—a difficult shot, but Alejandro knew he could do it. The president was probably wearing a bulletproof vest. It made no sense to aim for the torso or heart.

McGrath and Elena were shoved and jostled around

like everyone else in the noisy confusion. "What did you say?" he asked her, all the shouting drowning out easy conversation.

She had not taken her eyes off the man in question, trying to fix the binoculars on him. "Neal, I think it's him. No ponytail, but yes, I do believe it."

"See the scar on his face?" McGrath asked, just as a loud gasp suddenly erupted from the crowd. "What the hell?" McGrath turned to see what had happened, then, "Elena, the president's down!"

Up front, President Fox was on his knees, his hand covering the side of his bloody face. Secret Service types abruptly sheltered his body with theirs, orders barked out authoritatively as they tried to sort out what had happened, or more to the point, who fired the weapon and how badly was the president injured?

One of the Secret Service men assigned to McGrath and Elena grabbed the other. "Bill," he said, "look there, that cameraman backing out of the crowd. See . . . see . . . the guy backing out of the scene. All the others are still filming. That's our man. Gotta go—" he said. "Stay cool, OK?" They shot off in the direction of Alejandro and Miguel, now backing out of the crowd.

Moreno turned and started to walk casually away from the crowd, McGrath and Elena following him.

Inside a minute the Secret Service agents had bullied their way through the writhing crowd to about five feet from Alejandro and Miguel who saw them coming. It was obvious, because everyone else was scurrying around up front near the president and the ranks of the press and camera people. "OK amigo, here we go," Miguel hissed to Alejandro. Miguel had already taken out his stiletto, which glinted in the sunlight. "We got to take these two guys."

One agent went forward another two feet and stopped dead in his tracks. A bullet from Alejandro's camera weapon tore through his chest. He staggered and collapsed on the sidewalk. The second agent kept coming and managed to knock the camera out of Alejandro's hands. He unfortunately had not seen Miguel's stiletto. He plunged it into the agent's side and sent him to the pavement, blood gushing from the wound—but not before the agent fired his own weapon at Miguel. Miguel staggered back, hit in his side, bleeding, but alive. He decided to abandon Alejandro. Every man for himself in a crisis. Words he lived by.

Alejandro's time was running out. Two FBI agents with weapons drawn came at him from behind, as Miguel disappeared into the crowd and headed in the direction of Moreno. Alejandro stooped down to pick up the camera, then stood up, camera ready to fire. He turned around just in time to see Miguel's other two henchmen closing in from behind three agents now coming at him. He knew that he would have to aim carefully not to hit his own man behind the agents. His heart pounded frantically, and he found it difficult to steady his hands.

The man McGrath and Elena thought was Moreno, joined now by another man, was almost at the end of the block. They walked swiftly, McGrath and Elena following some distance behind. McGrath, on impulse, shouted, "Moreno . . . stop." The man they believed was him paused for just a fleeting second, then kept going. The pause was enough for McGrath. "That's gotta be him," he said.

Alejandro fired just as somebody jostled him from the side. The muzzle of the gun inside the camera sent the bullet ripping past the target, the agent, and directly into the forehead of his own man. His head flew backward with the impact. Before Alejandro could react, two FBI agents tackled Miguel's last remaining goon and took him to the pavement with a thud and groans, while three other FBI men surrounded Alejandro. He and the henchman still alive on the ground were handcuffed in seconds.

Moreno and the Miguel climbed into the blue Pontiac, as McGrath pulled out the cell phone and quickly punched in Goodwin's numbers. "Sam . . . we think we've spotted him. Not a hundred percent sure, but Elena thinks its him. He's getting into a blue Pontiac. He's with another guy. We're out here on Fourteenth Street. We're going to follow Yeah, sure, sure . . . we'll be careful. We won't do anything stupid."

By now people were shouting and running in all directions, some crying, holding hands up to their faces in disbelief, parents shielding children with arms wrapped around them, hustling them away, policemen bellowing and blowing whistles, attempting to clear traffic and regain some semblance of order. Terror, already on everybody's mind, spread like wildfire.

Without giving it a second thought, McGrath did the obvious. The car in front of them was a yellow cab. He should have used a D.C. police car, he knew. But in the confusion he wasn't certain he would have the authority to command one nor time to try to explain his and Elena's identity to the police and why they needed the car. Their Secret Service escorts were back at the National Press Club. He grabbed Elena, jumped in the back seat with her and shouted, "Follow that car," pointing in front of them. I'll triple your fare," he said urgently. That's all the Iranian cab driver needed to hear. Rubber squealed. They were off.

"Stay with him," McGrath said firmly, as he contacted Goodwin again and explained what had happened. The blue Pontiac they were following shot across Constitution Avenue, leaving McGrath and Elena's cab facing a yellow light.

"Gun it!" urged McGrath, "Go through it! Go! Go!"

Their driver seemed to enjoy the chase. He sped right

through the red light, wheeling in and out of traffic, just missed one car by inches, slipped through narrow spaces like an eel. He almost hit a woman and child trying to cross the street. McGrath could see pedestrians stopped on the sidewalk to stare as they sped by in a blur of action.

They followed the fleeing blue car, passed the Washington Monument, left onto Independence Avenue, and right into L'Enfant Plaza.

They flew the length of L'Enfant Plaza like they were in the Indy 500. They slammed around the curve at the end where the road angled down and to the left and dumped them out on Ninth Street. The Pontiac turned right on Ninth Street and headed toward Maine Avenue.

"Looks like he's headed for the fish market," McGrath said. "If he gets in there, he'll be hard to find. It's always so damn crowded." He was back on the phone. "The fish market, Sam. Yeah, OK . . . how soon?" He turned to Elena. "Reinforcements are on the way."

Up front, Miguel had made an instant decision to change plans. He knew he could not go directly to the power cruiser, not with that damn cab right behind him, so he instructed his driver to turn right on Water Street and go straight into the fish market. The market wasn't that far from his boat and it would be crowded. You *could* get lost in here. When they reached the circular drive in front of the market, the turn-around place, he said, "Slow down! We're jumping out here." They leaped out and slammed their doors.

By the time McGrath and Elena's cab reached Maine Avenue, the light had turned red, and the typical bumper-to-bumper traffic prevented them from crossing. When the light finally changed and they crossed and turned right onto Water Street, at first there was no sign of Moreno's blue Pontiac. It had simply disappeared into the jammed traffic circulating around the fish market area. When they reached the busy circular turn-around, McGrath said, "He's got to be in here somewhere. We didn't see the car come out. We might as well get out here. Listen, here's an extra twenty bucks. You did a great job. I want you to use your radio and let the authorities know that the man who shot President Fox is now here at the fish market."

The taxi driver said he would, collected his fare and pulled slowly away. McGrath and Elena stood there for a minute, trying to get their bearings.

The place was alive with people, an ethnic mélange of faces and dress, languages, and sounds. Noisy and confusing. A huge crowd of people milled around, talking, laughing, lots of shouting by the fish salesforce. Several huge fish barges floated there on the Potomac, offering sumptuous displays of every kind of fish and shellfish imaginable—piled high on stacks and stacks of crushed ice, behind which the fast talking, rubber-booted sales force hawked the day's catch. Where were they, McGrath thought.

The 200-foot wide pier extending straight ahead out into the Potomac lay before them, barges aligned along the right side, at the end at river's edge, and back down toward them on the left. Each barge had a long 60–80 foot display of fish and crabs—from flounder to blues, giant crabs and all manner of shellfish—piled appealingly high on mounds of crushed ice. Behind these dazzling displays, lower down on a walkway, paraded the sea of fish salespeople in slippery scaly-wet walkways about five feet wide. There they did the weighing and adding, tossing and bagging their wares.

"Listen," said McGrath, his heart pounding, "the best thing for us to do now is to stay together. It's possible Moreno won't recognize you. He doesn't know you're here in the U.S. And he sure as hell doesn't know me. But we might recognize him. Let's see if we can spot him. He's got to be here somewhere. It shouldn't be that hard to see him."

"OK. Good idea," Elena nodded in agreement. She sounded determined and in control.

"We can work our way straight ahead, down that way, toward Cap'n White's . . . see," he said, pointing, "there at the end of the pier, at the river's edge."

"OK," Elena responded, as if she were certain of what they were doing.

McGrath took Elena's arm and elbowed his way methodically through the crowd. They took their time, letting their eyes scan across faces. McGrath could feel his pulse race, fascinated by the chase, musing over how he had got himself into this situation, wondering exactly what in the hell he was going to do if they actually spotted Moreno. They came closer and closer to Cap'n White's busy barge at the far end of the fish market.

"God, Neal," Elena said, so close to him that he could hear her whisper, "maybe he's already slipped out a back way. Wouldn't surprise me one little bit, if . . ." then she froze. She squeezed McGrath's arm so hard her fingernails dug into his flesh.

"Neal," Elena whispered, catching her breath so loudly, McGrath could hear it. "Over there. By that vegetable and fruit stand. The man in the blue shirt and red tie. It's him." She moved even closer to McGrath, her right elbow close to her side, using just her upraised hand and index finger to jab in the direction she wanted McGrath to look. McGrath sensed that she was excited about finding their quarry, but not as scared as he might have expected.

Bernardo waited patiently in the cabin of the boat tied up near the fish market. He checked his watch for the tenth time in the last fifteen minutes. They should be back any minute now. He was ready. He had waited for this moment for a long time. Ever since the incident with the leather sack Miguel had ordered his men to place over his head. Yeah, he thought, he was ready. He looked at the revolver resting in his lap. His first shot would be for Miguel. The second for Moreno. He would aim for the heart in both cases. The silencer would muffle the shots. He thought again how he would dispose of the bodies. He saw himself dumping them down river in the dark into the Potomac. Each body wrapped in anchor chain attached to a small Danforth anchor. In time, he thought, fish and decay would do the rest.

He had his story all worked out. The two men, who he knew from the trip up from Reedville disliked each other intensely, got into an argument on the return trip. He would say that Moreno shot and killed Miguel who fell overboard and then tried to shoot Bernardo. Bernardo would say that he then shot Moreno who fell overboard. That would keep Bernardo in the clear and play to Miguel's lieutenants' probable paranoia about Ramiro and Moreno double-crossing them. Yes, he thought, it's believable.

Then he heard someone step aboard outside. The boat rocked ever so slightly. Miguel's voice came through the door. "Bernardo," he said. "Come quick. I need help."

"Down here," Bernardo replied. Then he saw Miguel's feet stepping down into the cabin. His shirt was covered with blood. He apparently was alone. All the better, he thought. He slipped the revolver into his belt under his shirt. He would get Miguel into his stateroom and eliminate him there. That seemed safer. He didn't want Moreno to come in and find Miguel dead on the floor of the main salon in a pool of blood. But as soon as he saw Miguel, he had a second thought. Miguel must be wounded bad. He looked white as a sheet, about to faint. He would help him into his cabin. Bernardo walked across the floor to Miguel to lend him his shoulder.

"Where's Moreno?" Bernardo asked.

"Don't know . . . maybe still in the fish market," his voice a shallow whisper, barely audible. His feet scarcely helped move him in the direction of the state-room. "Water." Miguel said in a fading voice.

Bernardo helped Miguel onto the bed, stood up, and said, "I'll be right back with the water." He made no effort to stop the bleeding from the wound. In the galley, Bernardo took his time pouring the glass of water. He wondered when Moreno would come in. Miguel was one thing, he thought. An old score that needed settling. Moreno was another fish. A big fish. He knew, from what Miguel had told him, that Ramiro wanted Miguel to kill Moreno after the hit on the president. Miguel had made Bernardo a party to his plans, expecting him to help take out Moreno. Bernardo was at first frightened, then excited. It would be enough money to go home and live the fat life with his family. It was an offer he could not refuse. Yes, for money like that, he could find the courage. In the back of his mind, he ran through his story again . . . he would say that Moreno killed Miguel when Miguel tried to shoot him and he, Bernardo, killed Moreno in self-defense. He could see himself then approaching Ramiro for the money that would have gone to Miguel for killing Moreno. Perfect, he thought.

Bernardo returned to the stateroom, heart racing, concentrating on what he was about to do. He could see that Miguel was either sleeping or had fainted, his eyes closed, breathing thinly. Time to get to work, Bernardo thought. He went outside the room to his duffle bag and removed the dark brown leather bag, just about the size to fit a bowling ball—or a man's head. But first he stepped up the ladder and peered outside down the dock. No sign of Moreno.

He went back to the stateroom where Miguel was lying on his side on the bed. Bernardo walked around to the side of the bed where he could see Miguel's eyes. They were closed. He put his ear up to Miguel's mouth—shallow breathing, barely audible. Ever so gently he slipped the bag over Miguel's head, drew it down snugly over his eyes, nose, and chin. He carefully pulled the tie strings tight and made a firm knot at the back of Miguel's neck. He made the knot double firm so that it would be impossible for the man inside to untie it before he suffocated to death. Bernardo stepped back, admired his handiwork, paused for a moment, his face a mask of sweet revenge. He stepped outside the stateroom and closed the door. He went back to the cabin ladder and stepped up to peer outside to see if he could see Moreno coming.

"Where?" McGrath whispered "Which one? There're three men standing there."

"The big one," Elena replied in a soft voice. "The one holding the cantaloupe." McGrath was struck by how cool and intelligent she sounded and acted in this threatening situation. She focused on Moreno like a lab retriever. He felt almost as if he had to hold her back, like hanging onto a leash.

"You sure that's him?"

"Yes. Yes. The ponytail's gone. But, yes, it's him for sure."

"Hang on a minute." McGrath pulled the phone from his pocket and punched in the numbers. Then he hit the "send" button. Nothing. He repeated the sequence. Nothing. "Shit, the phone's not working . . . OK, listen, Keep an eye on him. I'm going to use that public phone over there and call Sam. You OK for a minute or two?"

"Yes . . . sure . . . I'll be right here." She turned away and fixed her gaze on Moreno.

"OK I'll be back in a second."

"Neal," she said. She turned to look into his eyes. "I love you."

It took him by surprise, because she had seemed so distant and preoccupied lately.

"I love you too," McGrath said. He held her close and kissed her, then moved off in the thick crowd. He made his way to the telephone hanging in the little half-booth on the side of the nearby building. He reached it, hurriedly dialed the number and waited. Busy. OK, he thought, he could wait a minute. From where he was positioned, Elena and Moreno were in his line of sight. He could see Elena standing there. Moreno had not left the produce stand. Again he dialed. On the second try, his call went through. "We've spotted him, Sam. Yes. The fish market. Yes . . . yes . . . she's right here with me. OK . . . OK. We won't do anything. Right, right . . . we'll just stick with him. No, I won't approach him. Yes, understood."

As he spoke to Goodwin, McGrath momentarily lost sight of Elena, the crowd blocking out his line of vision. He hung up the receiver, listened to it click into place, glad to know that Goodwin was on his way down there, his heart pounding like a racehorse, then turned to go back to Elena. He didn't see her at first. He thought he caught a momentary glimpse of the top of her head through the crowd. But as he looked hard at where she had been standing, elbowing his way through the crowd toward where he had left her, it became clear she was not there. Where was she? Where was Moreno?

TWENTY-EIGHT

Washington, D.C. = Havana

McGrath was stunned. Elena was missing. So was Moreno. Was that her on the other side of the crowd? No, somebody else. He looked in another direction. Over there? No. My God, he thought, she's disappeared. He tried to stay calm. He pushed into the crowd

toward the spot where he had left her. Come on . . .
come on . . . Elena, his mind raced, for the love of God,
where are you?

Then he saw them. Elena *and* Moreno. *Close together*.
Moreno leaning against her from the back, and it looked
like, yes, for certain, McGrath could see Elena's right
arm bent up tight behind her, held by Moreno. He
leaned forward, pressing her forward in front of Cap'n
White's barge not more than twenty feet from McGrath.

Elena's face was drained of color as Moreno forced
her along in front of the huge fish-laden barge at the end
of the pier. He seemed remarkably unperturbed, smiling, walking along, saying something into her right ear.

McGrath looked around for help, but saw no reinforcements. He dared not shout for fear of spooking
Moreno into harming Elena. His eyes fixed on the two of
them, his mind racing through his next move. Then
Elena's face grimaced, as if Moreno had raised her bent
arm a notch higher up behind her back. That did it.

With a turbo thrust of adrenaline, McGrath shoved
aside the man in front of him, dug in and plunged head-
long across the short open space separating him from
Moreno and Elena. Neither of them saw him sprinting
toward them, their faces turned away.

McGrath raced across the open space, put his shoulder down and hit Moreno on the left side with every
ounce of energy he could muster. On contact the three of
them half-staggered, half-fell, reeling downward onto a
pile of freshly cut, slippery flounder laid out on a huge
mound of crushed ice. They slithered across the stacked
fish, McGrath grappling to get his hands around
Moreno's neck, determined to squeeze the life out of
him there on the spot.

The three of them entangled as they kicked and
thrashed—knocking scallops, squid, and live crabs into
the slippery barge walkway. Elena's head crashed into

the wall on the other side of the walkway, four feet down from street level into the barge. She looked unconscious. Two fish hawkers rushed over to attend to her and another acted as if he might jump into the melee, but he seemed unsure who was the good guy and who was the bad. McGrath glanced at Elena, then back to Moreno.

Down on the ice-covered wet floor behind the fish counter, in a pile of flounder and slimy squid, McGrath closed on Moreno and smashed his face three times with his right fist. Blood spewed from Moreno's nose, now broken and McGrath was about to hammer a fourth blow, when Moreno twisted free. In a second McGrath saw the knife and the look in Moreno's eyes. Moreno, left hand out as if to mesmerize McGrath, lunged with a deft right arm underhand jab, like he was pitching a softball. The abrupt move made him slip on the squid and wet floor and miss his quarry. McGrath sidestepped and shouted, "Somebody call the police . . . this guy's a killer wanted by the FBI."

Still nobody jumped in, and Moreno now was getting up from the floor. He was on one knee, knife in hand with intent to kill written all over his bloody face. McGrath looked around and grabbed a basketfull of soft shell crabs and slammed the basket upside down on Moreno's head. Live crabs caused him to drop his knife, which skidded across the floor over the side and plopped into the water. At this point, Moreno decided that as much as he wanted to kill McGrath, of higher priority was escape. McGrath grabbed his left leg and hung on, dragged along the floor as Moreno tried to kick himself free.

By the time Moreno had dragged McGrath five or six feet, he saw a way down a corridor that led to the back of the barge, the opening to which lay in front of him. Thinking fast, Moreno allowed Neal to get up—in fact

Moreno reached down and pulled Neal to his struggling and slipping feet, then got him into a neck collar hold with his left arm, smashed him hard in the right eye, and threw him over his hip and through an open door into a six-by-six foot room filled with crushed ice. McGrath thudded upside down in a loud crunch of loosely packed flying ice, and Moreno was convinced he had knocked him cold, or better broke his neck. But he did not have time to check out his handiwork. This thing had gotten out of hand.

With McGrath lying dazed on the ice, Moreno dashed down the thirty foot corridor to the back of the barge. He briefly thought he'd like to slam the door and lock this man in the ice room, but the clock was ticking. No time to lose.

McGrath shook off his disorientation, wiped at the warm smear covering his eye, stumbled off the ice, and brushed aside help offered him by two men standing by.

Moreno had raced down the corridor, turned left, run another fifteen feet, only to discover that he was in a cul-de-sac. When he turned back along the walkway by the river's edge, he found himself face to face with McGrath, now stumbling toward him down the corridor. Moreno knew he was positioned on the barge's deck floating on the murky Potomac River just two feet below and behind him. He had no doubt he could handle this man coming toward him.

McGrath staggered forward, his head tilted to the right so he could see through his left eye. Moreno prepared himself in a balanced karate stance. McGrath sized up the situation quickly. He knew Moreno was a specialist in martial arts. But he remembered Elena telling him that the report on Moreno mentioned that he was afraid of water. He looked directly into Moreno's steely cold eyes and calculated what he would do next. Karate kick came to mind, given the man's stance. Mc-

Grath noticed the deck was wet and slippery. The next second he let out a bellow and lunged at Moreno for the second time that day.

Moreno's kick was exquisitely timed, executed perfectly. The blow, however, missed McGrath's body by less than an inch and wound up in his hands. McGrath grabbed the foot, twisted it sharply, and raised the leg high into the air causing Moreno to lose his balance and stumble backward. This movement, coupled with McGrath's charging weight, sent both men over the edge. They plunged into thirty-two feet of warm, murky dark, Potomac River water.

McGrath knew instantly that Moreno was in a state of panic. It was obvious in the wild thrashing and flailing arms, wide open eyes and heavy gasps for air. The playing field suddenly seemed level for McGrath, for Moreno's alarm nullified some of his strength and agility in martial arts. McGrath sensed it immediately as he struggled with Moreno deep down in the watery depths that engulfed their slowly turning bodies. Still, McGrath knew he was dealing with a psychotic killer who could kill someone easily in close physical contact. Though terrified by the water, McGrath understood that Moreno could kill even in these conditions.

The first time they came up for air, McGrath saw fear in Moreno's eyes as he beat away at the water, heard him suck in a loud gasp of air, trying to get McGrath off his back. They went under again, but not before McGrath caught sight of a helicopter coming in for a landing. Under water, McGrath could not see his opponent, but felt his writhing body, which he used to manuever around behind him to pull him farther away from the barge. McGrath had taken a huge gulp of air as they went under the second time, and down in the brackish depths he hung on to Moreno, sensing his confusion and fear.

When he tackled Moreno at the edge of the barge and flew into the water with him, McGrath's first impulse was to end this man's life under the water. He would hold on and take Moreno under with him. But in the struggle under water, his lungs signalled for air and Moreno's thrashing stopped. His body went limp. McGrath decided that Moreno should be kept alive. Secret Service would want to question him. So he decided to bring him to the surface, get him revived back on the barge, and turn him over to the authorities. Let them decide his fate.

They surfaced about ten feet from the barge, as all the people who could squeeze into the narrow door opening looked out at them.

"You need help?" someone shouted. McGrath saw the two D.C. policemen taking off their shoes and socks. Sam was there too, shouting encouragement.

"Hang on," somebody yelled. "Here comes the life line!" McGrath saw the man heave a life buoy toward him, and it splashed into the water within his grasp, tiny ripples flowing out from where it hit.

Gasping for air, McGrath managed to get out words indicating he could make it, as he pulled the unconscious Moreno to the surface and reached for the buoy. The two D.C. policemen dived into the water. Then it happened. Moreno suddenly came alive, reached over and pulled McGrath in close to him, got his left arm around his neck and began to force him under water, before McGrath had time to catch an extra breath of air. For a moment in suspended time, their roles had unexpectedly reversed.

McGrath knew he had to do something quickly. He could not last long under water. His lungs screamed for air, and he did the only thing that came to his wildly churning mind. With his free left arm and hand, McGrath reached down between Moreno's legs, clutched his testicles in a tightly closing fist and squeezed with every ounce of energy he possessed. Moreno writhed in pain as McGrath squeezed harder and harder. Moreno's grip on him lessened, and gave him just the second he needed to maneuver. McGrath came around and up again behind Moreno.

He saw to his shock that Moreno had produced a knife that must have been strapped to his leg. Moreno lashed at McGrath's midsection, but McGrath was quicker in this element. He grasped Moreno's wrist, bent it backward, and got the knife away from him. With his head above the surface of the water, McGrath took a huge gulp of air and, with his own hammer lock, pulled Moreno's head back down under water with him, and plunged the knife into his midsection. Blood began to mix with the churning water, and this time McGrath did not try to save the bleeding and drowning Moreno. He held tightly—until bubbles trickled out of Moreno's gaping mouth.

It was then, and only then, when Moreno again went limp, eyes open, that McGrath rose to the surface, pulling up Moreno's body behind him, now aided by the policemen who had now reached him. Together they manuevered Moreno back to the barge, where extended hands pulled all of them out of the water. Sonny and Billy White, the barge owners, were on the scene, along with more D.C. policemen, Sam, an FBI guy, and a couple of Secret Service men.

They hauled Moreno's heavy bleeding body up first and laid it on the barge deck, where the FBI man began to try to revive him with old-fashioned artificial respiration. Moreno lay on his stomach, head to one side, dark brakish water, and vomit gushing out of his mouth.

McGrath slumped down on the deck and leaned his back against the wall in the puddle of water that collected around him. He tried to catch his breath, breathing hard, watching Elena come down the corridor, helped along by a policewoman. Behind them he could see three more paramedics racing down the corridor with their life-rescuing equipment. Elena hurried over to him, kneeled down and threw her arms around him tightly, tears welling in her eyes, as she murmured, "Neal, Neal . . . I'm so glad you're alive. My God I thought he had killed you."

He smiled, then coughed and wiped his mouth with the back of his hand. He returned her hug.

They held onto each other, resting against the barge wall, and McGrath nodded to the paramedic that he was OK. He gazed over Elena's shoulder at Moreno, five feet away. A paramedic was down on his knees, face close to Moreno's, checking for breathing, and now had rolled him over, looking at Moreno's chest. His fingers were on his carotid, looking for a pulse. Another paramedic was beside him, standing by with an ambulance bag, the stretcher lying on the deck next to Moreno. "His pulse is thready. No respiration," said the paramedic.

"Throw me a mask," McGrath heard the paramedic say to his assistant. They slapped what looked like an oxygen mask with a tube in it on Moreno, and the man working on Moreno blew into it several times. "He has airway, but still not breathing. His larynx isn't blocked." Then, without warning, Moreno started coughing up more water and vomit. "Roll him, Jim. Bill, get over here quick."

"One, two, three, roll," at which point the three paramedics gently rolled Moreno onto his right side, as he continued to cough up murky water and vomit. "Suction!" and they efficiently suctioned out the liquids in Moreno's mouth and throat "He's breathing."

From where he was sitting, McGrath could see Moreno's dusky, bluish gray face, with blue around his lips. His nail beds were grayish-blue as well. "Blood pressure's ninety—palpable, pulse in the fifties. Not good," he said anxiously. "Get the IV and stretcher ready."

"He's probably going to die, Elena," McGrath whispered, his voice weak with exhaustion. They watched the paramedics lifting Moreno's blanket-wrapped body onto the stretcher, an IV in his wrist, neck in an immobilizer, dirty water running from his mouth. "Sam could have used Moreno for information to nail Ramiro."

"For God's sake, Neal. Don't worry about it," Elena replied softly, hugging him. "The agency will piece it all together."

Another paramedic appeared on the scene to take McGrath's blood pressure, while others worked on Moreno. They now had him on "high flow" oxygen. A mask covered Moreno's face, and on a backboard on the stretcher they put a cervical collar on him should his neck be broken. His head was taped to the backboard. McGrath watched as they attached spider straps on him, one long nylon strap running down the length of his body, with other lateral straps running off into holes along the edge of the backboard. Moreno was unconscious, but the oxygen was flowing. McGrath's blood pressure was high, one hundred forty over ninety, heartbeat at one hundred ten, adrenaline still pumping from the struggle. He and Elena were both wrapped in blankets. They asked him if he was he strong enough to walk back to the ambulance for a check-up.

They escorted McGrath and Elena back down the corridor out to the front of Billy White's barge. Television panel trucks and media newspeople were there, interviews underway, police cars everywhere. An ambulance with doors open stood not far from where McGrath had fought with Moreno, while a second peeled away with its siren on. It was taking Moreno, handcuffs on his wrists and ankles, to the nearest hospital. Everyone seemed to be talking at once, and McGrath heard a police car's siren howl toward them from out on Maine Avenue. Goodwin walked alongside him with Elena.

"What happened to the Mexican president?" McGrath asked. "Was he killed?"

"We thought so at first," Goodwin said. "But the bullet just grazed his ear."

"Did they get the shooter?"

"Oh yeah, and some of his buddies too. A real round up. How you feeling?"

"Like I've been hit by a mack truck. Light-headed."

I can imagine," Goodwin said softly. "Let's go over here. We've got an ambulance waiting." McGrath heard the words only faintly, far distant, as he sank to his knees and felt arms around him.

The next thing McGrath knew he was lying on a stretcher inside an ambulance, racing to the hospital, sirens wailing, Goodwin by his side. Elena lay on the other stretcher. He closed his eyes, listening to the siren, and faded into unconsciousness. His last thought before he drifted off was of Elena.

On Monday afternoon Ramiro made his last minute telephone calls in a state of intoxicated exhilaration. As the hours sped by while he checked in with each of his generals supporting Operation Rebirth, his adrenaline rushed at the prospects of eliminating the two men who stood in his way for control of Cuba—*el Comandante* and his brother. They were in a countdown to tomorrow's explosive change in government, and he marveled at the brilliance of his plan and orchestrated success in putting it into motion. As Ramiro completed one call after the other, the aphrodisiac of power surged through him. He could not remember a time when he felt as excited as he did now—except, perhaps, when he had paraded into Havana on the day they overthrew Batista years ago. But this was different. This day would be his to celebrate—his creation. His triumph.

Sure, there were two other individuals he thought about. Elena was one. But Miguel or Moreno would dispatch her. Miguel should check in any time now. Ventura was the second problem. But what Ventura told the CIA about the drug operation wouldn't be important once the coup was sprung and everything in Cuba was in chaos. Unless, of course, Castro was right and the U.S. was preparing to launch an attack. But this was pure speculation. Castro could be dead wrong.

When he finished speaking with the last person on his list, Ramiro's telephone rang to bring a message from Quintero. Esteban, whom they had hosted on his trip up from Colombia, was in great spirits after his "remarkable" night with Yolanda. Quintero reported that he was fantastically impressed with their capability to handle massive drug shipments to the U.S.

"Esteban is ready to deal," Quintero told Ramiro. "He's prepared to ship through Cuba as much stuff as we want to handle. We've struck it rich!" Quintero shouted at the other end of the line, unable to contain his feverish excitement. Ramiro put down the receiver, leaned back in his swivel chair and lit up a huge rich Cohiba cigar. A new era loomed on the horizon.

TWENTY-NINE

Antonio De Los Baños, Cuba—Langley, Virginia

By the time Castro's jeeps left the Plaza de la Revolución, Herrera had arrived at the airport. He was there as part of the send-off delegation with Ramiro and his staff. Later he would fly over to Pinar del Rio to review the Territorial Troops. He sat nervously in the Flight Office with Castro's physician, Dr. Torres, a small man wearing dark horn-rimmed glasses and a white *guayabera*. He would ride on the helicopter with Castro. Normal procedure.

Herrera stood up, walked to the coffee urn, poured two cups of coffee, his cold, perspiring hands trembling slightly. He came back and handed a cup to Torres. "You have those magic blue pills, doctor?" he casually asked the physician, smiling and sitting down while looking around to make certain nobody could hear.

"*Sí* señor," said Dr. Torres uneasily. He patted his shirt pocket.

"You will have Castro take them before he boards the helicopter?"

"*Absolutamente*. He will want to swallow them, from what I know about the lady in waiting." The physican smiled knowingly.

"The stroke occurrs within four hours after he takes them?"

"Precisely. Rest assured it will occur." His voice was thin and tinny.

"*Bueno*," Herrera said.

Five minutes later Castro's jeep caravan wound into view down the road, a sand trail ghosting along behind it. Castro's jeep passed by the flight office and skidded to a stop in front of the massive hangar. The huge helicopter soon would be wheeled out.

Back in the hangar, Ricardo nervously checked the bag containing the bomb, which lay beneath the workbench with its spare parts and tools. Like the others, he turned around and snapped to attention when one of Castro's staff barked his arrival. In seconds his profile appeared at the hangar door. Behind him, Ricardo could see Raúl's much smaller figure. One of Castro's staff barked the "At ease" command, and Cuba's leader started discussing something with one of the chief mechanics standing beside him at the hangar entrance.

It was at this point that Ricardo bent down, as if to check for a lost tool under his bench, readying himself to grasp his bag with the device in it at precisely the right time. His hands were shaking like a leaf, but his timing was impeccable. As soon as he leaned under the workbench, he heard the cry of "Fire!" from the other side of the hangar.

That word unleashed the panic and confusion Ramiro anticipated.

Each person involved in the fire diversion played his part to perfection. Yelling erupted, and several mechanics started running toward the fire. Ramiro jumped into action. He ran in direction of the fire, and when he darted by the security guard standing by the door to Castro's helicopter, he shouted authoritatively, "Come on man, we can use your help."

The guard, conditioned to follow orders, left his helicopter post and followed Ramiro.

Ricardo grabbed his bag, jogged to the door of the helicopter, hurriedly looked around, then bolted for it. He leaped up the steps to the cockpit, tripped on the third step, regained his composure, and scrambled inside. He pulled the door shut behind him, panting heavily. In just seconds—he had practiced this move over and over again late at night when no one was around the hangar—he secured the device behind the instrument panel. No one would ever find it, and it was set to go off just as General Ramiro had determined. Then, he peered out the window to see if the coast was still clear. Within a minute he was back out of the helicopter, making his way to the scene of the commotion.

They got the fire under control five minutes later, and Castro instructed that the helicopter be wheeled outside, where he, Raúl and the other officials would board and fly to Pinar del Rio.

Ramiro and Ricardo—from their different perspectives—watched intently as the lumbering tractor hauled out the giant locust onto the hot tarmac. Ricardo signed deeply in relief, because his work on Operation Rebirth was done.

Herrera stood outside now with Dr. Torres, watching

the helicopter preparations, surprised, like everybody else about the fire. "Strange," Herrera commented to Torres, "that's the first fire in the hangar in a long time." He had a puzzled look on his face.

When the MI-24 *Hind-D* monster lay at rest on the tarmac, glistening in the morning sun, Castro strode over to the door with his arm around his pilot. The whole thing was going like clockwork, Ramiro thought. Soon it would all be over. He felt a surge of confidence as the hint of a smile played around the corners of his mouth.

It was at that point that Castro's physician, Dr. Torres, sidled up to him, spoke a few words to him quietly, and handed him a little blue pill with a glass of water. The old leader looked at it and paused. Then, instead of putting it in his mouth, he abruptly stuffed it in his left shirt pocket. The physician looked concerned and Herrera, who could not believe what he had just witnessed, could see from where he was standing that Dr. Torres was whispering something energetically to Castro. The gray-bearded head of state looked irritated and brushed off the physician, as he might a fly.

Herrera watched this episode in stunned disbelief, all his senses on instant alert. What was going on here? Castro was supposed to take the pill. He didn't swallow the pill. Herrera's pulse raced. Something was wrong. Dramatically wrong. He had a sudden urge to go to his car and drive away. Perspiration trickled down the small of his back.

Ramiro, preoccupied in a discussion with Castro's brother, completely missed the incident. Either that, or he simply ignored it as of no importance. Ramiro stopped talking when he heard Castro bark out the name, "Ricardo." That he knew the mechanic's name was not so unusual. Castro knew most of the men's names at this and other airports. It was the tone of voice. Something sinister about it, Ramiro thought. "Come here, please," Castro said, motioning to the mechanic.

Ramiro saw Ricardo's face turn ashen, the young man in a state of shock as he walked slowly toward Castro. When he stood before Castro, Ramiro began to feel uneasy himself. Had Castro, or somebody on his staff, seen Ricardo plant the explosive? Something darkly ominous about this scene, he thought. Why Ricardo? What's going on here? He glanced over at Herrera, whose face was granite stone, impassive. Ramiro shifted his weight. Hard to tell what Herrera was thinking behind those sunglasses, but yes, Herrera was worried too. Ramiro could see it at the pinched corners of his mouth. Nobody else seemed concerned.

"I have a surprise for you, Ricardo," Castro said. "We're going to take you out to Pinar del Rio with us. We'll need a good mechanic if anything goes wrong," he smiled. "You're the man I want," he said, scratching his beard. Castro's eyes seemed to twinkle with his words.

"Oh," he added, looking over at Herrera, "General Herrera will be our pilot today. We'll use my main pilot as co-pilot, to give him a little rest. I think General Herrera would enjoy arriving early for the exercises, right Julio? And you, Manuel," he said, looking at Ramiro, "I want you to come along for the ride too. We need to talk."

Ramiro's mouth went dry. For a minute he could make nothing come out. He stood there and looked blankly at Castro, not knowing exactly what to do. To run would be foolhardy. To board the helicopter certain death. He knew at that instant that he, Herrera, and Ricardo would be blown to pieces within the half hour. Obliterated in the twinkle of an eye.

Ramiro looked at Herrera who seemed relatively unaffected by the whole situation. But, then, why should Herrera be concerned, Ramiro thought. He knew nothing of the bomb in the helicopter. To plant the bomb was Ramiro's decision. He had made it without telling Herrera, who was dead set against it. Herrera staunchly insisted on the pill to induce a stroke. Ramiro visualized that evening when he and Herrera had argued heatedly. Operation Rebirth had nearly unraveled right then and there. In an effort to paper over their fragile alliance, Ramiro had promised Herrera that he would go along with the pill—a chess move promise to buy time.

"OK, climb aboard, *mis amigos. Vamos,*" Castro said in that thin, high-pitched voice of his, walking toward the giant locust basking in the sunshine.

Ramiro looked at Ricardo, as if to ask if the device were in place. Ricardo gave a slight, tremulous nod *"Sí."* He seemed to be blinking hard to hold back the tears. They both knew that once the timer had been set on this particular explosive device, it could not be stopped, short of cutting wires. The timer definitely was set.

"Fidel," Ramiro said, in as calm a voice as he could muster, removing his sunglasses, locking his eyes on Castro as they walked toward the helicopter, "I have an extremely important meeting this morning back at MININT. We're taking a hard look at the causes of recent defections. I should be there. I'm in charge of the meeting."

Castro stopped. He paused for a second and stroked his beard. He checked his watch. He looked at Ramiro and said, "Let it wait. What we have to discuss is far more important. Let's go." He started walking again. Ramiro could feel his heart pounding, as he thought frantically for some way out. His feet felt like lead as he worked to lift them to place one foot down in front of the other.

Herrera overheard this brief exchange and looked closely at Ramiro. He could swear the man's hands were trembling. He looked pale. Positively ill. It was catchy. It made Herrera more nervous. Something definitely wrong here, he thought. The image of Castro turning down the pills lingered vividly in his mind. What's going on?

Herrera followed Castro up the steps, climbing up and into the cockpit. He took the pilot's seat beside Castro's regular pilot and clicked the safety harness buckle into place. Castro sat in seats directly behind Herrera with his brother, Ramiro, Ricardo, and the others. Dr. Torres was with them. Three Castro security guards were riding today.

"Manuel," Fidel said, turning to Ramiro, in a tone of compassion, "You are strangely quiet, my friend. I trust you are well. You look a little pallid."

Ramiro gave him a blank stare. His mind raced. What could he do? "You're certain you'd rather have me here than at that meeting?" he asked.

"*Absolutamente,*" Castro answered suavely.

Herrera, seated in the pilot's chair, convinced something had gone wrong, automatically began his preflight check out procedure. He switched on one button. Then another. Why had Castro treated his physician so disdainfully? Why bring Ricardo along? What was the story with Ramiro? Why was he sitting there? Why am I flying this goddamn thing? He glanced back at Ramiro. The guy was white as a sheet. Herrera could see that the mechanic, Ricardo, looked like he was about to vomit.

Herrera glanced at Castro. He seemed totally in control. He turned back to the controls and started the engine, trying to keep his hands from shaking. The rising whine of the engine and thudding of giant rotor blades overhead drowned out conversation. Herrera tuned the radio frequency to check for tower clearance and prepare for take-off. With his heart beating wildly, he struggled to keep his wife and son in focus as he concentrated on flying this beast.

As the motor's resonating hum and whirring blades churned overhead—dirt, paper, and anything not tied down swirling around outside in the tumult of wind—Herrera looked at the waving bystanders watching them take off. He gave them a smile and a jaunty "thumbs up" sign, swallowed hard, and prepared to lift off.

Ricardo seemed to be praying. He rubbed his hands hard up and down his pant legs to dry the palms of his hands. He was acutely aware that Castro was watching him closely out of the corner of his eye. A look of utter disgust lay on his face like one of those Mexican masks in Ramiro's living room. He felt for a moment that he might need the sick bag.

The giant helicopter shuttered off the hot tarmac, its huge metal frame vibrating convulsively from the engine's pulsating thrust. Inside, at about one hundred feet of altitude, Ramiro watched as Castro shifted his weight and held his left hand high, as if he had made up his mind about something. Or was it a signal of some kind? He watched, locked in spellbound anxiety as Castro, sitting beside him, reached forward in his seat and thumped Herrera on the shoulder. Herrera glanced back, and Castro motioned with his thumb pointed down. He wanted the helicopter returned to its pad. What the hell? Ramiro wondered, relieved they were returning and he could get out of this flying deathtrap. What now?

Herrera too was confused as he worked the controls to shift the helicopter's direction. Why go back? Was Castro ill? Did he forget something, some detail he wanted to attend to before they departed? OK, if the old man wants to go back, let's do it. He looked out the cockpit window as they descended back to the tarmac and saw the crowd gathered below, faces turned up in puzzlement.

Ramiro, meanwhile, worked hard on the story he would tell Castro. As they vibrated downward, his mind raced, calculating his options. Time was running out fast. If Castro was onto them, how could he lay the blame on Herrera?

The rumbling MI-24 *Hind-D* craft shuttered down in a

churning cloud of dust and settled heavily near the crowd. More people emerged from the hangars and flight buildings, as the giant rotary blade slowly turned after the engine had been cut and sand and dust settled.

The first to materialize from the helicopter were two of Castro's security staff. They told everyone to back away. One of them jogged toward the flight office to make a telephone call. Castro appeared, followed by his brother, General Ramiro, and Ricardo. Ramiro and the mechanic looked confused and worried. When Cuba's flying ace, General Herrera, stepped out into the sunshine, he seemed perplexed.

Security guards quickly stepped out from the crowd, weapons drawn. They walked directly up to Ramiro, Herrera, and Ricardo, who looked stunned, in a state of shock. When the guards pointed their weapons at them, the crowd's gasps and murmurs were all they could hear in the otherwise eerie silence. Castro's own revolver was out and pointed at Ramiro. More security guards arrived and silently forced the three men to put their hands behind their backs. Handcuffs appeared, sun glinting off steel. They snapped in place with audible clicks, and the three pale prisoners stood awkwardly as Fidel, hands locked behind his back, eyed them impassively. Seconds passed. Time itself stood still.

"You disgust me," he said finally, his words uttered in a distinct tone of subdued anger. "After all these years. All our progress together. And you call yourselves revolutionaries. You should be ashamed. This is treason in its most evil form." Another long pause as he glared at them. "Take them away," he said

Herrera felt his knees go weak. He could swear Ramiro was about to faint. Again the question rolled across his mind like thunder in the mountains. How did he find out? Surely, it was not the Viagra. Not Dr. Torres. The physican loathed him. Was it something Ramiro had done? Then he thought about his wife and son, whom he probably would never see again. His dreams of a better Cuba and those wondrous goals of José Martí . . . all for naught. He felt all energy drain from his body. How had Castro uncovered the conspiracy? What had gone wrong? He sensed himself falling into a deep state of limbo. *Shangó* had deserted him.

"Wait a minute," Castro said. He motioned to two more security guards. "Take the mechanic to the helicopter. Find the explosive. Disarm it. Hustle. We don't have much time." They grabbed Ricardo, unlocked his handcuffs, and ran him, arms locked in arms, across the tarmac toward the huge rotor-bladed bird.

Explosive? Had Herrera heard correctly? Explosive? A bomb? A timer device to disarm? He looked at Ramiro, who glared back at him like a trapped hyena. Herrera shot him a glance of disbelieved questioning. A goddamn fucking . . . bomb? He silently mouthed the questioning words at Ramiro, whose eyes locked onto his, right through the sunglasses. Ramiro's head nodded gravely, furtively, in the affirmative. In that one quick look, Herrera got the message. Yes, goddammit, I used the bomb. It was my idea. I'm in charge. I call the shots. Ramiro glared the message at him.

You arrogant, power-hungry, greedy, self-serving sonofabitch, Herrera thought. You double-crossing bastard. You used the bomb. How could you be so fucking, utterly senseless? It was then that Herrera realized in bitter clarity that his dreams of himself as a pioneer looking for his idealized Cuba had been sabotaged by the very man who had promised to make those dreams come true. He cursed himself for making a covenant of faith with the devil, Ramiro—a fatal error of judgement.

Ramiro had destroyed them all, and with it the promise of a new Cuban heartland. Herrera's heart ached as they led him away. He looked at Ricardo, back now from disarming the weapon, tears running down his cheeks and wondered how Ramiro had entrapped him in this web of deception. A glance at Dr. Torres told him that the man might be on the verge of a fatal heart attack. It would be better for him, Herrera thought, wishing he might experience the same fate. Death from natural causes would be far better than what otherwise awaited them.

Juan and Martina Espinosa got the whole story about the incident out at Antonio de los Baños late that day, when their friend at the U.S. Interest Section dropped by for coffee. The friend learned about it from her son who worked as a mechanic at the airport and from other contacts with Cuban security. She told the Espinosas how Generals Herrera and Ramiro, Ricardo, the mechanic, and Castro's physician, Dr. Torres, had been hauled away in military police cars. They apparently were driven immediately to the central military prison in Havana, where they experienced intense interrogation for hours.

Castro, although subdued, had controlled the events. In fact, her son said he thought that Castro seemed to enjoy it, especially when they found the explosive on the helicopter and disarmed it. When they handed the device to him, he received it reverently, as if he were holding a sacrificed human heart from the days of the Aztecs. Something that would help protect his *patria* and make it strong in the future. In fact, the inside scoop was that Castro would use this act of disloyal treason to his great advantage. Yet another asset to mobilize the people to defend the *patria*.

McGrath sat down with Elena, Goodwin, and McGinnis in Goodwin's CIA office that afternoon. They arranged themselves around the polished conference table, cups of coffee in front of them. Goodwin had just picked up McGrath and Elena from Bethesda Naval Hospital, where they had spent the night under observation. Mc-

Grath received a clean bill of health. Elena had suffered a mild concussion when she slammed into the wall at the fish market. McGrath looked tired but rested after his ordeal in the Potomac River with Moreno.

"How you feeling, Neal?" McGinnis asked.

"Better than yesterday about this time," he replied, smiling at her.

"You both look well enough," McGinnis said, "considering all that you've been through in the last two weeks."

"Yeah," McGrath said, "I think we'll survive."

"I asked you both to come over," Goodwin said, "for a number of reasons. But first, take a look at this report that just came through from our Interest Section in Havana. I think that you will find it interesting." He handed a copy to McGrath and one to Elena, then looked at McGinnis, sat back in his chair, and smiled.

McGrath was the first to exclaim. "A coup d'état . . . against Fidel Castro?" He sucked in his breath and looked at Elena, who stared at him.

"You don't look so surprised, Elena," McGrath said, watching her calm reaction.

"I'm not . . . really," she replied. "Remember how I told you that we couldn't go to Herrera for help because he seemed to me to be a confederate of Ramiro's. I was afraid we couldn't trust him, remember? All those meetings between Herrera and Ramiro in Ramiro's office? No, can't say that I'm totally surprised at this, but I can tell you one thing for damn sure. I feel sorry for Herrera and his family . . . sorry he got wrapped up with Ramiro."

"Yes, of course, you're right," McGrath said. "But y'know, I really liked Herrera. Can't help but think his heart was in the right place." He took a sip of black coffee. "He's a Cuban patriot, that's for certain, even if he got mixed up with Ramiro. He allied with the wrong man."

"Not a holy alliance, that's for sure," Goodwin said. "If ever there was an alliance of opposites, that was it."

They discussed Ramiro and Herrera and the coup conspiracy another ten minutes, then Goodwin looked at Elena, then at Neal. He played with the yellow pencil in his hand for a second, then said, "Neal, don't be surprised, and I don't think you will be, when I ask Elena this next question. You're a smart guy and I suspect you figured this out a long time ago. If you have any lingering doubts, this will clear it up. But remember that so long as you are connected with us, this information is strictly on a need-to-know basis. Will not leave this office, clear?"

McGrath gave Goodwin an inquisitive look and nodded agreement.

Goodwin turned to look at Elena and said, "You found out nothing about Ramiro's involvement in the coup?"

It was out. Clear as a bell, McGrath mused. He was right in his initial hunch. He took in a deep breath. Elena. CIA, a CIA mole in Ramiro's office.

"No, Sam, nothing . . . drugs yes," she said, looking at McGrath, "but Ramiro's role in a conspiracy against Castro? I knew Ramiro and Herrera were together in something big, that much I suspected, but I assumed, if anything, it was the drug operation, not working a coup together." She took a long drain on her coffee. "So Castro must have had his own mole in the office, someone who knew about the coup."

"Now Moreno's dead," she said. "Ramiro and Herrera in prison . . . along with that mechanic and Castro's physician. All in red letter, front page news in *Granma*. A conspiracy against Castro led by Generals Herrera and Ramiro, and who knows how many others. More heads will roll before this is over. Question is how many others were involved. Right there in front of my nose in MININT. My God. So that leaves the big question, doesn't it?" Elena looked at Goodwin.

"Right. It does indeed. Who informed on Ramiro and Herrera?"

"Right," Elena said.

"We have a good idea," Goodwin said. "We don't know for certain of course, but the logic seems solid."

"Oh?" Elena said.

"The key question is who's running Ramiro's office now? I mean, since he was arrested?" Goodwin said.

"And the answer is . . . ?" Elena said.

"We understand that it's Ramiro's cousin, Victor. He's the guy now in charge. Buddy-buddy with Castro and his brother. That guy, Quintero, has been moved up too. He's Victor's chief staffer."

"Victor?" Elena asked. "and that scuz ball, Quintero?"

Silence. McGrath and Elena stared at one another as the idea took hold.

"Oh my God," Elena said. "That rat. He always envied Ramiro. Wanted power, but didn't know how to get it. It must have been *Victor* who told Castro . . . can you imagine that? Ramiro's cousin. The guy Ramiro brought along with him. You know, Sam, I never trusted Victor, right from the beginning. I disliked Ramiro intensely. But he was what he was. Victor was something else. A weasel. Maybe worse even that Quintero. In some ways, I'm not surprised. That whole MININT operation, even much of the military, was a hornet's nest. Guard your rear and sting thy neighbor seemed to be the operative credo."

"Victor makes a lot of sense," Goodwin said. "We need more intelligence on it. Sooner or later we'll know for certain. But, yeah, it's believable all right."

McGrath looked at Elena and said, "Well at least I'm glad to clear up the matter of your CIA connection," he said. "Better us than them," he smiled.

"I owe you an apology, Neal," Goodwin said. "I could't tell you everything when I asked you to look up Elena," he smiled. "It would not have been prudent."

"You're forgiven," McGrath said. "We're still alive, and it was one hell of an adventure."

"Right," Goodwin said. "You had good company too. Elena, to put it mildly, was our top spy in Havana. Strategically placed in Ramiro's MININT office." He stopped for a minute, looked at Elena and smiled. "She's the best."

"But why involve me?"

"We did not have much choice," Goodwin answered. "We knew Elena was in trouble given Ramiro's paranoia about everybody."

"I managed to contact Kincaid about the file cabinet incident," Elena said. "We met at El Moro. But Kincaid was in no position to do anything." She paused. "I feel terrible about him."

"Why couldn't he help?" McGrath said.

"Why?" Elena replied. "Because he feared for my safety if Cuban intelligence put the two of us together in any way. Ramiro watched him like a hawk. Ramiro knew that Kincaid might be on to him. Diamond couldn't help either, because Ramiro tracked him too. Anyway, getting out of Cuba, other than taking to the sea like we did, is no easy matter. The place is an island prison if you're suspected of anti-government activities. Crawling with watchdogs. So Kincaid passed the message to Sam here in Washington, who got the idea that you could help me . . . and that you did," she added, taking his hand.

"We needed Elena to stay with Ramiro as long as possible," Goodwin said. "we wanted to pursue his drug connection. 'Course, nobody dreamed that Ramiro had launched this coup operation at exactly the same time."

"So you were our natural plan of action," McGinnis said. "If anybody could help her, it would be you. You have the skills to deal with the situation. The right person at the right time. Our street-smart man in Havana," she chuckled, referring to the old Hollywood film

"I couldn't have made it without you, Neal," Elena said in a subdued voice. "You saved my life."

"Neal," Goodwin said, grinning, pausing, "I'd like to introduce you to *El Caimán*." Goodwin gestured with his hand to Elena sitting across from him.

"*El Caimán*?" McGrath asked. "Crocodile?"

"Right," Elena said, "a big bubble-eyed crocodile. Resting just underwater at the edge of the river. Waiting for some tasty morsel to float by. Good name for a spy, don't you think?" She chuckled lightly.

"When I said Elena was our top spy in Havana, I wasn't kidding, Neal. Tell him, Elena."

"OK . . . what happened, Neal, is this. In effect I was a double agent."

"Right."

"Well, first, I worked for Castro, aka el Señor or *el Comandante*. I reported to Castro and was in his confidence. He wanted me to keep an eye on things in Ramiro's office. He didn't exactly trust him, you know. My uncle, who knows Castro, introduced me to him, and he placed me right there in MININT. Then, of course, I work for CIA, my primary allegiance."

"But you didn't go to Castro with information about Ramiro and the drugs?" McGrath asked.

"Right. For one thing, I thought the drug trafficking might go as high as Castro himself. I didn't know for certain. So I couldn't risk telling him."

"Was your uncle involved in all this?" McGrath asked.

"My uncle works for us too," Elena said. "But he really was out of country, so I could not go to him."

McGrath sat there for a minute, gazing at her in utter fascination. "That's why his boat was so well equipped . . . all that electronic equipment . . . short wave radio and all?"

"Correct. Prepared for an emergency."

"So what do you think Ramiro was trying to achieve?" McGrath asked.

"Here's what we surmise," Goodwin said. "Correct me if you think I'm wrong, Elena. You too, Kim. Ramiro essentially wanted to control Cuba in order to make Havana the drug trafficking capital of the Caribbean. His goal was to run the place like the old dictator, Batista. Get back to gambling, prostitution, and high stakes drug deals. He and his colleagues would lead the life of powerful fat cats."

"Moreno?" McGrath asked. "What about Ramiro and Moreno?"

"Ramiro," Goodwin explained, "in all likelihood convinced Moreno that by killing the Mexican president, the Mexican military would step in to rule the country. That would set up conditions for Moreno's leftist movement to gain a healthy following. Moreno probably believed that he could assassinate President Fox and escape undetected. He undoubtedly had lots of help. That way, nobody in Mexico could pin the assassination on the leftists. So Moreno's leftist guerrilla movement would be free to win popular support to overthrow the unpopular military and bring a socialist government to Mexico, in which," Goodwin said, "Moreno would see himself playing a prominent role."

"But a leftist government in Mexico would be ideologically opposed to Ramiro's corrupt dictatorship in Cuba, right?" McGrath asked.

"Indeed," Goodwin said. "That's why we think Ramiro intended to have Moreno killed after he did his job here. That would leave the leftists without their leader. It would undermine the guerrillas and leave the military in power. Just like Ramiro's new military rule in Cuba. Blood brothers, you might say."

"Do you know that for certain Ramiro intended to eliminate Moreno?"

"Yes. We have solid evidence. I can tell you only that an informant of ours, a new contact we have established in Key West, says that is exactly what Ramiro intended."

"How would he know?"

"He was involved in the plot to eliminate Moreno."

"So if Moreno had not drowned, he would have been eliminated anyway?"

"That's what we believe."

"Incredible," McGrath said in a low voice, staring at all three of them. There was a momentary pause. Then McGrath said, "I would like to ask one more question."

"Shoot," Goodwin said.

McGrath turned and looked long and hard at Elena. "Are you going back?"

"Probably not." She smiled at him. She gave him one of her best, winning smiles. "I may just work as an analyst here at Langley . . . at least for the time being."

"Cuba would not be safe for her," Goodwin said. "Not with Victor in charge. Certainly not with everything that's happened in the last week. It just wouldn't work. No, we can safely say that *El Caimán* has been relocated."

That evening McGrath and Elena were seated at a table in *DeLuca's* in Georgetown. They had spent the late afternoon briefly in McGrath's office at the University. There they had run into several students in the hallway who had peppered them with questions. The students had seen Professor McGrath's photo in The *Washington Post*. They had read the cover story on Professor McGrath of Georgetown University who had been involved in the strange and violent incident at the Washington fish market shortly after the assassination attempt on the Mexican president. McGrath had dodged the questions, promising to tell them about it later, after classes began in September.

He did find time to drop in on the chair's office to tell him that his research trip to Cuba had been successful, that he had good information for his book project. Things looked more promising on the tenure front anyway, he learned. The department's Tenure and Promotion Committee had voted to give him another year's extension on the decision. Turns out, he was told, that Goodwin had given the University a little call, claimed extenuating circumstances working for the government. There would be time enough to finish his book.

McGrath sat there staring across the table at Elena. She looked absolutely stunning in the candlelight, he thought. Pale blue sleeveless dress. Pearl necklace. "What's on your mind?" she asked softly, gazing back at him, sipping chardonnay.

"I was just reflecting on these last days," he said quietly. "How fortunate we are to be alive. How lucky I am to have met you again. How good it feels to be free from the Cuba snakepit . . . or hornet's nest, as you called it. I'm glad Sam asked me to look you up."

Elena reached across the table to clink her wine glass to his. "The pleasure has been all mine," she replied. "You saved my life, Neal. I wouldn't be sitting here had it not been for you." She reached across the table for his hand.

The looked at each other for a minute. "In many ways, you saved mine too." McGrath explained to her how his melancholy over Rebecca had faded. He had loved her deeply, treasured his time with her, but was eternally grateful that Elena had pulled him back from the brink. "You truly are an incredible individual . . . I can honestly say that I feel whole again. Alive. Strong. Ready for the future . . . with you if that can be arranged."

She sighed. "I hope you can forgive me for not levelling with you from the beginning," Elena said. "May I take this moment to officially apologize for my flagrant duplicity." Her words sounded playfully disarming, yet genuine and from the heart, carried to McGrath on the wings of a beguiling smile.

"Apologies accepted," he replied, with a faint grin.

"Neal, you need to know one thing about which there is no doubt." Her tone of voice became low and serious.

"Yes?"

"Just this. I do care for you deeply, far more than you might imagine." She gazed into his eyes. "If I seemed distant recently, it's because I was so focused on Moreno, so consumed by the mission, so to speak. I hope you understand."

Of course he did, although he told her that there had been moments of bitter doubt about their relationship. Then he said, "There is one thing, Elena."

She looked at him inquisitively.

"Why did you go work as a secret agent in Cuba? What possessed you to do that?"

"Why did I wind up in Havana? . . . Good question. Basically because I wanted to do anything possible to help bring a change in government. I love Cuba, you know. I'm a Cuban patriot . . . love my *patria* . . . much like General Herrera. His ideals were my ideals."

"Not like Ramiro?"

"Hardly. Ramiro was no patriot. He wanted to use the *patria* for personal greed."

"But you wound up working in his office."

"Right. Which gets us back to your basic question. Why did I choose CIA? Truth is, CIA recruited me after I got down there. Remember, I started working at the National Library. When they approached me, I had already decided that we needed a government overhaul if Cuba was going to make progress anytime soon. So I thought that by working in his office, I might find myself somehow in a position to help things along."

"You mean bring down Castro?"

"Well, if not that, then anything to open up the political system . . . you know, try to make it more democratic, more participatory, better human rights conditions."

"But you told me you believed in Castro and his revolution."

"Look, what he did for Cuba in the beginning was tremendous. I mean he got rid of Batista and launched a whole new society."

"But the revolution went astray somewhere along the line?"

"Yes."

"Your *patria*, Herrera's *patria*, is not Castro's kind of *patria*?"

"Correct. But now Herrera's in prison. Who knows what will happen next."

"Ramiro deserves what he gets," McGrath said. "But Herrera? Herrera was something else. I can see why you identified with him and his vision for Cuba." McGrath could see Herrera in that dark prison room stinking of urine, where not so long ago he and Samuels had been held captive. A shudder ran up his spine. He genuinely hurt for Herrera. "Herrera was a good man," he said. "A true patriot ruined by Ramiro, Cuba's Machiavelli."

"And you, Neal? What are your plans for the future?"

McGrath gave Elena a pensive look. He paused before answering, then said. "Me? I want to get back to academic life. My classes. Students. Friends. Surviving this whole experience has taught me one thing."

"That would be . . . ?"

"The importance of loved ones. Family ties. Friends. You know, quality of life issues. I always knew life is not a dress rehearsal. But after all you and I have been through, I value quality of life more than ever. I plan to spend more time with my father, for one thing. Give more time to my students. Here's another thing. After seeing those human rights conditions in Cuba, I'm going to be more active on public policy issues. You know, like international human rights. Individual effort can make a difference. If you and I have learned anything over the past days, it's that, don't you think?"

Elena nodded in agreement, contemplating his remarks.

"America has become too nonparticipatory," McGrath said. "Civic action is low. Volunteerism's low. Voting's deplorable. I wish my students could meet Juan and

Martina Espinosa. Look how hard they struggle for what many of us take for granted. A simple chance to voice their opinion."

"Maybe I should sit in on one of your courses," Elena said, grinning.

"You're more than welcome. But for now," McGrath said, smiling back, extending his hand across the table, "let's go home. We have to make plans."

THIRTY

The Potomac River, Virginia

Bernardo dropped anchor in the Potomac River fifty miles south of the D.C. marina at ten-thirty Tuesday night. He had left the marina shortly after Moreno had been dragged from the river and headed away from D.C. to hole up for awhile. The incident had been all over the news. He knew that cops, FBI and Secret Service agents would be crawling over the marina area, trying to find Moreno's accomplice, Miguel, who lay dead in his boat. More to the point, one of Miguel's men in D.C. had called him on the cell phone to tell him what had happened outside the National Press Club.

In the moonlit dusk of night, the anchor holding against the tide, Bernardo struggled with Miguel's body up the cabin ladder onto the deck. The eerie leather mask was still around his head. Bernardo could see nobody around. His heart pounding, he retrieved the spare anchor chain and small Danforth anchor from the anchor chest on the foredeck. He carefully wrapped Miguel's body in the chain, not wanting to look at the leather mask. He bolted the anchor to the extra two feet of chain left over from the wrapped up body.

He stood up from his work, looked up and down the river and along the barren shoreline. He took out a red bandanna from his back pocket and wiped his brow. Nobody around as far as he could see. With some difficulty he rolled the body to the edge of deck, spat on it, gave it a firm push with his foot, and tossed the anchor. The splash echoed over the moonlit water. Bernardo peered over the safety line, his eyes fixed on the body of the man in the leather mask as it disappeared deep down into the murky water. Within seconds, the stream of bubbles left in its downward journey faded and the surface again was flat and calm, shimmering in the moonlight.

Satisfied with his work, Bernardo struggled to raise the boat's anchor, went to the bridge and started the engine. Soon he was underway on down the Potomac, a rippling white wake trailing off behind his boat, headed for Reedville. He smiled to himself. His future looked good. He had come a long way since that terrible moment with Sánchez off Cuba's north coast. He had dispatched Miguel, an act for which many individuals would thank him, he thought.

To make life complete, he had that new contract as informant for CIA. A huge source of revenue, some of which he had already collected, and his information should allow CIA to dismantle Miguel's organization and scatter his men. That meant that he could get himself hired by some other drug captain, so he could keep milking the CIA. Oh yes, he thought, life is sweet. Had anyone been within earshot, they would have seen the man on the bridge of that Bayliner cruising slowly down the mighty Potomac grinning broadly, humming a tune that had a distinct Latino beat.

HEAT SYNC
WES DEMOTT

Henry (HT) Thompson is a soldier eager to make his way into Special Operations, the best place, he feels, for a man with his skills to make a difference. When a covert military force known as Jaspers recruits him from the Navy SEALs, HT knows he's found his chance. He believes he is being trained to assassinate foreign enemies who pose a threat to this country. It's only when he receives his orders that he realizes what his true mission is—to kill the President of the United States.

THE PEGASUS SECRET

GREGG LOOMIS

What started as a suspicious explosion in a picturesque Parisian neighborhood could end in revelations that would shatter the beliefs of millions. American lawyer Lang Reilly is determined to find the real cause of the blast that killed his sister. But his investigation will lead him into the darkest corners of history and religion. And it may cost him his life.

Lang's search for the truth begins with a painting his sister bought just before she died. Could there be something about the painting itself that made someone want to kill her? Every mysterious step of the way, Lang unearths still more questions, more hidden secrets and more danger, until finally he arrives at the heart of a centuries-old secret order that will stop at nothing to protect what is theirs.